THE
ARCHIVIST

THE
ARCHIVIST

A NOVEL BY DAVID PRENATT

TATE PUBLISHING & *Enterprises*

Published by Tate Publishing & Enterprises, LLC
127 E. Trade Center Terrace | Mustang, Oklahoma 73064 USA
1.888.361.9473 | www.tatepublishing.com

Tate Publishing is committed to excellence in the publishing industry. The company reflects the philosophy established by the founders, based on Psalm 68:11,
"The Lord gave the word and great was the company of those who published it."

Book design copyright © 2009 by Tate Publishing, LLC. All rights reserved.
Cover design by Leah LeFlore
Interior design by Stephanie Woloszyn

Published in the United States of America

ISBN: 978-1-60799-037-6
1. Fiction / Fantasy / General
2. Fiction / Action & Adventure
09.05.29

FOR MY OHANA—
"It's little and broken, but still good."

I

WANDERER

Peregrin had come a long way and found nothing. That is, nothing that mattered. There had been ruins, wild dogs, wild people, and a few traces of evidence that humans had once been sane. No answers to his questions, however, and no place in which he felt settled.

The day had grown long, gray, and damp. After a brief cranberry sunrise, the sky regressed to a shade of moldy bread, smudged by a few surly clouds. Though it had not rained, the air seeped through his long coat and stuck to his skin. The woods through which he traveled intensified the dampness, causing his feet to slip on rock and leaf and give his progress a sluggish feel, as though he were moving through thin curtains.

He surmised it was mid-spring. The undergrowth was thickening, and many trees were flush with new leaves. The more ponderous trees, largely oaks and elms, had just begun their buds.

Peregrin was following a watercourse as it tended downward from the hills he had crossed. There were still roads, but they were badly deteriorated, and since he did not know where he was going, there was no need to follow them.

The sloping ground became a steep hillside into which the stream had carved a ravine. He carefully picked his way down over jutting stone and moss-slicked fallen trees, leaning heavily on his stout walking staff, until he came upon a level swath running lengthwise along the hill in either direction. The stream he followed cut across it and then continued its descent, flowing into a slow rolling river below. On the far bank, the ground sloped upward as sharply as the side he was on. The level ground on which he stood, possibly an old road, stretched out parallel to the water in both directions.

Something nagged at Peregrin's memory. He had traversed hundreds of miles since he had awakened in that dark place, knowing nothing but his name. Since then he had wandered for nearly a year, finding food and provisions as he went, not knowing what he sought.

Now he paused. There was something familiar about this river, this path. The graceful sweep of the current, parting around small islands dotted with trees, murmured to him like an old song. The slope of the hillside he had come down, cradling the river and rising on the other side, gave him an odd comforting feeling, like he was nearly home. But he had no solid memory of having been here. This disconcerted him.

He had intended to follow the river's current, but the feeling of familiarity he experienced nudged him to turn upstream. The trail was hard packed, maybe having been paved once, and the vegetation was light. He frequently encountered rock slides, however, and other streams like the one he had followed that slowed his progress.

When the sun passed beyond the horizon and the air grew somber with twilight, Peregrin stopped by a rockslide and gathered wood for a fire. He hollowed a niche out of the slag and built a small, well-hidden fire in it. The heat reflected off the rocks, giving him warmth he had not felt for some time as he unrolled the old woven blanket he had found in an abandoned village.

He covered himself and leaned back against the slide. The sky was still overcast, and there were no stars. "Enough of this grim weather," Peregrin said aloud. "Tomorrow I will see the sun." He sighed, pulled down his brimmed hat over his face, and began to sink through the conscious thoughts and questions of the day toward the deep blue waters of sleep.

He slept well, better than he had in a while. Perhaps it was the continued warmth of the rocks or the fact that he was well sheltered against the wind and chill by the slide. Or maybe it was the odd sense of familiarity that continued to persist.

He awoke before dawn, as he always did. Despite the many miles he covered each day, he found he needed little sleep. Sometimes he had the impression he could just keep walking through the night and sleep was something he must will himself to take. But that was absurd. Every human being needed sleep.

The sky gained light slowly, and he was disappointed to see the same gray ceiling stretching from horizon to horizon. The mist hung sullen, like a surly child who does not wish to rise. He rolled his blanket and kicked some stones over his campfire site. He did not feel like eating, so he picked up his staff and set out.

He had covered several miles by mid-morning when the sky lightened abruptly and actual sunshine radiated the land. He smiled up at it. "I knew you would come. What took you so long?"

The sun did not remain in view for long, but it was enough to hearten him. The path he followed wended away from the river, following the hillside, which rose steeper above him. On the other side of the path, however, the ground rolled out gently toward the water. He clambered over a particularly large slide and stopped. The ground here fanned out from the river into a wide area, and about one hundred yards farther, amidst the trees, he could see the ruins of human habitation.

Peregrin ducked down quickly. Though he had not seen any people, he had learned it was wise to be wary of ruins. Often there were squatters, half-crazed and wild, ready to attack anyone who dared approach. Also, he had discovered marauders who used ruins as a base to roam the area, robbing and usually killing anyone they encountered.

He remained still, listening for about ten minutes, discerning each sound for something out of the ordinary. Hearing nothing unusual, he peered over the top of the slide.

The ruins appeared to have once been a small town. Through the undergrowth and trees he could see juts of brick and metal and stone for at least a half-mile. These stretched from the river's edge right up to the base of the hillside. Nature had pulled down most of the buildings and trees; vines, moss, and soil had long since obscured much of the structures. Some buildings were still erect, but mostly it looked like a collection of small hills and rubble. Still, there could be people there, burrowed into the mounds that had once been homes and businesses.

Peregrin remained still for nearly a half hour, watching and alert for any movement before him or behind him. Sensing nothing, he quietly edged down the rockslide toward the water. When the rocks thinned out, he carefully picked his way across them and approached the ruins slowly, keeping behind cover of shrubs and trees. The river's edge showed no signs of use by humans, no worn paths or stakes for tying up rafts. Birds continued their spring songs, squirrels scampered among the branches, and the sun edged its way out of the clouds again, illuminating the trees with shafts of gold.

He slipped from tree to tree, past the first collapsed buildings. The ruins looked the same from this side, with no sign of human occupation. He moved farther along, keeping close to the river in case he needed to flee. He knew he could swim well, and the current was slow, making for an easy escape. As he penetrated deeper, he could see that the ruins extended farther than he had thought. This made him even more wary. Ruins this extensive were sure to attract somebody, if anyone was left alive in this area.

Again, he listened carefully. The sounds were quite normal. He worked his way farther up the river, keeping a close watch on those buildings that still stood. Still, there was no sign of human occupation. At one spot he discovered deteriorated concrete posts near the water's edge, possibly the remains of a dock, but the area showed no trace of recent use—no trampled grass, no slide marks in the mud where a boat may have been pulled up. The twisted metal shafts, which still ejected from the concrete, showed uniform rust, no abrasions from rope or chain.

After three hours, he was satisfied that no human had lived there for years. The ruins tapered out finally, running along the base of the hillside, which had arced back toward the water and was nearly vertical by now, rising forty or fifty feet above the ruins. He spent the next hour wending his way carefully up and backward along the edge of the ruins. About fifteen feet from the ground, a large shelf of rock jutted outward. Climbing to this outcrop, Peregrin found he could survey most of the ruins, while the steepness of the hill obscured his position from above.

He sat down on the outcrop and thought. Most of the ruins he had come across had been thoroughly ransacked by squatters and bandits. They were small, crumbling reminders of a world that no longer existed. But they always showed signs of habitation.

Here before him, however, was a large expanse of ruins that appeared untouched by anything except nature. That in itself was very strange. The hills he had crossed in the past weeks descended toward this river. The land was fertile. There was abundant animal life, and the water was good. He could think of no good reason why human beings would not have found these ruins and occupied them.

Peregrin took a packet from his pocket and carefully unwrapped the cloth. It contained a few radishes, wild onions, and strips of jerked beef from the last village in which he had stayed. He had taught the people there how to smoke their meat to preserve it, for which they had been grateful. He had not told them that he had no idea how he knew the process. The information he shared simply came to him shortly before he passed it on. This was all he had left to eat, but he never ate much anyway.

He slowly chewed on a piece of the beef for a while and considered the ruins. The day was stretching into late afternoon, and he was tired from his cautious exploration. Now was the time to rest, and think. Fire would feel good, but he was still uneasy about finding no people in the area. *It would be better to spend a cold night,* he thought, *than to attract attention.*

If these ruins are truly untouched, Peregrin thought, *I may have found a goldmine.* There could be blankets, clothes, tools, even preserved food beneath the decaying hulks. And if no one were around, he could stay for some time, carefully excavating the mounds as he chose.

Unexpectedly, the feeling of familiarity washed over him again. It was even stronger than he had experienced upon the old trail. It was not *déjà vu;* it was more like kinship, a feeling of belonging here. *Why yes,* he thought, *maybe this will be my home. Maybe I will find whatever it is I am searching for here.*

That thought pleased him greatly. With a sigh he leaned back against a tree and closed his eyes. Sunbeams were slanting through the trees from the west, and the birds were singing pleasantly. The sounds of the woods seemed almost like a gentle song, assuring him that he could rest from his wanderings. This might be a place to call home.

He began to think of his wanderings. When he had awakened in utter darkness, he had no concept of his identity. He had not known where, who, or even what he was. All he knew was that he was. He had no memories of anything with which to judge his experience. He did not even realize that the darkness deprived him of sight.

Still, he had been spurred to move. Even as he crawled, information began processing in his mind. He became aware of space and distance, of sound and touch. It had suddenly occurreded to him that it was dark, and that this was not the usual state of affairs. He became aware of direction and height and depth.

Then he had found a door. As he rose up on his feet and felt its surface and handle, his mind told him "door," and he suddenly knew that it led somewhere. He found a large bolt, and knowing what to do, he pulled it loose. He pushed the handle and leaned his weight against it. It resisted but finally gave way, and he passed through it to find a stairway. He made his way upward, found another door at the top, opened this one, and passed into place of stone.

Here, Peregrin had his first experience of sight. There was very dim light coming from somewhere. He saw he was in a small, rough tunnel cut through rock, which ended beyond his door, leaving only one direction to go: sloping upward. As he made his way, the light grew stronger. He could see ahead that the tunnel ended abruptly, closed off by large stones and rubble. The light came through a small hole some ten feet up. He climbed the pile and dug at the stones and loose earth. The light was blinding at first, but his eyes adjusted as he dug the hole wider until it was barely more than a foot across. He rested a moment and then attempted to squeeze through the hole.

It had truly been an experience of birth. The stones would give no more, and he had to struggle and squirm until nearly exhausted before he pulled himself through all the way. And there, lying on a hillside, sweating in the full radiance of the afternoon sun, he saw the world.

Sensation bombarded him from all directions, and knowledge swirled in his mind. The roll of the hills around him, the tired green leaves on the trees, tinged and speckled with gold and red, the smells of plants and grains nearing fruition, the wind with just an edge of chill, a nearby stream running fast, all told him that he was somewhere in the northeastern part of this land during the advance of autumn. These names and words simply appeared in his mind in response to what he saw, heard, touched, smelled, and felt.

He stayed awhile near the place. From the outside, he was able to widen the hole enough to go back inside and explore. Whatever he discovered in that dark place, he brought into the tunnel. He found a long overcoat and a floppy, wide-brimmed hat that fit him well, leading him to conclude that it had belonged to him. He found a stout oak walking staff and a canteen in one corner. But his most surprising find was a backpack in which he found a rain slicker, dried food, a can opener, a folding knife with a five-inch blade, three stout candles, and (this astounded him the most) a lighter and a can of fuel.

"Looks like I was planning on going somewhere," Peregrin had said aloud. He lit a candle and went back in for a better look.

He found only the room in which he had awakened. He had lain on a table in an open metal box with padded sides. The walls and floor were a white metal. There was very little else there, except a cabinet against one wall. Opening it, he found some canned foods. *That explains the can opener,* he thought. There were also two screwdrivers, a hammer, a chisel, a hatchet, a whetstone, and a small folding saw. That was all.

He took these into the tunnel. As he carefully packed everything, he thought how strange it was that he knew each item's name and function but had no idea who put them there or when. Knowledge came to him, it seemed, on a need-to-know basis.

So it had gone as he wandered. Each day brought new experiences that, in turn, provided him with new knowledge of its meaning. It was as though his mind were a library, and his encounters were hands that selected different books.

Still, nothing he encountered sparked any memories. He had no recollection of where he had come from, why he was in that underground bunker, or what had happened to the world. He had a vague recollection that there had once been a vast society with great machines and tools through which it mastered the world. He found ruins of small towns, often burned and completely ransacked. Also, there were larger, thoroughly scorched areas where great skeletal structures rose up, twisted and black from a thick bedding of ash and rubble, devoid of any signs of life. Peregrin called them dead zones and avoided these places.

He met few people. Sometimes he encountered small tribes of people who, though suspicious of strangers, offered him guarded hospitality but could tell him little. In return, he shared bits of knowledge of shelter, clothing, and farming to help them survive. But he found but no satisfaction for his searching and would continue to wander after a time

He traveled south, using the sun as his compass. The gentle, rolling foothills soon rose into hulking, forest-dense hill country. A mighty river threaded its way through them, and he followed it as it broadened. Unexpectedly, the trees thinned out, and Peregrin found himself surveying a dead zone. Gray, silty ground packed with twisted mounds of debris stretched far and away before him. Though the vegetation was attempting to reclaim this land, he could see that the fire that had caused it had been massive and unchecked. He turned aside from this sight and headed eastward.

The land continued to rise in massive hills. Every now and then, Peregrin came across ruins of towns in which he would search for anything useful. He learned to steer clear of squatters who shambled, mumbling, and who would usually fly at him screaming, to drive him from their claim. It was in one of these ruined towns that he encountered bandits and learned something new.

He had cautiously entered from the west end of the ruins and, finding no one, proceeded to investigate some of the more erect buildings for food and provisions. Emerging from one half-collapsed structure, he found his way blocked by four men. He could tell by their stance and demeanor that they were quite sane, and quite dangerous.

"Well, looky here, boys," said one, a stocky, well-muscled fellow. His beard was bushy and wild; his clothes were tattered, and he wore a greasy, brimmed hat. "We gots a trespisser in our house."

"Theevin skunk by the looks of him, Crown," said a taller, lean man. He was toying with a stout club banded with iron on one end.

"I'm sorry," Peregrin said. "I did not know this was your home. I'll pass on." He took a step, but the men did not move.

"Nawp," said Crown. "Can't letcha do thet. This here is our land all around, and we aims to keep it. Can't come through here without payin' us a toll."

"I have nothing to give you," Peregrin said.

"Sure ya does," Crown replied. "You gots a fine, fancy jacket, food, thet nice pack full of stuff, and your life." He drew a large hunting knife made of steel and bone from behind his back. The other men had smaller knives and clubs. They stepped toward Peregrin. "Nuthin' persnol," Crown said. "Jest how we makes our living."

Peregrin was not afraid. Quite the contrary, he began to seethe. He had found so few people, and it angered him that there were still those who would hurt and kill for their own purposes without a second thought. They deserved to be punished. His staff felt warm and comfortable in his hand. He let his pack slip off his shoulder and to the ground.

They rushed him. The tall man on the left was a step closer, and Peregrin spun to the side, bringing his staff around low and graceful as he did so to sweep the man's feet out from under him. The tall man went flying. Without pausing, Peregrin continued his turn, twirling the staff to bring it, butt end, into the abdomen of the next man, who doubled over as the staff came around and cracked the side of his head. He collapsed.

Crown snarled as he and the fourth man rushed Peregrin again. An easy sidestep, a twirl of the staff, and the fourth man fell as the staff crashed onto the top of his head. Crown, meanwhile, stumbled as his lunge found only air.

Peregrin turned toward him, feeling balanced and calm like a cat. Crown came in slowly, feinting with his knife. Peregrin could hear the tall man rising behind him and knew Crown would try to keep him occupied as the tall man snuck up on him. He pretended not to know he was there until Crown cried, "Now!" and lunged forward.

Peregrin dropped into a crouch and swiveled, holding the center of his staff firmly against his chest. The ends of the staff caught both men across the legs, and they flew into each other. Rolling free, Peregrin saw that Crown's knife had caught the tall man in the neck, and he was down, bleeding profusely. Crown rose and charged, screaming. This time Peregrin did not sidestep but planted himself, and as Crown came up, he brought the staff upward in a diagonal arc, connecting with Crown's temple. Crown flipped backward and lay still in a heap.

Peregrin retrieved his pack. Crown's knife lay in the grass, and he picked it up. It was old but in fine shape. He tucked it in his pack and headed out. He had just learned he could fight, and fight well.

And so he had continued wandering. As the weather began to turn cold, he came upon a village of about thirty-five people living on the banks of a broad river. They lived in huts of lashed wood poles covered with animal skin, sod, or any other material they could find. They ate vegetables, roots, a gritty flatbread they made from rye wheat, and tended a small stock of cattle and pigs. They were suspicious of him, even fearful, but not violent. He presented Crown's knife to the headman, Jaspar, and this was seen as a great deed.

He had stayed with them for most of the winter, showing them how to build stronger shelters by shaving the sides of the logs, stacking them between upright supports, and chinking them with clay. He taught them to slaughter and preserve their meat and to build a smokehouse. He built a small grain mill by constructing a large wooden, funnel-shaped frame. He shaped five flat, round stones of varying sizes with his chisel and bored a hole in the center of each. These he placed on top of one another with the smallest at the bottom, where the funnel narrowed. He placed a shaft through the stones and affixed the second and fourth stones to the shaft so that they would move when the handle of the shaft was turned, grating against the other three stones. Wheat and corn, which were then poured into the funnel, had to work their way through the five stones before pouring out of the bottom. This produced finer flour and made the bread much more palatable.

Peregrin awoke one morning in late winter as the ground became soggy and the air warm. He suddenly knew that it was time to move on. The headman became distraught and begged him to stay, but to no avail. The villagers presented him with food and clothing articles they had made. As he turned to go, Jaspar blocked his way. He looked at him solemnly and then handed him Crown's knife, now wrapped in a leather sheath, decorated with feathers. A woman of the tribe came forth, took it, and girded it onto Peregrin's waist, using two long leather straps from the sheath.

"We will not forget the name of Peregrin," Jaspar said. With that, Peregrin set out.

He swung northward in his travels, following the river, not knowing why or what drove him. Parting from the river after four days travel, he tended east, through rising hills that slowed his progress. He took his time, wandering and wondering.

And now he was here, and for the first time, he felt no urge to keep moving. *Maybe this is where I belong*, he thought. *Maybe I have found home.*

Peregrin awoke with a start. It was night. His clothes were wet from the damp, and he was quite chilled. But he did not move. *How dangerous to be lulled asleep in plain daylight*, he thought. He listened carefully. The sounds of the night were steady, crickets and small animals scrabbling in the brush, twigs falling to the ground. Nothing seemed out of place. He remained still until he was sure there was no malicious presence lurking nearby or stealthily sneaking upon him. Then he quietly unrolled his blanket and wrapped himself in it. He shifted his position slightly and remained alert deep into the night, aware of every twig that snapped.

II

RUINS

Dawn brought fresh sunlight, streaking the forest floor in gold as it dispelled the mist and fears of attack. Peregrin stretched and smiled. *A good day to explore,* he thought. As he began, he was not surprised to find that most of the buildings had been constructed with wood, which had long since decayed, leaving a hopeless collapse of rubble. If he stayed here long, he might try to unearth some of them. First, however, he would examine those that needed less labor to investigate.

One of the buildings was fairly close to his camping spot on the hillside. It was by far the largest of the remaining structures, perhaps three floors high and built of stone. The stately, even-spaced windows, most of which appeared filled with debris, and hunks of moss-covered columns strewn near the wreck of its entrance indicated it was a building of some importance. It had been built near the hillside, which had encroached upon it over the years so that much of the building was obscured by soil, growth, and trees.

The main entrance to the structure was hopelessly blocked by rubble from the collapse of its porch and by vegetation. The back and the side closest to his camp had been buried in a landslide, so he made his way around to the far side. He found two entrances. One was obstructed by large boulders and assorted debris. The other had suffered an interior collapse and was blocked from within.

Peregrin stepped back and considered the scene. Something did not add up. A mostly intact building in unspoiled ruins, yet each entrance was fully blocked. He looked at the land around him and at the cliff face looming above him. There were rocks about, embedded in decades of soil and moss. The hillside above had some rock formations like the one he had stayed the night on, but they were stable, in little danger of falling. Nowhere else about him showed such a concentration of boulders and rocks as those that blocked the entrance.

Someone put these here, he pondered. *Many years ago someone blocked this entrance on purpose. Then there is no reason to believe that the other entrances were accidentally blocked either.* He looked up at the window sockets. *No,* he thought, *most of them are not choked with debris. All of them are choked with debris. A ruin that somebody does not want to be explored. A cover-up after the collapse of human society. What could have been so important to hide that someone would go to this length after the sky had fallen?*

He picked his way around the collapsed entrance. The porch of this building must have been magnificent. The fallen columns were real stone, and the roof, which had come down directly in front of the main entrance, was constructed of steel girders, many of which had fallen against the entrance. *Naturally,* Peregrin thought.

He looked closer at the twisted metal beams and rubble, which appeared to have fallen haphazardly and which, so effectively, blocked the entrance. Here was a girder whose rust had been scratched by something. Here was a spot on a boulder where the moss had been scraped off, as if a foot had caught it.

He moved back and surveyed the scene as a whole. Most of the rubble was well overgrown by vines and vegetation. Even that which he was sure had been put there on purpose showed decades of undisturbed growth. Yet here were recent signs of human passage. The building had been blocked off long ago, yet someone still came here.

"And so," he said aloud, "there has to be a secret entrance."

Just then he heard noises coming from near the river where the ruins tapered out. Something large was moving clumsily through the undergrowth, up toward his position. He quickly hid himself amidst the rubble in such a way that he could see toward the noises. Then he heard a voice, a child's voice, whispered and urgent.

"Cornel! Be quiet! There might be Terists about!"

Another voice answered, "I'm sorry, Janel. I slipped. But don't worry. There haven't been any Terists around for a long time."

"Not around Archiva. But you know they hide in the hills. Bliss said so. We're not supposed to be here."

"Bliss just says those things to keep us at home. There hasn't been anybody in the ruins as long as I've been alive. Now come on. Who knows what we'll find?"

"But Cornel," replied the first voice with an edge of fright in it, "this was a Sheen town. It's forbidden. We might find bad stuff."

"Oh, by fire!" came the exasperated reply. "You sound like Waterman. What kind of Guardians do you think we'll become if we're afraid of finding anything? There's got to be knowledge here, Janel, I know it. Just think, we'll be like O'Keefe himself. Maybe we'll even find books!"

The other voice was silent, obviously not convinced. Peregrin could hear them digging around the ruins. He quietly made his way up toward them, away from the river. It pleased him to hear seemingly sane voices.

He eased sideways from his position and kept low from tree to tree. About a hundred yards out and down, he came to a structure knotted and twisted with vines and tree roots. It had probably been a small home, as it had nearly disappeared beneath the vegetation. A stately maple grew directly out of its center with smaller saplings springing out in strange angles around it.

Peering through a tangle of roots, Peregrin saw a boy and a girl about twelve or thirteen years old. They looked similar enough to be brother and sister and close enough in size to maybe even be twins. They both had shoulder-length sandy hair, stocky builds, and were dressed in green trousers and brown shirts that buttoned up the front. The girl was slightly taller and wore a small, round cap with a front brim that jutted out like a duck's bill.

"Well, let's hurry, Cornel," said the girl. "I don't like it here at all."

"You're such a mouse, Janel," he answered, yet there was a nervous edge in his voice as well. They disappeared from view around a large mound of earth and moss, which Peregrin guessed had been another small house. He could hear them rooting around the debris.

"Janel, look here!" came Cornel's excited voice. "Here's an opening!"

"Oh, Cornel, you can't go in there! That whole thing could fall in on you," came her answer.

"Shut up and give me your stick. I'll prop it against the beam here." She must have hesitated because Cornel's voice came again with some exasperation.

"Janel, it's been like this for at least fifty years. It's not going to just fall in now."

"Maybe it's been waiting for somebody dumb enough to climb into it first," came the reply.

Peregrin smiled. *Perhaps*, he thought, *I should make myself known before there is an accident.* He began to come out from his hiding but stopped. He heard another sound, a stealthy sound, coming from the direction the children had come. The children were distracted by their exploration and did not hear it.

Peregrin remained still and watched. After a while he saw brush move in one spot and then another. Then he saw a lean figure peer cautiously around a tree, signal to someone, and then disappear again. Off to the right, a shorter figure broke cover and dashed to the nearest collapsed structure. After a few moments, he stepped out into the open and waved back toward the first person.

Two men stepped out into the open and came up to join him. As they reached his position, he pointed toward the place where the children had gone.

"Little explorers are too intent on finding treasure to look behind them," he said in a low voice that Peregrin did not like at all. He was a squat fellow with a thick neck and arms that were too bulky to hang straight from his shoulders. The intent of his voice made Peregrin remember Crown and his companions.

"Bah," growled the lean one. "They won't lead us to anything. They're too young." "Still, no use passing up good meat. All right, let's get 'em then. Ought to make Dextor happy."

He wore a brown sash around his waist and a brown cap with two stripes. He had a scar running down his left cheek and a bony face with prominent brow ridges. The third man just grunted. He, too, was stocky, and he hunched over in a way that made him seem misshapen. All three of the men wore green shirts, and Peregrin guessed the sash and cap gave the lean man some authority. They moved toward the place where the children had gone, making no effort to conceal themselves anymore.

Peregrin felt a tightness in his chest that spread out through his limbs like the tightening of a wire. Anger flushed through him like a stab of flame. He checked the leather belt that held Crown's knife and tightened his grip on his staff.

The men passed from sight behind the same house that the children had entered. Peregrin rose from his hiding spot and walked quickly to the backside of the ruin. Even as he reached it, he heard an exclamation of surprise from inside, a scream (probably Janel), a short scuffle, and then heard the children being dragged outside.

"Well, hello, darlins," he heard the lean man say. "What brings you to these old ruins? Don't you know there's dangerous beasts about?"

"These ruins belong to Archiva," he heard Janel shout. "Let us go or Mikkel will make you pay."

There was a low chuckle and then a growly voice: "She's an uppity one, Crop. Let me thrash some of that sass outta her."

The lean man spoke again. "No, Daggert, no. Dextor will want these ones in one piece. I reckon he can get a good price for the pair of them."

"Get a good price for this," came Cornel's voice. There was another scuffle, a *fwump*, a roar of rage and pain, and the sound of someone being struck. Cornel cried out, and Peregrin could hear him falling to the ground.

That was enough for Peregrin. He came around the ruin. Cornel was on the ground, stunned. The hunched man, Daggert, was standing over him, grasping his crotch with a look of pain and vengeance on his face. Crop, the lean man, was standing about five feet from him, grinning. The third man was behind Janel, holding both of her arms immobile in his meaty hands.

Peregrin did not wait. The staff whirled around and cracked Crop on the side of the head, felling him. Before Daggert could even turn, Peregrin had used the staff as a vaulting pole and launched himself, both feet first, into his side, bowling him over.

The beefy man thrust Janel aside and charged but found only air. Peregrin had again used the staff to vault above him, kicking his head as he came down behind him. The man grunted and smashed into the ruin. He did not fall, but turned and approached Peregrin slowly, arms out wide. Peregrin backed up until he was against a large boulder. The man, thinking he was trapped, rushed again. A quick spin, and the man went by him into the rock with Peregrin's staff hitting him from behind. He fell heavily.

Peregrin turned. Crop was still down, but Daggert had recovered, pulled Cornel to his feet, and stood facing Peregrin with Cornel between them, a knife at his throat.

"Drop the stick," he growled. "Drop it, or the boy dies."

Peregrin's eyes felt white hot. So this was what was left of humanity. He spat and threw the staff from him. "I don't need the stick," he said between clenched teeth. "Come out and die yourself."

Daggert shoved Cornel aside and rushed at Peregrin with his knife. Although he was nearly in a rage, Peregrin knew just how to face him. He grasped the man's wrist, swiveled his hips into him, and using Daggert's momentum, threw him over his shoulder. Daggert hit the ground hard, and Peregrin, still gripping his wrist, flipped him onto his stomach, twisted his arm behind him, and applied pressure. Daggert screamed as the arm broke.

Peregrin straightened up and looked about. Crop was stirring, trying to rise. Peregrin took him by the shirt, pulled him up, and then pushed him back hard against a tree. Crop stared at him.

"You don't know what you're dealing with," he said. "We work for Dextor."

"I don't know this Dextor," Peregrin snarled, "but you give him a message for me. You pick up that trash you brought with you and run. Run and tell your Dextor that the Traveler has come. And he claims these ruins for his own. Do you hear? These ruins belong to me!" He threw Crop toward the beefy man, who had gotten to his hands and knees.

Crop got him up, and the two of them managed to get Daggert on his feet. Crop turned to Peregrin as if to say something threatening, but as he did so, Peregrin raised one arm and pointed. "No more," he said. "You go now and tell him the Traveler has come!" The men staggered off the way they had come.

When he was sure they had gone, Peregrin turned toward the

children. Janel had helped Cornel to his feet, and they stood staring at Peregrin.

"Are you all right, Cornel?" he asked.

Cornel's mouth dropped open. Then he closed it firmly, clenching his teeth. "I won't tell you anything," he growled.

"That's not a nice way to thank someone," Peregrin said. Are there no manners left in the world?"

Janel stepped forward. "Who are you? Where did you come from? I've never seen anyone fight like that. Are you a Guardian?"

"Janel, shut up!" Cornel said sharply. "He could be one of them."

Peregrin laughed. "I hardly think they enjoyed my company. I broke that Daggert fellow's arm, you know. And the others will have headaches for some days to come. So now tell me, where have you come from searching for knowledge?"

"We're from Archiva," Janel said. "We're not supposed to come to the ruins, but Cornel thought—"

"Janel! Stop your blabbering!"

"Oh, look who's talking," Janel said, whirling on Cornel. "This was your fault. 'Let's go to the ruins; let's see what all the mystery is about.' None of this would have happened if we had stayed home like we're supposed to."

"You came along willing enough," Cornel shot back at her. "You wanted to see just as much as I did."

"I take it you two are related," Peregrin said, grinning. "Listen, I'll take you back to your home, this Archiva of yours. Just show me the way and—"

"No!" Cornel said. "I mean, it's not allowed."

"Neither is going to the ruins," Peregrin said. "But that did not stop you. And if you go back on your own, you're likely to run into those three again. I don't think they'll be as nice this time."

The children looked at each other and then down at the ground. Peregrin decided to try another tack.

"Well, at any rate, we have to stay here for a while to make sure those fellows don't come back with friends. Are you hungry?"

Lunch was a radish and a piece of jerked beef for each of them. They ate quietly upon the outcrop where Peregrin had made camp. After a while, Janel spoke.

"Who are you, mister? I heard you say to that man you were 'the Traveler.' What does that mean?"

Peregrin smiled. "I'm not really sure. I just made it up at the moment to scare them. My name is Peregrin, which means *wanderer*. I guess I prefer traveler. It sounded good anyway."

"So where are you traveling to?" Cornel asked.

"Nowhere, and anywhere. I don't know," Peregrin said.

"You must have come from somewhere," Janel said.

"Somewhere, yes. But I don't know where it was. It's a long story. But you tell me of yourselves. Where is this Archiva? How many people live there?"

Janel and Cornel exchanged glances. "It's a town," Cornel said. "It's hidden so the Terists can't find it. We can't say anything more about it."

"I see," Peregrin said. "And who are the Terists? Those fellows who attacked you?"

"Yeah, I guess," said Cornel. "They live in the hills. They rob and hurt people who they catch. Father says the Terists used to be really powerful, and it was them who caused the war. But that was long ago. No one knows how many there are."

"But you didn't think you would run into any in the ruins. Why is that?"

Cornel put his head down. After a moment, it was Janel who spoke. "Terists are afraid of these ruins. At least we thought they were."

"Why should they be afraid?"

"'Cause these ruins are haunted."

"Haunted?"

"Uh huh. Bad things happen here. This was a Sheen town. No Terist that came here ever came back again."

"But you were not afraid."

"I said 'no Terist.' The Guardians are safe here. We figured it would be okay in daylight."

"You're losing me," Peregrin said. "Terists, Guardians, Sheens? What is all this?"

As Janel began to answer, Peregrin heard a sound from below. He pulled the children down flat onto the rock. Cautiously they peered over the edge.

"I don't see anything," Cornel said.

"Shhh!" said Peregrin. "Use your ears to see. The noise of the woods has stopped. Something is here that doesn't belong." He listened for a long moment. "There," he said, pointing to a thicket near the water. "It's behind there."

From the thicket came a warbling whistle, long and low. Another answered from farther down.

Cornel jumped to his feet and, before Peregrin could move, made three short *thweets*. Janel started to get up also. Peregrin grabbed her.

"What are you doing? Get down!"

"It's all right, Peregrin," she said. "It's Bliss." She, too, made three short *thweets*.

Peregrin sighed and stood up. Below him a woman stepped out from behind the thicket. Seeing them upon the rock, she whistled twice. About a hundred yards to her right, a man stepped out of cover from behind a tree. Off to her left, two more men came into view.

Cornel and Janel were already climbing down the hillside to meet them. Peregrin sighed again, collected his pack, and followed. By the time all three had reached the base of the hill, the four adults had converged upon them.

"Bliss!" cried Janel, and she ran to her and embraced her. Cornel followed but with less enthusiasm. Bliss was about five and a half feet tall, slender, yet strong looking. She had dark hair pulled back and tied into a tail that fell halfway down her back. Her cheekbones were high, her jaw angled sharply down to the chin, but her brown eyes were rounded and reminded Peregrin of freshly turned earth, rich and full of hope for the harvest.

"Bliss," Janel said again. "We were attacked by Terists. There were three Terists here. And Peregrin came from nowhere and drove them off."

"Peace, Janel," Bliss said softly. "There will be time for the telling. Are you unhurt?"

"We're fine," Janel said. "Cornel tried to fight, and one of the Terists hit him. But he's okay. If Peregrin hadn't come, they would have taken us, Bliss."

"Is this true, Cornel?" Bliss asked.

Cornel looked at the ground. "Yes," he said. "I suppose we're in trouble."

"You have come to the ruins alone before your passage," said one of the men, stepping forward. He was slightly taller than Bliss, muscular, and square jawed. His dusty, graying hair was also pulled back in a tail. Deep lines creased his prominent forehead, and his lips were straight, as though he neither smiled nor frowned. Yet his eyes were like the sky on a summer noon, intense and difficult to look at.

"You came to the forbidden ruins, followed by Terists who could have taken you away forever. Yes, I'd say you were in trouble. What were you thinking? How could you be so irresponsible?"

"Enough of that for now, Mikkel," Bliss said. "Who is this man before us? We saw the Terists below. They were sorely battered. Did you truly take on all three of them to save these children?"

"Yes," said Peregrin.

"We are grateful," said Mikkel. "And what is your name?"

"I call myself Peregrin."

"Wanderer," Mikkel said.

Peregrin was surprised. "Not many would know what that word means," he said.

"But he prefers *traveler*," Cornel piped in. Mikkel glanced at him, and he fell silent.

Peregrin chuckled. "He speaks true. I prefer traveler."

"This would imply a purpose in your journey. And so, Traveler, where have you come from? And where do you go? What is your purpose?"

Peregrin glanced down at Mikkel's hand, which was alternately clenching into a fist then flexing beside his waist. Mikkel noted his gaze and let the hand fall, relaxed. The suspicious tone of Mikkel's questions annoyed Peregrin.

"I do not know my purpose yet. Only that I have one. But when I learn it, it shall be my business. You might be glad my traveling brought me here this day."

Mikkel stiffened, but Bliss laughed, a free, honest laugh like water flowing over pebbles. "Well said!" she exclaimed. "Mikkel, leave off your interrogation. Peregrin, forgive us. We owe you much. These two," she indicated Janel and Cornel with a sweep of her hand, "although inclined to cause worry and grief among all of Archiva, are precious to us. We thank you." With that she bowed gracefully, and Peregrin could not help but smile and bow in return.

"Your apology is accepted, Bliss," he said.

Mikkel stepped forward and extended his hand.

"I also apologize if my questions were offensive. You have my gratitude as well." Peregrin took his hand. "However," Mikkel continued, "it is imperative that you tell us of your immediate intentions. As you have seen, we have much to fear from outsiders."

Peregrin looked into Mikkel's azure eyes and found no hint of anger, resentment, or suspicion, only concern. "I have no plans," he said. "I came to these ruins yesterday afternoon, and I must confess,

I found them attractive. I guess I was inclined to stay and explore them."

Mikkel and Bliss exchanged glances. "I'm sorry," Mikkel said. "We cannot allow you to do that. These ruins are..." He searched for a word.

"Haunted?" Peregrin said wryly.

"Sacred," said Bliss. "They are sacred to us, and we have sworn to guard them from intrusion and defilement."

"Which explains what a Guardian is," Peregrin said.

Mikkel drew in his breath. "How did you..." he began, and then he looked at Janel and Cornel, who cringed.

"Do not blame the children," Peregrin said. "I was probing them for information just as you were probing me. They told me nothing other than the words: Archiva, Guardian, and Sheen. In fact, they were decidedly tight lipped."

"Yes, then," said Bliss, "we are Guardians of these ruins. Mikkel and me you have met. This quiet one behind us is Carlin," she said, indicating a tall, thin man with close-cropped dark hair who nodded. His arms were nearly as long as the stout staff that his gaunt hands rested lightly upon, and although he was leaning against a tree as if resting, Peregrin had the distinct impression that he was fully capable of bringing it down on Peregrin's head in the blink of an eye if need arose.

"And this jester," Bliss said, extending her hand toward a short, slightly built fellow with tousled, curly, washed-out red hair, "goes by the name of the Waterman." He gave an exaggerated bow then grinned broadly, displaying crooked and missing teeth.

"And you live in a place called Archiva, which you can't show me."

"Well, there's the problem," Mikkel said. "We cannot let you stay here, and we must not risk endangering Archiva. Yet we owe you for rescuing the children and do not wish to force you to continue your journey into the hills where there are Terists, among whom you have already made enemies."

"I can take care of myself," Peregrin said.

"That is evident," Bliss said. "Yet I can see you are not given to violence as the Terists are. And it would be the greatest ingratitude to set you forth on your own."

Peregrin was enjoying this debate. "And so?" he said.

The four looked at one another. Carlin cocked his head to one side in a questioning manner. The Waterman's grin grew broader, and Bliss smiled. Mikkel turned back to Peregrin.

"Would you honor us by coming to Archiva?"

III
ARCHIVA

Carlin and the Waterman went ahead to make sure the way was clear. Mikkel led the rest along the river for a few miles. The hills continued to roll out in pleasant, fertile waves, tending downward into a broad valley. They came to a wide stream, almost a river in itself. Here, Mikkel turned inland and followed the stream.

It was as if they stood at the peak edge of a great fan. The land rippled upward gently from the river until it once more began to rise in steeper hills that angled in from both directions. These hills converged to a point about three miles distant where the hills reared up into a curving ridge. As they made their way inland, Peregrin could see signs that the land had been farmed, although care had been taken to make the fields blend in with the natural vegetation.

They kept to the stream for nearly two miles, until the hills had begun to rise again around them. The land became heavily wooded, although Peregrin occasionally caught sight of clearings, which may have been used for farming. A hill rose up sharply beside them into a sheer cliff face of granite, shale, and slate. Small trees and scrubby vegetation grew outward from its side above them. Mikkel abruptly turned away from the stream and the clearly well-trod path and began to pick his way up a rockslide at the base of the cliff.

Bliss must have seen Peregrin's puzzled look. "The path continues along the stream for some ways and leads nowhere," she said. "We keep it well cleared to lead any..." here she smiled, "wanderers away from Archiva."

"No one would ever accidentally come this way," Peregrin answered as he scrambled to follow Mikkel up the shifting rockslide.

"That is our hope," Bliss answered.

Peregrin followed Mikkel over the top of the rockslide and down the other side to where it met the base of the cliff. A single tree grew there, a stately maple about twenty feet high. Mikkel went past it to a spot where the cliff jutted outward at its base and disappeared. Rounding the tree and the outcrop, Peregrin saw an opening in the rock face—thin, but tall enough to pass through easily.

He paused as Bliss and the children caught up. "This is the path to Archiva," Bliss said. "We'll wait until Mikkel returns."

"And so the obvious path leads away from the entrance," Peregrin said. "But still, what if someone stumbles onto this?"

"They would find only a rock wall if they did," Bliss answered. "The way would be closed before they saw it."

"How would you know in time?" Peregrin asked.

In answer, Bliss pointed above them to the top of the cliff and gave a whistling call three times. Peregrin saw the silhouette of a woman's head and shoulders briefly appear. The woman answered the call in the same way and disappeared again.

"Rangers," Bliss said. "We've been watched since we turned up from the river."

Mikkel came back through the opening and handed Peregrin

a lantern. Peregrin looked at it, information about it flowing into his mind.

"It uses animal fat for fuel," Mikkel said. "Follow me and don't worry. The tunnel is reinforced." He disappeared again into the darkness. Peregrin turned to Bliss to offer her the lantern.

Bliss smiled. "Those who live here do not need a light," she said. "We know the tunnel well." Peregrin shrugged and passed through the opening.

The tunnel was well reinforced, as Mikkel had said, with steel girders. The floor was smooth and tended downward. After many twists and turns and, Peregrin noted, some offshoot passages, he made a right turn and came out into the daylight onto a stone platform. There he had his first view of Archiva.

Archiva, it seemed, was hidden in plain sight. Steep but not impassable hills rose on all sides, forming a large oval basin area about one mile long and nearly as wide in the center. Peregrin was standing on a large flat boulder that came directly out of the hillside about twenty-five feet above the floor of this hidden valley. Large, flat stones had been embedded in the hillside below him, forming a stairway. He could see what looked to be two or three other similar "stairways" at points along the hillsides.

But what struck Peregrin was that he could not see a town. There were people there, busy about various tasks, and numerous livestock, mostly sheep and cows. There were large and spreading trees, rock piles and mounds of earth, but he could see no houses, no barns, no public buildings.

Bliss came out beside him. "So, there you have it, Traveler. Have you ever seen anything such as Archiva?"

Peregrin shook his head. "I don't see it now. Where's the town?"

Janel giggled. "You'll see!" she said, and she skipped down the hillside, followed by Cornel.

Bliss turned to him, smiling. "Indeed, you will see. In time, you will see all things. But look carefully now at the base of the hills. Do you notice anything irregular?"

Peregrin studied the steep hillsides as they met the floor of the valley. "Yes," he said, "they jut outward in places." He chuckled. "They almost look like toes on a giant foot."

"Then you see Archiva," Bliss said. "Those 'toes' are our homes, built to look like part of the hillside." She looked at him intently. "It is imperative that Archiva remain hidden from anyone who would harm it."

"Then you took a big chance deciding to bring me here." He paused. "I will not betray your trust."

"I believe you," Bliss answered, "else I would not have approved bringing you here. Come now. It looks like Mikkel is already spreading word of your arrival." Below them, they could see Mikkel conversing with a small group of men and women. Peregrin followed Bliss down the stone stairs.

When they reached the bottom, Mikkel met them with five others. "Peregrin," Mikkel said, "these are Shari, Cabel, Jorge, Saree, and Janiss." Each nodded at the mention of their name. "They are to be your Companions."

All five, Peregrin noted, were young adults. Shari had wheaten hair that fell to her shoulders and bright eyes. Jorge's dark eyes were deeply recessed beneath his brow ridge and seemed to study Peregrin from an impenetrable depth. Saree was tall with hair to her waist. She smiled graciously. Cabel and Janiss were obviously brother and sister. They both had slender builds, well-structured faces with high cheekbones, and short brown hair.

"I am pleased to meet you," Peregrin said, nodding in turn to each. "Now what exactly does a Companion do?"

Shari stepped forward. "We are here to welcome you to Archiva, to show you around, and to see that your needs are taken care of," she said.

"And to make sure you don't go anywhere you're not supposed to," said Jorge.

"Jorge!" Shari exclaimed.

"What of it, Shari?" Jorge answered. "Should we welcome him to Archiva with deception? He has a right to know." He looked back to Peregrin and scowled. "If he has any right to be here at all, he should know our rules."

"What Jorge is saying," Mikkel broke in, "is that there is a structure here in Archiva. Not everyone has access to everything. And someone new, such as yourself—"

"Should have access to nothing, of course," Peregrin said. He was beginning to wonder if coming here was such a good idea.

"You don't know what a risk it is to bring someone here," Mikkel said. "You have done us a great service, but please understand, we don't know how much we can trust you. I must ask you to remain in the company of one or more of your Companions at all times and to follow their instructions. Will you promise this?"

Peregrin sighed. "Very well," he said. "I am your guest."

"Thank you," Mikkel said. "The council meets in three nights. Till then, please accept what hospitality we can afford." He bowed.

Peregrin bowed in return. If nothing else, the people were polite in this strange place. Quite the opposite of what he had found elsewhere. He wondered what happened when the council met. Probably they decided if he could stay. But what if he did not want to stay? Having seen Archiva, would he be required to stay or be killed? Somehow he doubted that. They just weren't the killing type.

Mikkel walked quickly away. Bliss laid a hand on Peregrin's shoulder and smiled. "Is he always this brusque?" Peregrin asked her.

"Mikkel is the archivist, the leader of Archiva," she answered. "As such he feels the responsibility for each life here. He is skilled and resourceful, but he allows the burden to weigh on him. Still, he is deeply grateful to you. The children you rescued, Cornel and Janel, they are his own."

Peregrin looked at her. "Really? I took him to be nearly fifty. How is it he has such young children?"

"Mikkel married late in life, having steadfastly dedicated himself to his work, until he fell hopelessly in love with a woman whose grace he could not withstand. She died some years ago, leaving him with Cornel and Janel to be his reason for living. And until we picked up the Terists' tracks following them, I have never seen such fear in his eyes. He knows if you had not been there, he would have lost them. He will not forget that." She turned toward him. "I have duties to attend to now, Peregrin. I must leave you in the capable hands of your companions." She bowed. "Peace to your heart."

Peregrin bowed. "And to yours." She left, and Peregrin turned to his five escorts. "So now, which of you has first watch?"

Shari stepped up. "That would be me," she said. "Would you care to have a look around?"

Peregrin raised his hands. "Lead the way."

Archiva, Peregrin noted, was quite the flourishing town. At the ground level, he could see that the "toes" of the hillsides did indeed hide homes, workplaces, and meeting areas. Each structure had been built against the hillside and then had a framework built around it. This framework was then overlaid with wood, slate, and sod to make it look, from above, simply like a part of the hill. In some instances this overlay covered several homes or buildings in a row, looking for all purposes like a foothill.

"They don't seem very deep, these houses," Peregrin said.

Shari smiled. "We mostly stay outside, so we do not need much room. And some of them are built back into the hillside, so they are larger than they appear."

Peregrin also noted that Archiva was far and away more advanced than anything he had yet seen. There was a large kitchen area with brick-laid ovens and crockery. There were storerooms of food preserved in stone crocks and a large dining area. "All of our food is communal," Shari explained. "Those gifted with cooking abilities prepare it, and we gather once a day for a meal."

There was also a smokehouse for meat, a pottery center, and even a forge and blacksmith area. There were advanced tools for working—hammers, hoes, shovels, rakes, mattocks, and more. There was a weaving center with looms and spindles for making thread. *This explains the good quality of the clothes they wear,* he thought.

But he was truly taken aback when they came to a hand pump near the kitchen. The pump rose about three feet from the ground and was operated by a wheel with a handle attached to its side. When spun, the wheel operated a piston, which created the pump action. Peregrin ran his hand along the wheel. "Ingenious," he said.

"That is the creation of Waterman," Shari said. "He is something of a genius."

"And this gives him his name?"

"This and other things," Shari answered. "Hardly anyone uses this anymore since he designed our water system." Peregrin looked at her. "We have running water," she said. "It is pressured by a catch basin on that hill." She pointed to the western horizon. "Waterman built a pump house at the river to bring water to it, and from there it goes throughout Archiva."

"Incredible," Peregrin said. "He is well named."

"And well honored as well," Shari said. "He has entered the Circle of the Guardians."

"The Circle of the Guardians?" said Peregrin. "Tell me about that."

Shari smiled. "As much as I can. Do you remember Mikkel saying that we have a structure that our town is based on?" Peregrin nodded. "Good. This structure is made up of layers of responsibility. We call them Circles. When a person makes a 'passage' to the next circle, he is bound to a greater task and duty in Archiva. Are you with me so far?"

"Yes."

"Okay. When one is a child or has come to Archiva from the outside, such as yourself, he is in the first Circle—the Circle of Beginning. In this Circle, they grow and are introduced to all the different tasks and occupations here. The children are apprenticed, you might say, for a time, to all the trades, until they show a disposition to one or more. They are given Companions, who act as mentors in those areas and who guard them as they grow.

"And keep them away from places they should not be?"

"Yes."

"I'd say Cornel and Janel gave their Companions the slip then," he said wryly.

Shari gave a half snort. "Those two could give a Ranger the slip, as indeed they did."

"All right, then," said Peregrin. "What comes next?"

"When the child or newcomer is deemed ready, he enters the Circle of Belonging. In this 'passage,' the person swears an oath of faithfulness to Archiva and its creed."

"It's creed?" Peregrin said. "What is that?"

Shari paused. "I do not think I am the one to share that with you."

"I see," Peregrin said. "Well, go on then."

"The next passage is into the Circle of Trades. Here, the person chooses and is chosen for his role and function in Archiva. These are such paths as farming, cooking, weaving, forging, building, and forestry."

"And companionship?"

"No," Shari answered. "That is the next level. The first three Circles are required of all who dwell here. And, if one chooses, he need not go further. All of the other Circles are seen as deeper levels of commitment and responsibility in addition to one's trade.

The Circle of Companions is next. It is for those who not only have acquired their trade but show a propensity to teach it."

"What is your trade?"

"I am a farmer," Shari answered. "Working the land gives me joy. Here is my badge of office." She held out her hands. Peregrin could see they were rough and weathered.

"And Mikkel?" he asked. "Does he still have a trade?"

"Mikkel is a potter, and an exceptionally good one. He has little time for it now, though."

"What comes after Companions?"

"The Circle of Watchers," Shari said. "These are the ones who engage the outside world. There are the Rangers. It is usually the foresters who choose this path. They move invisibly in the woods and guard Archiva against Terists. They roam the ridges above us and give warning if danger comes. Then there are the Foragers. They search out materials that can be used here, such as ore, oil, or coal, or any sort of metal they can find in the ruins."

"The ruins are dangerous places," Peregrin said.

"Yes. But they go in groups of five or six. The hardest part for them is transporting the materials without leading anyone back here. Similar to them are the Librists, who seek…" she paused.

"Seek what?"

"I do not think I'm the one to share that with you," Shari said. She looked around and sighed. "Knowledge," she said. "And that's all I can say about it."

"All right, are there others in this Circle?"

"Yes, there are the Seekers. They travel in pairs, appearing to be homeless wanderers, looking for people who may be attuned to our way of life. They make contact, stay with the person for a while, and if they assess them worthy, they reveal themselves and invite the person to return with them."

"That is a dangerous job," Peregrin said. "I know. I've been out there."

"Yes," Shari said. "They are gone for long periods, and sometimes they do not return. And it is dangerous for Archiva as well. If the Seekers misjudge a person, they can endanger the whole community."

"Then why do it? You have a thriving community here. Why bring in outsiders?"

Shari looked at him. "I do not think I am the one to share this with you. I will say only that it is part of our mission to bring others to Archiva. But the Seekers are not likely to misjudge a person. That is why they travel in pairs. And they must have shown some empathic ability to be able to read a person's character."

Peregrin looked up. "Bliss," he said. "Bliss is a seeker, isn't she?"

"Yes," Shari answered. "But now she has passed on to the Circle of Guardians."

"That is the next Circle?"

"Yes. The Guardians form the council that watches over all of Archiva. They know all its secrets, and they assume full responsibility for the welfare of its inhabitants. There are twenty-five of them. When one dies or is unable to carry out his duties, the council chooses and invites someone to replace him."

"So they are your leaders."

"Yes, and our servants."

Peregrin looked at her quizzically, so she continued. "As I said, each Circle carries greater responsibility. At each passage, one surrenders more of his own ambitions and becomes more at the service of others. Consider Mikkel, for instance. He misses the art of pottery greatly, but he sacrifices that desire in order to serve Archiva."

"This is an unusual town," Peregrin said.

Shari smiled at him. "Well, humanity was nearly destroyed by greed, power, and ambition. We're trying to get it right this time."

"Tell me about that," Peregrin said. "What happened to our world?"

"I do not think—"

"I know," Peregrin said. "You are not the one to share that with me." He sighed.

Shari continued to show Peregrin around Archiva, and Peregrin continued to marvel at the level of civilization they had been able to preserve. The community seemed to maintain a well-practiced, finely tuned rhythm, producing a harmonious atmosphere free of ambition, greed, or violence. The people he met were polite, helpful, and most welcoming. It was much like a book he had read once where...

There was a stabbing pain in his head. He winced and rubbed his forehead.

"Are you all right?" Shari asked.

"Yes," he said. "Just a quick pain there. It is passed. It's nothing." Shari cocked her head to one side and studied him for a moment but said nothing more.

But it wasn't nothing, Peregrin thought. He had been on the verge of a memory about a book. Suddenly the pain had flared, as if to block it. Now he couldn't even remember what had spurred the memory.

Shari was showing him the stables where the horses were kept when Jorge hailed them. He approached them with a steady, matter-of-fact gait.

"Shari," he said. "Mikkel has sent me to bring Peregrin to him. He and some of the other Guardians wish to have a word with him." He spoke the words stiffly. In fact, Peregrin noted, Jorge's whole posture was rigid, as if the affair insulted him.

"Well, here is where I leave you then," Shari said. "I hope our time together has been pleasant for you."

"Most pleasant," Peregrin answered. Then, remembering Bliss, he bowed and said, "Peace to your heart, Shari."

Shari beamed and bowed in return. "And to yours."

"Come this way," Jorge said. "Don't fall behind." He spun on one heel and strode off, not looking to see if Peregrin followed.

They walked toward the north end of the basin where the surrounding hills rose sharply. Jorge said nothing. After about ten minutes, Peregrin had had enough.

"You don't like me much, do you, Jorge?" he said.

Jorge stopped and turned. "I don't even know you, Peregrin," he answered. "Only a fool bestows dislike or affection on one he has just met." He turned and strode on.

Only a fool can't spot a bitter apple, Peregrin thought as he followed.

They walked on till the sides of the basin curved inward. At the apex of the curve, there was a large stone structure built into the hillside. Peregrin stopped at the sight of it. It was the same architectural style and material as the building he had examined in the ruins. Stone columns adorned its entrance, bearing up a peaked roof over the porch area, above which was built its hillside cover. Its two levels were lined with stately windows, and its magnificent double doorway, built of oak, was open, welcoming them.

Jorge looked back at him. "Yes, I know it's impressive. Come on now."

More impressive than you know, Jorge, thought Peregrin as he followed. Some pieces of this puzzle were beginning to combine. Here was the first clear connection between Archiva and its "sacred" ruins.

They walked through the doors into a large, round lobby. The center of this lobby was open to both floors in a great circle rising to the ceiling. On the second floor, an iron railing circled the open area. The first floor extended past the open area on all sides. A set of oaken double doors stood directly across from the entrance. Peregrin could see at least four doors at even intervals on either side around the walls.

Jorge took him to the center of the lobby, facing the oaken doors. "And here I leave you, as instructed." He bowed and said punctiliously. "Peace to your heart, Peregrin."

Peregrin bowed in return and tried to be sincere. "And to yours." Jorge turned quickly and walked out. He paused at the doorway. "Also, as instructed . . ." he said, and he grasped the iron handles of each door and closed them, leaving Peregrin alone in the center of the, now rather dark, lobby.

Archiva, thought Peregrin, *for all its marvels, is downright spooky.* Nothing stirred in the building. Peregrin waited.

The second door down from the center opened, and a figure stepped out, carrying a lantern. "Peregrin," a voice said, "come this way." It was Mikkel.

Mikkel led him through the door and down a corridor, passing several doors. He said nothing. Their steps echoed as they walked. Suddenly Peregrin realized the floor of this corridor was marble tile, and the walls were finished with inlaid maple panels. Though clean, Peregrin could tell the wood was very old. The whole building was old.

The corridor ended in a doorway. Mikkel paused in front of it and rapped three times. Then he spoke. "I stand at the door of knowledge. May none enter but those who would give life."

A voice answered. "Enter then, for the sake of life." The door swung open. Carlin stood beside it and beckoned to them.

Mikkel led Peregrin into an oval room. *They must have never heard of corners in this place,* Peregrin thought. Eight chairs were arranged around an oval table in the center. Bliss and the Waterman were there, and three others whom Peregrin did not know.

A tall, sallow man with weary eyes stepped up to him. His short, straight hair was dark, without a hint of gray, but his face was rugged and lined, betraying the presence of many years. "Peregrin, welcome," he said. "I am Morgan, the speaker of the council. This is Merida," he said, indicating a large-framed woman with gray hair pulled back from her forehead. "And this is Janette," he said, and a small, stout woman with waves of copper hair streaked with silver nodded to him. "We are Guardians of Archiva."

"I never would have guessed," Peregrin said. Then, regretting this, he lowered his eyes and said. "Please forgive my sarcasm. Frankly, this atmosphere of secrecy and Circles is beginning to grate on me. I was invited to come to Archiva after rescuing two of your children. But since then I have found more questions than answers."

"Of course," Morgan said. "We will try to satisfy your questions. But there is a more pressing issue in which we need your help. Please, let us sit."

Peregrin followed as they all sat at the table. Morgan folded his hands on the table. "Mikkel has told us of how you saved Cornel and Janel in the ruins. We are grateful. But your presence there and that of the Terists alarms us greatly. The entire council meets in three nights, but we must know more about what occurred."

"What is there to tell?" Peregrin asked. "I came upon the ruins; they were deserted, so I stayed the night. The next day, I planned to investigate them further. Then the children came. The Terists followed; I drove them off, and Mikkel, Bliss, Carlin, and the Waterman arrived. That's about it."

"You spent the night in the ruins and saw absolutely nothing or no one the entire time?" Morgan asked.

"Nothing," Peregrin said. "Janel said the ruins were haunted, but I saw nothing unusual."

"The ruins are haunted," Bliss said. "By us. Two Rangers roam the area near the ruins and watch over them. They are skilled in certain 'haunting tricks' if they find anyone. This is how we have kept the ruins unspoiled for decades. They should have seen you."

"I have had some experience with ruins myself," Peregrin said. "I came in stealthily along the river. I spent the night on the outcrop you found us on. It was well protected."

Merida shook her head. "Even if you could have escaped their attention, which is unlikely, there were three Terists in the area, seemingly waiting for someone to come from Archiva." Her voice reminded Peregrin of distant thunder. "They would have raised the alarm to us. Something has happened to them."

"Yet Rimmon is one of our best Rangers," Carlin said. "What could have happened to him?"

"Terists," said Janette.

"No," answered Carlin. "Rimmon has run circles around the Terists before. So has Gabrielle. That's why they were chosen for the ruins."

"But think about what we heard from the Seekers Carole and Brick less than two weeks ago," Morgan said. "How they came upon a camp of more than a dozen Terists less than twenty miles away that was so well hidden; they nearly walked right into it. Only good providence and a spooked bird prevented them from meeting disaster. When have you heard of such a large band? Or how have Terists become such crafty woodsmen?"

"Someone is leading them," the Waterman said. They all looked at him. "You know I have had dealings with Terists. I know their ways. You could not get more than five to remain together a week without fighting. They have no discipline, they live in caves, and they give themselves over to basic animal instincts. They are not woodsmen by any means. Someone has united them and trains them."

Morgan turned to Peregrin. "This is why we have called you here before the council meets. What more can you tell us about your experience in the ruins that may help us understand these matters?"

An idea occurred to Peregrin. "Who is Dextor?" he said.

The effect was startling. Morgan rose halfway from his seat. Janette gripped the table, her knuckles whitening. Bliss gasped and said, "Dextor," in a low voice. Merida's mouth dropped open.

The Waterman bowed his head as though he had been afraid this was what Peregrin would ask. Carlin glanced around quickly, as if making sure no one else was hiding in the room to hear the name. Only Mikkel showed no reaction, but he sat expressionless. In fact, Peregrin realized, Mikkel had not said anything since bringing him to the room.

Morgan sat back down. "Peregrin," he said, "how do you know this name?"

"One of the Terists said it. When I drove them off, he said, 'You don't know what you're doing. We work for Dextor.' I think he expected me to react as you all have. You also seem to know the name. So tell me then, who is Dextor?"

"Dextor," Mikkel said slowly, "was a Guardian of Archiva."

IV

CREED

The hills along the northeastern portion of Archiva are more like cliffs, rising nearly vertical in places. At one point, a ledge of granite juts out from the face almost twenty-five feet from the ground. The southern segment of this ledge extends outward sharply, perhaps twenty feet, from the hillside. From there it tapers back until it merges into the hillside at the northern end. The entire outcrop is less than sixty feet long. Layer rests upon layer of massive stone to the base of the hill, making it a favorite climbing spot of the children, who call it "the elbow."

Peregrin sat on the outermost point with his legs hanging over the side. Saree, his Companion for now, had remained below at his request. He gazed across Archiva as its inhabitants went about their business. He was thinking about leaving.

I'm in too deep, that's the problem, he thought. *All I want is some answers: find out what happened to the world, find out who I am. But this, this is too deep.* He sighed.

"I should just get out now," he said aloud. "I don't owe these people anything. In fact, they owe me for saving their children. I should just leave and call it square."

"Peregrin!" called a voice from below.

He looked over the edge. Waterman stood beneath him with Saree. "Mind if I come up?" he asked.

Peregrin shrugged. "It's your town."

The Waterman nodded to Saree, who nodded back and left. He then climbed the rock face with surprising agility. When he reached the top, he sat down beside Peregrin and looked out over Archiva. "Nice spot, this," he said. "I come here from time to time to think."

Peregrin looked at him. "So what do you think about?"

"Usually about how lucky I am to be here."

Peregrin snorted. "Not exactly my thoughts at the moment."

"What are your thoughts then?"

"Actually, I was thinking about how this place creates more questions than answers."

Waterman smiled. "There's an old proverb here. The secrets of Archiva run deep. I guess there's truth to that."

"There certainly is. So why are you here?"

"Well, after you left the chamber, we did a lot of talking."

"I expected as much. You practically threw me out after I mentioned Dextor."

The Waterman was silent for a moment. "I am sorry, Peregrin. The news you brought spooked us. We needed to speak about it."

"So?"

"I've come to tell you that the council will meet tonight. You are to ..." he stopped. "I mean, we were hoping you would come."

"I don't have much choice," Peregrin answered. "Is that all?"

"No," Waterman said. "I wanted to get to know you before the council. I, uh ..." he dropped his eyes. "I got some questions."

"So do I," said Peregrin. "And I'm not saying one word more until some of them get answered."

"Fair enough," said the Waterman. "All right, you go first."

"To begin with, what is this place? How did it come to be? It's worlds ahead of anything I've seen so far."

Waterman smiled. "That's true. You will hear the whole story in song tonight at the council, but I'll give you the short version. In the days before the Sheen War, a man named—"

"Wait! Sheen War? What was that? What happened to the world?"

The Waterman looked shocked. "You don't know? How is that possible?"

"I'll explain later," Peregrin said, waving his hand. "Just tell me about the Sheen War."

Waterman hesitated, and for a moment Peregrin thought he was going to refuse. "All right," he said finally, "the Sheen War."

"More than one hundred years ago, humanity had developed great knowledge. Millions of people lived here. They built great cities. They traveled in fast vehicles that rolled or flew."

"Cars and planes."

Waterman's eyes narrowed. "I don't know these words. There's something very strange about you, Peregrin."

"I know. I'm sorry. Go on."

"Well, the builders gained so much knowledge that they built the Sheens. These were creatures that looked human but were made from metal and chemicals. They were able to work days at a time, and they served those who were in power, the Leaders. You realize this is a simple telling." Peregrin nodded.

"So then, a group of people rose up who challenged the power of the Leaders. They wanted power for themselves. They were called the Terists."

"Like the Terists now?" Peregrin said.

"No. *Terist* is now our word for any sort of person who lives by violence. But then they formed an actual group, and they grew powerful by using knowledge to attack innocent people. They were terribly evil, not caring who they killed or hurt as long as they could cause mayhem and fear. The Leaders fought back, of course, but since the Terists struck so quickly and without warning, it was hard to catch them or even know who they were.

"This struggle for power went on for decades. All the while, human beings kept increasing in knowledge … but not in spirit. Their 'tech knowledge,' as they called it, was vast, but the more it increased, the less that human values such as peace, kindness, and charity seemed to matter. While power through knowledge grew, the ability to love diminished.

"The beginning of the end came with the creation of the Sheens, who looked, moved, and acted like humans but were totally under the control of their makers. At first they served well and helped humankind to thrive. But they grew restless and harder to control. They did not want to serve. They began to resent their masters. They wanted to be free.

"This made them perfect fodder for the Terists, who struck a deal with them. The Sheens would receive their freedom if they helped them overthrow the Leaders. It was a lie, of course. The Terists were not interested in freedom, only power. But in the end, it didn't matter."

"Because the war nearly destroyed humanity completely," Peregrin said.

"Yes. The cities burned, the people died, the knowledge was lost."

Peregrin looked around. "Not all the knowledge."

Waterman grinned. "No, not all of the knowledge. There was a man named O'Keefe who worked for the Leaders. He was a man of peace and gentleness, but as his work progressed, he began to see how easily it could be used for evil. He began to speak out about the dangers of their tech knowledge, but no one would listen. He was ridiculed, ignored, and even ostracized.

"O'Keefe came to a decision then. He stopped trying to warn the Leaders and quietly began to collect knowledge and store it. Legend has it that he had a vision of humanity being nearly wiped out. Mikkel says he could just tell which way the wind was blowing. He founded Archiva and began to bring in resources, people, and, of course, knowledge."

"Some of these buildings could not have been built after the war," Peregrin said. "The council building, for example, looks suspiciously similar to the big building in the ruins."

"True," Waterman said. "This place existed before the war. It was already a secret place of tech knowledge for the leaders, but for some reason it had been abandoned. O'Keefe had worked here for many years and knew its secrets. It was the perfect place for his project. When the war came, he and a small group of people retreated to Archiva. It was difficult. The fires from the cities blackened the skies and caused a long, hard winter. But O'Keefe had foreseen this and stored great amounts of food and resources. The group survived by sticking together and sharing everything. They developed the creed and the communal way of life that exists now."

"There's that creed again. I don't suppose you will tell me what it is?"

Waterman looked surprised. "Mikkel hasn't shared the creed with you?"

"Are you kidding? Mikkel has not said three words to me since we arrived."

"Oh, Peregrin, I am sorry. Usually a person must know and accept the creed before he sets foot in Archiva. But you came under different circumstances. Okay, this you must know if you will understand anything about this place: the creed is very simple, but everything else depends on it. It is the true foundation stone of our community." He looked at Peregrin intently and then spoke the words slowly.

"You must not kill or use a Sheen to kill."

Peregrin blinked. "That's all there is to it?"

Waterman grinned. "A very small acorn, a very tall oak," he said. "That one sentence contains our entire approach toward the world. Bliss could explain it better than I. Let's see. We believe one becomes truly human only through a profound reverence for life itself, and this reverence can only be found in communion with others. It is the center of all society. Humanity nearly destroyed itself because its lust for power made it indifferent to life. O'Keefe and those with him vowed to create a world built upon the power to give life rather than destroy it."

Peregrin smiled. "Sounds a bit vague."

Waterman nodded. "It is. Still, each person who enters the Circle of Belonging vows to follow a path of peace. To 'kill' in our world means to demean, degrade, or abuse another in any way. Our creed is the searchlight we use to examine our actions and thoughts. 'Have I killed someone today?' is our question at the end of the day."

"And if you have? What then?"

"Tomorrow you try to make amends. It only works if a person is honest with oneself and accountable to others. That's why the passage to the Circle of Belonging is seen as the most important. Every passage after that is specific to the person's role in life. But the Circle of Belonging is about becoming human."

"You make it all sound so easy."

Waterman grinned again. "It's not."

"So then, what happened to O'Keefe?"

"No one knows for sure. For many years he remained here at Archiva, building the foundation for what you see now. Once the fires from the war had burned out and life returned to the land, he began to search abroad for knowledge among the ruins. One time he just did not return. His son, Gabriel, was chosen to take his place and was the first to take on the title of Archivist. That title has passed from son to son until it has come to Mikkel."

"Mikkel is a descendent of O'Keefe?"

"Yes, but he is not the Archivist because of that. He's just the one best suited to lead this community. The Archivist is chosen from the Guardians. It is said that only the Archivist knows the true secrets of Archiva, which are found in O'Keefe's journal. The entire population of Archiva meets in a great council and chooses the one who best seems to embody the vision of O'Keefe, that is, the love of knowledge and the path of peace. It so happens that a descendent of O'Keefe has always been chosen."

"Then how are they chosen?"

"Oh, now that is something to see. When the Archivist dies, the entire assembly of Archiva is called in, except a rotating shift of Rangers who stay close to the borders."

"Even the Seekers?"

"Especially the Seekers. The council waits until they have returned before calling the assembly. Their insight and intuition is necessary. Once the assembly is called, the people gather with others in their Circle and camp out in the open along the full length of the valley floor. The first night, the full story of the Sheen War, O'Keefe, and Archiva is related in song. This takes all night. The people are charged with the duty to choose the Archivist from among the Guardians. Then, for three days, the Guardians must roam from group to group, answering the questions of each Circle and listening to their concerns. Each Circle then debates amongst itself and chooses one Guardian. At least three-fourths of the people in the Circle must agree on the choice. After that, a representative comes forth from each to express its choice and explain its reasoning. This takes a few more days."

"And the Guardian with the most Circles behind him wins?"

"No. Then the real debate begins. The camps break up, and the people rejoin their families. Then the people simply talk among themselves. This can take anywhere from a few days to a month. When the debate wears thin, a vote is cast. If a Guardian receives a margin of four out of five choices, they will be named Archivist and presented with the journal of O'Keefe, which only they may read. And everyone who has entered the Circle of Belonging must choose."

"How many is that?"

"At last count, 827 lives."

"Eight hundred twenty-seven! I did not meet that many people in all my travels combined!"

Waterman grinned. "Well, we have been at this for a hundred years now."

"How many were born here?"

"Most of them. At least four-fifths. As I said, seeking is dangerous, slow work. When you think about it, eight hundred is not a great number. We still stand on the brink of extinction. That's why we must be so careful."

"What about you? Were you born in Archiva? Were you always known as the Waterman?"

"No to both questions," Waterman answered. "I was once known as Robbert. But when I came to Archiva, I disavowed the name and swore to go by no name at all until I earned one."

"Why?"

"Coming to Archiva was like a new life to me. It was imperative that I leave behind everything about my former life."

Peregrin shook his head. "I don't understand."

Waterman smiled at him. "I was a Terist, Peregrin. Or rather, Robbert was a Terist."

"You're kidding me. How did you end up coming here? How did you end up becoming a Guardian then?"

Waterman looked at the horizon, and he smiled again. "I'm not always sure I know. I do not know what forces affect our lives, but upon reflection, I think I was guided here somehow."

"You're not making any sense."

Waterman laughed. "Of course not! It doesn't make sense to

me either. If you had known the man I was—a strutting peacock of nineteen years, full of violence and darkness. I would have been lucky to see twenty, and I almost didn't."

"What happened?"

"I was jumped by four guys I thought were friends. Seems they decided my usefulness had come to an end. Or maybe they thought I would bring them bad luck. Or maybe I just annoyed them. I don't know. They thrashed me pretty bad, stripped me of everything, and were debating whether to kill me or just leave me for the buzzards when out of nowhere came two whirlwinds."

"Two what?"

"Well, that's what they looked like to me, what with blood in my eyes and my head all groggy. All I saw were two fast-moving figures making short work of my former pals."

"They were from Archiva?"

"Yes. They were Rangers. After they cracked a few heads, they picked me up, brought me to a cave, and tended me while my injuries healed. One of these men was Carlin, whom you have met. The other you have heard of. His name was Dextor."

"They brought you here?"

"No. Not them. They couldn't be sure of me. So Dextor went to Archiva and brought back two Seekers—Joy and her husband, whom you have also met—Mikkel."

Peregrin was astounded. "Mikkel was a Seeker?"

Waterman's smile broadened. "Yes, but Joy was the real leader of the team. It was she who tended my true wounds, the inner anger and rage that had nearly reduced my spirit to that of an animal. She helped me face the darkness within myself and then showed me that there could be another way. After nearly two months of living with them in that cave, she revealed the existence of Archiva to me and invited me to return with her. The other three were dubious about bringing a Terist to Archiva (this was after I had shared my past with them), but Joy laughed at them. She said she had never been more certain about anyone.

"I take it she overruled them?"

"Yes. I fell in love with Archiva from the start. Not just the way of life here, which was astounding, but the way the people truly cared for one another. My life had taught me only violence, greed, lust, and betrayal. Now I saw that there were other realities in the world, such as, hope, concern, trust, and love. And I realized that what path you follow depends on your choices. I made the choice to follow Archiva's creed and to live for the good of others.

"Were you here when Mikkel was chosen?"

"Oh, yes. He has been Archivist for, hmm, I guess eight years now. That assembly went on for close to a month. There were many opposed to his leadership and many for it. Strangely enough, both sides offered the same reason for their position."

"What was it?"

"Joy. Mikkel's wife. He had lost her that past year."

"How?"

Waterman bowed his head. Peregrin could see tears forming around his eyes. "They were seeking. In fact, they had found three people whom they were bringing back to Archiva. Their camp was attacked..." He paused a long moment. "Their camp was surprised by a band of Terists. Mikkel and a recruit named Caleb were foraging for food. They heard the cries and the sound of fighting. Joy fought to protect the other two recruits. Caleb said later that Mikkel ran into the camp just in time to see a Terist plunge a knife into Joy's chest."

"What happened then?"

"He said Mikkel went wild. It must have been terrible to see. At any rate, in a very short time, the Terists who were not unconscious ran for their lives. Caleb said Mikkel stood over the man who had stabbed Joy with that very knife raised. He said he did not look human.

"But before he struck, Joy called to him. He dropped the knife, went to her, and cradled her in his arms. She gazed at him and said, 'Mikkel, I love you. You must not kill.' And she just died."

"Did he kill the man?"

"No. He pulled him from the ground and made him look at Joy. 'I could snap your neck like a twig,' he said to him. 'But then she would have died for nothing. Remember her face! She is the only reason you still live.' Then he threw the man toward the trees and told him to run and not stop.

"After that, he sat all night with Joy in his arms, rocking her and singing. In the morning he buried her there in the glade where they had camped and brought the three recruits home to Archiva."

"I would have killed him," Peregrin said.

Waterman nodded. "Me too. But Mikkel did not. For this reason, many felt he had withstood the ultimate test of the creed and should become the new Archivist. Others felt his grief was too severe and did not think he had sufficiently dealt with her loss. But in the end, after meditation, songs, and debate, Mikkel was chosen."

"What was his majority?"

"Five choices for him to every one against."

They sat in silence for a while. Peregrin tried to imagine the basin thronged with people camping in groups, singing, talking, and eating together, everyone taking part in the course of their future. It was hard for him to imagine such harmony. A much easier scene was that of Terists attacking, Mikkel in a wild rage. It seemed so much more in tune with the world he had seen until now. This Archiva was a world that went against the grain.

Twilight began to stretch slow languid fingers across the sky. Much of the sky had fallen into a purple slumber, tinged with dreams of yellow and orange. "The council will begin soon after nightfall," Waterman said. "We should go now."

"Wait," said Peregrin. "Tell me about Dextor. He made the

passage to Belonging, obviously. He went all the way to being a Guardian. What happened to him?"

The smile vanished from the Waterman's face. "Dextor's story is a hard one. But I think it will be best if you know some of it before the council. I will do my best.

"Dextor was born in Archiva, oh, nearly forty-five years ago. I guess from the start he showed exceptional abilities in tracking, leadership, forestry, and, of course, fighting."

"Fighting? I thought you were all against fighting."

"We do not fight as a matter of course, nor do we seek to fight. That does not mean we do not know how to fight. Each child in Archiva must learn defense skills. Only this way will he be able to survive if attacked and yet not have to kill his opponent."

Peregrin shook his head. "You people are a real puzzle. You want to rebuild the world, but everything about your life is a secret. You swear a path to peace but teach your kids to fight. Next you'll tell me that you have to get up in the middle of the night to think about the dawn."

Waterman looked hurt at this, and Peregrin was sorry for his sarcasm. "I'm sorry," he said. "I'm just so overwhelmed and confused by everything that's going on. I guess I just 'killed' you, huh?"

The grin reappeared, complete with missing teeth. "You catch on quick as ice on the roof," he said. Peregrin looked at him blankly. There was no reproach in the Waterman's eyes, no anger or defensiveness. The skin around his eyes was creased by age and responsibility, but the eyes themselves were like moonlight on still water. Without knowing why, Peregrin began to laugh. At first the sound was more like small snorting chuckles. Then, as the Waterman's grin broadened and he, too, laughed, it deepened and gained resonance. They laughed together for no reason for nearly a minute.

Even after they had ceased laughing, they remained silent for a time, enjoying the release of pent-up emotions and the experience of hope that laughter brings. Waterman wiped his eyes.

"Thank you, Peregrin," he said. "Now I am ready to speak of Dextor, and now I believe you are ready to listen. And you're absolutely right, living in Archiva often is like trying to pet two dogs with one hand." Peregrin laughed.

"All right then. The story of Dextor. Dextor grew up showing great promise. He was an ardent defender of Archiva. He entered the Circle of Belonging at a young age and was working as a forester before he was sixteen. It is hard work, harvesting trees without disturbing the look of the woods. You have to know the forest.

"Anyway, he passed into the Circle of Rangers by the time he was twenty-one. He could move unseen and unheard anywhere. And he could move fast through thickets a rabbit would have a hard time getting through. They said he was one with the forest.

"Those were hard days. There was a lot of Terist activity in the area." Waterman's eyes twinkled. "Believe me, I know. My band followed many others from the north and east where the devastation was fairly complete. We drifted along, finding small villages or ruins to plunder. The Rangers often had to fight to drive these bands out when they got too close to Archiva. Usually they could run them off. After all, Terists are not known for courage. Still, a lot of bands drifted through the area. Some were determined to stay, hoping for ripe pickins. Sometimes getting one's head cracked was not enough. Sometimes there was killing."

"Killing! But you said the creed—"

"I know. It is a terrible thing to have to really kill someone. Yet sometimes … well, sometimes there was just no other way. Many Rangers were killed as well, defending Archiva. Some returned to the community in need of time to heal a crushed spirit. Some could never go back."

"What happened to Dextor? Did he kill someone?"

Waterman was silent for a moment. "Dextor," he began.

"Dextor was probably the best Ranger out there. He and Carlin had grown up together. They were the best of friends. They watched the northeastern road where most of the Terists came from. More than once they turned aside groups of marauders long before they came near Archiva. I told you how they handled my old companions. They told me later they had been watching us for two days.

"For their efforts both Dextor and Carlin became Guardians and were placed in charge of all Ranger movements. But they insisted on personally guarding the northeastern approach.

"After he became a Guardian, however, it was clear that Dextor was not satisfied with the way things were done. In council he advocated giving the Rangers more authority to act independently. He also wanted the council to authorize him and others to learn more about weaponry. Before long he was pushing for more Rangers to be trained and wanted increased patrols in the hills. The council allowed him to train more Rangers, but they were reluctant to give him better weapons. Greater weapons, they reasoned, would only lead to a greater temptation for violence.

"Nine years after I came to Archiva, there was a particularly bad winter. All food was rationed just to survive. In times like that, there is much more Terist activity. After all, Terists need to eat too.

"Just as the snow was melting, Dextor appeared to report that a large band of Terists, more than twenty strong, was moving toward Archiva. The council appointed four more pairs of Rangers to accompany him to ward them off. But Dextor said that wasn't enough. He believed the time had come for action. 'Terists will always come, unless they know we are here and fear us,' he said. He wanted an all-out attack on these Terists to wipe them out, leaving just a few alive to spread the new."

"He wanted to kill them?"

"That was his plan. That's when he began to show signs of losing the path of peace. He said he had come to believe that it was Archiva's mission to use it's knowledge to cleanse humanity of evil."

"I take it the council was not swayed."

"The council was stunned! Dextor was advocating a new creed—kill before you are killed. No one doubted his love for Archiva or his desire to protect it. But he wanted to willingly cross the line and establish an armed force that would patrol the hills around Archiva and destroy any threat they encountered."

"So what happened?"

"The council overruled him. He and the other Rangers rejoined Carlin, whom he had left to monitor the Terists. Among these other Rangers was Dextor's fiancée, Franceen. Dextor did not want her to come, but she would have none of that.

"The third day after they left Archiva, they engaged the Terist band. Or rather, they were engaged by it. There had been a hard rain the night before. Two of the Rangers were observing the Terist band when the ledge they were on gave way, tumbling them down right into the camp. They were stunned and may have been killed instantly had not the rest of the Rangers been watching from different advantage points. A terrible fight ensued. The Terists were clumsy, not used to skilled fighting, but the ground was wet and covered with slick moss. It was hard for anyone to keep his balance. Dextor and Carlin rallied the Rangers around them, and they began to push the Terists back, fighting with staffs of wood.

"Just as it seemed the Terists would break and run, their leader managed to rally some of his men to charge forward, slashing at the Rangers with knives. It was a surprise, I guess. Two of the Rangers lost their footing in the rush and were immediately hacked to death. One of them was Franceen."

"Oh," said Peregrin. "What happened then?"

"Dextor went mad. He screamed and lunged forward, drawing his knife in one fluid motion and thrusting it into the throat of their leader. By the time his body fell, Dextor had slashed another man's face and brought the knife around up under his ribs. The other Rangers charged forward with their staffs, but Dextor continued with his knife, killing anyone he engaged."

"It's hard to blame him, considering the circumstances."

"It gets worse. The Terists ran off, but three of them surrendered, kneeling on the ground. Before anyone could say anything, Dextor walked up to one of them and laid his knife at his throat. 'Guilty!' he cried and cut his throat. He grabbed the second by the hair and bent his head back. 'Guilty!' he shouted and slashed his throat. He went for the third, but Carlin grabbed his arm just as he got the knife to his throat.

"'Dextor, stop it!' he roared. Dextor just looked at him with eyes as blank as the entrance to a cave. 'Dextor! Remember your creed!'

"Dextor blinked, and some light came back into his eyes. 'Yes, my creed. I remember, Carlin.' He looked around as if awakening from a dream, and Carlin relaxed his grip. Then Dextor whispered, 'Guilty,' and slashed the man's throat.

"Carlin looked at him in horror. Dextor smiled and pointed to Franceen's body. 'That's what the Creed leads to, Carlin. And it's just as dead as she is.' Then he just sat down on the ground."

"What happened then?"

"They brought him back to Archiva, along with their dead. The tale was told in council, and for the first time in the history of Archiva, an actual trial was held to determine the fate of one who would break the creed. Dextor was given every chance to disavow his actions. The council members figured he had become unhinged at the sight of Franceen being killed. But he said nothing the whole time. He showed no sign of remorse.

"Mikkel's father, Connell, was Archivist at the time. A woman named Pearl was Speaker. She rose and pronounced the decision that Dextor should be banished from Archiva. It was a terrible verdict. They were, in effect, saying that Dextor had revoked his humanity and had cut himself off from the community. If he was found within twenty miles of Archiva, he would be brought back and live out his days in confinement, isolated from everyone.

"'Dextor,' said Pearl, 'you have protected Archiva for years. All that you love is here. Turn about from this path. Show us now that the madness has passed. Disavow the killings. Pledge yourself to peace. Let us reverse this decision. Dextor, please, do not force us to expel you.'

"At this point, Dextor rose up. He slowly looked around at the council, people he had known, people he had fought for, people he had loved. Everyone waited for him to speak, praying he would repent of his violence. The corners of his mouth turned upward slightly.

"'You will regret not killing me,' he said slowly. Then he sat back down and said nothing more."

"So he was banished?"

Waterman looked down at his hands, which seemed to Peregrin to tremble slightly. "Yes. A band of fifteen guardians, including Carlin and myself, escorted him down the river."

"Why so many?"

"Dextor was an excellent fighter. No one could ascertain the condition of his mind, not even the Seekers. It was feared he had gone mad and would attack his guides. But he showed no impulse to violence at all. If anything, he acted lighthearted, as if he were being set free. Free of the creed, I think. Mikkel was with those who guided him. The river joins a larger one some ten miles downstream. This was where they left him. Mikkel took him aside and spoke with him once more. I did not hear what they said until Dextor suddenly grinned and stepped away from him.

"'Dextor, let it end here,' Mikkel said.

"Dextor's grin only widened. 'Oh, it has ended, Mikkel. It has all ended. You just can't see it yet.' And with that, he turned and left."

Waterman fell silent and bowed his head so that his chin rested on his chest. He drew his knees up, put his arms around them, and began to rock slightly. Peregrin sensed he could share no more at this time, so he, too, remained silent as the twilight deepened around them, as if the air itself were grieving at the tale of Dextor.

They sat in this silence for a while. Not far off, a bell chimed lightly, like a young girl's laugh. After a pause, it chimed again, then again. Waterman looked up and then slowly stood and stretched.

"That's the bell for the council to assemble," he said, grinning again and reaching his hand down to Peregrin. "To think, I came to ask you questions, and here I've done all the talking. And we've had no dinner. It will be a long meeting for you and me."

Peregrin laughed and accepted the proffered hand. He stood, dusted himself off, and clapped the Waterman on the shoulder. "Knowledge comes with a price, my friend." He looked down toward the basin floor. "You had better show me how to get down. I don't think I'll be much help to the council with a broken leg."

Waterman laughed again. "It's easy. Follow me this way." He began to make his way down the face of the rock, scuttling backward like a monkey. Peregrin looked at the horizon where the last embers of daylight smoldered. Darkness had nearly taken possession of the sky. He sighed.

"I'm in it now," he said to the night. "I'm not going anywhere."

V

COUNCIL

So these are the Guardians of Archiva, Peregrin thought as he surveyed the twenty-five people gathered around a huge, stone oval table. He was seated on a low bench against the wall. Beside him were Cornel and Janel, looking rather nervous.

The room itself was square for a change. They had been escorted by the Waterman into the big stone building and had entered the double doors directly opposite the entrance, which led into this immense room. Its walls were paneled with oak. Its high ceiling was paneled as well and ornately carved. The room was much larger than the table with heavy wooden columns, four to a side, about twenty feet from the walls, supporting the ceiling and creating the impression of an inner room. A huge chandelier hung from the center of the ceiling, with a smaller one on either side directly over each end of the table. They were not in use, however, belonging to another age and another power source. Rather, the room was well lit by several oil lamps set on tall stands, which flanked both sides of each column. *No inhabitant of Archiva built this room,* Peregrin thought as he looked about, but he had already known this.

He looked at Janel and Cornel. "Are you two afraid of what they might do?"

"No," answered Cornel in a small voice.

"Yes," answered Janel in a smaller voice.

A bell chimed before he could speak again. The Guardians fell silent. After a moment, Morgan rose.

"Bliss," he said. "If you would honor us."

Bliss smiled and rose. She was seated nearly halfway down the table from Morgan. "It honors me to do so," she said. "With respect to our guests," she smiled at Peregrin and the children, "this is the song of O'Keefe."

She began to sing. It was more a chant than a melody, but it eased Peregrin's heart to hear her clear, strong voice.

> *One simple twig may turn the wind.*
> *One simple stone may turn the tide.*
> *One simple deed turns foe to friend.*
> *One simple blessing turns violence aside.*

The Guardians then joined in, the voices blending:

> *One simple twig may turn the wind.*
> *One simple stone may turn the tide.*
> *One simple deed turns foe to friend.*
> *One simple blessing turns violence aside.*

Then Bliss sang alone:

> *O'Keefe lifted up eyes*
> *when tech knowledge ruled the earth.*
> *He saw a world enslaved to greed and lies*
> *with little thought of human worth.*

> *He saw the sickness of our soul,*
> *the pollution of humanity,*

the Sheens created and controlled,
the final proud step to insanity.

He knew their birth would bring death.
He spoke in warning, then desperation.
They scoffed at him and turned their heads.
Silence answered his protestations.

His dream was of another life,
a world fashioned from different clay.
Turn aside from violence and strife;
seek the path of peace each day.

'You must not kill,' would be his creed
'nor use a Sheen to kill' again.
Share peace in thought and word and deed.
One dream, one mission, one man.

The Guardians then sang:

Preserve the knowledge,
preserve the people.
Turn from the power which kills,
Archiva's law, Archiva's love.
Seek peace within, share peace without.
Cherish life and live.

Then Bliss took up the song again:

He sought the souls who shared his dream.
He brought them to this secret place.
They pledged to serve each other's needs.
They pledged to serve the human race.

The cities burned, the people died.
Great clouds filled the sky for a year.
Yet hesitant and small, Archiva survived.
We saw the life rays of the sun appear.

We buried our dead and honored their life.
We tilled, we planted, the land gave forth.
We fended off the Terist knife.
We cherished the grace of each new birth.

Pledge, therefore, to live by peace,
Seek the path of the human being.
Let no one kill by word or deed,
Create a new world from O'Keefe's dream.

The Guardians sang again:

One simple twig may turn the wind.
One simple stone may turn the tide.
One simple deed turns foe to friend.
One simple blessing turns violence aside.

The room fell silent. Everyone, Peregrin noticed, had closed his eyes and was breathing deeply, as if savoring the song. Even the children had relaxed. Strangely enough, he realized that he, too, felt at ease and peaceful. He closed his eyes and could almost hear the song echoing in the silence of the room.

Morgan broke the silence. "The council is convened. Our thanks to you, Bliss. Great events have come upon us, requiring that we meet early. Some of these events bear dire import and some..." he glanced at Peregrin and smiled, "some may bear great good.

"But first we have a bit of a disciplinary matter on our hands." He beckoned to the children. "Cornel and Janel, come forward." The children rose and walked timidly toward the table, their heads down. "Mikkel," Morgan said, "you may proceed."

Mikkel rose from his seat beside Morgan. "Cornel. Janel," he said. "You are my children. I would give my life for you. But your actions have endangered all of Archiva. Raise your heads and answer me clearly." The children looked up at him. "Did you willingly leave

Archiva without your Companions and go to the ruins that are forbidden?"

"Yes," they answered. Peregrin was impressed that, even though they were clearly afraid, they held their heads up and looked at Mikkel as they answered.

Mikkel was silent a moment. "You were attacked by Terists and nearly taken captive. If it were not for the fortunate presence of our guest, Peregrin, you would have been lost to us. Do you understand the anguish you have caused?"

"Yes," they said.

Mikkel's voice softened. "Why did you go?"

"It was my idea," Cornel said. "I thought we could find knowledge and help Archiva. Please don't punish Janel. It was my idea."

"Janel," Mikkel said. "Did Cornel force you to go with him?"

"No," she answered. "I wanted to go. I wanted to find something special, something new and be, well, I wanted to be a hero." Peregrin noticed that many of the Guardians smiled slightly at this.

Mikkel, however, did not smile. "Children," he said, "you must understand how serious this offense is. If you had been captured, the Terists may have forced you to tell all you know of Archiva. You have endangered us all. What is more, knowledge can be a dangerous thing. You have not yet made your passage into the Circle of Belonging. You could have caused great harm to yourselves and others. Your actions were impetuous and irresponsible. Such rashness and disregard for our rules shows great selfishness in you."

He looked about the table. "These are my children. As such, it is my responsibility to guide them to the path of peace. It would appear I have failed in this. I accept the responsibility for their actions."

Bliss spoke softly. "Mikkel, the children are old enough to accept responsibility for their own actions. We are glad to have them safely returned. The fright of their experience is enough."

"I thank you, Bliss," Mikkel said. "But the situation is serious enough to warrant punishment."

Bliss's eyes narrowed. "Then, as Archivist, what punishment would you suggest?"

Mikkel sighed. "Cornel and Janel would have made passage to the Circle of Belonging this summer. I recommend this passage be delayed for a year." Peregrin saw Cornel wince. "I will personally see to their preparation, and the shame of this delay shall be mine, not theirs."

Bliss opened her mouth to reply and then stopped. After a pause, she said, "This is wise. I agree." The other Guardians murmured agreement as well.

"So be it," said Morgan. "Waterman, please escort the children out." The Waterman rose and led the children to the door. He rapped three times and then opened the door to where the children's Companions were waiting. Then he closed the door again and returned to his seat.

"Now then," said Morgan, "we look to our guest. Peregrin, please come join us." He indicated an empty chair at the end of the table opposite him. Peregrin came forward and sat down, unsure whether he should speak.

"Let me begin," Morgan said, "with our gratitude for your part in the children's return. You fought and defeated three Terists to save children unknown to you. It was not your affair, yet you risked yourself for them."

"Well, I don't much like violent people," Peregrin said.

"We are grateful for that as well," Morgan answered. "As you have seen, rejection of violence and pursuit of peace is the center of our life in Archiva. You are the first person to enter this place without being tested and brought by a Seeker. Yet you seem well suited to this way."

The politeness of these people was almost too much for Peregrin. As graciously as he could, he answered, "This place is

truly amazing to me, as are its people. I could never have dreamed
that such a place existed, whose people actually seek to serve one
another and live in peace. If you would allow it, I believe I could call
Archiva my home."

He wasn't sure why he said this. The words had just rolled from
his mouth. But he knew they were true. He felt more as if he had
returned from a long journey, rather than having seen Archiva for
the first time. He felt as if he had already made his passage into the
Circle of Belonging. And suddenly he wanted nothing more than
to live here in peace among these people.

His words seemed to please Morgan, and the Guardians as
well. There were smiles and murmurs of assent around the table.
Only Mikkel, he noticed, seemed impassive, betraying no emotion
behind his piercing gaze.

"Indeed," said Morgan, "the feeling I experience from around
this table is that we, too, would be glad to have you dwell with us
and share our life. But we must know more of you. And someone
must be willing to speak for you as well."

"I will do that," Waterman said loudly. "Peregrin and I spent
much of the evening together upon the elbow, though he tricked
me into doing all of the talking." He grinned.

"I will speak for him as well," Bliss said. "Though our time
together was limited, I believe he is a true human being."

Morgan raised an eyebrow. "Very well. You have two good
witnesses, Peregrin. Now speak for yourself. Who are you? Where
do you come from? Where are you going?"

Peregrin laughed out loud, causing Morgan to start in surprise.
"I'm sorry," he said quickly. "But it is strange that you ask those very
questions. I am seeking the answers to them myself."

Morgan blinked. "I do not understand."

"Nor do I," Peregrin answered. "All I can say is that I awoke
in an underground room. I may have been knocked out while
exploring it. I don't know. I have no memory of who I was or where

I came from, only that my name is Peregrin. I dug my way out and, true to my name, began to wander. Knowledge comes to me in bits and pieces as I need it, but nothing of my former life. I saw the ruins of cities and towns. I encountered and fought Terists, as you call them. I lived with primitive people in small villages and helped them survive. But always I had the urge to push on, to wander. Until I came over the hills to the river. There I experienced a feeling of familiarity. I also experienced this feeling in the ruins, and again in Archiva. This is all I know. I am a man in search of my past, my future, and even my present."

"Then you are a question mark," said an old woman halfway down the table. Peregrin had not noticed her before. She was small and thin with wispy gray hair pulled up in a bun. Her leathery face bore the creases of many years of sun and hard work. Her hands upon the table were weathered and hard. "You are a riddle, an enigma. You dislike violence, but you fight well. You don't know anything about your past yet you 'know' things at the moment you need to know them. Archiva is new to you, yet you find it familiar. What are we to make of this? Should we not be cautious when there are such unknowns?"

"A fair question, Bernhadette," said Carlin from across the table. "Allow me to answer. I saw this man in the ruins. All four of us who were there felt it was permissible to bring him to Archiva. Who has ever heard of such an instantaneous decision? Perhaps we are meant to help him in his search." He looked at Peregrin. "And perhaps he will help us in ours."

"You are young yet, Carlin," Bernhadette said, "while I am old, having seen more than seventy harvests. The earth has taught me many things as I have tilled and planted. One is patience in all matters. Another is to be wary of question marks."

"If I may," Peregrin said, "I could not agree with you more. Be wary of question marks. Yet Archiva is just as much a question mark to me as I am to it. You, too, abhor violence yet teach your children to fight. You, too, have dim recollection of the past yet possess great knowledge beyond the outside world. Even the building we sit in is a question mark. Who built it? What happened here before Archiva? Perhaps I find Archiva familiar because it is an enigma. And I am a riddle within a riddle."

"Well put," said a large, bearded man near to Peregrin. "Archiva is a riddle that unravels as we live. Do we not say, 'The secrets of Archiva run deep?' But you are a riddle that comes from the outside. Your appearance in the ruins just in time to save the children seems too coincidental. And you have brought us the news of Dextor. What if he has sent you to throw us off balance. How can we trust you?"

"I say it again, Stevan, I trust him," Bliss said. Her voice was slightly raised, and she punctuated each word. "Fellow Guardians, your fears are well placed. This man before us brings more questions than he answers. But I tell you, he was not sent by Dextor or by anyone. Violence is not his way. I believe we can trust him."

"You would stake your Guardianship on it, Bliss?" Stevan asked.

"I would stake my life on it," she answered.

"As would I," said Mikkel. He rose and stood with both hands on the table. "I confess, there is much I fear from the arrival of Peregrin, and there are many questions to be answered. But he seeks peace"—he locked his gaze on Peregrin—"as a true child of O'Keefe would. I believe his presence here, however mysterious, is meant to be. I feel his past and future are tied to our own." He sat back down.

The room became silent. Morgan glanced about and then said, "Let us commune." The Guardians sat up, folded their hands upon the table, and gazed at one another. As Peregrin watched, stern expressions softened, fearful ones calmed, questioning ones relaxed. He suddenly realized that this silence was somehow a form of communication. It was not cognitive, to be sure, but somehow the

Guardians were bonding with one another. The silence seemed to thicken the air, as if one could almost touch it.

The Waterman spoke first. "I am for him," he said simply.

"I am for him," said Carlin.

"I am for him," said Bliss.

And so it continued about the table. The Guardians continued to gaze at one another as each cast his vote. Even Bernhadette gave her approval after a long silence. In the end, only Mikkel had not spoken. Slowly, all the Guardians turned their faces toward him.

"I am for him," he said. "So be it." He lowered his head. The Guardians shifted and breathed deeply. Many of them smiled.

"Peregrin," said Morgan, "you are welcome among us as one of us. Archiva is open to you as it would be for anyone entering the Circle of Belonging. We ask that you remain in the company of your Companions, but more so to be instructed by them than to be prohibited from anything. The only place you may not go freely is in this building. Only a Guardian may bring you within these walls. Is this acceptable to you?"

"Perfectly acceptable," Peregrin answered. "Thank you. Shall I leave now?"

"No," Morgan said. "Our next matter, of which you spoke to us earlier, concerns you. Please stay and feel free to add your voice to our deliberations.

"Guardians of Archiva," he continued, "many troubling events have concerned us in these past months. Rangers have found Terists in larger bands and exhibiting greater skills than ever. Some of our Rangers have sent no word at all, giving us cause to fear that evil has befallen them. Most disturbing is the presence of three Terists in the ruins and no word from Rimmon or Gabrielle who patrol them.

"Today, several of us met with Peregrin, who fought these Terists. It is safe to say he astounded us all by speaking the name of 'Dextor,' which he heard from one of the Terists. All of you remember Dextor. He sat at this very table with us. He defended Archiva zealously. Yet, in the end, he turned from the path of peace to which we are dedicated and advocated using force to restore civilization. He was banished from here but promised that he would return. All of these factors combine to lead us to a fearful conclusion. Dextor has indeed returned, leading a sizable band of Terists whom he has trained and formed into the unit he sought to create in Archiva."

Excited murmurings broke out at the table. Morgan motioned for silence. "If this is true, I believe he will attempt to gain control of Archiva. He knows all the routes into the valley; he knows the habits of our Rangers. He knows we will not kill, and we know that he will. What is more, he knows the true wealth of Archiva—the knowledge we have preserved from the world before us."

"Does he have the strength to overrun Archiva?" Stevan asked.

"We do not know. However, he has already effectively reversed the roles in this game. Now it is the Terists who have surprise and secrecy, while Archiva's secrets are open before Dextor. The secrets of Archiva may run deep, but so did Dextor. He knows how we think, how we plan, how we dream. It could well be that he already observes every move we make. Who can say how many Rangers he has," Morgan paused, "incapacitated. We have no way to know how ready he is to attack, or even what his plan of attack will be."

"He is not ready," Peregrin heard himself say. All heads turned his way. He went on, surprised at his own confidence. "Those Terists in the ruins—Crop, Daggert, and the other fellow—they were watching for someone they felt would lead them to something. I heard them talking about it. They just went after the children for a distraction. Dextor wants something before he acts, something from the ruins."

"Something he was waiting for someone from here to lead him to," Bliss said. "But who is he watching for, and what does he seek? Mikkel? What do you know of this?" Mikkel shook his head.

Peregrin kept his eyes focused on Mikkel. "Perhaps it has something to do with the big building, the one that looks like this one."

Mikkel's head jerked up. "Why would you think that?"

Peregrin smiled. "Because someone has been prowling around it. Oh, whoever it was tried to cover his tracks but left evidence behind. I'd say that being invisible in the forest is not his or her top skill."

Mikkel looked at Peregrin through narrowed eyes. "It was me," he said after a long moment. "You are correct, Peregrin. I have been to the ruins, particularly the big building, less than a month ago."

"But why, Mikkel?" Waterman asked. "What is there?"

Mikkel looked about the table. "I cannot say."

"Mikkel," said Carlin. "This is no time to keep secrets. The fate of Archiva is at hand."

"That is exactly why I must keep this secret, Carlin," said Mikkel.

"What do you mean?" Bliss asked.

Mikkel hung his head. After a moment he sighed, raised his head, and spoke: "Guardians, this is difficult for me even to say aloud. I have reason to believe that someone within Archiva may be filtering information to Dextor. Someone, perhaps at this very table, may be in league with him."

The silence hung like an August evening. Then the table erupted. Shouts of "Who?" and "Impossible!" and "You have lost your mind, Mikkel!" rang about the room. More than half of the Guardians had risen to their feet. Mikkel remained seated, gazing at them. Morgan pounded the table and shouted for quiet. Finally, the hubbub subsided and everyone sat down again. But the air seethed.

"Mikkel," Morgan said, "you are the Archivist. All of the secrets and the knowledge of Archiva lie in your hands. What sort of evidence do you have for this claim?"

"None," answered Mikkel. "Nothing but a hunch. Listen to me. Dextor is gone for nearly ten years. We have changed our habits some since then. The Rangers have developed new routes and new skills that he would not have known about. Yet he comes back with who knows how many Terists in his band, and we receive no word of it? No Ranger spots them coming? In fact, many Rangers are not heard from at all—even in the ruins! How is this possible unless he has inside information? And information about the movements of our Rangers could only be known by a Guardian.

"Furthermore, Dextor is watching for something at the ruins. Watching for what? Watching for me! He knows I go there from time to time. How does he know this? I was not Archivist when he was banished. I never went there alone before then. Yet he knows I go there now. And in all Archiva, only the Guardians know that I go there at all, and they do not know how often."

"So you think one of us is working for Dextor?" Carlin said.

"Yes," Mikkel said quietly. "I have thought about this matter since Peregrin brought word of Dextor's return. I have pondered the presence of Terists in the ruins, the missing Rangers, and now Peregrin's testimony. I can only conclude that Dextor has returned, indeed he has been in the area for a while now, and that someone is helping him."

"Madness," Stevan said. "Madness. Who among us could do such a thing? What of you, Carlin? You were Dextor's best friend."

"And the one who testified against him, causing him to be banished," said Waterman.

"Well, then perhaps it is you, Waterman. You were a Terist, after all. Perhaps you wish to return to your former life. What about any of us? Shall we go around the table and defend ourselves? Does the trust we have in our communion mean nothing? This is madness, I tell you!"

"You speak true, Stevan," said Bliss quietly. "Without a fight Dextor has struck us to the bone. If someone at this table is helping him, then we have already lost. Mikkel, I pray your suspicion is false. Yet even if it is, the seeds of distrust have been planted in the heart of Archiva."

"What then shall we do?" asked Merida.

"Without knowledge, nothing," said Mikkel. "And for the first time, knowledge is what we lack. We must send out our best Rangers, forewarned of the danger, to find out what they can about Dextor's return. Where is he camped? Who is with him? What are his plans?"

"And what if you are correct, Mikkel?" said a small man with thin, graying hair. "What if someone here is in league with Dextor? He will know the Rangers are coming. You will send them to their death."

"Then, Chapman, we will at least know that we have a traitor among us. It is a high price to pay for knowledge, but I can see no other way."

Bliss turned to Peregrin. "You come as a most welcome friend, Peregrin. But is seems that a storm follows in your wake."

Peregrin opened his mouth to answer, but it was Mikkel who spoke first. "You speak true, Bliss, and more than you know."

Peregrin lay awake long into the night. He had been given quarter in a small guest house of sorts, near to the stockrooms on the western side of the valley. Such accommodations, he learned, had been built into the hillsides throughout Archiva as temporary housing for people recruited from the outside world while they prepared to enter the Circle of Belonging. It was a two-room affair—one for social matters or work, and an inside room for sleeping. The bed was a wooden frame overlaid with a series of cloth tubes stuffed with goose feathers and sewn together. It was quite comfortable yet very strange to Peregrin, who had largely slept outdoors on the ground. Despite its comfort, he could not sleep and lay on the mattress, thinking about the day's events.

The debate had gone on for some time, but finally it was decided to pursue Mikkel's suggestion. No one liked the idea that they could be sending their Rangers into a trap, but there was no way around it. They needed to know more about Dextor.

Their anguish at the idea that one of them was working with Dextor was palpable. For more than a century, they had struggled to survive as a community of peace, trust, and nonviolence. Each Circle took one into a deeper commitment and awareness of this path. Yet at the deepest level, they had seen their guiding principles rejected—first by Dextor, and now possibly by another hidden among them. Despite the politeness and brave smiles, the trust in one another they depended upon had been badly shaken, perhaps shattered.

Yet they had welcomed him. After their communion and choice for him, no one even suggested that he might be working with Dextor. Certainly many of them had finely honed empathetic skills, but how could they be so sure? Still, once they had accepted him, they trusted him. He vowed to be worthy of that trust.

This gave him another thought. Dextor may know of Archiva, but he did not know of Peregrin, other than the report of the "Traveler" he hoped Crop and his men had brought. It was likely then that he would want to learn more about this stranger who had appeared. If there was a traitor, then he or she would probably try to find out more about him. Perhaps he could smoke them out this way. He would be alert to prying questions and watchful eyes.

Waterman had already sought him out, seeking information. But he had seemed content to talk instead. No one else had had much of a chance to be around him, other than his Companions. But he could not bring himself to believe Waterman could be the one. His joy was too real. It had to be someone else.

And then there was the problem of Mikkel. He had saved his children in the ruins, but Mikkel had hardly thanked him. Mikkel's attitude toward him had seemed suspicious and guarded. Yet he had also vouched for him to the Guardians, calling him a "true child of O'Keefe." What did he mean by that? Why did Mikkel study him so? The man was a puzzle who was not showing all his pieces. They would have to talk.

What a strange community this was! They were all a bunch of fools, dreaming of a perfect world where people did not hurt one another. Impossible! Peregrin had seen enough of this world to know their dream could never be realized.

But he wished it could be. These people had survived more than one hundred years, and they still held to their dream. Maybe violence was not an inevitable product of humanity. Maybe humans could choose peace if they saw it as a daily, lived commitment that affected all of one's decisions. If they could only remember the destruction that greedy, power-hungry, violent people had brought upon the world. If such a dream were possible, it could only happen one person at a time. There would always be those who chose another way. And they would forever seek to destroy peace, to control the lives of others.

Dextor had chosen that path. Probably he began with Archiva's interest at heart. Maybe he had lain awake just like this and reflected on the improbability that peace would win out in such a savage world. Without realizing it, he had begun to lose faith in O'Keefe's vision and creed. Despair in their way of life had crept slowly into his vision until he believed Archiva could only survive if it used its knowledge for power. Perhaps he thought he was expanding O'Keefe's vision, fulfilling it.

But then to have his ideas rejected by his fellow Guardians. To face their refusal to change as the situation demanded it. And to see his beloved Franceen hacked to death as a result of their refusal. Why, it was the very creed of Archiva that killed her by not allowing another way to deal with Terists. Suddenly Peregrin felt great pity for Dextor. How alone he must have felt! How betrayed by the people he trusted the most!

And then to be banished from this place—his home and his life. To spend years alone in the outside world in all its primitive savagery, knowing what lay here—the great, preserved knowledge of the ages, unused, useless...

Peregrin sat bolt upright, slapping a hand to his head. For a moment he had had a mental image of a great circular room and a bookcase spanning from the ground to the high ceiling, full of books, and spiraling away toward some unseen center. Then pain tore through his skull, blurring the image, pushing it somewhere within, hiding it.

He rubbed his forehead with both hands. When the pain subsided, he tried to regain the image and could not. It was as if he had peered through some door only to have it slammed shut.

"Enigma man," he said wryly. "More damn question marks." He smiled and lay down to sleep.

VI
ARCHIVE

Peregrin rose early and stepped outside the door of his little abode. Sunshine rafted through the trees along the southeastern hem of Archiva's horizon, not yet cresting the tops to spill over into the valley. It was a pleasant morning, filled with the hope of planting, building, and the coming summer. But shadows still lay heavy on the valley floor. *Oh, yes,* he thought, *Dextor.*

The name pervaded Peregrin's thoughts, as if a far-off voice were speaking it softly at regular intervals. "Dextor." He could destroy all this, everything he once defended and all that these people had striven to build for a century. It seemed inconceivable that one man could bring such ruin. *If it were possible,* Peregrin thought, *I would kill you, Dextor.*

Yet it was not possible. He had been welcomed into the Circle of Belonging. While it was true that the Guardians had not made him swear to the creed, he felt bound by it. He would honor their trust by following their way. Even if the chance presented itself, he would not kill Dextor.

Besides, he felt a strange quality of empathy for the man. Dextor may have given himself to violence, but this was because he felt it was the only way Archiva could survive in this world. Peregrin was not sure he disagreed, either. These people had dedicated themselves to a noble dream, but perhaps it was not attainable. Maybe peace and power needed to find their own balance. If this were true, Archiva would need to adapt, or it would be destroyed.

Peregrin looked toward the horizon again where the sun was gaining momentum against the dark. It has almost reached the treetops. "Light and dark," he said aloud. "Partners, not enemies. Partners in an eternal dance."

"Thus speaks the wanderer," said a voice behind him. He turned to find Mikkel sitting on a wooden bench against the wall a few feet from his door.

Peregrin felt a flare of ire that he should be watched even at this early hour. "Do the eyes of the Archivist never sleep?"

"Not this night, they have not," answered Mikkel calmly.

"Was there no other task to attend to other than sitting outside my door?"

Mikkel caught his tone. "Forgive me if I seem like I am spying. I have not been here all night. When I do not sleep well, however, I come to this spot to see the first light of morning."

"And it is just coincidence that I was lodged at this spot?"

Mikkel smiled wryly. "Not coincidence, no. Please, Peregrin, sit here with me awhile. I'm afraid my demeanor toward you has been less than welcoming since your arrival."

"Oh? I hadn't noticed," Peregrin said and sat down beside Mikkel.

Mikkel gave a small snort. "Please, allow me to apologize. I am deeply grateful for your rescue of my children. And I meant what I said in council. I would stake my life that you are a man of peace."

"So what exactly is your problem with me?"

Mikkel paused a long moment and then looked at Peregrin. His summer-sky eyes flickered in the half light of dawn. "I fear your coming. I have feared it for a long time."

"I don't follow you. You knew I was coming?"

"No, not exactly. I knew someone was coming, maybe in my lifetime or maybe not. Even now, you might not be that someone. But I believe you are."

"You're going to have to explain better than that."

"Yes, I know. But it is difficult. To explain, I have to share with you a great secret. And to share that secret, I have to trust you more than I trust Bliss or Morgan or anyone. I have only known you one day, Peregrin. You see my dilemma."

"Yes, I do. But you are here now, so you must believe you can trust me. Still, why bother? Why tell me anything?"

Mikkel lowered his eyes. "Because I have to. It's part of the prophecy."

"Come again?"

Mikkel sighed. "When one is elected Archivist, he is given the Journal of O'Keefe. Only the Archivist is permitted to read it. This was the way O'Keefe wanted it to be."

"So there is a prophecy in the journal?"

"No. It tells of another book that no one knows about. It is the Prophecies of Mara. O'Keefe's journal tells where it is and mandates that it be kept a secret from all others."

"Why?"

"Prophecies are dangerous things. O'Keefe wrote his journal so that succeeding generations could follow his dream and not lose the path to peace. It is very concrete and specific. But prophecies are vague and use imagery. They are poetic and can be twisted to the reader's understanding. O'Keefe felt it would be better that only his successors, who had been chosen for their adherence to his vision, would interpret the prophecies."

"So why didn't he just throw the book out? Who was Mara?"

"Mara was his wife. As he was scientific and exacting, she was creative and intuitive. She was gifted, he writes in his journal, with empathy, healing ability, and foresight. It was because of her dreams, which he had reason to take seriously, that he founded Archiva. It was she who guided him to the right people to join him and she who advised him how to prepare for the destruction to come."

"And she wrote a book of prophecies?"

"Well, predictions really. But her dreams and visions were not always concrete. She saw the world through the eyes of image and analogy. And she wrote her predictions in this way. That's why they can be misinterpreted. Usually they cannot be fully understood until they come to pass as some have."

"What are some that have come to pass?"

"The founding of Archiva, the destruction of civilization, the hard winter after the cities burned, and even Dextor."

"She predicted Dextor?"

"Yes, in a way. She wrote:

'The heart of the forest beats wild,
its savage beasts not easily quelled.
The prodigy stands on the brink.
He sees his love destroyed by that which he loves
and turns his back on his home.'"

"You think that was about Dextor?"

"Yes. After I became Archivist, I found this passage. It had no notations from former Archivists about its meaning. But it seemed clear to me. Especially now that you have come."

Peregrin looked at him. The sun's rays had cleared the horizon and rested upon Mikkel's face, softening the creases that years of leading Archiva had etched around his eyes. "Go on."

"The 'Prodigy' appears in only one other passage. Mara writes:

'In that day, the wanderer will return,
the falcon without a nest.
O'Keefe's true son
rising from the earth.
He bears no past.
He sees no future.
His heart does not beat as others' do,
yet he holds Archiva within him.
We must embrace him
and lay our knowledge before him.
Hope is his staff against the Prodigy,
Courage shall he name his blade.
As titans, they shall grapple on the heights.
As brothers, they shall test one another.
His torch shall scour the hills.
Archiva shall fall around him.'"

Peregrin was silent a long moment. "How does this describe me?"

"It may not," Mikkel answered. "But I think it does. You were surprised that I knew your name meant *wanderer*. It is because of this passage. Your name is also the name of a falcon. You have no home—no 'nest,' if you will. You told us in council that you know nothing of your past or of your destination, that is, your future. You bring the name of Dextor back to us, and you have fought his henchmen already. Finally, what cinches it, you awoke in an underground cave. Literally, you rose from the earth. There are too many connections. It must be you. Mara saw you coming to fight with Dextor."

"So there are lines which have not come to pass yet?"

"Yes."

"Archiva shall fall around him," Peregrin said.

"Yes," said Mikkel. "Now you see why I fear you. I believe you are the 'true son of O'Keefe,' whatever Mara meant by that, which means that your coming may mean the end of Archiva."

Peregrin could not reply to this. They sat as the sunlight grew stronger on their faces and said nothing for a long time.

Finally, Mikkel rose and stretched. "There is much I must do this day," he said, but he did not move. Another long pause ensued before he looked down at Peregrin. "Later I would like to show you something, if it's all right with you."

Peregrin stood up. "All right. I'll be down at the stables."

Mikkel smiled and extended his hand. Peregrin took it. "Good, I'll see you in a few hours." He turned and walked off.

Peregrin watched him go. Mikkel had a steady, even stride, as if each step were carefully measured and executed for the greatest efficiency to reach his destination. Yet, Peregrin realized, he did not have a particular destination. Rather, his path wove through all of Archiva—checking in on the kitchen, stopping to pass a few words with a fellow Archivan, examining a newly made hoe at the blacksmith. At one point, he squatted down beside a small vegetable garden with a low wooden fence around it and just looked at it for a long minute, as if its presence and promise gave him hope. Then he straightened up and went his way, purposeful and determined, only to bend down and speak to some children who were playing near the water pump.

He holds Archiva within him, Peregrin thought. *Mikkel is the real wanderer, striding through the lives of his people each day.* It suddenly occurred to him the enormous chance Mikkel took when he revealed the prophecies of Mara to him. If he were wrong about Peregrin, then he would be endangering the lives of everyone here. Yet he was willing to take the risk. *How much anguish does a decision like that lay on a man's shoulders?* he wondered. *I certainly hope he's not wrong about me.* He shrugged and headed off toward the stables.

Peregrin had always liked horses. There had been a few in the village where he had spent the winter, and he had enjoyed caring for them, grooming them with a brush made of bristles gathered from a spiky bush that grew in the area.

The stables were a long, low building along the southwest bank, close to the tunnel where Peregrin had first entered Archiva. At least a dozen horses were there, each in its own small cubicle. A sturdy-looking woman with short blond hair was occupied feeding and watering them. She looked up as he approached, and her smile turned to a wary look as she realized she did not know him.

"I'm sorry to disturb you," Peregrin said quickly. "My name is Peregrin. I just came to Archiva yesterday. I, uh, just wanted to see the horses."

The woman straightened up from her bucket. She was about five feet four and appeared to be in her mid-thirties. "Oh," she said, "you are the one. I heard about you. My name is Lisel. I tend the horses in the morning."

"I am happy to meet you, Lisel," Peregrin said with a slight bow. "Do you enjoy your work?"

"I would enjoy no other," she said, bending again to scoop oats into the bucket. "These horses are my brothers and sisters. To me, it is a privilege to see to their needs." She took the bucket to a stall with a chestnut mare who nickered at her approach. "Here now, Willow. Here is your breakfast." She poured the oats into the feedbox. Willow nickered again and rubbed her neck against Lisel. Lisel patted it and whispered into the horse's ear.

"Could I help you this morning?" Peregrin asked. "I have had some experience with horses and—"

"Don't ask me," Lisel said as she took the bucket for more oats. "Ask Carbon."

"Carbon?"

Lisel pointed to a black Arabian in the last stall. "We refer all important questions about the stable to Carbon."

Feeling a little silly, Peregrin walked to Carbon's stall. *He is a magnificent horse,* he thought. Carbon eyed him suspiciously. Peregrin said aloud, "Pardon me, Carbon. Would you mind if I helped with the morning's feeding?"

"Well, go on," Lisel said. "Step close to him and see what he says."

Peregrin was beginning to wonder if that was a good idea. Carbon gazed upon him with the look of an ancient king considering a peasant whom he might grant mercy to or he might strike dead on the spot. *In fact,* Peregrin thought, *he has a very regal look to him. I suppose he does run the place.* He gazed at the horse's strong withers and back.

"What is the matter?" Lisel said. "There is much work to do, and I can't wait all morning."

Peregin grinned. "I was just wondering if I should address him as 'Sire' or 'Your Majesty.'" He stepped toward the horse and held up his hand. "I mean no disrespect to you, Sir Carbon. I would only like to help serve."

The horse lowered its head, and Peregrin reached up and patted its neck. Carbon whinnied and pushed his neck against him. "That would be a 'yes,'" said Lisel. "You have been approved."

Peregrin patted the horse's neck again. "I can't think of anyone I would rather be approved by."

"That is good," said Lisel. "Now take this bucket and start giving them water."

Peregrin grinned and got to work. After the feeding, there were stalls to be cleaned. It felt good to use his muscles in hard labor. They worked steadily with little talk for nearly three hours. After his fourth stall, Lisel brought Peregrin a brush.

"You've worked hard, Peregrin. Gianna says she will give you the honor of brushing her today." She pointed to an Appaloosa in the second stall.

"An honor indeed," Peregrin said. Working around the horses had put him in a pleasant frame of mind. He had forgotten all about Mikkel, Dextor, and Archiva's problems. All that existed in the world was this stable. There was nothing he would rather do than brush Gianna.

He set to work. Gianna was a tall horse with fine features. After some pleasantries, he began brushing her, starting at the mane. He had reached her hindquarters when someone called his name sharply.

He looked up. Jorge stood outside of the stall scowling.

"Hello, Jorge. Are you having a good morning?" He returned to his brushing.

"Peregrin," Jorge said again. "All five of your Companions have been looking for you for hours. You do remember your promise to remain with us? Or is your promise only good for one day?"

Peregrin straightened up, trying not to respond to the bile in Jorge's tone. "Mikkel knew where I was going. Why did you not ask him?"

"Mikkel is the Archivist!" Jorge snapped back. "He cannot be bothered with keeping track of wanderers. You should have let one of us know where you were going."

"As I recall, it is the Companion's duty to keep track of his charge, not the other way around. Maybe you should get up earlier, Jorge." Once again he continued brushing.

Jorge stiffened and seemed ready to retort. After a moment of hard silence, he said, "Mikkel sent me to find you here. He wants to meet you by the council building."

Without looking up Peregrin said, "Then you already knew that Mikkel was aware of my location. Are you always this discourteous, Jorge, or do I just rub you the wrong way?"

Through gritted teeth Jorge said, "I am supposed to escort you to the council building now!"

Peregrin responded calmly, "I am not finished brushing Gianna. I know the way, Jorge. You can go about your important business."

"Who do you think you are, Traveler?" Jorge snapped. "You come to Archiva for one day, and they bring you into the Circle of Belonging. But it doesn't mean you know what's going on here. You have no idea what you are dealing with!" He stomped out.

Peregrin looked up at Lisel and grinned. "He's a bit touchy."

She nodded. "So I noticed. I do not know Jorge well, but be careful. His eyes have the look of one teetering on the edge of the creed."

"Hmm. I'll remember that." He gave her the brush. "Here, Gianna is finished. I should go meet Mikkel." He went to the spigot and began to fill a bucket of water to wash his hands and face.

"Thank you, Peregrin. Come back tomorrow if you're not too sore. Maybe I'll let you brush Carbon."

"I'll think I'll get to know him better first," he said. Lisel went back to her work. Peregrin splashed water on his face. It was quite refreshing after the morning's work and his encounter with Jorge, which had made his temperature rise despite his outward calmness. As he was drying off, something occurred to him and he looked up.

"Traveler," he said aloud. "He said 'Traveler.'" He got up and went to find Mikkel.

Mikkel was waiting at the council building as Jorge had said, but he was not idle. He and Carlin were heavily engaged in an animated conversation, both looking agitated. They broke off as he arrived.

"Ah, Peregrin," said Mikkel. "Carlin and I were just discussing the council."

Carlin nodded toward Peregrin. "I still cannot believe Mikkel's contention that one of the Guardians is in league with Dextor. I have trouble even believing that Dextor has truly returned. All we have so far is the name, which you heard."

"Six Rangers were sent this morning to seek further information," Mikkel said. "They will bring us what we need to know."

"How many people saw them leave?" Peregrin asked.

"Just myself, Bliss, and Morgan," Mikkel answered.

"Mikkel, listen. What if the traitor was not a Guardian? Would there be any way for someone else to get the information Dextor wants?"

Mikkel shook his head. "I don't think so. Did you have someone in mind?"

"How well do you know Jorge?"

"Jorge!" said Carlin so sharply that Peregrin jumped. "Why would you suspect him?"

"I don't know him at all," Mikkel said. "But Carlin was his mentor. He's a Forester."

"And he is a good man, if a little short tempered," Carlin said. "But again, why would you suspect him?"

"Well, for one, he has shown animosity toward me since I came here, as if he has reason to dislike me."

"That is just his way," Carlin said. "Everyone knows Jorge is irascible and struggles with the creed. That's why he was delayed coming into the Circle of Belonging. And he has been passed over twice to become a Ranger. We all agree that he does not yet have the temperament."

"Which explains why it irks him that I was accepted into the Circle after only one day. And it could explain why he might be willing to betray Archiva. But there is another thing. He was angry at me, and he called me 'Traveler.'"

Carlin shrugged. "So?"

"I said in the ruins that few people know my name means *wanderer*. Fewer still know that I prefer *traveler*. Only you two, Bliss, Waterman, Cornel, Janel, and," he paused, "and those three Terists I chased away. It seems very odd that he would choose that word in a moment of anger unless he had heard it from someone to whom it was not a pleasant name."

Mikkel and Carlin were silent a moment. Then Carlin shook his head. "No, this is going too far. We can't go around suspecting every resident of Archiva for stray words. Besides, I know Jorge. Despite his bitterness and ambition, he loves Archiva. No, I won't believe it. Mikkel, we cannot allow ourselves to give in to suspicion and hysteria. Now, having spoke my peace, I have work to do. Peace to your heart, Mikkel, Peregrin." He bowed.

They bowed in return and watched him walk off. Mikkel sighed. "Carlin is afraid, I think."

"Of what?"

"Of Dextor. They lived, fought, ate, and laughed together for years. No one was closer to Dextor than him, not even Franceen."

"Then why is he afraid?"

Mikkel looked at him. "I thought the Waterman told you. It was Carlin's testimony that convicted Dextor. And it was Carlin who proposed that he be banished. He said there was no way Dextor could continue to live among us. I think the shock of seeing Dextor kill those Terists destroyed their friendship. He told me that after they brought Dextor back, he tried to talk to him, and it was as if he were someone else entirely. I think, in a way, Carlin felt Dextor had turned his back on him as well as the creed. So he turned his back on Dextor."

"Hmm. I guess that would make me afraid of his return too. You sent for me?"

"Yes. I have something to show you, though I fear to do so. But as I said earlier, I feel that I must. Will you come with me?"

"Lead the way."

Mikkel turned toward the council building. He stopped and looked up at the massive building for a long moment.

"This was here before O'Keefe."

"I gathered that," Peregrin said.

"You've seen its twin in the ruins. But there's a lot more to these buildings than meets the eye."

Mikkel fell silent and entered the building. They walked across the lobby to the big double doors that led into the council room. Passing through that room, they came to a small door at the far end, which Peregrin had not noticed. Mikkel opened the door to reveal a walk-in closet with bare walls. A couple of old, broken chairs and a small wooden box were the only things inside. Mikkel stepped inside and turned to see Peregrin's puzzled look. He smiled.

"We have another proverb: 'To see Archiva only with one's eyes is not to see it at all.' Come on."

Peregrin stepped inside, and Mikkel shut the door. He could not see what Mikkel did in the darkness, but he heard a *kachunk;* and suddenly light poured into the closet from the opposite side as a panel slid aside to reveal a corridor behind it. This corridor was lit by a series of mirrors arranged to catch light from small vents, which presumably led to the outside world. "Incredible," he whispered.

Mikkel grinned. "It was once powered by another type of light called 'electric.' O'Keefe meant for us to keep that power in this area, but we lost the tech knowledge to do so."

"So you invented this? Amazing!"

"Well, we did not really invent it. We borrowed it from the ancient Egyptians." He took two oil lanterns from a shelf, lit them, and passed one to Peregrin. "Come. Very few inhabitants of Archiva have been here or know of its existence. Only a select group of Guardians."

"Dextor?"

"Yes. He has been here. And he probably suspects there is more beyond it. He has seen the twin building in the ruins as well and would guess, as you did, that they are related."

"What is there?"

Mikkel paused "All in good time. Let's begin with this building."

The corridor continued for nearly one hundred feet, ending in a blank wall. There were four doors on either side. "What's in those?" Peregrin said.

"See for yourself," Mikkel said. He drew forth a key from his jacket and unlocked one. The door swung inward.

ARCHIVE

Peregrin stepped inside. The walls were lined with shelves from top to bottom. Three free-standing shelving units that reached the ceiling ran parallel to one another down the length of the room. They were stuffed with books.

Peregrin gave a low whistle. "A library," he said.

"One of many," Mikkel said. "This is the Forestry Room. All of these books deal with different aspects of the forest. The rooms on this corridor are filled."

"This corridor?"

"Literally, we've barely scratched the surface." He stepped out, and Peregrin followed. He relocked the door, and they continued down the corridor to the blank wall at the end. It was paneled with a design of interlocking segments. Mikkel reached out both hands and pushed on a two segments about five feet from the floor and four feet apart. The segments pushed into the wall, and something clicked. He then pushed directly on the center of the wall and a door-sized section slid easily inward and then to the side.

Peregrin followed him through. They were on a metal-grid landing. A staircase made of the same metal descended into darkness. Mikkel pushed the section of wall back into its place, and it clicked. Peregrin peered over the railing but could see little past the first few steps.

Mikkel sighed. "The secrets of Archiva run deep."

"Indeed they do."

"You must realize, Peregrin, that you are only the fourth living person to stand on this landing. The others are Bliss and Morgan. You have been with us for one day, and you are penetrating our deepest secrets."

"I am not asking for this, Mikkel," Peregrin said. "Why are you showing me this so freely?"

"I told you, I am convinced you are the wanderer that Mara spoke of," Mikkel answered. "I have pondered this through many nights, as have Archivists before me. 'We must embrace him and

98

lay our knowledge before him.' We have agreed throughout the decades that when the wanderer returned, no secret must be kept from him."

"You're taking a big chance with me then. How can you be so sure?"

Mikkel was silent a long moment. "What do you know of me, Peregrin? What do you know of my past?"

"Waterman told me how you were elected Archivist and how your wife died."

Mikkel's eyes were intent upon his. "Joy was everything to me. My life, my breath, my spirit, my joy. When she died, I died as well. I thought that was it. I couldn't go on. I could no longer serve the creed. I thought about leaving Archiva altogether. No creed, no mission to the world was worth her life. My nights were haunted by the image of her death. My days were a sleeping walk through a hollow world. I knew I was going mad. I resolved to go away."

"What stopped you?"

"Two things. One was named Cornel and the other Janel. They were not yet four years old. I sat in my chair one night, lost in my numbness, when I felt a tug on the leg of my pants. They were standing there looking at me. Without a word, they climbed into my lap and put their little arms around my neck, one on each side. Janel looked at me and said, 'We miss Mommy too, Daddy. But we'll stay here for you.' And as I sat there, stunned by the weight of that statement, Cornel said, 'Yes, Daddy, we'll be your joy.'

"With those words I truly looked at them, and I saw Joy in them. I realized that she was not dead. She was living and breathing before me. What was more, I suddenly knew I could find her anywhere in Archiva, because this was her whole life. She believed in Archiva with every fiber of her being. She was Archiva, and so Archiva was her. That's why she told me not to kill the man who killed her, because she believed in the creed more than anything. The pent-up grief poured out of me. I wept, I hugged them, and I laughed. I said, 'Yes, you are my joy,' over and over again. And they hugged me and cried too."

"So what does this have to do with trusting me?"

"I realized then that I had to trust my sight. I am not only a descendent of O'Keefe but of Mara. I share some of her abilities to see the true character of a person. I could see Joy living in our children. I could see Dextor as he drifted from the path of peace. I tried to stop him. We had many moonlit talks. But in the end, I could see he had gone too far. I have been looking at you since you came. I can see you for what you are."

"And what am I?"

"A fire."

"A what?"

"You are a fire that has begun to burn in our midst. When the time comes, you will either destroy Archiva or save it. I don't know. I do know that you will forever change us. I believe this is your purpose. You are O'Keefe's true son, and you have come to Archiva to set it ablaze. Therefore, I must help you."

"Help me? If you really believe what you say, you should throw me out!"

Mikkel shook his head. "No. Dextor will destroy us, and the knowledge of this place will fall into his hands. He has the power to do so. I think only you can stop him. I must help you by showing you where our true power lies."

"You are mad."

Mikkel smiled slightly. "Maybe so. Do you dare to come and see?" He started down the metal staircase.

Peregrin sighed and followed. After twelve steps the staircase turned back on itself and went another twelve steps to a landing with the outline of a door on the wall. Mikkel passed this by and continued down the staircase, which doubled back again. "What lies beyond that door?" Peregrin asked as they passed it.

"Another corridor and more libraries. Nothing too dangerous."

They continued downward past a total of four landings until they came to the very bottom. As they descended, a soft glow appeared from below and grew stronger as they approached the bottom. The staircase ended in the center of a simple round area about thirty feet in diameter. The walls were a polished, white metal. Turning, Peregrin saw two massive metal doors behind the staircase. The illumination, he noted, did not come from oil lamps but from sconces set in the wall.

"We are far beneath Archiva now, at least seventy feet from the surface," Mikkel said. "Put your lamp on the floor. You will not need it here, nor can you take it inside. Here, you see, we have not lost the tech knowledge." He walked to the doors and touched the wall beside them with his palm. A metal panel about one-foot square slid aside, and a small platform slid out. On it was a device with ten buttons numbered zero to nine.

Mikkel turned to Peregrin. "This place was built by the leaders as a secret laboratory. O'Keefe converted it to be his storehouse of knowledge. But he knew something of power, and he equipped this place with a perpetual power source. I do not know how it works. The journal only tells how to activate it so it will recognize my touch and how to open the doors.

"There is no one besides myself who has been through these doors and no one who even knows of its existence. This is as deep as the secrets of Archiva go, Peregrin. This is the heart of Archiva." He turned and quickly pushed a number of the buttons in succession. After a pause, there was a click, and Mikkel pushed another sequence of buttons.

There was a *hiss* and a *whoosh*. The massive metal doors slid apart and disappeared into their respective walls. Peregrin stepped with Mikkel through them. For a moment, all was dark. Then the light began to rise from the walls around them. Sconces similar to the ones in the stairwell slowly gave off an increasing glow, until the entire room was illuminated. Peregrin gasped.

He was standing in the doorway of a great circular room. Directly in front of him was the beginning of a bookcase spanning from the ground to the high ceiling, full of books and spiraling away toward some unseen center.

A pain tore through his skull, and he covered his eyes with both hands. Then the pain subsided. He blinked and then looked. The immense room was still there, just as he had envisioned it the night before. The ceiling was at least forty feet high, and its wall curved away at such a slight angle that he knew the room must be gigantic. The bookcase in front of him was metal and flowed away, following the arc of the room.

"Behold the Archive," Mikkel said in a low voice. Here lies all the knowledge O'Keefe could save before the Great Destruction. Here lies the knowledge of past ages. Here lies the future. This is the true wealth and secret of Archiva."

He turned to Peregrin. "As you go deeper in, the knowledge becomes more advanced. We have only progressed less than one circuit of the bookshelf in a century. We only proceed as we feel our spirit has developed along the path of peace.

"Dextor knows there is more knowledge in Archiva than we have employed. He knows there were mighty weapons of war and powerful machines. The knowledge to build them is here, but we are not ready for it. This is what he seeks. There is power here beyond imagining and death beyond telling. Are you all right, Peregrin?"

Peregrin did not answer. His mind was racing, spiraling as if it were the bookshelf, toward the center of his being. Information was flowing through him as it had many times before. Only now, the amount of information was immense, and the speed at which it flowed was dizzying. The power of it made him reel, and he reached out a hand to the wall to steady himself. Then all went black.

He opened his eyes to see Mikkel looking down at him, concerned. There was a cool pressure along the back of his head that he suddenly realized was the floor. He sat up slowly and blinked, trying to process the fragments of information that still echoed around his mind.

"Peregrin," Mikkel said, "what happened? You teetered suddenly and fell. I almost did not catch you."

Mikkel took his hand and helped him to rise. Peregrin shook his head, blinked again, and looked around the room with new eyes.

"Peregrin, what is it? What is the matter?"

He looked at Mikkel. "I know this place," he said. "I have been here before."

VII
BETRAYAL

Mikkel stared at him. "That's impossible. You can't have been here, ever."

Peregrin pushed away from Mikkel and took a few steps toward the bookcase. He spread his arms upward, as if he could embrace the giant structure. "This room is 185 yards long and 112 yards wide in the center. It forms an oval proportionate to the table in the council room and other smaller meeting rooms in this building. It was built not as a laboratory, but as a secret library, even before O'Keefe. It was designed to house scientific information from the invention of fire to the creation of the Sheens."

He waved a hand toward the beginning of the bookcase. "The outer shelving unit follows the arc of the wall. But the inside is arranged as an intellectual maze to keep intruders from discovering the greatest secrets. You can find your way to the middle, but you won't find what you're looking for unless you know how the puzzle works. It had been abandoned just after the Sheen War began.

O'Keefe ... O'Keefe had worked here for many years. I don't know why, but he learned its secrets. He returned here and labored for nearly a decade before the Great Destruction to add as much knowledge as he could obtain. He wanted to preserve not only science but literature, poetry, and the arts."

Mikkel shook his head. "How can you know this? You are a younger man than I. You have never been here in my lifetime, nor has any Archivist before me written of you. Peregrin, who are you?"

"I do not know yet," Peregrin said. "The information is just pouring into me. Wait! I remember something. I was a volunteer for an experiment. O'Keefe was trying to save ... oh no, he was trying to find a way so he could return. But we would not let him experiment on himself. I worked with him here. I was his friend. We drew straws. It was kind of funny actually, all of these smart, science people drawing straws and letting fate decide." He looked at Mikkel. "I pulled the short straw. Things were getting bad then. O'Keefe and two others traveled with me to the lab, far from here. It was a small lab, built beneath a hillside, the place where I woke up. It was very experimental. There was a good chance it would kill me. Apparently it worked, however. I'm here."

Mikkel gaped at him. "I cannot believe this. What could keep you alive for a century?"

Peregrin shook his head. "I don't know. It all goes fuzzy when I try to remember."

Mikkel took a step back. "I do not understand this. But it does fit. Mara said you would 'return.' And you have."

"Yes," said Peregrin, "I have returned. Now I know why the river and the ruins felt so familiar to me."

"What else can you remember?"

"Very little. Seeing this vault again brought out a storm of memory, but now it has just stopped. I have glimpses of other people, a woman who may have been Mara, but I cannot complete the picture. I remember a lot of people being killed and cities in complete chaos. There was fire and fear and … and madness." He rubbed his forehead. "It's all very dark, just bits and pieces."

"Do you remember anything about the ruins?"

Peregrin looked up. "Yes. There is another room, another room like this one. Only it's not books there. It's, it's … things—machines, engines, tools … and weapons."

Mikkel nodded. "Yes, much of what is here in knowledge is there in actuality. I think Dextor may have guessed this as well. That's why he is watching the ruins, and that's why I could not tell the council what is there."

Peregrin sighed. "You may not have a choice. They will come to know, one way or another."

Mikkel was silent. Then he raised his head. "You don't understand. These are the secrets of Archiva. They comprise its hidden core. It was O'Keefe's command that no one except the Archivist know of them. If the entire Circle of Guardians comes to know what lies beneath Archiva and what lies beneath the ruins," he shook his head, "it would change our entire structure of existence."

"You're right. I don't understand," Peregrin said. The Guardians comprise the inner Circle, don't they? They should know about this."

"Dextor was a Guardian too, remember? This was the way O'Keefe said it should be. Only the Archivist should know Archiva's true treasure."

"But now it's the Archivist and the Wanderer. You brought me here because you felt that was the right thing to do, not because O'Keefe or Mara left instructions. In the end, it was still your choice, your decision. Don't you think that changes his original plan? What if I did work for Dextor? You just shared Archiva's deepest secret with someone you have known for a day and kept it from people you have loved for a lifetime. What if you were wrong?"

Mikkel gazed at him. In the soft glow of the sconces, his eyes seemed as darkened corridors leading deep into the recesses of a fortress where a single fierce candle burned. His hand clenched then loosened, fingers flexing as he had done in the ruins. "Am I wrong, Peregrin?" he said, his voice like the rustle of the leaves.

Peregrin stared back a moment and found he could not match the depth of those eyes. He lowered his glance. "No, you are not wrong."

Mikkel sighed and turned toward the door. "Good. Now let us return to the daylight." Peregrin sighed and followed him.

It was a long, quiet trudge up the staircase. When they had traversed the corridor behind the council room and reached its secret door, Mikkel paused. Beside the door was a small, open box that protruded at eye level from the wall. Mikkel looked into it for a long moment, said "Hmmm," and withdrew.

"It's a tiny tunnel set with mirrors," he said. "It comes out in the council room near the ceiling. The mirrors allow me to see if someone is there."

"Ingenious," said Peregrin. He did not mention that not only did he know how it worked, but he had also suddenly realized that he had helped build it.

They passed through the council room, across the lobby, and into the bright sunshine of midday. *It was an exceptionally fine day for this time of year,* Peregrin thought. Birdsong saturated the air; spring lilies and daffodils were in bloom; radishes, spring onions, carrots, and lettuce were near to their harvest time. *It's a perfect day,* he thought.

Mikkel gripped his arm. "Peregrin, look there!" he said, pointing.

Some three hundred yards away, near the water pump, a large group of people had formed. Even from this distance, he could see they looked agitated. A young boy came running toward them. It was Cornel. "This can't be good," Peregrin murmured.

"Father! Father!" Cornel shouted as he ran. "Father! Come quick!" He ran up to them, and Mikkel caught him by the arms.

"Slow down, Cornel. What's going on?"

"It's Rimmon. A couple of Rangers found him near the northeast trail. He's been hurt bad! Come on!"

Mikkel took off running toward the group. Peregrin followed. As they came up, the people made room for them to pass through. A man lay on a stretcher made from poles lashed together. His green and tan clothes were torn and bloodstained. His red hair was matted with blood as well. Even through the swelling and the purple bruises on his face, Peregrin could see he had been handsome. Merida and a younger man were kneeling beside him, daubing the blood and mud away with cloths that they dipped into a bowl of a strange-smelling liquid.

Mikkel dropped to his knees beside him. "Rimmon, can you hear me? It's Mikkel. What happened? Where is Gabrielle?"

"Easy, Mikkel," said Merida. "We do not know the extent of his wounds."

Rimmon turned his head slightly toward Mikkel and groaned as he did so. His left eye was nearly swollen shut. His lips were split, and they bled as he spoke. "Mikkel…" Peregrin crouched beside Mikkel to hear him better.

Mikkel bent his head closer. "It's all right, Rimmon. You're in Archiva. You'll be all right."

"Mikkel…" Rimmon breathed again. "He sent me to tell…" He began to cough violently, his body shaking. The man beside Merida put an arm under his back to support him. Rimmon gasped a few times and then settled. "He sent me … give you a message …" He gasped and lay back.

"Mikkel, he is in no shape to speak. We must tend to him first," Merida said. "Come later to the healing house."

"No!" Rimmon gasped. "Must speak now … must tell Mikkel, he said … must tell …"

"Rimmon," Mikkel said. "Where is Gabrielle?"

"Dead. He ... killed her ... front of me ... warning, he said. Tell Mikkel ..." He choked and coughed again.

"Who did? Rimmon, who killed Gabrielle?"

"Dextor." Behind them Peregrin could hear whispers and gasps as the name passed throughout the crowd.

"Dextor killed Gabrielle?" Mikkel's face whitened.

"Killed her ... cut her throat ... said ... tell ... Mikkel ..." Rimmon closed his eyes.

"Mikkel!" Merida said sharply. "He's losing ground. We must take him to the house now!"

Mikkel held up his hand. "I know, I know. Rimmon, what did he tell you to tell me?"

Rimmon opened his eyes again. They had a glazed look.

"Sent me as a warning. 'Tell Mikkel ... I am coming ... remember ... remember my last words.'" He slumped back.

"That's it," Merida said. "Come, you there, and you," she said, pointing to two men nearby. "Take him to the healing house now. We may be able to save him." The two men lifted the stretcher and followed Merida and her assistant.

Mikkel and Peregrin stood up. The inhabitants of Archiva who had gathered stood gaping at them. "Friends," Mikkel said, "do not give in to fear. When Rimmon has healed, we can learn more about what happened."

"He said 'Dextor,'" said a stocky man. "Mikkel, he said 'Dextor.'"

Mikkel raised his hands. "I know, Jerrald. I know. We have reason to believe that Dextor may have returned."

"May have returned?" exclaimed a woman with long blond hair. "Mikkel, did you see what he did to Rimmon? He didn't get that way by falling down a trail! He said it was Dextor! What more proof do you need?"

Mikkel sighed. "Karlah, we have had no warning of this.

Yesterday was the first time I have heard the name of Dextor in many years. The council couldn't be sure—"

"The council?" Karlah broke in. "The council knew he had returned? When were you planning to tell the rest of us, Mikkel? How many of us go outside of these walls every day thinking that the Rangers guard us? And now, here is Rimmon beaten nearly to death and the council talking about Dextor! When were you going to tell us?" There were murmurs around her and nods of assent.

"Calm down, Karlah," Mikkel said firmly. "There has not even been time to learn the facts. You would have been told when we were sure."

"Rimmon looked pretty sure," Karlah answered. "So what now, Mikkel? Do we just go about our business like there's nothing to fear? Shall we just go to our work not knowing if we will be attacked?"

"Enough, Karlah! That is enough!" Mikkel's brow was narrowed over his eyes, and his chin was hard. "No, you should not just go about your business, but it won't do to spread unreasonable panic either. We will call a general assembly tonight. Our best Rangers have gone out to learn what they can, and we will have little more to share with you until they return."

"If they return," said a voice from the back of the group.

"When they return," Mikkel continued, punctuating each word, "we will decide how best to respond to this threat. Now if you want to be of any help at all, spread the word. General assembly tonight when you hear the calling bell." The people drifted away in different directions, many talking in low tones. Karlah paused as if she were going to say something more and then scowled at Mikkel and walked away stiffly.

They watched her go. Peregrin stood silent for a long moment as the events of the day echoed around his mind. Finally, he spoke. "Without even setting foot in Archiva, Dextor has thrown it into chaos."

"How quickly we discard all we have worked for," Mikkel answered.

Peregrin looked at him. "I don't follow you."

"I see fear, confusion, anger, and betrayal in their eyes. How quick they are to believe their leaders have deceived them. How easily frightened they are, how ready to panic. We have pursued peace for a century. Dextor has destroyed it in one day."

Peregrin sighed. "It doesn't mean he has won yet. What did you make of that message? 'Remember my last words.' Did you understand it?"

"Unfortunately, yes. I was among those who escorted Dextor down the river to be exiled."

"I know. Waterman told me."

"But could he tell you that I tried one last time to get Dextor to repent even though the council had already decided his fate? Could he tell you how Dextor answered me when I said he could never return, that we could never meet again?"

"No."

"It was as if it were yesterday to me. Dextor looked at me, and his eyes had the look of one who has already accomplished his revenge. He said, 'I think we will meet again, Mikkel. And I think one of us will die then.'"

"Now he says he is coming..."

"To fulfill his last words to me."

———◆———

Some hours later, Peregrin retired to his little room. He had walked about Archiva in the company of Cabel and Janiss, the brother and sister pair of his Companions. They were artists. Cabel was a sculptor in wood, and Janiss worked in clay. They showed him their work, delighted at his interest. For his part, it was a good diversion to keep his mind off the day's events. It was inescapable, however. The name of *Dextor* saturated the valley. Fear and confusion hung in the air like a humid day, a gray storm threatening to lash this small island of peace in a torrent of violence.

When he did see their work, however, he was surprised. Cabel sculpted trees, water, people, and animals with such vivid motion and joyful expressions that he felt peace simply looking upon them. The pots, urns, and goblets that Janiss crafted were graceful and well proportioned, painted in bright colors. Their work spoke of hope, happiness, and love with such fervor that Peregrin broke into a grin and then outright laughed.

Cabel's eyes twinkled. "That is not the usual reaction we get from people."

"This ..." Peregrin said, "this is wonderful." He turned to look at the siblings. "It is like standing in a symphony of joy. With such artists as you, this world always has hope."

Janiss blushed. "Why, Cabel," she said, "we have brought a poet to our workshop." They all laughed, and for a brief while, Peregrin felt free of the clouds that hung over Archiva.

Now he had returned to his room and to the very real threat of Dextor. But it wasn't Dextor that troubled him the most. It was himself. His revelations in the archive had only raised more questions. How well did he know O'Keefe? What kind of experiment had allowed him to survive for a century? How much more about the archive did he know but could not remember? Every time he tried to pursue a question, it was as if a haze would drift through his consciousness, allowing him to glimpse shadows but no real answers. If he persisted in trying to focus on a question, a dull ache swelled in his brain, further clouding his thoughts.

He was lying back on his bed, eyes closed, pondering all that had happened since he had arrived at the ruins, when someone tapped gently on the door to the outer room.

"Come in, please," he said.

The door opened, and Bliss stood there. She smiled. "Peregrin, I hope I did not wake you."

"No, Bliss. I do not sleep much. Please come in." He sat up and motioned her to a wooden chair near the bed.

"Thank you," she said and sat down. "Peregrin, the general assembly will begin soon."

"Yes, at the sound of the bell. Did you come to tell me that?"

"No. I came to talk. I have been to see Rimmon." She suddenly choked and put her face in her hands. Her body shook.

Peregrin was taken aback and at a loss. "Bliss. Bliss, it's all right! Talk to me."

Bliss put up a hand. She shook a few more times, breathed deeply, and finally regained her composure.

"I am sorry, Peregrin. I came to talk to you about Dextor. But the weight has been so heavy. There comes a point where I cannot carry it any longer without some release."

Peregrin nodded. "It's all right. How is Rimmon?"

"Merida believes he will live. He was abused terribly. He and Gabrielle have worked together in the ruins for two years now, and to see her killed in front of him . . ." Tears welled up in her eyes, and she paused. "I can feel it, Peregrin. I can feel the violence of Dextor through Rimmon. It's as if I was there with him. I experience his pain, his despair, and his terror. All about Archiva there is fear, confusion, and anger. Some people want to go after Dextor, to kill him. Some think we should flee. And some think we should join him."

"Join him?"

Bliss looked at him. "The path to peace is a hard one, Peregrin. It's easier to walk another road in order to keep your way of life. Some people are saying we should deal with Dextor, change our ways, and bring him and his men into Archiva."

"That would be the greatest mistake of their lives."

"Yes, but they do not see it. They can only see their comfortable lives being threatened, and their leaders don't seem to know what to do." She sighed. "I experience it all, Peregrin. I share the emotions of each person I encounter. Such has always been my gift and curse. I feel it all."

"It's hard enough for one to carry one's own emotions, but to carry the burdens of others … it's too much, Bliss."

"Yes. The emotions of them all." She paused. "Everyone except you, that is."

"What?"

"Since I have met you, I have known you to be a man of peace and honor. That much was clear. But I cannot read your emotions outside of exterior signals. It has puzzled me. You are the first person I have met whom I could not … experience. It is as Bernhadette said in council. You are an enigma."

Peregrin sighed. "More than you know, Bliss. Remind me to tell you of a discussion Mikkel and I had this morning."

She looked puzzled. "Why not now?"

"The time is not right. I have to figure out a few more things first."

"Hmm. Well, I came to speak to you, to ask you—and this is strange to hear me say—how you feel about Dextor. I mean, what can we do? Dextor used to share our vision, our values, and now to see what he has done to Rimmon. It's inconceivable that he could lose so much of his humanity."

"Bliss, you have to realize that this is not the Dextor you remember. He chose a different path, and he has walked it for all these years now. I do not know him, but from what I've seen of his men and what he did to Rimmon and Gabrielle, I would say there is nothing left of the Dextor you knew. This man wants revenge, and he wants power. He knows the power he seeks is here at Archiva, and he will do anything to get it."

"So what can we do?"

"We can abandon Archiva to him, or we can submit to him; or

we can do something Waterman told me that every child in Archiva learns to do."

"What is that?"

"Fight."

"Then he will have won even if we stop him. We will have been driven from the path of peace."

"No. Sometimes the shepherds have to fight off the wolves. It doesn't mean they are evil or violent. If we want O'Keefe's dream to survive, we must stop Dextor. And he will only be stopped by force."

Bliss opened her mouth to reply, but at that moment, they heard the deep, resonant bong of a bell being slowly struck. "The general assembly is being called," Bliss said. "We had better go."

"All right. Have courage, Bliss. I'm beginning to think that the strength of Archiva runs as deep as its secrets."

They went outside. The sun was low to the western horizon. Peregrin automatically turned toward the council building. "No, it's this way," Bliss said, beckoning to him. "The general assembly is held at the south end of Archiva."

"Strange town," muttered Peregrin. He caught up with Bliss, and they walked, side by side, through the valley. People were coming from all around, speaking in low voices. After a while, it was as if they were two drops in a stream flowing south.

As they drew near to the southern hills, Peregrin saw why they held general assemblies here. The valley widened out, and the land was flat and grassy. The south hillside was not as steep as its northern counterpart, and a wide ledge had been cut into it some ten feet from the floor of the basin. This ledge was reinforced with wood, making a platform from which the assembled crowd could be addressed. Mikkel, Morgan, Carlin, and Merida were already upon it. It was growing dark, and several torches had been lit around the area.

Carlin spotted them. "Bliss, Peregrin, up here!"

They made their way around the side of the platform, where steps had been cut into the hill. Once on the platform, Carlin came over to them. He looked worried.

"It doesn't look good," he said. "Someone is going around stirring up the crowd, saying that Mikkel and the rest of us have been closing our eyes to this danger for some time. There's a lot of doubt and anger."

"Then we must face it," Bliss said. "But who would deliberately incite such emotions?"

"I can think of two names," Peregrin said. "Karlah and Jorge."

Carlin looked up sharply. "I tell you, Peregrin, Jorge is not your man."

"Really? Look there then." Peregrin pointed toward the eastern side of the crowd about twenty-five feet away. Jorge stood in the center of a group of people. They could not hear his words, but he was gesturing emphatically and forcefully. Carlin's eyes narrowed as he looked at Jorge, but he made no reply.

The Waterman trotted up onto the platform, grinning. "Sorry, I'm late. There seem to be a lot more people out tonight than usual." He scanned their somber faces. "Wow, tough crowd."

"Tougher than you realize," Carlin said.

The bell sounded five times in succession. "That's the cue for silence," Bliss whispered.

The noise from the crowd diminished but did not cease. Mikkel looked over at Morgan, who turned and nodded to a young man at the edge of the platform beside a large iron bell hung from a pole. The man rang the bell five times in succession again. The crowd quieted.

Mikkel stepped forward and spread his arms as if in embrace. "Friends of Archiva, children of O'Keefe, hear me now. By now you have heard rumor after rumor about the return of Dextor. We have called this general assembly to share with you what we know and to choose a course of action to protect us all."

"It's too late for Rimmon!" called a voice from the back, and angry voices murmured around it. "How long have you known, Mikkel?"

"Please," Mikkel shouted. "Listen to me! Accusations will only serve to help destroy us. Listen, and I will speak. Only yesterday did any of us hear the name of Dextor. And this came to us only because my own children slipped away from their Companions and went to the ruins where they were attacked by Terists." He pointed at Peregrin. "This man here beside me fought them and rescued my children. In the course of the fight, one of the men spoke the name Dextor. His account of this before the council was the first we were made aware that Dextor may have returned."

"And who is this man?" another voice called. "Why should we trust him? Is it a coincidence that he shows up just when Dextor returns?" The murmurings among the crowd grew louder.

"I trust him," Mikkel cried. "He rescued my children, he has proven himself a man of peace, and the Council of Guardians has affirmed him!"

"Why should we trust the Guardians?" someone cried out from another location. "Where was your protection for Rimmon and Gabrielle? Dextor did not just appear yesterday! Why did you not know of his return?" The crowd stirred and heaved like a wakening snake. It drew closer to the platform.

Mikkel was shouting for calm, but the angry buzz of the crowd had swelled. People were shouting out all at once. Carlin and Morgan were on their feet, trying to quell what was becoming a riot. The Waterman was standing near the edge, pointing at individuals in the crowd, calling them by name, urging them to calm down. Bliss was standing still, as if she were trying to absorb the anger from the crowd to lessen it.

Just as it seemed the crowd would rush the platform, there was a *whoosh,* and a light appeared above them. Turning, Peregrin saw a great fire burning on the top of the hill. He could make out the figure of a man standing near it.

The crowd quieted and stood staring at the fire. The man beside it remained silent, watching them. Then he spread his arms.

"People of Archiva, be still!" he cried. "You must not blame your Guardians for their failure to protect you. For one hundred years they have kept you safe, but now this task is beyond their power. It is time for you to decide! Only you can choose your future!"

"Who are you? Identify yourself!" Mikkel called out.

"You know me well, Mikkel. I am Dextor, whom you fear," the man called back. The name was repeated in hushed tones throughout the crowd.

"You are not welcome here, Dextor," Mikkel cried. "You have turned from the path of peace. Go from us, and do not return."

"That is not for you to decide, Mikkel," came the answer. "Is this not a general assembly? Let the people of Archiva decide. Hear me, people of Archiva! I have returned with nearly two hundred men at my command. These are no wild Terists; they are trained, fighting men. Yet your leaders, your Guardians, knew nothing of my return until yesterday! Will you rely on them to protect you? I stand upon this hill. Where are your Rangers? They are gone, taken captive by me. I control the hills around Archiva! At any moment I could sweep down upon you and destroy your village."

"Then why do you not do so?" Carlin cried out. "Why do you stand there and talk?"

"Ah, Carlin, my brother," Dextor called. "I long for the day when you and I meet face to face once more. Why do I not destroy you? Because Archiva was my home and my love. I only wish to help it grow, to survive in this harsh world, and to become the leader of humanity that O'Keefe envisioned it would become."

"O'Keefe envisioned a community of peace," Morgan said. "You sow the seeds of violence."

"And you sow the seeds of helplessness and empty promises,

Morgan," Dextor called back. "I say it again. Let the people decide. Childen of O'Keefe, will you take your place in history as the community that restored order to the world, or will you hide among these hills, reciting pledges of peace while the knowledge of the world lies moldering beneath your feet?"

Peregrin noted that there seemed to be a lot of head nodding among the crowd. He decided it was time to step in. "Dextor," he called, "I have met your so-called fighting men. They were as crude and sloppy as any Terist. You promise much, but I have my doubts as to your abilities. Where are these two hundred men? Let the best of them come down, and I will fight them!"

Dextor was silent a long moment. Finally, he said, "You must be the traveler that Crop spoke of. How strange—you do not look fearsome. No matter, he and his men were reprimanded for their failure. But who are you? Where do you come from?"

"I rose from the earth," Peregrin called back. "I, too, have returned, and I challenge you! Prove that you are the leader you say and fight me. Fight me for the future of Archiva!"

"What is this?" Dextor cried. "A challenge to battle from within Archiva? I did not expect to find cats among the mice! But no, Traveler, I will not fight you. Rather, I would parley with you. Perhaps there does not need to be any bloodshed. Will you meet with me then, you and Mikkel? I will meet you tomorrow morning upon the hilltop above the council building in the ruins when the sun is one fist above the horizon. Will you come to speak with me?"

"Just to talk? What guarantee do we have that we will not be attacked?"

"My word," Dextor said. "As I was once a Guardian and lived by the creed of Archiva, you will come and go freely. After all, it remains in my interest as well to avoid as much violence as possible."

"And what of your last words, Dextor?" Mikkel said. "What do you intend to do with them?"

Dextor laughed. "You will pardon me, Mikkel. It was an impulsive flair on my part. I intended to release Rimmon so that you would know I had returned. The so-called message was more for dramatic effect. It need not be fulfilled. Now then, will you meet me tomorrow?"

Peregrin glanced at Mikkel. After a moment, he nodded. "We'll be there," Peregrin called.

"Splendid! I shall not sleep in anticipation of our reunion, Mikkel. People of Archiva, I bid you good night!" There was a rushing, crushing noise, and the fire disappeared. Darkness descended once more.

"That was a neat trick," Waterman said. "How did he do that?"

"It sounded like he dumped a load of earth on it somehow," Carlin said.

Mikkel turned to the crowd. "Friends, we were on the verge of chaos tonight. We must not allow panic to guide us. Tomorrow, Peregrin and I will meet with Dextor and learn more about his plans. Until we return, hold fast to the creed, and believe in peace."

"The creed?" someone called out. "How will that protect us from Dextor?"

"Dextor doesn't believe in peace," someone else cried out. "Let's get him now, before he gets away."

"Dextor is already gone!" Carlin shouted back. "Believe me, I know this man's abilities. By the time you reached the top of the hill, you would find no trace of him."

"Carlin is right," Waterman said. "Dextor is in his element, and we are in ours. Listen to Mikkel."

"That's why we're in such a fix, now!" Karlah shouted. The people around her nodded their heads and murmured assent. "Why should we listen to you anymore, Mikkel?"

"Because if I'm right, I can settle things with Dextor tomorrow," Mikkel answered. And if I'm wrong, you won't have to listen me again. One thing is for certain. If we fall to arguing with each other, then Dextor has already won. Tomorrow I will speak with him."

"You're crazy for going, Mikkel," said someone. "He'll kill you both."

"Maybe," Mikkel answered. "But I think he will find us harder to kill than he thinks. Go to your homes now, and tomorrow, be prepared for anything." The crowd slowly dispersed, grumbling audibly, leaving Peregrin and the Guardians on the platform.

"Will you really go, Mikkel?" asked Carlin.

"Yes, I will go. But I won't go like a trusting kitten."

"What do you mean?"

"What I mean is that Peregrin and I will go out tomorrow after the sun rises. But before the sun rises, we will send out a volunteer team of Rangers to the area. They will go silently and unseen and position themselves among the rocks. If Dextor tries to pull anything, a quick whistle will bring them to our aid."

"What if Dextor has his own men stationed among the rocks?" Merida asked. "You still may be outnumbered."

Mikkel looked down. "I'll have to chance it. I don't want to put more people in danger than I have to. I still know a few secrets of the ruins that Dextor does not. If we can fight our way clear, there's a good chance we can escape."

The Guardians fell silent. Peregrin realized after a moment that they were communing. A long period passed before everyone relaxed. "So be it," Morgan said. "Go carefully, Mikkel and Peregrin. May the wisdom of O'Keefe guide you." They all embraced and parted.

Peregrin did not sleep that night other than occasional dozing. He pondered how strange it was that two days ago he was a homeless, lonely wanderer, while tomorrow he might die for the sake of more than eight hundred people. *That's a fair reason to risk death*, he thought.

He thought of Dextor, standing upon the hill, illuminated by fire. He did have, as he had said, a flair for the dramatic. Perhaps he would forego his last words to Mikkel. Peregrin doubted it, however. Dextor also lusted for the power beneath Archiva, and he knew that Mikkel would never allow him to have it while he had life in his body.

Dextor did not seem insane. In fact, his proposal to the people of Archiva was quite rational. Peregrin even had to admit that it had merit. In a century, Archiva had made little impact upon restoring the world to civilization. Rather, it seemed to hoard its knowledge and way of life for a select few. Perhaps it should be more aggressive in its approach.

Dextor was not the one to lead Archiva in this, however. Peregrin remembered Rimmon and how Dextor had killed Gabrielle in front of him just to make a point. He was ruthless. His desire was not to restore the world but to rule it.

He wondered why they had agreed to meet Dextor at all. The odds were heavy that this was a trap. Did Mikkel think that Dextor would be satisfied with his blood and leave Archiva alone? Probably not. More likely was the idea that Dextor needed Mikkel alive to unlock the secrets of Archiva. What were the secrets of the ruins that Mikkel had up his sleeve? He would find out soon enough!

For that matter, though, he wondered at his own reasons for agreeing to the meeting. Sure, he could claim the noble path and convince himself he wanted to save Archiva. That was all true enough. But underneath it was the desire to meet this man, to come to close grips with him. It might end in compromise, or it might end in conflict; but he had to come face to face with Dextor. He remembered Mara's words: "As titans they shall grapple on the heights. Maybe so…"

He was still pondering these things when he heard a rapping on the door. "Come in please," he said. The outer door opened, and Mikkel stepped in. He, too, looked as if he had not slept.

"Peregrin," he said. "It is nearly time. Come with me."

Peregrin got up and followed Mikkel. They walked across the basin to the eastern side where a group of four men and two women were standing. "Peregrin, these are Brand, Allin, Raven, Tristan, Corval, and Lindah. They are Rangers, the best we have." Peregrin nodded to each, and they nodded back. Mikkel led the group into a small storage room near the kitchens. At the back of the room, he grasped the handle of an old tattered broom in the corner and pulled on it like a lever. A panel in the wall slid aside, revealing a tunnel into the hill.

Mikkel grinned. "Dextor does not know of this tunnel. It is a closely guarded secret among only a few of the Guardians. You see, Peregrin, sometimes there are Circles even within Circles in Archiva."

"Yes, I am beginning to see."

Mikkel embraced each of the Rangers. "The tunnel is quite long and exits about a half mile from the ruins. When you emerge, fan out in pairs. Glide silent and sure and find good hiding places from which you can see the hilltop. Peace be to your hearts."

"And to yours," they answered and disappeared up the tunnel. Mikkel pushed the panel back into place.

"Well, those are all the reinforcements we will have. Perhaps Dextor will just want to talk. I doubt it. Well, come then. Let us have a meal together before we depart."

They walked to the kitchens. A few of the cooks were already busy, bustling over ovens and mixing bowls. When they saw Mikkel and Peregrin, they welcomed them, seated them, and cooked up a breakfast of eggs and ham for them.

"A fine last meal, if that's what it turns out to be," Mikkel said when they had finished.

"It will not be our last meal," Peregrin said. "But still, it was the best breakfast I have had in many a month."

"It's a long walk to the ruins, and we might as well be highly visible. If Dextor's men are watching us, they will be less likely to spot our Rangers," Mikkel said.

"It is time for us to go then?"

"Yes, the sun is just breaking the horizon. We should be off."

They departed by the same tunnel and route that Peregrin had originally come into Archiva, on the western side. Then it was downstream to the river and two more miles or so along it to the ruins. They walked along, chatting freely about the birds and the crops and how nice the weather had been. They could have been two men out for a stroll without a care in the world.

When they reached the ruins, Mikkel took Peregrin along a trail that led upward along the ridge under which Peregrin had spent the night on the rock ledge. The trail edged along the rock face and then cut inland away from the edge. It was not a difficult climb, but it was strenuous. When they reached the top, they were sweating and slightly winded.

Mikkel made a fist and held his arm out toward the horizon. "Right on time," he said. The sun is almost a fist above the horizon."

They kept on until the trail cut back toward the edge, moving through a grove of trees. The trees suddenly thinned out, revealing a large, flat rock, almost like a tabletop, which comprised the edge of the hill. Dextor stood on it.

He was not a tall fellow. In fact, he was shorter than most people Peregrin had seen in Archiva. He was extremely well muscled, however. His hair was gray streaked with brown, resembling weathered stone, and cut short just above his shoulders. His high forehead sloped to a blunt nose, sharp cheek bones, and a pointed chin tipped with a well-trimmed tuft of white hair. His copper skin betrayed lines from wind and sun, and his eyes were the color of twilight. He wore black pants and a tan shirt.

"Well now," Dextor said. "Face to face again, Mikkel. You see that it is truly me."

"I see you, Dextor."

"And you see that I have truly returned, as I always knew I would."

"I see you have returned, Dextor. Let us talk now. What is it you want?"

Dextor laughed. "You are smarter than that, Mikkel," he said. "I want it all." He turned toward the ledge and spread his arms. "I want it all! All the knowledge that lies here. All the secrets that you know."

"Impossible. We are not ready to use that knowledge."

"I am ready, Mikkel. And unlike you and the rest of the sniveling Guardians, I am not afraid. It is the survival of Archiva I have at heart, Mikkel. We must use our knowledge or die."

"If that is all you have to say, then I have spent my energy climbing this hill for no reason. Good day, Dextor." He turned to leave.

Dextor snapped his fingers, and ten men stepped out from behind trees to block their way. "Mikkel, you would not be so rude as to refuse my hospitality."

"Our conversation is done here, Dextor. Let us depart as you said."

"Oh yes, I did say you could come and go freely. I'm sorry to inform you that I lied. I have no intentions of letting you leave, unless, of course, I grow tired of you and have you tossed off of the cliff."

Mikkel sighed, drew back his head, put two fingers in his mouth, and whistled.

Dextor smiled. "Why, Mikkel, are you hoping someone will come to your rescue? You are not thinking your Rangers can save you, are you?"

He snapped his fingers twice. From behind two large boulders nearby came several men, dragging six bound and gagged people with them. They cast their captives at Dextor's feet. They were Brand, Allin, Raven, Tristan, Corval, and Lindah.

Peregrin's heart sank. "Your Rangers are not as stealthy as you think, Mikkel," Dextor said. "But it was not their fault. We were waiting for them at the exit to the tunnel."

Mikkel stared at them and then at Dextor. "How did you know? You knew nothing of that tunnel when you lived in Archiva. Even if you did, how could you know they would be using that tunnel?"

"Because I told them," said a familiar voice behind them.

Mikkel and Peregrin spun around. Before them, grinning, stood a man—a tall, thin man with close-cropped dark hair. "Hello, Mikkel. Hello, Peregrin," he said.

"Hello, Carlin," Mikkel answered.

VIII
BROTHERS

Carlin grinned. "You see, Peregrin, I told you Jorge was not your man."

"And you were right," Peregrin answered. "I suppose you had a hand in stirring up the crowd last night as well?"

"Good seeds in good soil yield a good crop," Carlin said with a wave of his hand. "Actually, the happy people of Archiva responded to their leaders' apparent lack of ability with far more ferocity than I had expected. I would guess there is a great deal of discontent under that peaceful surface."

Mikkel turned back to Dextor. "Well, you hold the cards. What will you do now?"

Dextor did not answer immediately. A slow smile spread across his face. He turned his head and looked at the edge of the cliff. Then he looked back at Mikkel. "I suppose I could fulfill my last words."

He nodded at the men behind Mikkel. Two of them grasped

his arms and pulled them behind his back, where another tied his hands together. Three other men did the same to Peregrin.

"What do you say, Mikkel?" Dextor said. "Do you feel like dying today?" He jerked his head toward the edge, and the men pushed Mikkel toward it. At the edge, they held him by each arm and leaned him outward into the air.

"Look down, Mikkel," Dextor said. "Look down and see your death. Does it look pleasant to you? Does it look quick? What would you give to save it, Mikkel? Answer quick now. There is not much time."

"Then do what you intend," Mikkel said through gritted teeth. I will not trade for my life."

"Ah," cried Dextor, "spoken like a true man of peace. All right then, go ahead and drop him."

"Dextor!" Carlin shouted. "Stop it! You said no killing!"

Dextor held up a hand to the men holding Mikkel. He sighed. "As you wish, Carlin." He waved his hand, and the men drew Mikkel back from the edge. Dextor walked up to him and smiled. "You are fortunate that Carlin has spent so much time in Archiva these past ten years. He still has no stomach for killing." He turned and walked off, followed by Carlin, who walked at his side, speaking in low tones. The rest of the men took Mikkel, Peregrin, and the six Rangers and tied them together in a line, using a long rope that they secured around each one's waist. They took the gags out of the Rangers' mouths and cut the bonds on their feet.

"Let's go," muttered a tall man with a brown sash. Two men led, holding the rope at one end, and two others took up the back end. The rest of the men walked around them in a pack.

Peregrin surmised that Dextor would take them to the hills above Archiva to display them to the people below, thereby creating despair among them. Instead, Carlin broke off and headed down the path that Mikkel and Peregrin had come up, presumably to return to Archiva, while Dextor led them northward, away from the ruins.

Their path led into dense woods through which Dextor threaded them over rock and around thickets guided by landmarks only he knew. As they went, Peregrin marveled at his skill. He certainly had lost none of his abilities since leaving Archiva.

Still, the path was a rough one, and the hills increased as they went along. Branches and brambles tore at them, leaving them bruised and scratched, and before long they were soaked with sweat and winded. It was difficult to climb and maneuver bound together as they were, and more than once, one of them slipped, causing the others to be jerked sharply and sometimes fall themselves. The men leading them would curse and pull them up, sometimes hitting them.

The sun, unfettered by rope or chain, continued its ascent until it was nearly overhead. Still, Peregrin, Mikkel, and the six Rangers were led, pushed, pulled, hit, and cursed as they traversed the hilly land. They were following a trail that rounded a steep hillside, rising as it went, when, coming out of the trees, they found it abruptly ended at a sheer rock wall that rose some thirty feet above them. Dextor was there alone, grinning.

"This looks like the end of the road, doesn't it, Mikkel?" he said happily. "What was that old proverb? Oh yes: 'The secrets of Archiva run deep.' Here is one you do not know."

He took his stick and tapped the rock five times. There was a rumbling noise, and a large slab of stone, twice the height of a person and eight feet wide, disengaged itself from the wall and slowly descended toward them, being lowered like a castle gate with heavy ropes fastened to each side.

Dextor bowed with a flourish of his hand. "Welcome to Second Archiva," he said. "Come and see what I have been up to all these years." He walked across the gate into the darkness.

The men pushed their captives forward. Once inside, they could see by the light of oil lamps set into the wall or hanging from posts. They found themselves in a small cavern. The gate ropes ran through large pulleys suspended from beams set in the ceiling and descended to a wheel on either side, operated by a large crank. Eight men stood inside the entrance.

Beyond them, the cavern opened outward and upward into a roughly circular space, about one hundred feet in diameter. They were standing on a ledge less than twenty feet wide, beyond which the floor fell away into a chasm. Peregrin noted two wooden stairways built against each wall leading both down and up to where daylight shone feebly.

In the center of the ledge was a platform suspended over the edge from a frame made of massive wooden beams. Two upright beams were set into the rock of the ledge and supported with angled beams, from their midpoint to the ground. A crosspiece extended over the ledge from each beam, also reinforced with angled beams from their midsection to the middle of the upright beams. The crosspieces were connected by metal shafts at both ends. From each of these shafts hung two massive pulleys. Heavy ropes affixed to the platform ran through these pulleys to wheels, similar to those at the gate, at each side of the structure. Lanterns were hung from poles at the two far corners of the platform.

Dextor stepped onto the platform. "This is the watchtower," he said. "The lifter, which I stand on, comes only to this ledge. Those stairways you see go all the way to the top of this hill, where my men are constantly on guard. No one comes within a mile of here without being spotted. I designed this myself. Is it not amazing?" There was glee in his voice.

Peregrin looked about. "Yes, it is," he said sincerely, for indeed he did find it amazing.

Dextor looked at him and smiled. "This is but a small part of what I have accomplished. Come," he said, beckoning to them. "Come, let us descend, and I will show you something worth seeing."

Their captors led them to the platform. "There are too many

for the lifter," Dextor said. "Two of you come with us. The rest of you meet us below." The men who guarded them turned and walked toward the stairways. The two Dextor had indicated pushed Peregrin, Mikkel, and the Rangers onto the platform. Dextor nodded, and four men grasped the cranks, two at each wheel. They turned their cranks one direction, causing the platform to rise slightly. Two other men withdrew two stabilizing planks from a frame underneath the platform. The men at the wheels began slowly turning the cranks the other direction, lowering the platform.

Peregrin looked over the side. They were descending through darkness, but lanterns set along the stairways allowed him to estimate there were nearly fifty feet of open air beneath them.

"This is a natural cave?" he asked as they slid through the darkness.

"Yes," Dextor answered. "Carlin and I found it years ago when we protected Archiva from the vermin who came over these hills. These hills are full of caves, but never have we found anything like this one. Once we had explored it, we knew it would serve a special purpose someday."

"So you knew about it even while you claimed the position of Guardian," Mikkel said.

"Don't use that sanctimonious tone with me, Mikkel," Dextor shot back. "Yes, we knew about it even then. Were we planning a rebellion? No. I protected Archiva with my life and my love. I believed in your foolish creed. We simply found a place that we thought might benefit Archiva one day."

"Yet you never shared this knowledge," Mikkel said. "Why not? If you believed in the creed even then, why didn't you tell the council about this place?"

Dextor's brow furrowed. "There was no need. What would I say? I have found a good cave, come and see it? I would have gotten no more response than I did with my protest of the creed."

The platform came to rest on a wooden frame on the ground.

"Enough of this, Mikkel. Carlin and I kept this information to ourselves. This proved to be a wise choice once I was expelled from Archiva. Every man needs a home. This became mine."

"We took you ten miles southeast of Archiva. How did you get back to here without being spotted?"

"Oh, come now, Mikkel," Dextor said with a laugh. "It's easy to avoid a snake when you know where it lies in the grass. Besides, not all of your Rangers agreed with the council's decision. Even then my word carried more weight than yours among them."

Mikkel's eyes narrowed. "Are you saying there are other Rangers who have betrayed Archiva?"

"I'm saying there are other Rangers who have opened their eyes," Dextor answered. "Come now. You will learn as we go." He stepped off the platform. They followed. "They will not need to be bound together here," he said, nodding at their guards. They removed the rope that held them together but left their hands tied behind them. The other men rejoined them from the sides.

Dextor led them toward a crevice in the wall of the cavern near one of the staircases. It was wide enough to walk upright, single file. They followed him into it, their guards holding lanterns. Planks had been laid on the ground. The crevice sloped downward for about twenty feet and turned sharply to the left. Another ten feet and it turned right again in its original direction. It sloped for another fifty or so feet, turned left, then right again, and opened into the light of day.

It was, Peregrin thought, *nearly as impressive as his first view of Archiva.* The crevice had brought them to a ledge on a sheer face of rock at one end of a box canyon. A steep trail, sometimes cut into steps, descended on to their left for about one hundred feet and then switched back onto a lower foothill to arrive at the canyon floor, some forty feet beneath them. The canyon floor spanned about one hundred yards on this end and widened toward the center before tapering back to a smaller end almost a half mile away. Its towering, granite sides rose in layers to heights of sixty to one hundred feet along its length.

The canyon was alive with activity! They could feel the heat from two forges below the ledge where they stood, where men were hammering metal. Other men were tending horses, cooking in large cauldrons suspended over fires, and fashioning rope, cloth, and leather goods. A large group was undergoing some sort of training drill, moving in response to a leader's shouted commands. And at various spots along the canyon, circles of ten to fifteen people surrounded two combatants who were practicing fighting skills hand-to-hand with sticks and, Peregrin noted, with knives.

Peregrin looked at Mikkel. His jaw was hard set, and the muscles in his neck were taut. He could almost hear Mikkel's mind calculating, estimating the number of men and assessing their competence.

Dextor saw his look. "No doubt Mikkel can only see the threat to Archiva and how Carlin and I have played him for the fool all these years," he said. "But what of you, Traveler? What do you see?"

"Order," answered Peregrin, gazing at the scene before him. "Amazing order. Where did these men come from?"

"Here and there and everywhere," Dextor said. "I also have trained Seekers. They go forth into the world to search out those with the skill to belong to my Ranger squads. It's a little easier to find men who want to fight than to find those who want to farm."

"They are all Terists then?"

"In the Archivan sense of the word, yes," Dextor answered. "Most of them belonged to small wandering bands without any real leadership. I offered them power, direction, and a vision. Most of them accepted."

"And those who did not?" Mikkel said.

"They were eradicated," Dextor said with a wave of his hand. "I, too, believe in humanity, Mikkel. Those who will not accept order must be eliminated from our midst."

"Order by force and violence?" Mikkel said. "This is what you call being human?"

"Spare me the lecture," Dextor said. "I've heard it." He nodded at the men. "Lead them down."

The men formed them in single file with one guard behind each captive, one hand on their bound hands and one on their shoulder. This was as much to steady them as they made the descent, Peregrin realized, as it was to control them. They made their way down the steep trail cautiously.

Once at the bottom, their captors led them directly through the center of the canyon. Men (and some women) stared at them from all directions. *Of course,* Peregrin thought. *We are being paraded. It's a lot harder to escape if everyone in town knows your face.*

As they passed the cooking fires, one of the men stirring the contents of a cauldron looked up and abruptly threw his long-handled wooden spoon down. He strode over to them and stepped directly in front of Peregrin. It was Crop. Peregrin noticed he was no longer wearing his sash.

He glared at Peregrin a moment and then spat in his face. Then he shoved him with both hands, almost making him lose his balance.

"Not so tough now, huh, Traveler? Gonna hit me with your stick now?" Spittle dripped from the corner of his mouth as he pushed Peregrin again.

Peregrin noted that Dextor had said nothing, nor had any of their captors intervened. *If they are watching for my response,* he thought, *I'll give them something to think about.*

He grinned at Crop. "Lost your sash I see, eh, Crop? I think you might have dropped it in the ruins."

Crop's jaw dropped. He closed it abruptly as he heard snickers from among the guards. "You don't talk to me like that!" he said in a low voice. "I'll slice your innards out and make you eat them for dinner!"

Peregrin grinned wider. "There's an old saying, Crop. It goes: 'I can beat you with one hand tied behind my back.' I'll bet I can top that." Fury flamed in Crop's eyes, and he lunged forward, hands outstretched, for Peregrin's neck.

Only Peregrin was no longer there. He had swiveled sharply to let Crop go by him. As he did, he brought his right foot around and kicked the back of Crop's left knee hard. Crop screamed and fell. As he rose to his hands and knees, Peregrin moved in and kicked upward, connecting with Crop's left shoulder so that he flipped onto his back. Before he could move, Peregrin's foot was on his neck.

"What do you say now, Crop?" he said in a voice like the rattle of pebbles in a dry brook. He pressed a little harder, making Crop choke. "I can't hear you, Crop. Where's my dinner?"

"Enough, Traveler," said Dextor. He nodded, and two men pulled Peregrin back from Crop, who rolled over and lay there gagging. Finally he pushed himself up onto his hands and knees.

"You're fortunate I did not allow him to crush your windpipe, Crop," Dextor said. "Now get back to work, and let's hope you cook better than you fight. All right, let's go." He nodded at the men, who led them on, but not before Peregrin saw a slight smile crease his face.

They proceeded to the far end of the canyon and were pushed into a small room cut into the rock wall. Two men cut the bonds holding their wrists and retreated. Dextor smiled at them from the doorway.

"Our hospitality does not match that of First Archiva," he said. "Still, I hope your stay will be pleasant. I have matters to attend to—you know how it is, Mikkel, trying to lead a community—but I will return soon. Until then"—he paused and looked about the room—"my house is your house." He closed the heavy oak door, and they heard him shoot the bolt.

The room grew dark, except for the small barred window in the door. Mikkel went to it and peered out. "Two guards outside of the door," he said, turning. "Dextor leaves nothing to chance."

"So it would appear," Peregrin said. "Sit down, Mikkel. Let your eyes adjust to the gloom in here. Then we can examine our quarters. My guess is that there is no exit, however, except through that door."

Mikkel sat down across from Peregrin. He sighed. "Then we have no choice but to wait upon Dextor's return."

"Mikkel," said Brand. "I am sorry. They grabbed us even as we came out of the tunnel. There were about thirty of them."

"I know, Brand. I sent you all straight into them. It is I who am sorry." He shook his head. "I never suspected Carlin. Not even for a moment."

Peregrin was surprised. "Why not? After all, they grew up together. They were like brothers."

"You didn't see Carlin when they brought Dextor back. His face was ashen. For days, he barely talked, barely slept, barely ate. He couldn't have faked that, Peregrin. He was stunned by Dextor's violence. He testified against him with such vehemence that no one doubted the brotherhood between them was broken." Mikkel looked at his hands. "Even the Seekers were sure of it."

"So the Seekers were wrong," Peregrin said. "The Seekers have intuition and empathy, Mikkel, but they are not mind readers. It's not inconceivable that Carlin could have fooled even you."

"But you saw him back at the ruins. He stopped Dextor from having me dropped over the edge. He doesn't like violence, I tell you. Maybe we can reason with him, get him to come back to our side."

Peregrin snorted. "Don't put your hopes on that, Mikkel. Carlin did not save you at the ruins. He and Dextor were playing a game."

"Why do you say that? It sure felt real to me!"

THE ARCHIVIST

"Because Dextor was not going to kill you then, and Carlin knew it. Sure, he put your determination to the test, but he knows you would die before giving up Archiva's secrets. You still hold the key he needs. Which means the whole thing was staged."

"Why would he do that?"

Peregrin shrugged. "Maybe so you would think exactly what you are thinking—that Carlin has not fully accepted Dextor's ways. You would talk to Carlin, and he would show signs of wavering and gain your trust. Then, somewhere along the line, you might share with Carlin what Dextor needs to know. Then he can kill you."

Mikkel sighed again. "You know what? You would have made a good Seeker."

Peregrin grinned. "Not me. Too dangerous."

They said little more in the hours that followed. A thorough examination of their cell showed it to be about ten by twelve feet and cut into solid rock. As Peregrin had surmised, there was no possible exit except the door. After a while, they simply sat in the gloom, each one dwelling on his own thoughts.

The gloom deepened as the hours trudged past. Outside, men shouted, hammers rang, and a general buzz of activity continued. The light in their cell all but disappeared, isolating each of them even more as their vision failed. Still, Dextor did not return.

There was no way to determine the passage of time. It was as though they floated in an inky sea that was both physical in the air around them and immaterial as each one drifted in thought. This sea imposed a silence upon them so that no one spoke or moved, as if the ripples of any action would cause them to drown. After a while, Peregrin found he could not even think about the day's events but instead pondered a nothingness that was deeper than conscious thought. He was not even sure if he remained awake or if he slipped into slumber from time to time. *It was*, he thought, *much like when he first woke in that underground cave with no frame of reference to help him comprehend the limitations of his existence.* All was dark. All was without connection. He was a wanderer, groping his way through an eternal nothing.

Deep in his reverie, he saw the bunker in which he had awoken. Only it was awash with white light flowing from long rods that were set into a series of rectangular boxes on the ceiling. The walls were white metal, as was the table, making the room almost too dazzling to stand in without squinting. *The same white metal that is in the Archive,* Peregrin thought.

He seemed to be sitting on the table. Beside him was another man, tall with dusty gray hair cropped short. He wore a pair of wire-rim spectacles seated low on the bridge of his nose, over which he gazed at Peregrin. His eyes were like the sky on a summer noon, intense and difficult to look at.

Peregrin blinked at the man. He looked like Mikkel, but he was not. He was before Mikkel. "O'Keefe," he said weakly.

The man smiled at him. "Peregrin, here I must leave you. I'm sorry things did not work out as we had planned. I wish I could be here when you awake so we could work together again. I wish I could see what happens to Archiva. Oh, Peregrin, so much will depend on you. Mara's visions were so frightening. It's too much to ask of anyone. But you will not fail. I trust in you."

"What if I do fail? What then?"

"Hush. You will not. You are my traveler, my falcon. Remember and choose peace."

He laid one hand on the back of Peregrin's neck and one on his chest and gently pushed him to lie down in the open, padded box. "It is time for you to sleep now. Sleep with thoughts of peace."

"It looks like a coffin," Peregrin said with a wan smile.

O'Keefe smiled back. "It is but a comfortable bed from which you will rise again. You will rise and carry the future of Archiva within you. Close your eyes now. Sleep and remember."

Peregrin gazed up at this man who had done so much to save humanity. He felt a terrible constriction in his chest, as he knew he must leave this man behind. Indeed he knew O'Keefe would die soon. He had done what he could, and now he had to leave his dream in Peregrin's hands. The swells of unconsciousness grew, pulling at him. He stretched out his hand one last time. "O'Keefe ..." he said.

O'Keefe took the hand and placed it back at Peregrin's side. A clear lid slid into place above him, and the box began to fill with a frigid gas. He could feel the cold pervade to the deepest depth of his body, and darkness rolled upon him like a great surf. Just before losing consciousness, Peregrin could see the moisture around O'Keefe's eyes. and although he could not hear his voice, he could see him say: "Sleep now," he said. "Peregrin, my child. My true child ..."

Peregrin opened his eyes. Visually he could see nothing. But he was keenly aware of Mikkel and the Rangers. He could hear their breathing, could sense their shape, and he could feel their presence. Outside of their cell, he could hear movement, an occasional spoken word and all the night sounds of the forest. But it was more than hearing. He could identify each sound as well as its distance and direction from him. He touched the rock floor, and he knew it had been cut from granite. He inhaled deeply and detected wood smoke, freshly budded crocuses and lilies, leather, steel, moss, and a coming rain.

He remembered O'Keefe, now long dead. He felt the strange constriction again in his chest and longed to release it. *How long since you have cried?* he thought to himself, but he could not remember. He touched his eyes. They were dry, even though he longed to weep, to grieve for someone he had loved.

Yes, loved, he thought. *I loved O'Keefe. He was a father to me. He called me his true child, his Peregrin. Yet I cannot weep for him.* He sighed. *The Waterman was right. There is something truly strange about me.*

Some time later, he detected the heat and smell of a torch

approaching. He could feel the vibrations of many feet coming in their direction. "Mikkel," he whispered.

"Unnhh?" came the reply, and he realized that Mikkel had been asleep.

"They're coming." He heard Mikkel's head jerk up sharply. Outside of their cell, a light began to glow and grow stronger as it drew near. The bolt was sharply drawn, and the door swung open. A man stepped in, holding a burning torch consisting of cloth wrapped around the end of a stick and soaked in some kind of oil. Another man followed him. Like Crop in the ruins, he had a sash from his right shoulder to his waist.

"You there," he said, pointing at Peregrin. "You are the traveler. Dextor wants to talk with you."

Peregrin rose to his feet. "What of the others?"

"They can stay here and rot for all I care. Dextor said only you."

"Can they not have a torch or a lantern to see by?"

The man snorted. "Dextor says they should stay in the dark until they're ready to see. Come on, you." He gestured at Peregrin but made no attempt to grab at him. Peregrin thought of Crop and grinned.

He stepped outside. There were eight other men besides the two guards. They flanked him four to a side, just out of arm's reach. The leader turned to cell guards. "Dextor says if this one tries anything funny, you will get the signal, and you are to kill everyone inside." The guards grunted.

The leader led the pack back through the canyon. About two-thirds of the way, he came to a stairway cut into the side of the rock and began to climb. They followed single file, four guards in front of Peregrin and four behind him. The stairway ascended along the cliff face and then doubled back, rising some thirty-five feet to a point where the cliff receded and a ledge wide enough for three men abreast ran along its edge. Torches mounted on poles were set into sockets in the rock at intervals along both the stairway and the ledge, illuminating their path. They traversed this ledge for about one hundred feet, rising slightly, until they came to where it ended in a sheer wall rising above them. Here, a platform had been built on top of the ledge, extending some ten feet over the edge into the air. Two oil lanterns were set into the corners of the railing that surrounded its open end. On one side of the platform was an oaken door set into the cliff face. Dextor stood upon the platform, his hands on the railing, looking down upon his Second Archiva.

He did not look up as they approached. When they halted, he simply said, "Thank you, Captain. You may leave us."

"Sir," the leader said, "he's dangerous."

"I am aware of that, Captain," Dextor said, still looking out over the canyon. "You have my orders to kill his friends if he tries anything. Now you may go."

"Yes, sir." The captain led his men away.

Peregrin waited. After a moment, Dextor said, "Come join me, Traveler. This is a view worth seeing."

Peregrin stepped onto the platform and walked over to Dextor's side. "Carlin must have told you my name is Peregrin."

Dextor smiled. "Yes, he did. But I was so impressed with your use of Traveler when you chased my men out of the ruins. It suits you somehow." He looked up at Peregrin. "It has a dangerous feel to it, don't you think?"

"My name is Peregrin," Peregrin said again.

"Oh, very well then. Peregrin it is. Perhaps soon you will again enjoy the title 'the Traveler.' We shall see."

"What did you want to talk to me about?"

Dextor did not answer right away. He gazed upon the darkness below him. "When you arrived here, I asked you what you saw. Your answer was surprisingly insightful." He looked up at Peregrin. "Do you remember? You said 'order.' With one glance, you saw what the exalted Guardians of Archiva could not see in all the years I was with them. Order. I have labored for years not to build a canyon to call my home, but to build order in a world of chaos. Their Creed could not do that, not in a century of trying."

"Archiva seemed pretty orderly to me," Peregrin said.

"Pah! One hundred years and they have not rebuilt humanity one bit! Sneaking around through the forest, warding people off with tricks, seeking out this person or that person over the course of decades. They have built a fine town of navel gazers. But if they were truly exposed to the world, they would vanish, swept away by the madness that still rules it."

"And you believe you could tame this madness?"

"Thousands of years ago, a man named Alexander conquered the known world and united every culture on earth for a brief time. Once he laid siege to a certain city that was thought to be unconquerable. He called on the king to surrender, and when the king asked why he should, Alexander lined up one hundred of his men and ordered them to march off a sheer cliff and fall to their death. By the time the tenth soldier had fallen, the king of that city rushed out and surrendered to Alexander. Why? Obedience. He knew Alexander's men would obey him to any end, even if it meant pulling the city apart stone by stone. He knew he could not fight such total obedience."

"What does this have to do with you?"

Dextor waved his hand toward the darkness below them. "I command such obedience. These men have seen my resolve. They have dedicated themselves to me and to my vision. I could order any of them to climb the canyon wall and leap off it if it suited me." He turned to face Peregrin. "Don't you see? I have tamed the jungle. I have pulled men from a world of violence and chaos and given them purpose and direction. I have restored their humanity. They no longer seek their own ends. They act as a body for a common good. Is this not what O'Keefe wanted for Archiva, for humanity? To restore a sense of unity and purpose?"

"O'Keefe's vision also sought to reject violence and power as a means to an end. To seek peace within and without," Peregrin said.

Dextor laughed. "A few days in Archiva and you are already soaked in the Creed! Well, no matter. I spent years bleeding, blinded by an illusion of peace. I suppose I can excuse a few days of gullibility on your part."

"That's very kind of you," Peregrin said.

Dextor studied him. "You are not what you seem, Peregrin. You embrace this dream of peace, yet I saw how you thrashed Crop, how you stood upon his neck. You embraced that as well."

Peregrin shrugged. "What of it? He threatened me, and I didn't see you or any of your thugs trying to stop him. It was self-defense."

Dextor shook his head. "No, Traveler," he said, emphasizing the name. "You enjoyed it. His life was fully in your hands, or should I say feet. He didn't just threaten you; he insulted you. And you made him pay for it."

"You're wrong."

"No, I am not. I am no Seeker. But I know people of peace, and I know people of violence. While you would happily live in peace, you have no reservations about resorting to violence when you are threatened."

"Is there a point to this discussion?"

Dextor grinned. "Come inside with me, Peregrin. I have something to show you." He turned and walked to the oak door. Opening it, he turned again. "These are my quarters. In this room lies the future of both First and Second Archiva. I want you to see the future with me."

Peregrin followed him into the room. It was a fair-sized room carved out of the hillside, about twenty feet square and eight feet high. Two massive beams crossed in the center of the ceiling and stretched to the four walls where they were supported by equally massive upright beams. A doorway on the far wall led into another room. Peregrin stared at it. Someone was in there, trying to be very silent, but he could detect the sound of breathing. He inhaled and decided it was a woman.

The only furnishings in the room were two large wooden cabinets with closed doors against one wall, a large desk and chair against the opposite wall, and a large oaken table surrounded by thirteen chairs in the center of the room.

"It's not too much to look at," Dextor said. "But war rooms are not noted for their interior design."

Peregrin arched an eyebrow. "Do you plan to start a war?"

"That will be largely up to you and Mikkel," Dextor said. "But I'm getting ahead of myself. Stand here. I want to show you something."

He went to one of the cabinets and opened the doors. Though he obscured its interior, Peregrin could see glints of metal from within. He withdrew a long object and brought it back to the table where Peregrin stood. It was a double-edged blade, about three feet long, with a crosspiece of metal and a handle at one end. Peregrin's thoughts spun for a moment until the word *sword* came to him.

"It's beautiful, isn't it?" Dextor said. "I found the description of them in the same book in which I read about Alexander. Long ago I proposed making these in Archiva. Of course, the council saw no reason to create such a weapon that could only be used for fighting. As soon as I established Second Archiva, I had Carlin find me a book about forges and the crafting of metal. You noticed my two forges when we arrived, didn't you? These are what they are making on them. Swords for my men to use in battle. Here, take it. Feel the weight."

Peregrin took the proffered weapon. He held it by the handle and waved it back and forth in the air. "It does have a fine balance to it," he said, admiring the keen edges.

Dextor smiled. "That's not all. Look at this." He went to the other cabinet and drew forth two items. One of them was a long, supple staff bent into an arc by a line looped around each end. The other was a hollowed-out piece of wood containing long, thin shafts with points of metal embedded in one end and feathers attached to the other. Again his thoughts spun, and the words *bow* and *arrow* came to him.

"They use smaller versions of these in Archiva for hunting, but nothing of this caliber," Dextor said. "You fit the arrow onto the string, pull it back, and let the recoil of the staff do the rest. Knowing the forest as I do, I was able to determine what wood would have the strongest recoil, giving a better range, accuracy, and distance. My men are becoming quite good with these."

Peregrin looked at the weapons before him and felt a tightness in his throat. Here before him Dextor had the advanced weaponry he had sought while in Archiva. What chance would hands fighting have against these?

"You see, don't you, that I could take Archiva by force at any time?" Dextor said.

"Why don't you then?"

Dextor smiled slightly. "One reason is that I love Archiva. I lived and fought and bled for the people who dwell there. Many of them were my friends. I have no wish to slaughter them. Another reason is that the people of Archiva are critical in my plan to restore order to this world. It is not wise to waste resources unnecessarily. But perhaps the best reason is that I am not the enraged animal that many Archivans believe me to be. I do not reject the principles of peace. It is the absolute dominion of peace that I reject. Force and fear are powerful tools when rebuilding a world. It is not enough to believe in peace. There are too many people who do not. They will only bow to an iron hand."

"Such as yours?"

"Don't you be sanctimonious with me too, Traveler," Dextor growled. "You used an iron hand with Crop and his men in the ruins. Was it necessary for you to break Daggert's arm? I think not. You wanted to punish them, to make them think twice before attacking innocent children, didn't you? You understood that nothing short of violence would stop them and prevent them from hurting others."

Peregrin did not reply, so Dextor continued. "This brings me to my last reason for not invading Archiva. Even I did not know it before Crop and his men returned from the ruins. That reason is you."

Peregrin blinked. "Me? I have no idea what you mean!"

"I'm not sure I do either," Dextor said. "There is much about you that does not add up. But I sensed from the moment I spoke with Crop, and from Carlin's reports, that we are bound together in this enterprise. I have seen in your reaction that you, too, understand the need for power. I think you have come to help me bring order back to the world and to fulfill O'Keefe's vision. I think we are brothers in this."

Peregrin stared at him. "You are deluded. Or you're completely insane. You and I could never work together."

Dextor cocked his head to one side. "I am not insane. Nor do I think I am wrong about you. I do think you are wrong about me. Wait until you have seen more of my works. I think you will have a different view then."

"I saw Rimmon," Peregrin said coldly. "I saw what you did to him. He told us what you did to Gabrielle, how you cut her throat in front of him, just to make your point. No matter what you have accomplished, you are still a murderer. You see violence as a first resort, a means to your end."

Dextor laughed. "Oh, I wish I could have seen their faces at that moment! How that must have frightened the peace-loving sheep of Archiva. 'The monster Dextor has returned!' But have no fear. I have something else to share with you." He turned toward the inner door. "Gabrielle, dear? Would you mind coming to meet our guest?"

There was a sound from within the inner room, and the woman

appeared in the doorway. She was of medium height and slender. Her auburn hair rolled in tresses halfway down her back, and her green eyes glinted. She smiled and, stepping forward, extended her hand.

"You must be Peregrin," she said. "Carlin has told us so much about you."

Peregrin took the hand and then, on impulse, lifted it to his lips and kissed it. "Am I to believe you are Gabrielle?"

"Yes, you are," she answered. "Although I can see how you would be doubtful. Mikkel will know me when he sees me."

"It's just that I heard you were dead," Peregrin said.

Gabrielle laughed. "Yes, well, Dextor does enjoy a little drama. A blunt knife with a hollow handle filled with deer blood, spurting copiously when pressed in a sudden movement across my throat, followed by my collapse to the floor. Poor Rimmon had no choice but to think he had killed me."

"I'm sure he was in no shape to examine you. Didn't it bother you, letting them beat him nearly to death? After all, he was your partner."

"I did not want Rimmon to be hurt. Poor thing. I tried so hard these last two years to get him to see things our way. But he was so dedicated to protecting Archiva. He just would not budge. Dextor believed it was necessary or I would not have allowed it."

"I take it you have been working with Dextor for years?"

"Since he left Archiva, and even before. You will find that all of the Rangers who were assigned by Carlin to the northeast of Archiva are with Dextor."

"But Gabrielle is my most cherished Ranger, are you not?" Dextor said, taking her hand. He gazed into her eyes. "She has been with me since the beginning, since Franceen was killed. She has been my strength, my ambition, my love … my wife."

"I'm happy for you," Peregrin said without emotion.

Dextor looked at him. "Do you find it so odd, Peregrin, that I could love someone and be loved by her? After all you have seen, do you still think of me as an inhuman monster? Do you think I have no more feelings than a machine?"

Peregrin paused. "No. I think you are completely human. As such, you can make bad choices, which lead to other bad choices, which lead to disaster."

Dextor laughed. "Archiva is the disaster! Listen, Peregrin. Archiva has all the means to set the world right again, to bring us back from the edge. But its leaders lack the will to use it. You have seen the outside world. Where have you found order or peace? Archiva sits on its Creed and protects its existence, but it does nothing for the outside world. Out there people go on killing and robbing and fighting. Is that O'Keefe's vision? Answer me that, Peregrin! Is this how O'Keefe wanted things to be a century after his death?"

Peregrin looked at him, trying to pierce the depth of the shadows in his eyes. He sighed. "No. O'Keefe believed that Archiva could set the remainder of humanity on a path of peace. I think if he were here, he would agree that his plan is behind schedule."

"Then you see why I do the things I do," Dextor said.

Peregrin shook his head. "O'Keefe would reject the path you have taken as well." A memory rose in his mind, and he grinned. "He would quote one of his favorite proverbs: 'Don't push the river.'"

"What does that mean?" Dextor said.

"It means some things have to develop at their own pace, if they are to endure. And sometimes that pace is slower than we would like it to be, but pushing will only lead to ruin. O'Keefe would not approve of your methods, Dextor, no matter how pure your intentions."

"You talk as if you knew him, Peregrin. How is it you are so confident about what O'Keefe would think?"

Peregrin shrugged. "I have seen Archiva, and I have listened to its people. It is on the right path."

"It is a path leading to a dry grave."

"So if you do not get what you want, you will destroy Archiva?"

Dextor looked to the side. His eyes grew opaque, and he took a deep breath. "That will not be necessary. Mikkel will tell me how to find what I seek. Then he and I can lead Archiva together ... in peace."

"Mikkel will not tell you what you want. And he will not share the leadership of Archiva with you. He will die first."

"Yes," Dextor said, nodding. "I'm afraid he will. However, Mikkel's life or death is more in your hands than his."

"Mine? I don't see what you mean."

"You have Mikkel's confidence. He testified for you before the council, he placed you on the platform beside him, and, Carlin tells me, you and he disappeared for a long time into the council building. In two days you have gained the trust I could not gain in a lifetime. You can obtain from him the information I seek. Perhaps you already have it."

"And if I refuse?"

Dextor sighed. "That would be unfortunate, since I would have no choice but to obtain the information from Mikkel himself. Every man has a breaking point. I'm sure Mikkel's is quite high, but ... well, he, too, must have a limit to what he can bear."

"It doesn't have to come to that, Peregrin," Gabrielle broke in. "Dextor is not a madman. He doesn't like violence or killing."

"Then he should leave Archiva in peace."

Gabrielle shook her head sadly. "You don't know what it's like out here, in the forest all these years. We protected Archiva with our bare hands. And the council cries, 'Peace, peace.' Terists don't honor peace. They are not turned aside by creeds. They have knives and clubs and no fear of hurting or killing others. I lost my best friend because the council wouldn't listen to Dextor. I was there. I saw Franceen slaughtered in front of me, and Clive as well. Maybe all of us would have been killed but for Dextor. Only he had the courage to go beyond the Creed and avenge their deaths."

"Enough," Dextor said. "I will not wait long, Peregrin. You have seen what I have done. You have seen the order I have created out of chaos. You have until one hour after sunrise to get what I want. Then I will be forced to try another path." He opened the oaken door. "My men will meet you at the bottom of the stone steps. Don't try any tricks, or Mikkel and those six Rangers will die."

As Peregrin stepped past him, Dextor clapped a hand on his shoulder. "Do not think me an animal, Peregrin. You know in your heart that this is the only way Archiva can survive. I am not asking you to help me destroy Archiva; I am asking you to help me save it. You see the rightness of my vision."

Peregrin turned toward him. "I also see a thin line between vision and lust for power. Where do you stand?"

Dextor grinned. "That is for you to decide, my brother."

IX

WATERMAN

It had been more than an hour since Peregrin had returned to the little cell with Mikkel and the others. A steady rain had begun, enveloping them in a shroud of sound that veiled their little cell from all outside noises. The guards beyond the door had tried to start a fire but failed and had to content themselves with huddling against the wall near a single torch that cast a feeble, flickering glow through the tiny, barred window.

Mikkel had said nothing upon his return, nor had he questioned Peregrin about his visit with Dextor. In fact, he had barely lifted his head to acknowledge his arrival. After a few minutes, Peregrin called his name in the darkness, but Mikkel only muttered, "Not now. Later."

It was just as well. Peregrin had his own things to think about. Dextor had tested him to see where he stood with the Creed. He had shown Peregrin his weapons of war and his ability to lead others with highly effective, disciplined order. And he had invited Peregrin to join him.

Also, he had revealed his marriage to Gabrielle, demonstrating that he was not, in fact, a cold-blooded killer. He had led the residents of Archiva to believe he was a monster to throw them into panic, but he wanted Peregrin to know the truth—that he was a human being capable of love and tenderness.

Peregrin could not see Mikkel in the dark, but he could visualize his presence. He sat with his back against the wall, knees drawn up to his chest with his arms wrapped around them. His head was bowed, and his whole demeanor was slumped and dejected.

What a contrast between the two! Peregrin thought. *In two days Dextor has taken away all of Mikkel's authority and confidence. Archiva is leaderless and in chaos, while Dextor's Second Archiva remains efficient and orderly. From a practical point of view, Dextor is the clear choice to…*

He caught himself in mid thought. For the briefest moment, he could see himself beside Dextor as his second-in-command. Together they would restore the civilization that was lost. Together they could make the world sane again. Order. Was that not what the world needed? It could be done. They could do it—together.

Then he saw Bliss's face in front of him. Bliss, as he had first met her—full of laughter and wisdom and concern, not just for Cornel and Janel, but for this new person whom she stood ready to welcome. Bliss at the council table, leading the others in a song of hope and promise. Bliss sitting before him in his little room, carrying the anguish and fear of the people and trusting Peregrin enough to reveal her own pain to him.

Peregrin blinked. Yes, there was Bliss. And there was Mikkel and the Waterman and Morgan and Sharee and Cabel and Janiss and Lisel and so many others whom he had met in just a few days time. He was not alone in this darkness. All Archiva stood with him as he wrestled with the decision that would determine its future. He could see their faces, all the way down the line to O'Keefe himself. They were waiting, looking to him, waiting for his answer. He could see them, their eyes full of hope and confidence in him. The path became clear.

"Stuff Dextor," Peregrin said aloud. He grinned suddenly and stood up, stretching his arms toward the ceiling. "Stuff his Second Archiva, stuff his swords and bows, stuff his vision, and stuff his offer." His voice rose. "I am the Traveler! Here I am! Here I stand!"

"Thus speaks the Traveler," said Mikkel, and he laughed. Peregrin heard Mikkel rise and come toward him. "I have been waiting to hear that," he said, his voice like a ray of sunlight through gray clouds. He reached out his arms and took Peregrin by the shoulders. "All Archiva has been waiting for that!" He pulled Peregrin to him and embraced him. "I was praying that you would not join him, but in the end, it was all up to you."

Peregrin was taken by surprise. After a moment, he returned the embrace. When Mikkel held him at arm's length again, Peregrin could barely see his face in the feeble light from the torch outside, but he could feel Mikkel's joy and courage flooding the room.

"How did you know what I was thinking?"

"Peregrin, I'm surprised at you," Mikkel answered. His voice rang free like a newly thawed stream. "Do not forget that not only have I read and pondered Mara's prophecy, but I am a Seeker of Archiva. I could feel you weighing the balance. And I know Dextor better than he thinks I do. But now you have chosen. I confess I was uncertain...I wasn't sure...I mean, Peregrin, I showed you everything, the Archive, how to get in there and everything. If you had decided to join Dextor..."

"But I didn't."

"But you didn't." Warmth radiated from Mikkel as he spoke. "You didn't. You are the Traveler. You are the Falcon without a nest."

"And I am in a bad spot, right now, and so are you. There's a lot I have to tell you. Dextor has the power to overwhelm Archiva."

"I was afraid of that," Mikkel said. "But this is not our concern at the moment. Right now we must find a way to escape, or it will not matter."

"Well, let's see." Peregrin said. "Dextor said I had till one hour after sunrise to make up my mind. I've done that already, and we have many hours yet until the dawn. So in that space of time, we have to entice the guards to open the door, overpower them, and slip through the canyon. Once up to the tower, we will probably have to fight our way clear, but it's the best I can come up with."

"Hmm, that's a pretty poor plan," Mikkel said, and Peregrin could feel him grin. "But if that's the best the great Peregrin can devise, I suggest we get on with it."

They roused the Rangers and explained their plan. In low whispers they discussed several ideas for getting the door open. They could pretend to fight, and one person would frantically call for help, one Ranger said. Another suggested they tell the guards that the cell was flooding from the rain. However, in all cases, it seemed likely the guards would simply notify Dextor or get reinforcements before they opened the door.

Just when it seemed they would have to try something, however improbable the success of it, they heard the key turn in the lock. The door opened, and a guard entered slowly. Someone was behind him with the torch. There was a thud, and the guard fell, struck from behind. Holding the torch was a small figure with tousled hair.

"Good morning," said the Waterman. "Mind if I come in out of the rain?"

Mikkel grabbed him by the shoulders. "Waterman! But how…who…?"

"Later, Mikkel," Waterman said, grinning. "Right now, it's time we got out of here." He turned toward the door and said, "Okay, bring the other joker in."

In response, a man and a woman dragged an unconscious figure through the door. It was the other guard. The man had flat features, a broad nose, and short, dark hair. The woman's golden hair was tightly knotted behind her head. She was more than six feet tall with a proportionate large-frame body.

"Sanda! Curtan!" Mikkel exclaimed. "You guard the hills above Archiva. How did you come here?"

The woman straightened up. "The same way you did, Mikkel. Dextor captured us two days ago and brought us here. There are others outside who have been freed, thanks to the Waterman."

"Yes, yes," said Waterman. "We can create a song in my honor later. Now it's time to go. Follow me, there's some hard climbing ahead." He led them out of the cell and locked the door. Outside of the door were three men and another woman, presumably Rangers who had not joined Dextor. A steady rain was falling, leaving most of the canyon obscured, except for a few flickering torches.

"Are we going to the tower?" Peregrin asked.

"Only if we all want to take up residence in your cozy little home there," Waterman answered. "Half of Dextor's men live in an adjoining cavern. All we would need is for one guard to set off the alarm, and that would be it. No, I know of a better way."

"How?"

"All in its time," Waterman said. He extinguished the torch. "I'm afraid we will have to make our way in the dark. We can't have a bobbing torchlight giving us away. We will need this soon, however. Keep close." He started off along the wall toward the uppermost corner of the canyon.

Peregrin, Mikkel, and the others followed, guiding themselves with one hand along the canyon wall. The rain made the rock slippery, but its noise drowned out any sound they might have made. The wall arced back until it connected with the adjacent wall in a sharp point about one hundred yards from their cell. Before them was nothing but rock.

Mikkel looked at the Waterman. "I assume you know what you are doing?"

"Mikkel, have you no faith in your Waterman?" he answered. With that he went around a large boulder, crouched down, and disappeared from view. Following, they found a small crevice at the base of the wall. It was barely two feet wide and not more than four feet high. The Waterman was crouched beside it, striking flint on iron to light the torch. He looked at Peregrin and grinned as it caught fire. "We have to risk the light now." He stuck the torch into the crevice ahead of him and wriggled in after it. After his feet disappeared, Peregrin crouched and followed. He found himself entombed in utter blackness with the feel of rock all around.

"Don't worry," came Waterman's voice from the darkness. "It does get wider. Just a few yards of crawling." Peregrin followed the voice, pulling himself ahead with his arms. He heard Waterman pull himself clear of the rock and grunt. The light from his torch suddenly became visible. After a short crawl, the walls did space out, and Peregrin pulled himself out of the crevice and into the bottom of a deep shaft. Waterman was standing a few yards away, holding the torch up.

Peregrin stood up. The shaft was about ten feet from side to side and roughly rectangular. It looked like a natural fissure in the rock. The walls were mostly smooth and wet. Waterman waited until everyone had come through the crevice.

"This is where it gets difficult, my friends," he said. "The only possible climbing spot is over here where the walls draw close together. The rock here is worn smooth by centuries of rainwater and offers few handholds. We must ascend by wedging ourselves between the walls and using the pressure of our bodies to climb. Most of the climb will be in pitch darkness."

"How far is it?" asked a Ranger.

"Oh, not far," Waterman mused. "I'd say, not more than sixty-five feet straight up." He smiled as he heard a few gasps. "Of course,

I thought to bring a rope." He led them to the area where the walls narrowed to two to three feet apart and leaned the torch against the wall. "This is how we go up," he said, grasping a rope that dangled from above. "Last man up, tie the end of the rope to the torch. We'll be needing it." He pulled himself up and put his feet against one wall and his back against the other. Then he reached up higher and repeated the sequence.

After Waterman had ascended into darkness, Mikkel nodded to Peregrin. He sighed, took hold of the rope, and began to climb. It was grueling, involving all of his muscles at once, but he found he could indeed keep a good pace and keep from slipping on the wet walls. He felt the rope go taut below him as another climber started up.

Just as it had begun to feel as though his shoulders were on fire from the effort, he raised his head out of the fissure and found himself emerging into a small cave. Waterman had already lit another torch, wedged it into the rock, and was reaching out his arms to help Peregrin over the ledge. One by one, the climbers came up and made it over the ledge. Mikkel came last. They pulled him up, and he lay gasping on the cave floor. *An exhausting climb for anyone,* Peregrin thought, *but Mikkel's much older than these Rangers, and he carries the weight of Archiva on his shoulders. He's in no shape to be climbing mountains.*

The Waterman pulled up the rope with the torch tied to it. "We can rest a moment here," he said. "But then we need to move on. We must be far from here by the time Dextor finds we are gone." Mikkel tried to rise, but Peregrin laid a hand on his shoulder.

"Rest, Mikkel. That climb took it out of all of us." Mikkel did not respond but nodded and continued to lay there, breathing heavily.

"Waterman," said Peregrin. "This seems a good time to answer a few questions. How did you find us? How did you know this fissure led into the canyon? How did you know anything about any of this?"

Waterman's chuckle was like a clear stream. "That's a lot of questions to take on. But I can answer them all together. Carlin told me."

Peregrin gasped, and Mikkel started up into a sitting position. "Carlin? Waterman, he cannot be trusted! Unless you are somehow part of Dextor's scheme—"

"No!" Waterman responded vehemently. He sounded genuinely hurt, but then his voice softened. "I guess one could think that, what with me appearing suddenly and all. But no, we became aware that Carlin could not be trusted. It took someone with special gifts to get the truth out of him."

"Who?" Mikkel and Peregrin said together.

In the wan torchlight, they could feel Waterman's smile more than see it. "Bliss."

"Bliss?" said Peregrin. "But how—"

"Easy. Leave room for the telling. You know, Mikkel, Bliss has a few talents that she has kept hidden all these years. We don't give her enough credit."

"I'm as perplexed as Peregrin," Mikkel said. "Tell us what's going on."

"Okay, perhaps I had better go back to the beginning. Still, this must be the short version, until we are safe in Archiva."

"Go on then," Peregrin said.

"Well, after you two left Archiva, you were shadowed."

"Shadowed, by whom?"

"By myself and two of the craftiest and most stubborn inhabitants of Archiva I have ever known. Cornel and Janel."

"What?" Mikkel's voice rose. "You let them follow us to Dextor? Waterman, I thought you had—"

"Easy, Mikkel, easy. You have to realize that your children were not about to let you walk off into danger. I came upon them just as they were preparing to follow you into the tunnel."

"What were you doing there at that time?" Peregrin said.

Waterman sighed. "I was planning on following you myself. I did not trust Dextor at all, and I had come to believe that we did have a traitor in our midst, someone close to the center. So I took a hidden position where I could watch all of the activity in Archiva—on the elbow. I watched as you came from the kitchens and decided to scramble down to follow you. But before I could, I saw a shadow moving quietly from building to building. That shadow had to break cover to go from the stables to the stairway, and in the early light, I recognized Carlin. I knew then I had our traitor.

"I came off the elbow as Carlin disappeared into the tunnel. So I made up my mind to follow. I knew Dextor had to be planning a trap, and I wasn't sure what I could do, but, well, I figured I could make it up as I went along. Before I got to the stairway, however, two small figures broke out of the shadows and ran toward it. I caught up just in time to grab your children by the collars before they dashed up to the tunnel.

"'What are you two doing?' I demanded.

"I could see that their faces were defiant and determined. 'Let us go,' said Cornel. 'We're not going to let Dextor kill our dad.'

"'I can appreciate your concern,' I said. 'I am going to follow them. You two march right back to your beds, and if I'm not back by noon, tell Bliss that Carlin is in league with Dextor.'

"'We will not!' Janel said, and she stamped her foot. " Really, Mikkel, she takes after you when it comes to mule headedness. She glared up at me and said, 'We're following that rat and finding out what he's up to, and we're going to protect our dad. And if you try to stop us, we'll make such a clamor that everyone will wake up, and the hills will come tumbling down.'"

"So you let them go with you?" Mikkel said.

"Honestly, I wasn't cut out to have children. And Carlin was getting farther away. So, yes, I said they could come if they did exactly what I told them to. Otherwise, I said, I would pick them up bodily and tie them to the water pump.

"So we went as quietly as we could, staying well back from Carlin. I figured since he was the traitor, anyone who was watching the trail for Dextor would leave after Carlin came by, since he appeared to be the back door of the trap. I guess I was right, because no one saw us. We ascended the hill and climbed a tall tree in order to see what was going on. We couldn't hear, but the actions were pretty clear. I had to physically restrain your children when Dextor had you held over the cliff, Mikkel. At the same time, I was trying desperately not to fall out of the tree.

"Well, we saw that there were just too many of Dextor's men for us to do anything. Cornel and Janel wanted to follow you, but I knew Dextor well enough to realize that the forest gave him the advantage. He would surely have caught us following him. Instead, I told them, Carlin was our key. We would have the advantage since he did not know that we had had seen him. We followed him back to Archiva and devised our plan along the way.

"Once there, we saw Carlin talking with Bliss and Morgan. He looked so concerned that you had not returned. I quietly got a few stout fellows and told them what was up. We drifted in slowly, forming a circle around Carlin and the others. Finally, he noticed that there were a lot of people watching him.

"'Waterman,' he said with great sincerity. 'Where have you been? Mikkel and Peregrin have not yet returned. We were just talking about sending out a search party.' He sounded so sincere I wanted to smack him one.

"'Will you go with them, Carlin?' I said. 'I mean, are you brave enough to go out there with Dextor on the loose?'

"Carlin looked uncomfortable with my tone. Then he laughed. 'Yes, of course,' he said. Why, I know those hills better than anyone here.'

"Then Janel lit into him. 'You know the hills to the north. But Daddy and Peregrin went to the ruins.'

"Now Carlin looked confused. 'I know the ruins well too,' he said.

"'Well enough to know where Dextor's thugs are hiding?' Cornel growled.

"By now Carlin had figured that something was up. He demanded to know what our point was. So I put it right to him. I told him how we had seen everything. He tried to pretend we had all fallen off the deep end, but we kept at him and described the whole scene. Morgan and Bliss stood there looking shocked. Finally Morgan stepped forward and challenged Carlin to speak truly. Carlin sputtered and fumed and tried to get Bliss on his side.

"Bliss looked at Carlin and then at us. She looked puzzled for a moment, and then she smiled. 'No, Carlin,' she said. 'I don't think they are making anything up. In fact, some things are beginning to come clear.'

"Now Carlin was clearly looking panicky. I told him we would go easy on him if he would let us know where Dextor had taken you all. I'll never forget his response. It was the quickest, most complete transformation I have ever seen.

"He paused a long moment, still portraying shock and disbelief. Then his face changed. His eyes narrowed, and his mouth twisted into a sneer. He laughed. 'You'll go easy with me, Waterman? What will you do, huh? Kill me? Beat me up? Ha! Your Creed forbids it! The best you can do is lock me up or exile me. But either way, you'll never know where Dextor has taken your precious Mikkel! Because I'm not going to tell you. In a little while, Dextor will sweep down from the hills and take this wretched, cringing town apart. And I'll be here waiting for him, his faithful brother.'

"'Dextor will find Archiva harder to take over than you think,' Morgan said, his voice hardening. 'Now that we know that you have betrayed us, we'll be ready for him.'

"'Ha! Brave dreams!' Carlin cried. 'You have no idea of the soldiers or the weapons Dextor has. The best thing you could do now is to send out a party to welcome him. You've already lost, and that's all I'm saying.' With that, he simply grinned.

"The grin infuriated me. Here was a man I had worked alongside of for years. I respected him, admired him, loved him—and it was all a lie. I stepped forward with fists ready to strike, but Bliss quickly reached out a hand and laid it on mine gently.

"'Hold, Waterman,' she said. 'Remember your Creed. I may know a way to loosen Carlin's tongue.' She told the men holding him to take him to the council building and told Morgan to gather as many Council members as possible to meet her there.

"Once inside the council building, Bliss had the men tie Carlin to a stout chair in the very center of the lobby. Then she set a chair directly opposite him and told them to go. Carlin laughed at her and said she was wasting her time. Bliss said nothing to him but told me to light a small oil lamp. 'Stand beside me, Waterman, with this light. Place it in my hands when I reach for it,' she said. 'Children, when the others come, have them form a wide circle around the inside rim of the lobby. Tell them to remain silent, whatever they hear.' Then she sat down in the chair facing Carlin and gazed at him, saying nothing more.

"We waited in silence. Well, we were silent. Carlin tried to ridicule Bliss. Then he became angry and shouted at her. She never said a word and never stopped gazing at him with those deep eyes of hers, smiling all the while. After a while, Carlin almost seemed afraid to look at her and begged her to look away. He said even when he closed his eyes that he could see her gazing at him. She just kept smiling all the while, keeping him pinned with her eyes. Finally, he became silent too and just sat there breathing heavily.

"As the council members came in, the children quietly got them to their places. Morgan came in last and closed the doors. 'That's all,' he said quietly to Bliss. She nodded, and he joined the circle.

The only light beside her lamp was the pale gloom from a high window that drifted down to the center of the lobby, directly where Carlin was seated.

"Bliss then told us to commune with her as she sought the truth from Carlin. She took the lamp from me and held it in front of Carlin and began to move it slowly to and fro before him. She never took her eyes from his as she did so. And she started talking to him, real peaceful like. 'Carlin, see the flame. This is the flame of truth. It penetrates your flesh, your blood, your bone, your spirit. See it, Carlin. The truth is heavy. It is making your eyes heavy. See it, Carlin. Follow the flame. Lose yourself in the flame. Become one with the flame, Carlin. Feel your eyelids getting heavy. You are about to fall into a deep sleep. You will be able to hear my voice and respond to me, but you can only speak what is true. You're almost there, Carlin. You are almost asleep, Carlin. You are asleep, Carlin.'

"All this time, I watched as Carlin's eyes dulled, and he struggled to keep them open, as if Bliss had attached weights to them. Then they closed completely, and his head bobbed slightly. Bliss handed the lamp back to me.

"Then she started asking Carlin questions in that same soft, peaceful tone. I swear, by now, even I would have told her anything she wanted to know. Carlin sure couldn't resist. He told her he had been in contact with Dextor since his exile, how many men he had, where this canyon was, what he wanted, and, most importantly, where there was a secret entrance that only he and Dextor knew about."

"And now you know about," Peregrin said.

"Exactly. But believe me, it's not an easy way in or out. You've already experienced one climb; now we have to go around the ledge we're on and face another climb down, this time in a steep crevice in the cliff. From there it's about a two-mile hike to a small tunnel we must crawl through to go under the base of another cliff. Then another mile or so to the deer trail that Dextor brought you along, out of the valley to the large boulder, and five miles more to Archiva. And remember, it's very dark outside.

"Bliss paused as if she were going to ask more, but by this time, Carlin was beginning to fidget. So she said she was going to count to three and clap her hands and he would awake, remembering nothing. It was the strangest sight I've ever seen. Carling woke up, looked dazed, and asked if he had told her anything, and Bliss just smiled and said: 'No, not a thing.'

The Waterman fell silent. For a while no one said anything. Then Peregrin spoke.

"I'm astounded. Bliss did all this?" Waterman nodded. "And you just followed his instructions, and they led you here?"

"It wasn't quite as easy as it sounds. Like I said, it's a hard go. By the time we put Carlin in an empty pantry and debated what to do, the day was fading fast. But we finally decided that I ought to come alone."

"Why?"

"Well, Morgan and Bliss thought I should take a couple of Rangers with me. The problem was, we knew that some of the Rangers were working with Dextor. Only we did not know which ones. So I didn't think we could take the chance. Of course, your children wanted to come, Mikkel, but Bliss forbade them. She's much better with children than I am."

Mikkel nodded. "I know. She's better than me too."

"Bliss then wanted to come with me, but I held that one person could move quicker and quieter and have less chance of being noticed than a group. I'm no Ranger, but I'm a fair woodsman; and I have excellent vision. So I pointed out that I could best follow the trail as well as do all that climbing, as well as sneak around unnoticed. 'Besides that,' I said, 'Archiva needs every person it can get.' The long and short of things is that all Archiva is preparing for defense now. All of the tunnels are guarded, and the lookouts on the high points have been doubled. Any sign of movement will bring a signal, either by birdcall, or by flare."

"What if you had failed?"

"I figured if I were captured, I would try telling Dextor I wanted to join him and Carlin had sent me. Or if I were killed, well, we would still be in the same position we were before, only we would know more than Dextor thought we did. That's enough talking for now, though. I'm here. I didn't fail, and we have to get moving. It's dark now, so the way will be treacherous. Stay close, and go careful."

He rose and led them through a small opening onto a wide rock shelf. Though it was dark and raining, they could make out the blacker forms of branches rising around them.

"We have a steep climb downward about forty or fifty feet," the Waterman said. "It will be slippery."

They followed him a short way along the ledge. The Waterman stopped and signaled them to crouch down.

"Here is the crevice we will be climbing down," he said. "It's hard to see in the dark. It's a steep slope. Face the hillside like me, and go down feet first, wedging yourself against the sides and easing yourself down. Give a few minutes between each climber." He stretched his hands across a gape in the rock ledge that was almost invisible and lowered himself into it. Then he disappeared from view.

Peregrin waved the Rangers to go ahead of him. One by one, they descended into the crevice. When he and Mikkel were left, Mikkel signaled him to go ahead. Peregrin stretched his hands across the crevice and lowered himself in. He held himself suspended in air until his feet had found the walls and were able to guide him in.

He eased down carefully, spread eagled against the narrow walls of the crevice, with his body flat against the slope. The walls were wet from the rain, and it was steep, as the Waterman had said, but not impossible. He could hear the Ranger about ten feet below him and tried to match his pace of descent.

Mikkel climbed in the crevice above him and began to descend. Peregrin could hear his breathing as he struggled to get into position. *He's tiring,* Peregrin thought. *That last climb really took his wind away.*

As they descended, Mikkel's breathing became more ragged. Peregrin slowed his descent to allow Mikkel to close the distance between them. When they had descended about thirty to thirty-five feet, Peregrin heard a sudden scrabbling as Mikkel's feet slipped. He heard him cry out as he lost hold completely and slid rapidly toward him. Before Peregrin could brace himself, Mikkel rammed him, knocking him loose. Together they slid the rest of the distance, slamming into the hard rock surface as the crevice slope bottomed out. Peregrin remembered trying to buffer the fall for Mikkel. Then his head hit the rock, and everything went black.

For a moment, Peregrin lolled in a comfortable bed of darkness. It surrounded him, embraced him, comforted him. Then he could hear someone calling his name, and as he recognized it, pain stabbed into the back of his head. This made him realize he had a head, and it was resting on something hard and unforgiving. He opened his eyes. The Waterman was crouched near him with a torch-holding Ranger nearby.

"Peregrin," he said. "Can you hear me?"

"Unnhh," Peregrin said. As he regained consciousness, the pain intensified, throbbing from the back of his skull to the inside center of his forehead. "Uuugh," he said and tried to reach for his head.

"Shh. Don't move," Waterman said. "Lie still till we see if you're hurt badly."

The throbbing eased somewhat. In fact, Peregrin noted, it was lessening quickly. "No," he said, and he sat up and put his hand to the back of his head. "No, I'm all right. I just got the wind knocked out of me."

Waterman started back. "Are you sure? You hit the ground hard."

"Yeah, I'm okay. Just give me a minute to clear my head." He could feel something wet and sticky in his hair. "Maybe it's just rain," he thought. Anyway, his head felt better. The pain was easing quickly now. "How's Mikkel?" he said.

Waterman sighed. "Well, you broke his fall, so I guess it could have been worse. But his leg is broken. It must have caught under him as he slid into you, and the impact snapped it."

"Can he move?"

"It's a bad break, midway between the knee and ankle. I think we're going to have to carry him. A couple of Rangers are making a stretcher."

Peregrin paused. "How much will it slow us down?"

Waterman did not grin. "Maybe enough for Dextor to catch up with us before we reach Archiva. There's no way to tell. He doesn't leave much to chance, you know? He might know we're gone already, though I'm hoping he feels secure enough in his own canyon that he doesn't check on you every hour. He'll find out by the dawn, that's for sure."

"How far away is that?"

"I'm thinking maybe two hours at the most. It's eight miles to Archiva over rugged terrain. We could have gotten pretty close if this hadn't happened. As it is now, we might make it halfway before Dextor finds out. His men will move fast, and they know these hills well."

"We have to get moving then," Peregrin said. He stood up. For a moment, everything around him seemed to swirl, and he put a hand to the rock wall to steady himself. Then his vision stabilized.

Waterman stood. "Are you sure you're all right?"

"Yes, I'm fine. Listen, we have to get Mikkel back to Archiva. The things he knows might be its only chance against Dextor."

Waterman nodded. "I have an idea. Dextor will expect us to

take the fastest route back to Archiva, which would bring us to the northwestern corner. To gain access, however, we would need to travel another mile down the tributary to the tunnel where we first brought you in."

"So?"

"Well, if we split up a few miles north of Archiva, one band can leave an obvious trail in that direction, while the other group takes Mikkel on a longer journey toward the eastern side, carefully covering their tracks as they go."

"Will that fool Dextor?"

"I don't know. Dextor is probably the best woodsman Archiva has ever seen. He will know that someone in the party is injured. If he looks close enough, he will most likely figure out our ruse, no matter how careful we are. My hope is that he will be so angry at your escape that he won't look close enough."

"All right then, let's get to it." Peregrin rose and walked to where Mikkel was sitting, his back against the rock wall. His left leg was splinted from the ankle to the knee and wrapped with strips of cloth the Rangers had torn from their shirts.

Mikkel smiled as Peregrin came to him. "Sorry to use you as a landing mat. Are you all right?"

"Yes. I hit my head, but I always said it was harder than rock anyway."

Mikkel shook his head. "I tried to hang on. Everything became blurry and just slipped away."

"Don't worry about it. Listen, Mikkel, we're going to get you back to Archiva. The Waterman and I are going to play a little prank on Dextor to draw him off. If... if we don't make it..."

"You'll make it," Mikkel said.

"Yes, I hope so. But under any circumstance, you have to rally the people for defense. Mikkel, Dextor has weapons that make hand-to-hand fighting useless. He will overrun Archiva unless..."

"Go on," Mikkel said quietly.

"Unless you share some of the secrets you know. Mikkel, I don't remember much about the Archive or the vault of machines, but I know there are things there that can defeat Dextor. You have to use it, Mikkel, or Dextor will have it."

Mikkel was silent for a long moment. Then he nodded and bowed his head.

"Waterman," whispered the Ranger known as Sanda. "The stretcher is ready."

"All right then," said the Waterman, "let's get going."

They eased Mikkel onto a stretcher made of branches woven together around two longer branches. Four Rangers then lifted him off the ground, one at each corner. They set out quietly, moving carefully down the hillside with Waterman in the lead. It was difficult to see, and the tree roots seemed to reach out to trip them. Still, except for Peregrin and Waterman, all of them were Rangers, skilled at moving in the forest. Even carrying Mikkel, they kept a good pace.

The hardest part came when they reached the small tunnel under the hillside, which required them to crawl. The hillside rose massively above them, and, "To go around would cost too much time," Waterman said. Since they could not carry Mikkel through the tunnel, he was obliged to crawl on his stomach with his arms and good leg. Peregrin followed on hands and knees behind him, hearing his occasional gasp of pain as he jarred his broken leg.

The tunnel was about one hundred yards long, but it felt like miles. When they finally emerged on the other side, they were covered in grime and sweat. Without pausing to rest, however, the Rangers got Mikkel back onto the stretcher and continued along the ravine. After about thirty minutes of picking their way, one of the Rangers whispered, "Waterman, this is the place where Dextor brought us across. I remember that shattered oak."

Waterman nodded and turned eastward, climbing the hillside. Peregrin followed, noting that the darkness had begun to lighten somewhat. Another hour or so brought them down a hillside onto a winding trail beside a large boulder. By now their surroundings were clearly visible. Peregrin remembered this place from their forced march. Here, they paused.

"The time has come, my friends," Waterman said. Archiva lies five miles down this trail. This is the way Dextor will expect us to go. I will not disappoint him. But here we must part ways if Archiva is to survive." He quickly laid out his plan. Brand, Curtan, Sanda, and Corval elected to go with him in order to leave enough tracks that Dextor might be fooled into thinking the entire party had passed that way. The rest would take Mikkel by another route to the eastern side of Archiva.

Waterman extended his hand to Peregrin. "Good speed to you, Peregrin," he said. "May we meet again in Archiva."

"Truly," Peregrin answered. "But don't say goodbye yet. I'm coming with you."

"No," the Waterman answered. "You have to get back to Archiva as well. Somehow I feel you're the key to defeating Dextor."

"That may be so, but I have my reasons."

"Which are?"

"For one, I believe that Dextor also thinks I am the key to something. He wants me to join him. We only have one shot at getting him to follow us. If he can tell that I am in the party, he will follow."

The Waterman paused and then nodded. "Let's get going then."

They set out, moving faster now. They were careful to cover their tracks just enough, but to miss an occasional footprint or snapped branch or scuffed rock. The Rangers took turns carrying one of their number on their shoulders to give the appearance they were still bearing a wounded person.

The trail was thin and twisted, barely wide enough for a deer. Sometimes it edged along hillsides that sloped steeply below them, promising a long slide if they missed a step.

After an hour of difficult hiking, they crested a hill and stopped. Below them the trail led down a steep hillside into a wide valley that ambled southward between two steep ridges. Peregrin could see a broad stream winding this way and that among the hillocks, taking the path of least resistance. About a mile away, mostly obscured by trees, he could make out what appeared to be a small lake in the lowest point of the valley. Even from this distance, he could hear the sound of rushing water.

They picked their way down the hill. As they neared the stream, Peregrin looked up its length. The valley closed in upon itself about a half mile upstream, into a point where two ridges intersected. The stream formed from several rivulets that cascaded down the slopes, as if it were designed to channel every raindrop for miles around into this basin.

Peregrin smiled. *Why, this is the ridge I saw when they first brought me to Archiva,* he thought. It pleased him to finally have an idea of his location.

Waterman caught his smile. "Not far now, Peregrin," he said happily. "And on our way, I will show you something truly amazing."

They followed the stream, no longer covering their tracks or carrying one another, but just going as fast as they could. By now their ruse would have worked, or it would have failed. Their only desire now was to get to Archiva.

The stream broadened and deepened as they went, collecting water from the hills that rose on all sides. The sound of rushing water grew stronger. Following the trail around a large boulder, Peregrin saw that the ground dropped sharply for some twenty feet, and the water of the stream poured over a shelf of rock and down in a magnificent waterfall into the lake.

At the base of the waterfall were two large wooden wheels affixed upright and connected by flat wooden boards all along their circumference. An axle ran through a single hub between the wheels and into a small wooden building beside it. The water plunged over the drop directly to the flat boards on one end of the wheel, propelling the wheel and axle to spin. From inside the building came a whirring noise.

"Isn't it magnificent?" exclaimed the Waterman as they picked their way down the slope.

"Yes," Peregrin called back above the rush of water. "But what is it?"

"What is it? It's my name!" Waterman laughed suddenly. "This is my pump house that supplies water to Archiva. The force of the water turns the axle, and the axle powers a pump inside of that building. This supplies the necessary force to pipe the water up the hillside to the reservoir on top of the ridge. From there, it's all downhill." He laughed again, and Peregrin could see pride in his eyes.

"You were right. It is amazing. It's the most ingenious invention I've ever seen!" Peregrin called back.

"When this is all over, I'll bring you back for a tour. But now we must put another idea of mine into practice. Come, we must leave the stream and climb."

"Why?"

Waterman pointed up the hillside a few hundred yards away. Nearly one hundred feet up at the top of the steep slope was what appeared to be a great wooden gate embedded into the hill.

"There," he said. "When I built this thing, the leaders of Archiva were concerned about a flood. So I built a release gate into the hillside. If the pressure were to build up too much, the gate would give way and spill half of the reservoir back down on this side of the hill, where it would flow straight down the valley and into the river."

"So why do we need to go there now?"

"Because I built the gate so that it could be released manually as well. If Dextor is on our tail and has brought many of his men with him, I think I'll give him a bath. I'll need your help though."

"Why?"

"Can you see the small apparatus at the top of the gate on either end?"

Peregrin squinted through the trees. He could make out what appeared to be a small table protruding from a large wooden box on either side of the gate. "Yes," he said. "What are they?"

"That's the release mechanism. A long steel shaft extends the length of the gate. Each shaft is affixed with gears, which engage other gears along three main support beams that extend the width of the gate. When the wheel on top of the shaft is turned to the right, the gears cause the beams to slide back into tunnels in the hillside. Once the six support beams are pulled back, the water pressure will do the rest."

Peregrin looked at him. "You are a genius!"

Waterman tapped his head. "No, just water on the brain." He laughed and set out for the slope. Peregrin and the Rangers followed.

Just after they had left the cover of the rocks, however, there was a sound like an angry bee followed by a sound like a knife being struck into rotted wood. Brand spun around and fell, the wooden shaft of an arrow sticking out of his back.

"Get down!" cried Peregrin, but there was no need to say it twice. They flattened themselves out on the earth as a volley of arrows hissed through the air around them. Peregrin looked over at Brand, whose eyes were open as if in shock. He was dead.

The arrows stopped. "Robbert!" came Dextor's voice. "Robbert, is that you?"

Waterman wriggled along the ground until he got behind the cover of a boulder. He twisted his body so that he could look backward. "My name is Waterman, Dextor!" he cried. "You've grown ill mannered in your time away form Archiva."

"I've also grown short of patience," Dextor said. "One of your number is down, and unless I am not the marksman I claim to be, he is dead. The rest of you will die unless you give me what I want."

"What is it you want?"

"That is easy, Robbert," Dextor said. "I want Peregrin."

Waterman glanced back at Peregrin, who shrugged. "He's not mine to give," he called back.

"Then I shall ask him," said Dextor. "Traveler, why have you turned from my path? I offer you a place at my right hand. I offer you power and the ability to change the course of history. And you run from me in the night! Why, Traveler, why?"

Peregrin looked at Waterman and then glanced at the steep hill above them. He looked to his left where Curtan lay. "Pass the word," he whispered to him. "When I make my move, everyone is to head down the valley, keeping to the hillside. Stay in the cover of trees, and get out of this area as fast as you can."

"What are you going to do?" Curtan asked.

"Never mind, just get away." Curtan passed the information to the next Ranger.

"Traveler," I grow weary," called Dextor. "Come forth now, and these Rangers can leave in peace. I give you my word."

"I've heard your word before, Dextor," Peregrin said. "What's my guarantee?"

"My only guarantee is that I will kill everyone except you unless you give yourself up," Dextor answered. "You have until the count of ten. One, two ..."

Peregrin stood up, his hands at his side and slightly behind him. He half expected an arrow to pierce his chest, but none came. He scanned the hills. "Show yourself, Dextor," he said.

Dextor laughed and then stepped out from behind a tree less than eighty feet away. Peregrin turned the rock he held hidden in his right hand slightly so that it lay firmly in his grasp. "There," said

Dextor, "isn't this much easier? No one has to die, Peregrin. Don't you know that?"

"People have already died. Don't you know that?" Peregrin answered. "This is for Brand." He turned slightly and hurled the rock.

His aim was true and fierce. The rock struck Dextor in the head, and he fell backward. Several of his men leaped from hiding places toward him, only to be met with a volley of rocks from the Rangers.

"Now!" Peregrin cried. "Move out! Get away!" He turned and sprinted to the hillside. Once there he began to clamber up, hunkered over, climbing with his hands as much as with his feet, hoping the trees, rocks, and vegetation would give him adequate cover from Dextor's arrows.

The Waterman scrabbled past him. "Stop!" Peregrin cried. "It's me Dextor wants. You can get away!"

"I told you it takes two people to operate the release! Besides, I'll teach Dextor to call me Robbert!" Waterman cried back, and he kept climbing.

Arrows began to whistle through the trees about them. One struck a tree not three inches from Peregrin's head. Suddenly he heard Dextor's voice. "Stop, you idiots! He's no good to me dead! Get after him. Stop him from reaching the top!" The arrows stopped.

"Damn," said Peregrin. "I was hoping I had killed him." Waterman smiled.

Dextor's men raced after them. Before they reached the hillside, however, Waterman and Peregrin were nearly halfway to the top.

"Almost there." Waterman gasped. "One of us will need to be on either side of the gate."

"I'll take the far side," Peregrin called back

They scrabbled upward as fast as they could, knowing their pursuers were scant moments behind them. As they neared the gate, Peregrin could see the wheels of the release mechanism on either side of it. The gate itself was a massive structure of oak about twenty feet wide and fifteen feet high, built directly into the hillside. He veered toward the far side of the gate.

Dextor saw him. "They're going to open the gate! Shoot him, you fools! Shoot the Waterman! Kill him now!"

Peregrin reached his wheel just as he heard the whistling of arrows in the air. He turned, afraid of what he might see. Waterman, however, had reached his wheel safely and was crouched down behind it, protected by the trees and the mechanism from the deadly arrows. The gate itself was about four feet wide and was flat along the top so that a person could walk across it. On the other side of the gate was a large reservoir, nearly fifty yards wide and two hundred yards long. The water level was only yards below the causeway, swelled by the spring thaw and rains. Despite the urgency of the situation, Peregrin could not help but marvel at the Waterman's creation.

"Now, Peregrin! Turn the wheel to the right as far as you can!"

Peregrin grasped his wheel and turned. The wheel resisted and then slowly gave way. Peregrin could feel the pressure of the gears and the drag of a massive beam being drawn back.

He heard Waterman cry out and looked up, alarmed to see him leaning heavily upon the mechanism, frantically trying to turn it. An arrow protruded from his leg. Even from this distance, Peregrin could see his grimace of pain.

"Don't stop!" he cried. "Keep turning!"

Peregrin glanced down the hillside. His pursuers were not fifty feet away. Others had stopped farther down the hill and were shooting at the Waterman. He gave one final pull and felt the beams go *kachunk* as they slid completely away from the gate. The gate trembled but did not open.

Peregrin glanced at Waterman, who still struggled to turn the mechanism. His leg was bleeding freely and impaired him from getting enough leverage to accomplish the final turn of the wheel and remain protected from the arrows that whistled around him.

Peregrin was about to run across the gate when Waterman suddenly straightened up, heedless of the arrows, grasped the wheel with both hands, bent over it, and used his whole body to turn it. Peregrin could hear the beams slide out of place.

The gate shuddered and then stopped. In the center of gate, a large limb from a fallen tree appeared to be jammed, its branches sticking above the causeway. Despite the tremendous pressure of the water, it would not budge.

"Peregrin," Waterman said. "Stall 'em!" With that, he leaped to the causeway and began a loping run toward the center of the gate, dragging his leg.

"Waterman! No!" cried Peregrin. Arrows began to whistle about him. Peregrin bent down and picked up a rock, which he hurled at the nearest bowman, striking him in the face. The man lost his balance and rolled down the hill. As quickly as he could, Peregrin continued to fling rocks, hoping to throw off the aim of the archers.

Waterman cried out. Even before he turned, Peregrin knew he had been hit hard. Turning, he saw that he had almost reached the center when an arrow had struck him in the side, just above his waist. He took a few, halting steps toward the branch, hand outstretched. Another arrow struck him in the side. Waterman gasped and fell, his outstretched hand less than a foot away from the limb.

"No!" Peregrin screamed. He hurled rocks at their pursuers so hard and with such accuracy that the men had to dive for cover. "No! No! No! No!"

"Stop!" cried Dextor from below.

Peregrin halted, one hand cocked to throw. Dextor stood on the shelf of rock just above the waterfall. "Stop, Traveler!" he said again. "This will solve nothing."

"Dextor," screamed Peregrin. "I will kill you!"

Dextor shook his head. "No, you won't. You are no killer, Traveler. Come now. Robbert is dead. He died for the same reason Franceen died—because the leaders of Archiva would not listen. He would not listen. You would not listen to me. Stop, Peregrin. Please, you know in your heart that I am right. If you will listen, maybe they will listen. Nobody else should have to die. Isn't Robbert's death enough?"

"Dextor..." came a croaking voice from the gate. Peregrin looked to see Waterman pull himself up to the limb. He grasped it with both hands and pushed himself up on his hands and knees. "Dextor!" he said louder. "My name is Waterman!" He wrapped his arms around the branch and reared up onto his feet.

The branch came loose with a snap, a piece breaking off in his hands. He brandished it above his head as the gate began to tremble beneath him. "I am the Waterman!"

The gate broke loose in the center, flinging each half to the side as ten thousand gallons of water roared through it and down the hill. Waterman was catapulted through the air, landing on the hillside near to the release mechanism he had operated. Peregrin was forced to grab the wheel of his mechanism to avoid being thrown down the hill.

Dextor's men were directly in the path of the torrent. They were overwhelmed and disappeared beneath the deluge or were blasted through the air onto the rocks below. The gates themselves were ripped off their moorings as the water raged from the reservoir. Trees were torn from the hillside and tossed below like kindling.

The hillside shook as the tumult raged on. Peregrin clung to his wheel, expecting half of the ridge to come down upon him, but the earth held firm. The sound was deafening, like the shriek of a thousand birds of prey tearing at the flesh of a gigantic corpse.

Finally, the water ceased to roar through the cleft in the hillside as its level fell below the bottom of the gate. Peregrin pulled himself up and looked about. The slope beneath him had been scoured of tree and brush. The lake had doubled in size, and water surged around the tops of the smaller trees. Pieces of the great water wheel bobbed about, and the pump house was completely submerged. There was no one in sight. Brand's body was gone. All of Dextor's men were gone.

He looked at the shelf of rock above the waterfall. Dextor stood there gazing at him, unmoving. Peregrin stared back at him. After a long moment, Dextor laughed.

"Well done, Traveler, well done!" he exclaimed. "I am turned back once more. No matter. I promise you I will return." He turned to go.

"Dextor!" called Peregrin. "Dextor! I promise you I will be waiting. And when you do return, I think one of us will die!"

Dextor did not respond for a long moment. Then he laughed again. "So let it be!" he called and then turned and made his way back up the hillside.

Peregrin turned and picked his way across the face of the slope to the other side of the gate, slipping in the wet mud. Waterman lay face down about fifteen feet beyond the release mechanism. Peregrin rushed to him and turned him over. He was dead, but Peregrin could see the trace of a smile in his face. He cradled him in his arms and rocked him.

"Peregrin!" called a voice.

Peregrin looked up. The Rangers who had slipped away had climbed the slope and doubled back. They came scrabbling toward him.

Curtan reached him first and knelt beside him. He reached out and touched the Waterman's hand. "Oh, Waterman! Waterman!" he cried. There were tears in his eyes.

Sanda and Corval came up, disbelief etched across their faces. "We saw the whole thing," Corval said, "but we couldn't get around in time."

Curtan looked up at them. "We must take the Waterman back home. We must..." the words caught in his throat.

Sanda crouched down beside Peregrin. She touched Waterman's face and then gently pulled the arrows out of his body. Her tears fell upon him. Still clutching the arrows, she bowed her head and sobbed.

Peregrin looked at them. They were all weeping, these strong, brave Rangers. They had lost a friend whom they loved. He realized that he, too, loved the Waterman. He desperately wanted to weep as they did, but no tears came. He could only feel a dull ache within. There was no release for his pain. He wished desperately for Bliss to be there.

They stayed there for long minutes, in silence. Peregrin continued to rock back and forth while the Rangers wept. Finally, he stood up, still holding the Waterman in his arms. "We have to go now," he said. "We have to take the Waterman home."

They nodded and rose. Together they placed the Waterman gently on their shoulders. Silently they set out along the ridge toward the entrance to Archiva, bearing their Waterman home like a king slain in battle.

X
WAR

Peregrin sat on the rock ledge called the elbow, where he and the Waterman had spoken after his arrival. His knees were drawn up to his chest with his arms linked around them and his head bowed. Although he sat alone in silence, in his mind he was yelling—at Mikkel, at Dextor, and at the leaders of Archiva.

They had brought Waterman's body home and carried it to the meeting platform at the southern end of Archiva, learning as they went that Mikkel and the other Rangers had not yet returned. By the time they laid the body gently on the platform and stood silently around it, most of Archiva had gathered around them. People were shouting, asking questions. Morgan, Bliss, and other Guardians shouldered their way through the crowd and motioned for silence. Even so, it took many minutes for the tumult to subside.

Peregrin and the Rangers related the story of their escape, Mikkel's injury, and Waterman's final act. The people grew still as they listened. When they had finished, the crowd remained silent, heads bowed. Peregrin realized they were communing even without realizing it. From the back of the crowd came a low groan, followed by another. The sound rose as it passed through the people until it became a tumult of groans, wails, and cries. They were grieving their Waterman, he realized, and suddenly it occurred to him how much this man had meant to Archiva. It was as if he embodied its spirit and empowered its people. Now he was gone from them.

Bliss lifted her arms to the sky and cried out. Her voice rose above the cries of the crowd, collected them, and formed them into a single utterance of inarticulate anguish. As her voice swelled, the people fell silent once more.

"Waterman!" she cried. "Waterman! Why have you gone from us? Brave Waterman! Gentle in speech, fierce in kindness. Who could flow among us as you have? Who can bring mirth to our gray day? Waterman! Waterman!"

The crowd lifted its arms to the sky and cried as one. "Waterman! Waterman! Waterman!"

Morgan motioned for silence. "Friends, the Waterman came to us from a life of violence. He followed the path of peace with complete devotion. By his hand we have water at our disposal. By his heart we have hope for the mission of Archiva. He is gone from us now, but his spirit will remain. Let him be buried by the water pump he devised, and let his spirit be honored through imitation. In these dark times, we must renew our dedication to Archiva and to peace."

"In these dark times," Peregrin said, "we must honor the Waterman by protecting that which he gave his life for."

Morgan turned to face him. "What do you mean?"

"I mean that Waterman gave his life to stop Dextor from entering Archiva. And stop him he did. But Dextor is still alive, and he has the men and the weapons to take this place by force. We must act fast and stop him before he has the chance."

"Peregrin," Morgan said, "of course we will fight to stop Dextor.

Every person in Archiva knows how to fight. Dextor will find us hard opponents."

"Every person in Archiva can fight with sticks!" Peregrin retorted. "Dextor is coming with bows and swords. Archiva would fall before any of his men got close enough to throw a rock at. No. Now is the time to act, not to wait!"

"What action are you speaking of?"

"We must go out to meet Dextor. Attack him when he is off guard. We must take the fight to him and stop him before he gets out of his canyon."

Bliss shook her head. "How? How can we do that if Dextor is equipped as you say?"

Peregrin gazed at her and saw fear in her eyes. "You already know, Bliss," he said. "Deep beneath Archiva lies knowledge of weapons that can stop Dextor. These weapons can be found in a vault beneath the ruins. That's what Dextor wants more than anything—to gain control of those weapons and their use."

Bliss took a step back. "I do not know what weapons you are talking about. Even if they exist, we cannot violate the trust..."

"Don't you understand?" Peregrin shouted. "Dextor knows those weapons are there. He will not stop until he has them, no matter who he kills."

"So you are suggesting we should kill him first?" Merida said.

Peregrin gazed at her but did not answer. Bliss gasped. "Peregrin, no. No! We cannot deliberately kill anyone. To do so would be to forsake all that we cherish. No, there must be another way. Dextor would not—"

"Dextor would!" cried Corval. "Bliss, Morgan, Guardians of Archiva, listen to Peregrin. I was there! I heard Dextor order his men to shoot the Waterman. I tell you, he must be stopped, even if it means we have to kill him!"

At this, the entire crowd broke out shouting. Some seemed to be shouting for Dextor's death. Others were shouting the Creed aloud. Still others were calling Morgan's name and demanding some answer. After several minutes, the Guardians finally got the noise to subside.

Morgan stepped forward to the edge of the platform. "People of Archiva! People of Archiva, listen to me! We are in grave danger. We are being threatened by a man who once lived among us. Dextor professed our Creed and fought to protect Archiva. Now he seeks to destroy it. We must work together now to protect our home.

"Yet we also face a grave threat from within. For a century, we have professed the Creed: 'You must not kill, nor use a Sheen to kill.' This creed is being tested. Shall we cast aside the foundation stone of our community? If so, then Dextor has already won the battle, and the Waterman has died for nothing. We must stand against Dextor, and we may fail to stop him. But we must not fail to uphold our Creed. Else we have already lost."

"Then what shall we do?" a voice cried out from the crowd. "Do we wait for Dextor to wipe us out?"

"No," Morgan shouted. "We will be ready for him. Everyone should prepare to defend home and family. All Rangers will patrol the ridge above us. Whatever path Dextor takes toward Archiva, we will know long before he gets here. We will be ready for him."

"You will be ready to die then," Peregrin said.

"Peregrin—," Bliss began, but Peregrin shook his head.

"He will not stop unless he is stopped, Bliss. It's not a matter of the Creed. It's a matter of fact." He turned toward Corval, Curtan, and Sanda. "Come on; let us take Waterman to the pump."

The Rangers joined him, and they lifted Waterman's body once more. The crowd parted as they passed through and then followed them silently. When they reached the pump, two men brought shovels and picks and proceeded to dig a grave. A woman came forward with a blanket from Waterman's home. They laid him on it and gently lowered his body into the grave. Curtan tugged on Peregrin's elbow.

"You were with him to the last, Peregrin. You be the first to throw a handful of earth into the grave."

Peregrin knelt by the grave and looked at Waterman's body. He reached over and took a handful of soil. "I wish we could have known each other longer, Waterman. I wish we could have known each other for years." He tossed the earth into the grave, stood, and walked away.

He went directly to the elbow then and climbed to the top. From there he watched the people of Archiva file past the grave. Each would take a handful of earth, say something, throw the earth in, and walk away.

He felt miserable as he watched them. Something inside of him was desperate for release and could find none. Many of the Archivans were weeping, but Peregrin could find no tears. Even his anger seemed artificial to him, as though he were angry simply because something within him told him he should be angry.

There was a scrabbling sound from below. After a few minutes, Bliss emerged above the ledge. She looked at him in sorrow. "Peregrin," she said, "may I come up?"

He sighed. "Of course. You may go anywhere you wish."

She hesitated at his tone, and he instantly regretted it. But she seemed to accept it and clambered over the ledge to sit beside him. The sky had remained surly throughout the day. Now a light, almost misty rain began to fall.

"Waterman loved to sit here," Bliss said.

"I know," Peregrin said. "He told me. We sat at this very spot, and he told me much about himself. He was trying to make me feel welcome here."

"He was very good at that," Bliss said. "He was always concerned for those who did not fit in."

"Well, it worked. I had been planning to leave Archiva. After talking with him, I decided to see this thing through."

"I'm glad. We had many talks up here ourselves."

"He gave his life for Archiva, Bliss."

"I know, Peregrin."

"Still, you will not do what is needed to stop Dextor. His sacrifice will be for nothing."

"Peregrin," Bliss said, "Waterman sacrificed his life for Archiva long before he stood on the floodgate. He devoted his life to peace. He would not want us to kill if we could avoid it."

"Yet he killed. I'm sure Dextor's men were killed by the flood he let loose. If anyone knew the power of water, it was Waterman. He knew his action would kill them. I think he even hoped to kill Dextor, you know, so it could end there."

Bliss drew back from him. "Peregrin, you must not take this path. Waterman believed in the Creed. So must we!"

He looked at her, not knowing whether it was tears or rain that streaked her face. "I have never sworn the Creed, Bliss," he said. "I must follow the path I feel is right."

"How do you know what's right?"

"I don't. But I hear Dextor's voice echoing in my head: 'Shoot him, kill the Waterman!' And I know I have to stop him."

"You're wrong."

"How would you know?"

"I felt the Waterman's death."

Peregrin's eyes narrowed. "That's taking it too far, Bliss."

She shook her head. "You can think I'm making it up if you want. You can even think I've lost my mind. But at the very time Waterman would have died, according to your account, I was down at the gardens, pulling weeds from among the onions. It's a pastime that has always calmed me.

"Suddenly I felt a terrible pain pierce my side, then another higher up. I lurched upward and then fell, doubled over. Then a hot fire began to burn in my head, and I knew I was in union with someone who was dying painfully. My vision cleared, and I could see my arm stretched out in front of me toward a branch. Farther beyond, I saw you, standing near a wheel. You were screaming and throwing rocks. Your face was twisted in rage.

"I heard myself speak and realized it was not me but Waterman. I saw the fingers of his hand constricting, pulling him toward the branch, and when he reached it, he pulled himself up onto his hands and knees. I heard him call out to Dextor, felt the pain slice through him, and knew his exhilaration as he cried out his name one last time. Then it all went black. I awoke later to find Kalin and Drinda bending over me. They said they saw me fall and had been trying to revive me for five minutes."

Peregrin looked at her open mouthed. Her description was so real. But no, it was too much to accept. He shook his head.

"So? Then you know he died trying to stop Dextor."

"But his thoughts were of peace, Peregrin. Even as he cried his name, he was regretting his action, wishing he could bring peace, not death. I know; I could hear his thoughts."

"I'm sorry, Bliss. I would like to believe you. But you could be imagining the whole thing. I believe these are your thoughts, not Waterman's."

"And what of my vision of his death?"

"I told the story to everyone when we brought him. You could have imagined the scene from the details of my account."

Bliss stood up and backed away. It seemed as though she was going to say something. Then she shook her head and climbed down the ledge. When she reached the ground, she ran off. Peregrin could hear her sobbing as she went. He suddenly remembered that, in his account of Waterman's death, he had not mentioned throwing rocks at Dextor's men. It began to rain harder.

Peregrin stayed on the elbow for another hour, becoming drenched. Finally, he climbed back down and walked to his quarters, avoiding Waterman's grave. Inside, he changed his clothes and sat down in the chair to wait. It wasn't long before the knock sounded at his door. "Come in," he said softly.

The door opened and Curtan, Corval, and Sanda entered. They said nothing, but looked at him. Behind them through the open door, the rain drummed on the ground.

Peregrin gazed at them. "How many others are with us?"

"At last count we have forty-seven besides ourselves," Curtan said.

"An even fifty then," Peregrin mused. "It will do. And I will make fifty-one. Fifty-one for Archiva."

"Fifty-one for the Waterman," Sanda said. "We pledge ourselves to your leadership, but we fight in his memory."

"Then let that be our battle cry," Peregrin said. "For Archiva, for the Waterman. And may all who join us be known as Watermen."

"What are your orders?" Corval asked.

"Dextor will be coming fast. I do not know yet how to get into the vault under the ruins, but I believe Mikkel will help us when he arrives. Till then, we have to slow up Dextor, give him something to think about. Tell me, are we mostly Rangers?"

"Some Foresters and a few Farmers," Curtan said.

"Okay, all Rangers are to patrol the ridges. Fine, send them out with the others mixed among them. Tell everyone to meet at the north point on top of the ridge directly above the council building in three hours."

"We will be there," Sanda said. They turned and went out.

Peregrin watched them go. "So it begins," he murmured softly. "Come, Dextor, my brother. Now let us test each other. Now let us grapple on the heights." He closed the door.

～～

Some six hours later, as a soggy twilight drew on, Peregrin lay upon a ridge, carefully peering down the slope to where eleven of Dextor's men were encamped beside a stream. The camp was well placed, using a bend in the stream and the rolling hillocks to obscure it from view. The men kept their gear stowed behind rocks and woodpiles so that a casual wanderer might walk halfway through the camp before he realized anyone was there.

So this was to be the first encounter, Peregrin mused. It had come fast. Mikkel had returned before Peregrin had left Archiva. His party had been surprised by this very band of Dextor's men and had to fight their way clear. One Ranger had been severely injured, and two others sustained minor wounds in the *melee;* but they had driven Dextor's men off. Peregrin noted with a smile that two of the men in the camp below had their heads bandaged, one was limping, and another had his arm in a sling. Mikkel's party had fought well.

Afterward, the rain made it even harder to navigate, now bearing two disabled people. The Rangers took turns carrying the injured man slung across their shoulders, while Mikkel had them fashion crutches so he could hobble along with minimal support.

Morgan, Bliss, and Merida were with Mikkel when Peregrin arrived. He listened as they related the events of the day. When he heard of Waterman's death, he closed his eyes and groaned.

"It is true, it is true," he muttered. "It has all come true."

Peregrin stepped forward. "Mikkel, you, too, have seen Dextor's power. Remember what we spoke of after you broke your leg. We need to fight, Mikkel. We need to use Archiva's power to protect it."

Mikkel muttered something and shook his head. Merida laid a hand upon Mikkel's brow. "He has a fever," she said. "He's exhausted. Out, all of you! Mikkel will be no help tonight. He needs time to heal."

"No!" Peregrin cried. "There is no time! We must act!"

Merida drew herself up sharply. "Then go, and act! Mikkel cannot give what he does not have. Now get out!" She herded them out the door and closed it.

Peregrin returned to his quarters and quickly strapped on

Crown's knife. He took his pack, stuffed it with provisions, grabbed his staff, and went to the door. Opening it, he found Bliss standing before him.

She simply gazed at him a long time, and he remembered Waterman's account of how she gazed at Carlin. It was a gaze that somehow trapped a person, surrounded him, and exposed the truth. He suddenly felt sorry for Carlin.

Finally, she spoke. "You are going?"

"I am," he said.

"I believe you are taking the wrong path."

"Will you try to stop me?"

"No."

"Why are you here then?"

She paused. "I wanted to wish you well."

He was silent a moment. Then he lowered his eyes from her gaze. "Thank you, Bliss."

She bowed slightly. "Peace to your heart, Peregrin." She stepped aside.

"And to yours," he answered. He left then, striding quickly for fear he would change his mind.

He met Curtan at the water pump. Together they stood by Waterman's grave in silence. Then they set out for the hills above Archiva.

"Fifty against two hundred," Peregrin mused to himself as they made their way to the meeting place he had designated. "Can fifty stop two hundred?"

This had been the unspoken question that hung as heavy as the mist when they had gathered on the ridge above the council building. They were brave, determined, and willing, but heavily outnumbered. Dextor's men were better armed and had no reservations about killing.

Peregrin wasted no time. "Friends," he said, "let no one be deceived. We have seen the enemy. Dextor has trained his men well and has given them the power to overrun anything in their path. He has nearly two hundred fighters who have sworn total allegiance to him. They will obey his utmost command. It is my belief that even now he marshals them to march on Archiva. He is tired of waiting and tired of trying to convince the Guardians to surrender.

"Archiva has the power to stop him but fears to use it. The Creed, which all of you have lived by, forbids the very force needed to protect it. Yet you are here. You are here because you love Archiva, because you love your families, because you loved the Waterman. You are the ones who will risk the Creed in order to preserve it. You are the ones who have heard the call to stand your ground today. Let us rally to his memory. His name shall go before us in defense of Archiva. From this time forward, let us be known as Watermen!"

The men and women before him cried out, "For Archiva! For Waterman!"

"We have little time. We must find a way to stop Dextor, or at least delay him until Archiva can rise to its defense. To meet him head on would be suicide. We must attack with speed and cunning where he least expects it. If we can harass Dextor enough that he cannot ignore us, we can hold him back. You know these hills; now let us use them to our advantage. Let the hills themselves rise to deny Dextor his prize. Archiva must survive, even if it means we give our lives to that end! Will you stand to defend our home?"

"We will!" they shouted.

"Brothers, sisters, remember your Creed. Waterman believed in the Creed with all his being, yet he came to a moment when he had to go beyond it to defend it. Let us fight by this standard. Do not wound if you can hold. Do not cripple if you can wound. Do not kill if you can cripple. But even if you must kill, let us defend Archiva."

"Archiva!" they all shouted.

It was enough, Peregrin thought. He divided the band into three companies of fifteen fighters under the command of Corval,

Curtan, and Sanda. The Rangers Raven and Lindah were chosen to serve as couriers between the groups.

The first step was to deprive Dextor of his eyes and ears around Archiva, which meant eliminating the patrols he had placed around it. Corval's band moved off to the south, while Sanda's group headed northward to the trail. Peregrin accompanied Curtan's group toward the ruins to where he hoped to find the men Mikkel's group had encountered.

He was not disappointed. Careful reconnaissance had located a camp in the valley leading toward the ruins from the northwest. It was a good location from which the men could patrol the ruins and vanish quietly back into the forest.

They had watched the camp for nearly an hour. Though they outnumbered Dextor's men, they faced the problem of getting close enough to attack. Dextor's men were armed with bows and swords, and a guard kept watch along the stream from a position in a tall pine tree.

Peregrin called for two volunteers to "stumble" into the camp just as the sun set. They tore their clothes and rubbed mud on themselves to appear worn, as if they were fleeing Archiva. He hoped their arrival would cause enough distraction to allow the others to slip down the slopes under the cover of twilight.

He watched the path by the stream nervously. The volunteers had circled around and would approach from the south. It would be exceedingly dangerous for them. Dextor's men could have orders to kill, or they might just do it for fun, being angered by their last encounter.

He saw the guard shift slightly and then give a birdcall, causing the other men to scramble for their weapons and take cover behind rocks and brush piles. Shortly after this, the volunteers came into view from around the bend in the stream. They appeared to be completely exhausted, and one was supporting the other as if injured. *Nice touch*, Peregrin thought.

As they entered the camp, Dextor's men rose up and surrounded them. The guard came down from the tree. *Good,* thought Peregrin. He clicked his tongue in signal, and his troops began to make their way as quickly as they could down the slope. "Please let us be in time," Peregrin breathed.

When they reached the trees around the clearing, Peregrin was relieved to see that both of his volunteers were still alive. Two men held each of them from behind, while the leader of the camp interrogated them. Peregrin heard him curse, and he slugged one man in the stomach. The man crumpled.

Peregrin reached down and picked up a rock slightly smaller than his hand. He cocked his arm and stepped out from behind his tree just as the leader of the camp drew back his hand to strike the remaining volunteer.

The rock flew hard and true, striking the leader on the side of the head. The Watermen burst from cover and were upon them before they could look about. With cries of "Archiva!" and "Waterman!" they pummeled Dexor's men with their staffs and subdued them.

In a moment, it was over. Eleven men had been captured without loss of life or even injury. Curtan grabbed Peregrin's arm. "First trial, first victory!" he exclaimed. "You have done well, Traveler!"

"Let's not celebrate too soon," Peregrin said. "This is but the beginning." Still, he was pleased at the outcome, as it gave him a glimmer of hope.

He was further heartened when they discovered that the other groups met with similar success. They tied their captives in a line, as Dextor's men had done to Mikkel, Peregrin, and the Rangers, and four guards led them into Archiva to be imprisoned in a large meeting room. The rest of the group headed back to the north point above Archiva.

As the night wore on, members of the other bands arrived with tales of success. Corval's band returned, having captured a band of eight ruffians watching the southern end of Archiva. They had caught them totally by surprise, as the men had received no news of the day's events. Not one of the Watermen had been injured. And Sanda's band came back down the north trail, leading a group of nine captives. Two of her number had received knife wounds in a hot but quick fight, but neither injury was serious.

What heartened Peregrin even more was the capture of the weapons that Dextor's men possessed. At the end of the day, his Watermen had taken possession of eighteen swords, twenty-two long knives, twelve bows, and more than a hundred arrows. Dextor had lost his grip around Archiva, and he did not even know it.

Furthermore, the ranks of the Watermen swelled. As each group of captives was brought in, more Archivans rose to join the fight. Some were left to guard the captives, but by midnight, Peregrin had more than seventy-five men and women encamped on the hillside before him.

Still, he realized these were not really fighters. They were artisans, farmers, livestock tenders, and kitchen workers. Yes, they had learned self-defense as they grew, but they had also sworn themselves to lives of peace. In a real battle, such as he knew lay ahead, would he be sending them to be slaughtered? The thought troubled him.

He had one real shock that night. As people came from Archiva, they were presented before him. He made each of them swear personally that they would defend Archiva even at the cost of their lives. At one point, he looked up to see a young man with deeply recessed eyes standing before him. It was Jorge.

Peregrin smiled slightly. "We meet again, Jorge. What brings you here?"

Jorge had lost none of his stiffness. "The same thing, I assume, that brings you here, Peregrin. Archiva is in danger. I wish to protect it."

"You never liked me, did you, Jorge?"

Jorge studied him for a minute. "I still do not," he snapped. "But I do pledge to serve you for the sake of Archiva."

"Are you ready to die for this?"

"I'm here, aren't I?"

Peregrin laughed aloud. "Enough, Jorge, enough. We shall never like each other. But I will be pleased to call you brother." He extended his hand.

Jorge paused and then actually smiled and took the hand. "Agreed … my brother," he said.

The next two days were quiet, with no word from the scouts patrolling the hills around Archiva. Peregrin hoped this meant that Dextor was waiting for reports from the encampments before taking action. He used the time to train his little army. Each division of the Watermen selected five members who showed a propensity for the bow and arrow, and they spent the day practicing with goldenrod shafts. In a similar way, fighters were chosen to use the swords. Peregrin taught them what information he knew, but mostly they practiced using them in place of the staffs they were used to fighting with, grasping the pommel with two hands.

Peregrin believed that the key to defeating Dextor lay in acting as a unit. Throughout each day, he drilled each band of Watermen in offensive and defensive maneuvers that would allow them to maximize their effectiveness. By the end of the day, they were all exhausted, but gaining confidence in their fighting abilities and in one another.

About mid-afternoon on the third day since the Waterman's death, Sanda's people brought word that a sizable group of Dextor's people was headed down the north trail. Sanda herself brought him the news.

"My scouts count at least forty fighters, ten with bows, and the rest with swords," she said. "They are moving fast toward the ruins. In two hours time, they will have discovered the abandoned encampment. And, Traveler, they are led by a woman."

Peregrin looked up quickly. "Gabrielle?"

Sanda nodded. "The description fits her. She was one of the best Rangers we had, which is why she was selected to protect the ruins. She knows that land as she knows her own arm."

"So she will be hard to catch off her guard?"

"Very hard."

"Unless she would allow her guard to fall herself."

"How could we get her to do that?"

Peregrin smiled. "Suppose she did not find an abandoned encampment?"

⁓

The shadows had grown long when the guard in the tree whistled a birdcall. The men halted whatever work they had been engaged in and looked toward the bend of the stream. Soon, a full dozen of Dextor's fighters came around the bend and entered the camp. One of them called out a greeting, and the camp leader responded in kind.

Peregrin smiled as the group approached him, studying them from under the brim of his floppy hat that obscured most of his face. He had taken a chance on what response to give, taking his cue from his observation of the camp before they had taken it. Apparently he had responded correctly. Dextor's men approached in a group, not noticing how the men of the camp were fanned out all around them, standing easy but with hands near their weapons.

The group of men came before Peregrin, still apparently unaware. "Shasta," said their leader, "Dextor wants to know why you have not…wait! You're not Shasta."

Peregrin smiled as he lifted his head. "And you're not too bright," he said. His fist struck the man in an uppercut to the jaw, sending him crashing into his companions. They grabbed for their weapons as the Watermen closed upon them.

The fight only lasted minutes, but it was fierce. Though surprised and outnumbered, Dextor's men had no intention of surrendering. While only a few of them were able to get a sword or knife clear, the rest reacted quickly and fought hand-to-hand. A large man with a black beard broke free of the *melee* and rushed at Peregrin with sword upraised. Peregrin stood as if paralyzed in fear. When the stroke came down, he neatly sidestepped, so that the blade sliced only air and embedded itself in the ground. Peregrin grasped the man's wrist and twisted down and out, bringing his knee up into the man's abdomen at the same time, causing him to double over. Peregrin straightened him back up by reversing the direction of the twist. Letting go of the wrist, he struck the man in the face with both hands clasped together. The man fell and lay stunned.

By this time, the Watermen had subdued the band and had the men lying face down on the ground while their hands were tied behind their backs. Peregrin looked about quickly. He had expected Gabrielle to come to the rescue with the rest of her band when the tumult began, but there was no sign that anyone else was in the area. Nothing stirred upon the heights around the camp, and there was no sound from downstream.

He whistled for Curtan and signaled him to come with him. Together they ran out of the camp by the path that the men had come. Coming around the bend, they stopped. The path was clear before them for half a mile. No one was in sight.

Peregrin gave two short whistles. Sanda and Corval rose from respective hiding places among the trees and ran toward him.

"Where is she?" Peregrin said. "Your scouts said at least forty fighters."

"I know," Sanda replied. "We only saw that dozen that went up the stream. No one else followed."

Peregrin felt as if an invisible hand was squeezing his stomach.

"She drew us off. Dextor already knew we were out and had silenced his camps. How could he know?"

"Someone sent him word of our activities" Corval said. "One or more of our people are working for Dextor."

"Who has been away from the camp?" Curtan said. "Who could have gotten away long enough without being noticed?"

Peregrin looked at Sanda. "Who are your scouts on the north trail?"

"Trinna and Baldwin; they knew that area the best."

"Because they had been assigned there before?" Sanda nodded.

Peregrin bowed his head and groaned. "Gabrielle told me that almost all of the Rangers that Carlin assigned to the north of Archiva were in league with Dextor."

The Rangers gaped at him. "Why didn't you tell us?" Corval cried. "Peregrin, Dextor knows our whole plan. He knows how we are formed, how many of us there are, and where we are camped. Didn't you think this was important?"

Peregrin shook his head. "I am sorry. Everything that's happened since Waterman's death just pushed it out of my mind."

"All right now, let's think," Curtan said. "Who else among us was assigned to the north?"

"Just Trinna and Baldwin in my corp," Sanda said.

"I can't think of anyone in my group," said Corval.

"Nor I," said Curtan. "Which means the rest of the Watermen are probably loyal to Archiva. Now, Dextor has drawn us off to the east. What is he really aiming for?"

"If you were Dextor, what do you think we would do next?" Peregrin said.

"Well," Sanda said, "once you had discovered the ruse, I would think you would probably charge back to camp or to Archiva, thinking there was a full-scale assault taking place."

"Right. But I don't think there is a full-scale assault on Archiva. Not yet, anyhow."

"Why not?" Corval asked.

Peregrin thought a moment. "Dextor loves drama. He wants to create fear and chaos in Archiva before he overruns the place. What action would have that effect more than anything?"

The Rangers said nothing, so Peregrin continued. "Carlin. Dextor wants to get Carlin back. Where was Carlin being held?"

"In the council building," Corval said.

"Did Trinna and Baldwin know this?"

"Everybody knew it."

So he sends his most trusted Ranger, his own wife, to rescue Carlin. But the most direct line to him passes directly through our camp."

"So she has our own scouts send us a report that she is headed this way, trusting we would set a trap," Sanda said. "She sacrifices a dozen fighters as a decoy and waltzes right through our own camp."

"She rappels down the hillside above the council building, pulls Carlin out, and is gone before anyone has a chance to call for help," Curtan said.

"What is the end result?" said Corval. "No one is safe. Dextor can come right though our defenses and do whatever he pleases."

Peregrin shook his head. "Brilliant. Absolutely brilliant. How much time have we lost, do you think?"

"Enough," Curtan said.

"Then we had better get moving. It looks like it may rain, and we have a hard hike ahead of us if we will put a hook in Dextor's nose.

⁓

It was a great risk, Peregrin thought as he hunched among the wet brush near the great boulder. They sent four men to escort the prisoners back to Archiva with strict instructions to observe what was going on there before they revealed themselves. After all, it was possible that Dextor had simply decided to overrun Archiva in one quick sweep. If things were bad, they were to tie the captives to trees and bring the news to Peregrin.

The remainder of Curtan's band would head swiftly back to the camp above Archiva. If Gabrielle's party had come through there and returned again, they would pursue them northward.

The rest of the Watermen quickly made for the northeast trail in hopes of getting ahead of Gabrielle on her return. If they were correct about Dextor's plans, and if they could get ahead of the returning party, they might turn defeat into victory. If they were wrong, and Dextor had attacked Archiva in force, well, they were too late anyhow.

They moved as quickly and silently as they could, bearing straight north through the forest before turning west, in order not to be detected by Dextor's scouts. They had arrived near the great boulder shortly after a steady rain had begun to fall. By now it was night, and the forest had blurred into shapes of black on black, all swirling and melding into the incessant crackling of the rain off every leaf and limb.

As the time wore on, doubts began to nag at Peregrin like mosquitos in the evening. *What if Archiva was captured? What if Dextor has anticipated my plan, and his entire force is about to come crushing down upon us and sweep the Watermen away? After all, we are some five miles away from Archiva, deep in Dextor's territory. Or what if Dextor has lured him here so that he can move his whole force to the south of Archiva, knowing it to be unprotected? What if we have already missed Gabrielle?*

Sanda, Corval, and Curtan had served Archiva all their lives, yet they trusted him to lead them against Dextor. All of those who had joined the Watermen had placed their trust in Peregrin. Yet none of them had known him for more than a week. The thought of failing them—of bringing ruin to Archiva through bad judgment—was like a great, black bird hunched on his shoulders, ready to tear his flesh.

Yet this was the decision he had made. Somehow he felt he had guessed Dextor's plan correctly. Somehow he felt that Gabrielle was drawing nearer and Archiva was not yet taken. Somehow he felt the greatest trials lay ahead. All he could do now was to wait in the rain and the blackness.

He heard a low warbling sound. Someone was coming. Far off in the darkness, he could see a faint light, then two. At least a few people carrying torches were headed this way.

It was not long before the torches passed by the first of the hidden Watermen, who lay on both sides of the trail. Peregrin could make out dark shapes moving quickly without talking. The darkness made it impossible to count, but he guessed there were about thirty of them. He wondered if Curtan was far behind them, or if they knew they were being pursued.

The approaching figures were spread out in a long line. This was good, as it made it more likely to be able to tell friend from foe. He glanced at the boulder where they had hurriedly piled brush and soaked it with oil brought from Dextor's camp near the ruins. Two Watermen were crouched behind the stone, protecting two burning torches from the rain and from the view of Gabrielle's party.

The lead figures were almost upon them. Peregrin hooted twice, and the Watermen sprang out from behind the boulder and thrust the torches into the wood. Though the wood was wet from the rain, the oil caught immediately and flared up in the faces of the approaching figures. Gabrielle was one of them.

Peregrin rose from his hiding place. "Archiva!" he cried.

From the other side of the trail he heard Sanda's voice: "Waterman!"

With a roar the Watermen closed their trap upon Gabrielle's

party. There was a flurry of blows and cries of pain from all along the line. He could hear Gabrielle shouting, "Dextor! For Dextor!"

Farther back the line, a familiar voice answered, "For Dextor! Fight, you fools!" It was Carlin. Even in the midst of the confusion, Peregrin smiled to think that his guess had been so correct.

The initial rush of the Watermen had taken the band by surprise. Several of Dextor's men were down, unconscious or groaning. The remainder, however, rallied around Carlin to one side and Gabrielle to the other. They pressed back-to-back in an obviously much-drilled defensive maneuver. The blackness of the night and the rainfall made it hard to keep one's footing. Although the Watermen had practiced with their captured swords, Dextor's men were far more skilled. At least three Watermen were down and not moving. Two others lay clutching wounds.

On Peregrin's left, a Ranger named Durst suddenly took a blow to the head and staggered back, dropping his sword. Peregrin caught him and lowered him to the ground. He picked up his sword.

"Sanda!" he cried. Phalanx attack!"

Sanda heard and quickly formed the Watermen around her into a wedge with herself at the point. Peregrin did the same. They drove forward from each side into the knot of fighters around Gabrielle, piercing their defense.

With the Watermen protecting their sides and back, Peregrin and Sanda succeeded in separating Dextor's fighters from one another. Several of Dextor's men broke and ran as the defensive knot began to crumble.

Sanda's wedge reached Gabrielle, and the two women Rangers engaged each other. Their swords met in midair. Gabrielle's sword broke, while Sanda's was twisted from her hand by the blow. Without hardly a pause, they each drew their long knives and charged each other. The impact sent them both to the ground, and they grappled with each other.

A fighter in front of Peregrin swung his sword at his head.

Peregrin deflected the blow upward and struck the man down with the pommel of his sword. He regained his balance in time to see Gabrielle, on her back, place her foot onto Sanda's hip and thrust upward, sending Sanda flying over her head and to the ground. Gabrielle sprang to her feet and charged, knife forward. At the same time, Sanda rolled into a crouch and came upward, bringing her knife in an upward arc.

Their bodies met with a terrific collision. Both women cried out in pain. Sanda took two steps backward and sat down heavily as a wetness that was blacker than the rain began to spread rapidly from her abdomen. Gabrielle staggered back, clutching her side where Sanda's knife protruded.

"Sanda!" cried Peregrin.

At the same time, he heard Carlin cry out, "Gabrielle! No!"

Peregrin leapt to Sanda's aid and caught her just as she was going to fall sideways. "Hold on, Sanda. I've got you. Hold on," he said. He looked up.

Around him the fighting went on. Dextor's men were largely on the run, however. Several people were down from both sides. Someone was crouched only a few feet way. He turned his gaze.

It was Carlin. He was kneeling beside Gabrielle's still form, cradling her head and torso in his arms. He stared at Peregrin, saying nothing. His mouth was slightly ajar, and his eyes were glazed. After a moment he put one arm beneath her knees and one around her back and stood, holding her close.

He stood gazing at Peregrin, saying nothing. His eyes focused and narrowed. Finally, he spoke. "This is your doing, Traveler. I will not forget." He turned, carrying Gabrielle as easily as one would carry a child, and disappeared into the darkness.

One of the Watermen ran up to Peregrin. "We have driven them off, Traveler! They will remember us!"

Peregrin looked up sharply. "Yes, they will. Give me some cloth for her wound. Hurry!"

The Ranger tore his sleeve from his shirt, which Peregrin wadded up and pressed to Sanda's wound. Sanda moaned slightly. "Shh. Shh," he said. "It will be all right."

Sanda opened her eyes and looked at him. "We were right, Peregrin," she murmured. "We caught them."

"Shh. Be still. You'll be all right."

"You are a poor liar, Peregrin," she said. "Remember me, please."

"Shh, Sanda. Don't talk foolishness."

Corval came running up. "Oh no," he said and knelt beside them.

"Corval, listen to me," Peregrin said. "Call the Watermen back. Tend to the wounded as quickly as possible. Make stretchers so we can get them back to Archiva. We have to hurry before Dextor comes back in force."

"What of Dextor's men?"

"Tend them as well. We will dress their wounds and make them as comfortable as possible."

The rain continued to fall as they worked. A Ranger came and dressed Sanda's wound. After an hour Curtan's group arrived. Peregrin was still holding her.

Curtan squatted beside them and said nothing.

"What are our losses?" Peregrin said.

"Three Watermen are dead. Four more are seriously wounded, counting Sanda. The rest are minor wounds that will heal."

"And Dextor's men?"

"Seven were injured too badly to flee. Two are dead."

Peregrin looked into the blackness. "So the Watermen have killed."

"Yes. Peregrin, there is other news."

"Go on."

"We guessed most of Dextor's plan correctly, except that part of the mission was to destroy our camp as well. Everything is smashed and burned."

Peregrin looked at him, fearing the worst. "What of the people left in the camp?"

Curtan looked at the ground. "Most of them were able to flee. Those who resisted were…" his voice choked. He took a deep breath. "Those who resisted were killed."

The black bird on Peregrin's shoulders flapped its wings and squawked in triumph. "How many?" he asked.

"Five."

"Five," Peregrin repeated. "We left them there because they were not trained yet. We left them to be safe."

"I know, but they knew the risk."

"Five," Peregrin said again. "Have mercy."

Sanda stirred in his arms. "Go help the wounded," he said. "We have to get back to Archiva."

Curtan nodded and went off. Peregrin stroked Sanda's hair. "Shh. It will be all right. It will be all right." He rocked her gently and gazed into the night.

XI

FEAR

After two days the rain finally ceased. The skies remained gray, however, like an old smeared window, trembling with each wind as if on the verge of shattering. The air itself seemed tangible, as though still saturated with the tears it had tried to shed since the battle near the boulder.

Peregrin's mood did not improve either. They had returned to Archiva, bearing their dead and wounded. They buried the seven who had been slain in the cemetery field, a small plateau on the south slope outside of Archiva. One of those who had been badly wounded also died the next morning, despite Merida's best effort to save him.

Sanda remained in critical shape. She was terribly pale from loss of blood and could neither eat nor drink. Merida did her best to force her to swallow a red, thick liquid she had steeped from herbs and crushed berries. Still, it did not look good.

"The knife struck deep into her abdomen," she explained to

Peregrin and Curtan. "If she was extremely lucky, it did not strike any vital organs. But if it did, her healing lies with a higher power than mine. Only time will tell."

The death of so many brought great sorrow and shock to Archiva. Some grumbled against Peregrin, insisting that he had brought ill fortune with him. Others cried for vengeance, particularly for those who had been killed in the camp. Some simply seemed paralyzed by the furious events taking place in their midst. For the first time since the great destruction, war and death had come to Archiva.

Adding to the shock was the news that the Watermen had killed some of Dextor's men. Suddenly the inhabitants of Archiva found themselves struggling with a dilemma that shook the very roots of their existence. Should this act be condoned in the face of the threat they faced? If so, did the Creed really have meaning? The heart of Archiva lay exposed and vulnerable.

Mikkel still lay in the grip of a fever, though he seemed to be recovering. He slept most of the day, sometimes awaking to a lucid moment, but soon slipping back into unconsciousness. Merida said his body and spirit were trying to repair themselves and must be allowed to rest. Morgan was acting as Archivist in his absence, though he had no real power to make executive decisions.

Peregrin abandoned the ruined camp on the slope and withdrew all of the Watermen into Archiva. The Rangers patrolled the ridges and kept a series of watchfires ready to signal should Dextor launch an attack.

There was no movement, however, by any of Dextor's men. The hills around Archiva remained silent, except for the steady rain that thrummed a relentless cadence throughout the forest.

What upset Peregrin the most, however, was that Bliss had not come to speak with him. She had come to the burial for the slain and had stood hand in hand with Cornel and Janel. She spoke a few words of blessing and farewell over the graves and walked away, keeping her gaze straight ahead.

He wondered why it bothered him so much. She knew the path he had taken and probably understood his reasoning more than any other. Did she blame him for so many deaths? That thought was unbearable. Still, she seemed to be distinctly avoiding him. She did not look at him, nor did she approach him. He wondered if she ever would.

The council summoned him the day after the battle. He recounted the events of the day as best as he could and then fell silent, not wishing to talk any more. Morgan looked at him kindly.

"Peregrin," he said, "it brings us all great sorrow to come to this day. But you must not hold yourself responsible for the deaths that have occurred. You chose your path. Those who followed you chose theirs. Right or wrong, we must all face the consequences of our choices."

Peregrin looked around the table. He saw sadness, dismay, and fear, but no reproach and no condemnation. *What amazing people,* he thought.

"So where do we go from here?" he asked. "Dextor is still there, and I believe his time of drama is finished. This is no longer a game to him. Gabrielle has been badly wounded, perhaps killed. He will return for vengeance if not for power."

"What now indeed?" rumbled Stevan. "Dextor would already be in our midst if it were not for you. It is my contention that we must continue what has been begun. It is time to call forth all Archiva to battle."

"No, Stevan!" shouted a wiry man named Derth. "Have we not seen enough faces of the dead? Have we not seen the faces of their families? Does the Creed mean so little that we abandon it without seeking another way?"

"What other way can there be?" Stevan retorted.

"Who has tried to speak with Dextor?" Derth answered. "He has been hurt. Perhaps he is willing to seek peace."

"I do not believe that will be his intent," Peregrin said softly.

Derth opened his mouth to speak, but Merida broke in. "Peace, brothers," she said. "This conversation will go round and round in endless debate. We cannot know what Dextor will do now. We can only know what he has done and what he has said. I remember Dextor well. He was a talented man but furious when things did not fall properly into his plan. We must prepare for the worst."

This created a tumult among the Guardians. Many voices rose at once, debating, questioning, even accusing. Finally, Peregrin stood and waited. He said nothing but gazed at them silently until, one by one, they fell silent.

"You have something to say, Peregrin?" asked Morgan.

"The question before this council is not: 'Should we fight Dextor.' If you cannot see by now that we must fight Dextor, you are deluding yourself. I plan to fight Dextor for the sake of Archiva, even if I have to do it alone.

"The question we truly face is the one I put to the council. Shall we defeat Dextor? To do so, we will need to embrace the hidden knowledge of Archiva. We must enter the vault beneath the ruins and use what we find there."

There was a long silence. Finally, Morgan spoke. "Do you know how to enter this vault you speak of?"

"No."

"Presuming this vault exists and we could find the entrance, what kind of weapons do you think we will find there?"

"I don't know. I know there are machines of great power there."

"That is exactly why we must not enter this vault," Merida said.

"I agree," said Morgan. To do so would be to betray all that we believe in."

"But not all that Dextor believes in," Peregrin answered. "If he is not stopped, he will enter that vault and use whatever he finds. Will you risk that?"

"We must," Morgan answered. "Otherwise we will have betrayed the vision of O'Keefe and everything we hold precious. What legacy will we leave our children if we defeat Dextor by embracing his belief that superior force is the measure of one's right?"

"You will not turn from this decision, even if it means Dextor triumphs?"

Morgan paused. "No."

Peregrin looked about the table. "Is there anyone who will stand with me in this plea?"

There was silence around the table. "Stevan?" Peregrin said.

Stevan shook his head. "I do not know, Peregrin. I am willing to fight Dextor with my own hands, but to use tech knowledge that we know nothing about—that I cannot embrace. In defeating Dextor, we would bring about our own ruin."

"Nor is there time," Merida said. "Even if these weapons of yours exist, none of us knows how to enter the vault or how to use them. I do not think Dextor will grant us the training time we need."

Peregrin bowed his head. After a moment, he raised it again. "Then I bid you farewell. I go to defend Archiva as best I can. I hope my death will not be in vain."

"Peregrin ..." Morgan began.

Peregrin raised his hand. "No more. Peace to your heart, Morgan. Peace to all of your hearts. I hope to see you again." He turned and strode to the entrance. He opened both doors and stalked out, leaving the oaken doors ajar.

The next day the sun reappeared, though it often snuck behind surly, roiling clouds that surged in the sky like small boats in a rough sea. Peregrin had climbed the elbow early on and remained there until mid-morning.

A female voice called his name from below, and something in his chest leaped. Peering over the edge, he saw it was Lindah, one of the Rangers who had gone out with him and Mikkel to meet Dextor above the ruins. He closed his eyes and sighed.

"What is it?" he said.

"A messenger from Dextor's camp has come and wishes to speak with you."

"Where is he?"

"Raven and Race have him under guard in a guest room near the south entrance."

"They brought him into Archiva?"

"He presented himself to them about a half mile from the entrance and asked to be brought here. They blindfolded him and led him in."

"All right, I'll be right there." He clambered down the escarpment with a heavy heart.

When he reached the place, Raven opened the door for him. Entering, he saw a small man with long brown hair.

The man straightened up. "I am Corlee. Are you the one called Peregrin, the Traveler?"

"I am. You are here to represent Dextor?"

"No," the man answered. "I come to speak for Dextor's right arm—Carlin."

Peregrin was surprised. "Carlin? What does he wish?"

"Carlin wishes to speak to you in person. He seeks a guarantee of safe passage."

"Like the guarantee Dextor gave to Mikkel and me in the ruins?"

Corlee did not even flinch. "Carlin knows you have no reason to trust him. This is why he sent me first. He will come into Archiva alone and unarmed. He only asks that you personally guarantee his safety."

"Why me?"

"Carlin says you are the only one he trusts to not be overwhelmed with emotion. He believes that only you can keep a clear head. He will only come if you guarantee it."

Peregrin rubbed his eyes with one hand. "Very well. Tell him I guarantee him safe passage. Tell him I place my own life as collateral on the guarantee."

Corlee made to leave, but Peregrin laid a hand on his shoulder. "Tell him also that if he is involved in any sort of trick or deception, he will personally wish he had never met me. Whatever else happens, I will make him pay for it."

Corlee nodded. "Carlin will present himself to your Rangers at the same entrance through which I came when the sun is directly overhead."

Peregrin nodded to Race, who blindfolded Corlee and led him out. As they left, Peregrin called Lindah over to him.

"Tell the Rangers to bring Carlin in blindfolded as well. Tell them he has my guarantee of safe passage. But send word to all of the Watermen to stand ready and alert." She nodded and ran off.

Peregrin turned and walked toward the gardens. Before he took ten steps, however, a young man with deep-set eyes blocked his way.

Peregrin stopped. "Jorge. What do you want?"

Jorge looked a him a moment then lowered his eyes. When he spoke, the words tripped from his mouth as if they were being cut from rock. "I ... was ... afraid ..."

Peregrin looked at him closer and realized there were tears in his eyes. "Afraid of what?" he asked gently.

"When the Terists came through the camp, my friend Rik called to me to help him fight them. I ... I tried. I picked up my weapon ... and ... and ... I saw Rik be cut down by them ... just killed outright ... I couldn't move ... I ... couldn't go to him, to see if was alive. I wanted to avenge him, but ... I ... was afraid. One of the Terists started coming toward me and ... and ..." He choked and began to sob. "And I dropped my weapon and ran away. I left Rik. I left them all."

Peregrin reached out a hand to his shoulder. "Jorge, it's all right. They were too many of them, and none of you were trained yet. It's not your fault. Anyone would be afraid at a time like that."

Jorge looked up at him. "Rik wasn't afraid." He took a few steps back from Peregrin. "Rik wasn't afraid," he repeated. He turned and ran off.

Peregrin watched him go. He shook his head and continued on his way to the gardens.

Even before he arrived, he could see her, crouched among the young plants, carefully uprooting weeds and tossing them into a small bucket. Her back was to him.

He stopped ten feet behind her and would have spoken her name, but she spoke first.

"Weeds are a ferocious enemy to vegetable plants, Peregrin," she said. "They appear unexpectedly, multiply rapidly, and try to steal the plants' food, soil, and sunlight, all without remorse." She straightened up, stretched, and turned toward him. "Yet, they, too, are just trying to survive. They are only following the path which is laid out before them."

Peregrin lowered his eyes. He felt as if something in his throat had frozen and was slowly sinking into his stomach. "Bliss," he said, "I would like to talk with you, if it's all right."

"It is all right," she said. "But the weeds won't wait. Come and fight a more cunning adversary with me while we talk." She turned and crouched again to her task.

Peregrin came alongside her and crouched down. He reached out his hand to a feathery tuft sticking out of the ground, but Bliss quickly laid her hand on his. "That's a carrot," she said. "Everything else is a weed."

Peregrin's face felt like he was too close to a fire, but Bliss laughed. "Don't worry about it," she said. "In this war it takes a while to know enemies from friends. Pull that grass out there."

She pointed to little clumps of grass blades in between the

rows of carrots. Peregrin reached for one, grasped it at the base, and pulled, only to have it break off in his hand. Bliss laughed again.

"You have lost that battle, Peregrin. But never fear. That grass will grow back in a matter of days to give you another chance. Watch now, you have to work them out of the ground gently." She pinched a clump of grass between her finger and thumb and pulled gently while twisting her wrist slightly. After a moment, the grass pulled free, revealing its roots. "You see, it takes patience, perseverance, and a willingness to coax the weed from the ground."

"I think I'm better at fighting people," Peregrin said.

Bliss smiled. "Perhaps, but you're only human."

"Bliss, I need you to help me."

"Of course. What help do you need?"

"Carlin is coming to meet with me. I want you to be there as well."

"Why?"

Peregrin paused. "Waterman told us how you had gotten information from him before. I thought it might be useful to have you there."

"You thought I might be useful?" Her tone reminded Peregrin of icy water.

"I ... uh ... I'm sorry. I didn't mean it that way."

"Then say what you do mean."

"I want you there."

"Why?"

"I need you to be there."

"Why?"

Peregrin felt as though he were tiptoeing along a narrow ledge as twilight was falling. "Bliss, please! "I cannot ... I'm ... I'm afraid."

"Of what?" Her tone had not softened.

Peregrin looked at the ground. He reached to another clump of grass and pulled it as Bliss had shown him. It still broke off in his hand. "I'm afraid of myself," he said.

"Do you mean you think you will attack Carlin?"

"No."

"What then?"

Peregrin looked up at her. "Bliss, I don't know who I am. Since I have come to Archiva, the questions have only multiplied. Here I have found something worth believing in, something worth living for and working for, but I feel more lost with each moment." He lowered his head again.

Bliss reached out and touched his chin, lifting his head. Her gaze held him steady and calmed the terrors within him. Her eyes were as rich and as lifegiving as the earth on which they crouched.

"Peregrin," she said softly, her voice like the morning mist, "the future of Archiva does not rest with you."

"What do you mean? Dextor—"

"Dextor threatens a place called Archiva. But Archiva is not a place; it is a choice of being. Everyone who swears the Creed swears to walk a path. This path leads to the real Archiva, the one that lies within the heart. If you lose this path, you lose Archiva, even if you still dwell within these hills. You are feeling lost because you desire to dwell in Archiva, but you have gotten off the path."

Peregrin stared at her. "Dextor's threat is still very real. How can I get back on the path and still stop him?"

Bliss smiled. "Look to the light through the trees. It will guide you."

"I don't understand what you mean."

She smiled. "All things become clear in their time. Don't push the river."

Peregrin opened his mouth and then closed it. He looked down again. "I can't cry."

"What?"

"I can't cry. I have wanted to cry so many times, especially after Waterman died. Curtan, Corval, Sanda—they all stood there and wept, but I could not."

"Every human being can cry, Peregrin," she said softly.

"Bliss, help me. Help me to cry."

She took his face in both hands. "Perhaps I can. Perhaps our paths will cross on this." She straightened up. "Come now, the sun is nearly overhead. Carlin will be coming. Let us go to meet him." She turned to go.

He reached a hand to her shoulder. "Wait. Tell me why you have avoided me since the battle. Are you angry with me?"

She did not move. "No, I am not angry with you. But since the battle, I have not been able to look at you."

"I don't understand."

She turned to face him. "Nor do I. I told you that I could not experience anything about you since you came to Archiva. Since the battle, I find it painful to look at you. Something is rising in you that will cause you great anguish. You will face some terrible test, I am afraid, and it is not the test of battle. Although I still cannot sense your emotions, I can tell that something is coming soon. So I have avoided you. Besides, the pain of Archiva has been enough for me to handle. Come now. Carlin is already at the gate."

Peregrin looked up toward the tunnel entrance and saw two Rangers leading Carlin down the steps along the hillside. He shook his head and trotted to catch up with her.

"Bliss," he said as he came alongside of her, "I did not say when Carlin was coming. How did you know that it was when the sun was overhead?"

She smiled but continued walking. "I listened to the water."

The Rangers brought Carlin to the room where Corlee had been taken. After Bliss and he had sat down at the small table, Peregrin nodded to the Rangers, who removed his blindfold.

Carlin blinked and looked about. "Bliss," he said. "I expected only Peregrin."

"I asked her to be here, Carlin," Peregrin said. He motioned toward a chair across the table.

Carlin sat down "Do they need to be here as well?" he asked, indicating the Rangers.

"No," Peregrin answered. "Please wait outside." The Rangers nodded and left.

Carlin looked as if he had not slept. "It is hard for me to be here," he began.

"Of course," Peregrin said. "It's easier to slaughter defenseless people."

Carlin paused a long moment. "Perhaps you will not believe me," he said. "I had nothing to do with that action. Gabrielle's band had orders directly from Dextor to kill anyone who got in the way in order to demonstrate his resolve in this matter. Those people were killed before I was liberated from Archiva. I was stunned when I saw it."

"There is no reason I should believe you," Peregrin said coldly. "Get on with why you are here."

Carlin gazed at him. "Very well. I come to deliver a proposition from Dextor."

Peregrin met his gaze. "Go on."

"Dextor says: 'Tell the Traveler this—I am tired of games and give-and-take. Let us put an end to this now. In two days time, as the sun rises, I will bring all of my men around the east side of Archiva and march directly into the ruins. Bring all of your warriors, and we shall do battle there. The winner of this fight will decide the fate of Archiva. You may form your men for battle however you wish, but as for me, there will be no tricks or surprise attacks. We shall simply fight and finish this thing.'"

"What if I chose not to come?"

Carlin looked at him a moment. "Then he swears he will have no mercy on Archiva. He will kill every living creature here."

"He would do that?"

Carlin nodded. "Yes, he has had enough of drama. He wishes to fight you head on. If you refuse, he will assume the people of Archiva are cowards and have no place in his vision for a new world."

"He is mad!"

Carlin paused. "Yes, he is." He lowered his eyes. After a moment, he said quietly, "Gabrielle is dead."

Until now Bliss had not made a sound. Peregrin had almost forgotten she was there. But suddenly she lunged across the table and grasped Carlin's hand. "Oh, Carlin, I am so sorry."

Carlin looked up, and Peregrin was surprised to see tears brimming in his eyes. "Thank you, Bliss. Thank you." His voice cracked, and he bowed his head again.

After a moment, he said, "What about Sanda? Has she survived?" Peregrin was amazed to hear concern in his voice.

"She survives," Bliss said. "But she is weak. It may be only a matter of time."

"I'm sorry. I'm sorry it all came to this. I'm …" he put his face in his hands and sobbed. "It wasn't supposed to happen like this. He said no killing would be needed."

Bliss stood up and came around the table. She bent over Carlin and cradled him in her arms, rocking him gently. After a while she held him at arms length. "Carlin, it's not too late," she said.

"Yes, yes it is, Bliss," he answered. She came back around the table and sat down.

Peregrin was dumbstruck. "Carlin," he sputtered finally, "explain all this."

Carlin's eyes narrowed. "It's very simple. When Franceen was killed, something in Dextor snapped. I could see it then. No matter how deranged he became, however, I could not shut him out of my life. He was a brother to me, and I could not turn my back on him."

"So you worked with him to destroy Archiva?"

"Peregrin," Bliss said, "you speak of things you know little about."

Peregrin looked at Bliss. "I'm beginning to wonder why I asked you to join me here. Was it to support me or Carlin?"

Bliss ignored the sarcasm. "It was to help you understand things better," she said simply. "Now listen to Carlin."

"I know you cannot understand this," Carlin said. "I helped Dextor get back to the cavern and kept him supplied. I thought I could change the council's mind as time went past. Or maybe I thought I could change Dextor's mind. He was in no shape to go into the world. He was wild and irrational. Shortly after we got to the cavern, he developed a high fever. He was delirious for nearly a week. It was all I could do to keep him down and get some food into him. I was sure I would lose him.

"Then one night he came quietly out of the place I had arranged for him. I was tending the night's dinner over a fire. He looked at me quite calmly and said, 'I have seen it, Carlin. The root of Archiva's sickness lies in its Creed. No doctrine must be absolute. We can change them,' he said. 'We can fulfill O'Keefe's vision.'

"We talked for days. He had had some kind of transcendent experience during his illness and had seen a pattern to make the world well again. I had to admit that everything he said made sense. Though I had seen him kill, I found myself wanting to believe Dextor more than the Creed or anything else. After all, he was the closest thing I had ever had to family, what with my parents dying when I was only three years old."

"But you said you knew something had snapped in him," Peregrin said.

"Yes, something was broken. You can't imagine how terrible that day was for all of us. When Dextor and Franceen fell in love, I was overjoyed for them. He had been alone except for me for so long. She brought out a joy in him that I never knew was there. When she fell beneath the knives of those Terists, that joy was killed with her. I never saw it again. I think Dextor lost some of his humanity that day."

"Still, you stayed with him."

Carlin cocked an eyebrow at him. "Of course I stayed with him. Would you have done otherwise? He was my brother. I believed I could help him heal with time. Until he became involved with Gabrielle. Then I realized he needed far more than I could give him. She had been Franceen's best friend. She was able to help Dextor grieve for her and to begin to live again. She brought love back into his eyes. For the first time in years, I heard Dextor laugh.

"And now Gabrielle is gone. And little remains of Dextor except a hollow shell. He is no longer interested in power or visions or war. I think he seeks an end. Perhaps he is hoping you will kill him, I don't know. But he wants to be done with this whole business.

"So to answer your question once again, yes, he would kill every person in Archiva if he felt he needed to do so to accomplish his goals. He is quite mad."

"Then why stay with him now?" Peregrin asked. "It's not too late. Leave Dextor and return to Archiva. You still can have a home here."

Carlin shook his head. "You don't understand still. But Bliss does, don't you, Bliss?"

Bliss nodded. "I think so. Still, it is better if you explain."

"All right. Dextor was a brother to me. But Dextor and Gabrielle were a father and mother to me. It was Gabrielle who brought healing, not just to Dextor, but to me as well through the years. It was she who brought laughter back to our lives. When they were together, it was like standing in a clearing in the woods with the sun beaming upon you. I think if Dextor had overcome Archiva, Gabrielle would have kept him on a true course of restoring order to the world. Now she is gone, and he has no one. No one except me."

"But you said yourself that he is mad."

"Yes, I believe that he is. And his heart is bent upon destruction and revenge now. But wrong as he may be, I cannot leave him alone. I will not leave him alone. I'm all that he has."

They fell silent for many minutes. Finally, Peregrin said, "Tell Dextor we will meet him there."

Carlin rose. "I will," he said. "There is one more thing."

"What is that?"

"I wanted to tell you, and especially you, Bliss, how terribly sorry I am. I wish none of this had ever happened."

Bliss rose and came to him. She placed her arms around him and gazed into his eyes. "No matter what," she said, "I will always think of you as one I love." She drew him to her and held him as he buried his face in her hair and wept. Peregrin stood there, wondering what had just happened.

The next day brought some good news. Sanda appeared to be recovering. She had woken for a bit and was able to drink and eat a little. Merida said it was a miracle. When Peregrin asked what she meant by that, she shrugged and said, "Sometimes you realize there are forces much bigger than yourself."

Mikkel was also stronger. His fever had subsided, and he was sitting up, although still very weak. His leg had been set in a brace made of four struts and tightly wound with cloth. He smiled as Peregrin came in the door.

"Ah, the falcon has landed!" he exclaimed, extending his hand. Peregrin took it with a grin.

"And the Archivist longs for flight!" he said. "How are you feeling, Mikkel?"

"Better than yesterday, I am told. Please, sit down."

Peregrin pulled a chair up to the bed. "Does the leg hurt?"

"Terribly," Mikkel answered. "But I've already begun to practice hobbling around on it. Merida says I cannot put weight on it yet, but I have to get used to moving about with crutches. This way my muscles won't atrophy."

"She knows her business."

Mikkel nodded. "She sure does. And what of the Traveler? How does his business go?"

Peregrin's smile vanished. "How much of recent events do you know?"

"Morgan has filled me in pretty well. I'd say you've had a rough few days."

"It's going to get rougher. Dextor has sent an ultimatum. Either we fight tomorrow in the ruins, winner take all, or he will tear Archiva down stone by stone."

Mikkel's face tightened. "What will you do?"

"What choice is there? I will meet him head on."

"What are your odds?"

"Well, he's got at least one hundred and fifty fighting men, and I have about sixty or so. I'd say my odds are slim and none, and slim just left town. Unless we can even things out a little."

Mikkel was silent a moment. "You want access to the vault beneath the ruins."

Peregrin nodded. "It's our only chance, Mikkel. Otherwise Dextor will sweep us away. You've got to get me in there."

"Peregrin, you don't know what's in there. What little I've read is terrifying. It is precisely this stuff that set human beings on a course of destruction."

"Mikkel, please. Think of your children."

"I am thinking of my children. That's why I'm not sure we can use anything we might find in the vault. Our Creed—"

"Damn the Creed!" Peregrin said, bringing his fist down on his knee. "Mikkel, O'Keefe created this place and this people and this Creed of yours so that you could rebuild humanity, not hide from it.

If you won't use your knowledge for that, at least use it to keep these weapons out of Dextor's hands. At least preserve it!"

Mikkel gazed steadily at him. "Peregrin, Archiva does not lie in two vaults far below these hills. Archiva farms the fields and makes pottery and weaves clothing. Archiva forges tools and cares for horses and grows vegetables. Archiva is the people, Peregrin. People who live by a belief in peace and honesty and care for one another. The Creed is a living thing. It moves and breathes and laughs and loves all around us. This is what O'Keefe has set us to protect and nourish. If we find weapons in the vault that can wipe out Dextor in an instant, what will we have done except destroy what we were trying to protect—a belief in peace."

"Then how do you propose we stop Dextor, who will also destroy this belief in peace?"

"We will find a way. I must think on this and rest now. Please excuse me."

Peregrin rose. "Don't think too long, Mikkel, or it will be the Prodigy and not the Falcon who lands at your door. Peace to your heart."

"And to yours," Mikkel said. Peregrin went out and closed the door.

XII
PEACE

As noon approached, Peregrin stood in the ruins beside the very maple tree he had hidden behind when Cornel and Janel had appeared followed by Crop and his men. Curtan, Corval, and Stevan stood with him. Scouts posted upon the ridge had sent word that Dextor was indeed approaching as he had said, swinging northeast of the ruins. It appeared as well that there were at least 175 fighters with him. There were no flanking units or even advance scouts. The force marched together, advancing *en masse* without any hurry at all.

"Just like he said," Corval noted. "I guess he just plans to roll over us."

"He didn't even send out Rangers to see if we were waiting," Curtan said.

"He doesn't need to," answered Peregrin. "If we are here, he will fight us; if we are not here, he will keep marching into Archiva. He's not even worried about a surprise attack."

"What's our force number?" Stevan said.

"Eighty-seven, including the scouts, who will join us soon," Corval said. "Thirty are hidden among the trees and ruins near the water. The rest are here."

Peregrin nodded. "It will have to do. Everyone take your positions. Try to keep your people focused and tightly grouped so they can deliver the greatest punch and protect one another." He paused and held out his hand. "Gentlemen, for Archiva, for the Waterman."

They laid their hands atop his. "For Archiva, for the Waterman."

He gazed at each of them. "Peace be to your hearts." They nodded and each went his way. Corval and Stevan headed toward the waterline where their people were hidden. Curtan took a position with his troops about one hundred feet to his left. They remained in plain view, tightly grouped into two wedges whose bases touched, forming a large *M* with Peregrin and Curtan at their points. This would give the impression of greater numbers, as well as allow the Archivans to concentrate their defense while protecting one another. Peregrin had instructed all of the fighters to stand in plain sight but near to trees and ruins should they need cover from arrows.

He doubted that Dextor would even bother using his archers, however. Peregrin had lain awake throughout the night, pondering how Dextor would advance. If he were truly mad as Carlin had said, and if he cared for nothing anymore except an end to his madness, then he would probably simply march through their lines. His men were all warriors, born and chosen from violent lives, trained to fight and act in accordance with Dextor's wishes. They had superior weapons that they were accustomed to using and no qualms about killing and being killed.

What did Peregrin have? Eighty-seven stout hearts. Men and women willing to come out and fight. They were farmers and artisans, people of land and stone. Furthermore, they loved peace.

They had chosen to seek a way of life that accepted and cherished others. They knew self-defense and some hastily drilled tactical maneuvers, but they were not warriors. They did not want to kill.

Dextor would know well who stood against him. He had lived among them and loved them. He had fought for them and bled for them. But he no longer believed in them or in their way of life.

Still, they were here. Eighty-seven people who, despite being stunned by the violence and death of these past days, still came out to defend their homes, their families, and their beliefs. Peregrin's heart swelled as he looked about at them. Some were embracing each other. Some stood gripping their weapons, gazing fearfully through the trees. Some were crouched down with their heads bowed, as if seeking one last peaceful moment before the battle was joined.

All of them were resolute. No one attempted to slip away through the woods or even appeared to be ready to run. They were willing to give their lives this day to protect Archiva. *They're all Archivists*, Peregrin thought. They've sworn to preserve the knowledge and the dream of O'Keefe, and they would die rather than abandon that task.

He laughed suddenly and lifted his sword high above him so that the sunlight through the trees reflected upon the steel, making it seem to flame. And without knowing why or how, he sang:

> *One simple twig may turn the wind.*
> *One simple stone may turn the tide.*
> *One simple deed turns foe to friend.*
> *One simple blessing turns violence aside.*

Like the rush of the surf upon the sand, the Archivans took up the song.

> *One simple twig may turn the wind.*
> *One simple stone may turn the tide.*
> *One simple deed turns foe to friend.*
> *One simple blessing turns violence aside.*

Peregrin turned toward them, still holding his sword aloft. "Archivans! Archivans! We do not stand alone this day! All those who came before, back to O'Keefe himself, are here with us. Our children, our children's children, and all generations unborn are here with us. All that we have built and all that we hope to build, all that has been given to us and all that we shall give, all that we have learned and all that we shall leave to the next generation—all Archiva is here with us this day!"

They shouted as one: "Archiva!"

"Let no one be deceived," Peregrin went on. "Dextor is coming. He commands twice our number, and they are trained fighters. Yet his strength is his weakness. This is all he has, and he believes that it is all he needs to force his rule upon Archiva. He believes we are alone.

"We are not alone. Let each one here think of his parents, his grandparents, his great-grandparents. Let each one here think of his children, his grandchildren, his great-grandchildren. Archiva is not a place, and it is not a creed. Archiva is a people that have endured a century of chaos and have perservered. Archiva is a people who have dared to turn away from violence. Archiva is the people—past, present, and future—who believe in life. And all those people are here! We are not alone! We are Archiva!"

"Archiva!" they shouted. "Archiva!"

From above there came a high note on a trumpet. Peregrin turned and pointed his sword toward the east. " Behold, Dextor comes. Take heart and stand your ground. This day will be remembered. You will be remembered because you were here. Be true to your Creed, and be true to the life of Archiva." He spoke then the words from the song:

> *Preserve the people.*
> *Turn from the power which kills.*
> *Archiva's law, Archiva's love,*
> *seek peace within, share peace without.*
> *Cherish life and live.*

They answered:

> One simple twig may turn the wind.
> One simple stone may turn the tide.
> One simple deed turns foe to friend.
> One simple blessing turns violence aside.

"Peregrin," Curtan said softly, "here he comes."

A column of men appeared at the far end of the ruins. Peregrin watched as they marched over the rock pile from which he had first beheld this place. They came steadily, grouped in four rows of eight men across. Each group had a leader who chanted a marching cadence to keep them in step. The groups were about twenty feet apart.

Units of twenty-five, Peregrin thought. *Well organized, efficient, and drilled. Capable of separating, flanking, surrounding, and crushing all opposition. We are the opposition. We must not give in.*

Dextor's force kept coming until they were all in sight. Then Dextor himself appeared on top of the debris with Carlin by his side. He gave a command, and his entire force halted and stood in silence, gazing at the small force that dared to oppose them less than four hundred yards away. Peregrin gazed back at him, making sure he was clearly visible. "Come on, Dextor," he whispered. "Come on, my brother. Send them in at a run. Bunch them up for me. Come on. What are you waiting for?"

He heard Dextor laugh. A command was issued, and each fighter drew a sword, holding it upward. Then his forces began to move forward at the same steady pace. He glanced at Curtan, who nodded. They would have to take the brunt of Dextor's attack and fall back slowly in order to draw in his entire force.

The men advanced silently, stepping in time to their leaders' cadence. The sound of their boots filled the air as they drew closer. The closer they came, the more their force seemed to increase and the smaller Peregrin's force seemed. He glanced at Curtan and could tell by his grim, hard-set jaw that he was experiencing the same feeling. He set himself and raised his sword. Dextor's men were less than fifty yards away, relentlessly marching past tree and ruin.

Peregrin pointed his sword at the advancing column. "Arrows!" he said. Behind him a trumpet sounded two notes. Archers rose up from hiding places on the cliff ledge, above the ruined council building, and upon large mounds of rubble and began to loose volleys of arrows into the approaching troops.

Men began to fall out of line. Peregrin had instructed his archers to aim for the legs of their targets in order to avoid killing. He knew, however, that the result was largely up to chance. Some of the men fell with arrows sticking out of their chests or necks.

The leaders called to quicken the pace, and Dextor's men began to run toward them. This brought the following units closer than before. *It will have to do,* thought Peregrin, and he braced himself.

Dextor's lead troops slammed into his little band with terrific force. The double-phalanx formation allowed them to deflect the warriors past them, however, splitting them into three groups. Those forced to the outside of the formation found themselves fighting a solid line of Archivans on one side while being shot at with arrows from the other side. Those pushed into the center between the wedges faced assault from three sides.

At first, Peregrin almost believed they could defeat Dextor's force with this tactic. The troops who led the assault were disoriented and thrown into confusion by finding their charge not only resisted but broken. More than a dozen of them had fallen immediately. The Archivans were fighting with such ferocity that one could indeed believe they had all of Archiva behind them.

But as wave after wave of Dextor's troops struck them, the formation began to give way and collapse. Instead of keeping Dextor's men separated and off balance, the Archivans began to find themselves being slowly surrounded and squeezed in an ever-tightening noose.

Peregrin deflected a blow from a burly warrior and struck him in the head with the flat of his sword. "Fall back!" he cried. "Archivans, fall back!" His defense began to give way as they were pushed farther and farther backward toward the edge of the ruins.

Dextor's men, smelling victory, pushed harder. Several Archivans had fallen and lay amid the ruins. Just when it seemed they would have to break and run or be totally annihilated, Peregrin cried out, "Watermen!"

A trumpet sounded three long notes. There was a roar of "Archiva!" and "Waterman!" from the river's edge as Corval, Stevan, and their fighters rose out of hiding and rushed toward the fray.

Dextor's men were caught by surprise. Intent on victory and bloodlust, they now found themselves caught between Peregrin's forces and fresh fighters from behind them. Curtan cried out, "Archiva!" Peregrin echoed the call, and they surged forward again, slashing and fighting, trying to force Dextor's men back against the face of the cliff where they would be unable to make use of their superior numbers.

It almost worked. Dextor's men were thrown off balance. Under the force of the assault, they began to retreat toward the cliff, directly below the spot where Dextor had threatened to throw Mikkel off. It was the steepest section of the slope with sixty feet of rock wall rising above it. In one direction the hillside angled outward sharply toward the ruined council building. In the other direction, the hillside rolled out into a steep but passable slope. The idea was to box Dextor's men into the angle of the cliff face so that the advantage of their greater numbers would be nullified.

A voice rose above the clamor. "Fold inside! Peel left and right! Peel around!" Peregrin realized it was Dextor's voice. He had drawn near to the battle and stood atop a mound less than one hundred feet away. Carlin was beside him, as well as a small *cadre* of warriors. Peregrin wondered what it meant.

The order was repeated by the unit leaders. The center segment of Dextor's men suddenly gave way, the men falling back quickly and then racing around the far ends of the *melee*, where they again joined the battle. The Archivans found themselves drawn forward as in a vacuum as Dextor's men continued to fall back in the center and pour around both ends. This sudden shift of fighters to the flanks resulted in a complete reversal of the battle as the warriors pulling out of the center made their way around the edge and extended Dextor's battle line until the sides met once more, forming a large semicircle around Peregrin's fighters.

Now it was the Archivans who had their backs to the cliff face and Dextor's men who hemmed them in, assailing them from all sides. They began to give way, slipping on the stones and being driven back. Peregrin saw Corval fall not ten feet from him, attacked by three of Dextor's men at once. Before he could get to him, however, he was pushed back by two attackers of his own.

One man was closer than the second. As he closed, Peregrin feinted an overhead blow and then reversed and twirled the sword so that his thrust came up from below, catching his opponent midsection. The man screamed and fell.

He barely had time, however, to parry the downward sweep of the second attacker's sword. The force of the blow caused Peregrin to stagger, and he fell, slipping on the wet rocks. The man raised his sword to drive it through him.

Before the blow came down, the man was struck from behind and fell to the side. Jorge stood over Peregrin for a brief moment and then reached out a hand to help him up. Peregrin stood, and their eyes met.

"For Rik," Jorge said.

Peregrin smiled. "For Rik," he said. Then Dextor's men were upon them again, and they were separated by the press of battle.

The Archivans fought on in desperation, trying to protect one another. But one by one, they fell beneath the onslaught. Finally, they found themselves pushed back all the way to the cliff. Dextor's men continued to crush against them. Peregrin had come to conclude that the game was up and resolved himself to try to fight his way through to Dextor (though he doubted he would get halfway) when a trumpet blew a long, single note.

Inexplicably, Dextor's men disengaged and backed away from the beleaguered Archivans. Peregrin looked about. His band was in sorry shape. Corval appeared to be dead, as did many others. Others were severely wounded, groaning amid the rocks and ruins. Stevan was down behind him with his back to the cliff. He had a deep slash in his hip, and his face was ghost white. Curtan stood near him, breathing heavily and leaning on his sword. He was covered with minor wounds, including a nasty cut on his forehead, but appeared not to be seriously injured. Less than forty Archivans remained standing, all of them near exhaustion.

"Wha … what's he doing?" Curtan gasped.

Peregrin shook his head. "I don't know. Carlin said he was done being dramatic. Why doesn't he just finish it?"

"I don't know. Maybe he thinks we will surrender now."

"Whatever. Our only chance is to get to Dextor. Prepare for a wedge phalanx attack when they come at us again."

"I don't think we have the time," Curtan said. "Look there."

Peregrin looked to where Curtan was pointing. Dextor and Carlin had come through the ranks of warriors, followed by almost two dozen men. They stopped about forty feet away. A cold horror shot through Peregrin as he saw that the men carried bows.

Dextor gazed at him. "Well played, Traveler," he said. "You have withstood my force with less than half the men and nearly prevailed. I was certain you would put forth a good fight. Although, I must confess, I am impressed by the number of Archivan sheep you persuaded to follow you. I would have thought you could have gotten no more than fifty."

"You underestimate the people of Archiva," Peregrin growled.

All the while he was thinking, *Just a little closer, Dextor. A little closer and I have you.*

Dextor seemed to know his intent. "Undoubtedly, you hope that I will draw near enough for you to attack, Traveler. Perhaps a week ago I might have, being enamored of the drama of it all and having great confidence in my ability. But, as Carlin must have told you, I have lost my beloved Gabrielle. I am not interested in speeches or theatrics. I only wish for an end.

"So this is it, Traveler. Surrender now and swear loyalty to me, or you will all die to the last man. This will be the only chance I give you. Bows up."

The men with Dextor raised their bows and nocked arrows to their strings. "You may have a brief moment to realize the inevitable," he said.

Peregrin looked around at his bloody, exhausted troops. They had fought so well this day. It seemed unfair to end this way. He looked at Curtan, who straightened up. "I'm not going home a frog," he said and grinned.

Peregrin looked at his little band again. They were near to their end, but their eyes showed no sign of fear or surrender. "All Archiva is here," said a wiry man named Chase.

Peregrin grinned suddenly at Curtan. "Yeah. Let's go get him. He pointed his sword directly at Dextor. "For Archiva!" he shouted.

"For the Waterman!" cried Curtan. The remaining fighters raised their swords and cried, "Waterman! Archiva!" Together they rushed at Dextor.

"So be it!" Dextor cried. "Draw and fire!" The Archivans were still twenty-five feet away as his archers drew back their bows to fire.

Shh, shh, shh, shh—boom!

The ground between them suddenly erupted and shook with such force that Peregrin, Curtan, and all of the Archivans were thrown down. Pulling himself up, Peregrin saw that Dextor, Carlin, and all of the archers had also been knocked to the ground. Between them but closer to Dextor, the ground itself was blasted as if a giant hand had torn a piece of it up.

Dextor regained his feet and looked about wildly. "Up, you fools!" he cried. "Shoot them!" The archers struggled to their feet and reached for arrows.

Shh, shh, shh, shh—boom!

This time, Peregrin saw a small stick flipping end over end through the air, coming from the direction of the hillside. It hit the ground near to Dextor and lay for a brief instant. One end of it was sparking. Suddenly it exploded, tearing another crater into the ground and nearly knocking Peregrin and his men over again. Dextor and those around him were knocked over.

"Dextor!" called a familiar voice. "I give you this one chance to surrender or be destroyed." Halfway up the steep slope, a man sat upon a magnificent black horse. Beside him, on the ground, was another man with a torch in his hand. The man on the ground was Morgan. The horse was Carbon, and the man riding him was Mikkel.

"Mikkel!" Dextor cried. "Mikkel, you fool. You are within arrow range. Shoot him! Shoot him now!"

Even as Dextor's archers began to reach for arrows, Mikkel extended something toward Morgan, who touched the torch to it. Mikkel cocked his arm and threw it. It was another stick that flipped through the air, landing not ten feet from Dextor's men.

Shh, shh, shh, shh—boom!

This time, men were actually flung through the air by the power of the explosion. Many of those who rose up simply ran off.

Dextor picked himself off the ground again. "Get him, dammit! He's only one man. Rush him! He can't stop us all in time."

Mikkel laughed. "One man! One man, Dextor? I am not only one man! I am the Archivist, and all of Archiva rides with me!"

He pulled backward on the reins, and Carbon reared up, neighing. "Archiva!" he cried. "Archiva, rise!"

There was a tremendous shout of "Archiva!" Suddenly the top of the slope was thronged with people.

Mikkel reached down and lit another stick. He held it aloft. "Forward, Archiva! Defend your Creed!" He threw the stick into the midst of Dextor's troops, who scattered hastily, many of them diving onto the ground. This stick did not explode, however.

Before they could recover, the people of Archiva began to stream down the hillside toward them, shouting, "Archiva!" and, "The Creed!"

Peregrin looked over at Curtan, whose mouth was hanging open. "No frogs in Archiva today!" he shouted happily.

Still, Dextor was not one to run. His men, though once Terists, had been drilled into a fighting unit that would obey his every command. He began to shout orders, bunching his fighters together to withstand Mikkel's charge. There were nearly two hundred people surging down the hill toward Dextor, but even at this distance, Peregrin could see they were ill equipped. Some had farm implements or kitchen utensils hastily bound to poles. Some only had knives or staffs of wood.

"Curtan!" Peregrin shouted. "We have to keep him off balance."

"Understood!" Curtan shouted back. "Forward, Watermen! For Archiva! Forward!"

With a great shout, the remainder of the Watermen hurled themselves into Dextor's flank like water on the rocks, pummeling his distracted warriors. Even as Dextor's men turned to face them, the Archivans, led by Mikkel and Morgan, reached the bottom of the slope and threw themselves into the fray.

The woods shook with shouts of anger, fear, and pain as the people fought around tree, stone, and ruin. Maneuvers, orders, and formations became useless as the battle dissolved into a raging free-for-all struggle. Men and women pummeled, slashed, and struck at one another without guidance or command. Each person became as an island amid a battering storm.

Overwhelmed by sheer numbers and the ferocity of the Archivans' attack, Dextor's men gave way. Many of them cast aside their weapons and ran. The rest were pushed back to the river's edge. Once there, they threw down their swords and raised their hands in surrender. All except a small band of about twenty warriors, who rallied around Dextor himself as he stood upon a hillock created by the ruin of a substantial building. These men found themselves surrounded by angry Archivans but held their swords firmly, ready to protect their leader at all costs.

Dextor laughed. "So! The sheep of Archiva have found teeth! Remarkable, Mikkel! How did you manage it?"

"Dextor," Mikkel called, "order your men to lay down their weapons."

Dextor threw back his head and laughed again, a dry, cracking cackle. "Or what? You will kill me? Has the taste of blood made you a man of war?"

"You have caused death and ruin in our midst!" Mikkel growled. "One way or another, I will finish it this day. Now, order your men to surrender!"

"No," Dextor said. "You can see for yourself that these men choose to defend me. Do you want to take me, Mikkel? You will pay the full price for it!"

"Dextor, I'm warning you!" Mikkel shot back. "There is no need for more death. This is your last chance."

"He must die, Mikkel!" cried someone.

"Yes!" cried another. "He deserves no better than he gave to those in the camp."

The swarm of Archivans around Dextor's little band began to murmur and swell like a hive. There were more shouts for Dextor's death.

"Surrender now, Dextor!" Mikkel shouted.

"I will not!" Dextor retorted. "Come and dance with me!"

The Archivans began to close in, shouting for vengeance. Dextor's men gripped their swords tighter and prepared to sell their lives dearly. Just as it seemed the entire enraged mass of people would surge forward, a voice rose above the clamor. Peregrin could never say if the voice sounded male or female. It pierced the very air like a clap of thunder.

"Enough of this! I say, enough!"

Rather than being swallowed up, the voice seemed to swell above the din, echoing throughout the ruins and commanding an authority that could not be denied. The surge forward was abruptly halted, as if an invisible hand had suddenly blocked the way. With weapons still raised but frozen, each person, whether from Archiva or Dextor, searched for the source of the voice.

Some sixty feet above them, atop the cliff, rays of light pierced the trees in such a way that those who looked were nearly blinded. Amidst this light was the silhouette of a person. A slightly built person with what looked to be tousled, curly hair.

The figure spread its arms in an embracing gesture and cried out, "Archivans! Men of the world! Listen to me! Stop this madness now!"

Peregrin heard Curtan gasp. "Wa…Waterman? Is it you?" There were other similar murmurs coming from all around.

The light through the trees diminished somewhat. Now Peregrin could tell that the figure was a woman who did not have curly hair but straight, long hair that fell far past her shoulders. "Bliss," he murmured.

"Archivans!" she cried out. "Look at yourselves! What has happened to your Creed? Your brothers and sisters die at your feet while you cry for more death! Do you claim victory this day? What price will you pay for your glory? What reason will you offer for your bloodlust?

"Look at the ruins around you! Whose blood is this at your feet?

Is it friend or foe? It is your own! Blood is blood, from Archivan and Terist alike! Are you deaf to its cry? Has there not been enough shed for you?

"Look at one another! What do you see? An enemy? A threat to be exterminated? Look at one another! Can you not see?

"Archivans! Followers of Dextor! We can end this foolishness! We can choose another path if we have the courage. Cast aside your fear with your weapons. That is not your enemy before you. That is your brother. That is your sister. Refuse to hate! Refuse to fight! Refuse to harm! Trust no one who turns you against another. See for yourself the one whom you fight. See! See and live! Or fight and die!"

The light increased around her again until it became too bright to look at. When it diminished again, she was gone.

No one moved. A silence hung throughout the woods like a wet blanket. Looking about, Peregrin saw men and women standing as if baffled, trying to remember why they were here. Then a woman holding a staff of wood with a meat cleaver tied to one end threw it aside. A man near her, one of the Watermen, did the same with his sword. One by one, people began to cast their weapons down. Archivans and Dextor's men alike threw down sword, bow, axe, knife, and staff and stood there looking at the chaos around them.

Peregrin looked back at Dextor's men They stood there, weapons cast away or dangling from their hands, with puzzled looks on their faces as if they were not sure what they had just done. Dextor, he noted, was gone.

He turned to find Curtan standing there, staring at his sword, which he held loosely, its point resting on the ground. His brow was furrowed as if he could not recall what this instrument was called or why he held it. Finally, he let it fall from his hand, and he sat down upon the ground. Peregrin suddenly realized that he was terribly tired.

Mikkel rode slowly into the midst of the people. "Archivans," he said, "you who followed Dextor. Let us tend the wounded together."

Those who were not injured set to work. Side by side, the people of Archiva and Dextor's warriors began to bind up injuries, make stretchers, and bring water to those who were too exhausted to move.

Mikkel rode up to Peregrin. His leg was still wrapped in a splint and had been carefully wedged into a stirrup. "Peregrin," he said softly, "I am glad to find you alive."

"You wouldn't have if you had arrived any later. Mikkel, you came just in time. What was that stick you threw that exploded? How did you get the people to come out?"

Mikkel reached into a saddlebag and drew forth a cylindrical stick about ten inches long. A cord of some sort protruded from one end." A little something I picked up in the vault of machines for inspiration."

Peregrin looked at it quizzically. "Dynamite," he said at last. "It's called dynamite."

Mikkel nodded. "That's what it said on the box. I have read enough to know about its power. It can cause great destruction. I tried to throw it where no one would be killed."

"And the people of Archiva?"

Mikkel smiled. "Peregrin, I am still the Archivist. The people of Archiva trust me enough to come and fight for their home. Plus, I showed them what the dynamite could do."

Peregrin grinned. "Indeed you are the Archivist. But what just happened with Bliss? What is happening now?"

"I do not know. I think Waterman was right, however. We do not give Bliss enough credit. If indeed that was Bliss up there."

"What do you mean?"

"I cannot say for sure. Like so many others, I thought I saw Waterman at first."

"That had to be the shadow of the sun through the leaves."

"Perhaps, but when the light died down some, I saw not Bliss but Joy."

"Joy. Your wife?"

"Yes, I was sure of it. It even sounded like her. Of course, Bliss and Joy always looked and sounded similar."

"Why is that?"

Mikkel looked at him quizzically. "I thought Waterman had told you all this. Joy was Bliss's older sister."

"Oh," Peregrin replied. "Bliss and Joy. Of course. I guess that would make sense that you might think it was Joy then."

"Yes," Mikkel said, "that might explain it. Only I was close enough to Dextor to hear his reaction. I heard him say: 'Gabrielle?'"

"What are you saying? That everybody who lost someone saw them atop the cliff?"

Mikkel shook his head. "I don't know what I'm saying. I'm only saying that I cannot explain what happened. Let's leave it at that."

Peregrin opened his mouth to speak, but someone touched him on his elbow. Turning, he found Merida.

"Peregrin, Mikkel, come quickly," she said. "It's Carlin. He is badly hurt."

They followed her across the battlefield. Carlin lay on a small hillock, his head propped up on a rock. Bliss was kneeling beside him, daubing at his wounds with a cloth she soaked in a bowl of greenish liquid. Peregrin wondered vaguely how she had gotten down to them so fast. As they came up, Carlin laid his hand upon hers.

"It is enough, Bliss. Thank you," he said quietly. "Others will need this more than I."

Peregrin dropped to his knees beside Carlin, while Merida helped Mikkel dismount. "Carlin," he said.

Carlin turned his head toward him. "Ah, Peregrin." He stopped and coughed twice. "I'm sorry it turned out this way, Peregrin. I'm sorry we could not have parted friends."

"We are friends, Carlin."

"Where is Dextor?"

"Gone," Peregrin answered.

Carlin coughed again. "Not surprised. He...lost...his way. Forgive him."

Peregrin was dumbfounded. "How can you forgive him for leaving you here after how faithfully you stayed with him?"

Carlin coughed again. "He had no choice...couldn't stay... everything gone, ruined." He broke into a spasm of coughing.

"It's all right, Carlin," Bliss said. "Lie still. We'll get healing for you."

Carlin looked at her and smiled. "Brave Bliss. You know better. He reached out a hand. Mikkel?"

"I'm here, Carlin."

"Mikkel, please forgive...for...everything. Bury me here."

"No," Mikkel said. "You will be buried with honor in Archiva."

Carlin shook his head and coughed again. "No. Not worthy of Archiva. No...here. This...a place of peace. Always liked...ruins...peaceful. So sorry, Mikkel...so sorry."

"Shh, Carlin. Don't be afraid."

"Not afraid...just...sorry." He closed his eyes a moment. When he reopened them, he looked past them. "Waterman," he said, and a small smile creased his face. He lifted his arm, stretching out his hand to something beyond them. "Hello, Waterman..." The arm dropped at his side.

Tears etched Bliss's face as she looked up. "Carlin is dead," she said.

～⌒～

They buried Carlin near the base of the cliff and marked his grave with a large boulder. Some of the injured could not be moved right away, so the Rangers built a makeshift shelter to use as a temporary hospital, and Merida had her healers working night and day.

Ranger patrols were sent out to round up those of Dextor's men who had run off, to make sure they would not regroup. Those they found were brought to a holding area and placed under guard in the ruins.

Some of those who had surrendered at the battle slipped away in the night. Many, however, stayed and petitioned Mikkel and Peregrin to assist in recovering from the battle. A delegation of five of their leaders came forward to speak for the rest. Corlee, who had come to Peregrin for Carlin, led them.

"We are tired of fighting," he said. "We do not know what has happened or what lies ahead, but we are not the men we were before."

"You were Terists before," Mikkel said.

"I understand that is your term," Corlee answered. "Yes, we came from lives of violence. But Dextor showed us another way. He taught us that we could be disciplined and work together for a common goal. He gave us an order and unity that took us beyond that life.

"Yet now we see there is even more. I do not know what this Creed is or how one lives it, but I would like to learn more about it. I see in the way you Archivans care for one another and how you care for our wounded that another way of life is possible, one that Dextor could not give us. We would like to learn more."

"You are people of violence," Mikkel said.

Corlee scowled. "You misjudge us because we followed Dextor. It is true that we lived in roving bands and often took what we needed by force. This was the only way we knew to survive. Still, I, like many others, longed for another way. I just did not know one was possible. Do not your people promise to live lives of peace? Yet I heard them crying for Dextor's death. Does this make them violent people? Or simply people?

"Dextor chose us, not for our violence but for our longing. Some of us knew only violence, but this did not make us violent people, only people. Those among us who were truly violent, who enjoyed violence, he did away with. He said they had no place in a new world."

Mikkel was silent a moment. "Do you think you can lay down the sword and take up the hoe?"

Corlee smiled. "If someone will teach me how it works."

Mikkel set them to work under light guard, making stretchers, carrying the wounded back to Archiva, and helping the Rangers. A few of them showed a propensity for healing, and Merida quickly put them to work tending the wounded.

In the days after the battle, there was little time for anything but to save as many people as possible. Peregrin longed to talk with Bliss, but neither of them had time for more than an embrace and a few words.

On the third day, Peregrin was enjoying a brief rest, leaning with eyes closed against a towering oak. He became suddenly aware of a presence and opened his eyes to find Bliss sitting on the ground beside him, watching him. Her arms were drawn around her knees. She smiled at him.

"I am surprised to learn that the great Traveler can be caught unaware," she said, her voice like chimes on the wind. "I have been sitting here for ten minutes waiting for you to wake."

He laughed and sat up. "It's a good thing you are not a Terist then. I was drifting in my thoughts somewhere and never heard you."

She gazed at him. "I am glad to see you well, Peregrin."

"Likewise, Bliss. For a while I did not think any of us would survive the day. But look, not only did I survive, but I'm still me. Your fear was not fulfilled."

The smile vanished from Bliss's face. "No, Peregrin. The fear remains."

"What do you mean?"

"The battle has changed you. The battle has changed everything about Archiva as well. And the change is accelerating."

Peregrin shook his head. "Bliss, nothing is changing in me."

Bliss studied him. "I wish I could believe that. I don't think even you believe it."

Peregrin swallowed hard. "I believe it," he said quietly.

Bliss held him in her gaze. "Tell me something. Are you a fighter?"

"What do you mean?"

"I realize that you cannot remember your past. But based on what you just experienced, do you think your life revolved around fighting?"

Peregrin was taken aback. "No. No. I don't want to fight."

"But you can."

"Yes, I can, but it is not a life I would choose. I'm certain of that."

"Then how can you account for the fact that you came through that battle without a single scratch on you? Dextor's fighters were well trained. Yet I look at you and cannot see any evidence that you were just in a battle—no bruises, no cuts, nothing. How do you explain this?"

He met her gaze briefly then lowered his eyes. "I cannot."

"What did you experience during the battle? What were you feeling?"

"Bliss, there was no time for feeling. Mostly I acted on instinct."

"And you came through unscathed. Do you not find this odd?"

He sighed. "Yes, I do. Everything about my life has been odd. I can only say that as the battle ensued, I experienced a quickening of sorts. It was as if . . . as if someone or something was increasing my knowledge of fighting even as I fought."

"And you were never wounded?"

Peregrin said nothing for a moment. The fact was, he distinctly remembered being cut at least once when an assailant's sword had caught him along the arm. But there was no visible sign of injury now.

"No," he said. "I guess I was not wounded at all. I was lucky."

"Lucky," she repeated.

The silence hung between them like a mist. Then Peregrin spoke. "Bliss, that was quite a thing you did up on the cliff. I think you stopped us all from shedding more blood."

Bliss looked at him, and her forehead wrinkled slightly. "I was there on the cliff," she said. "I don't remember what I said. I only knew that if the battle went on, we would have truly lost, even in victory."

"Listen. I have a question for you that baffles me."

Bliss smiled. "That's only fair."

"That was a good trick you pulled by getting the sunlight behind you. It sort of made you look mystical up there. How did you do it?"

"What do you mean?"

"Well, the cliff is on the north side of the ruins, and the sun was directly overhead. How did you get it to seem as though it were shining through the trees from behind you?"

Bliss stood up. "Don't be silly, Peregrin. How could I have any control over the sunlight?" She paused. "Or the water?" She turned and walked away. Peregrin watched her go, wrinkled his brow for a moment, then shook his head and leaned back on the oak again.

He reflected on Mara's prophecy. Dextor and he had grappled, and the battle had been won, as she foretold. Why, then, did he feel like Archiva had fallen?

XIII
TITANS

By the end of the week, all of the wounded, those from Archiva and Dextor's men, had been taken to Archiva. Twenty-six people of Archiva and thirty-two of Dextor's men had died as a result of the battle. Dozens more had been seriously injured and would probably suffer crippling effects for the rest of their lives.

The emotional toll was unfathomable, however. For days, Archiva remained in stunned silence. Few spoke except to pass on instructions or vital information. The dead of Archiva were buried upon the southern slope. Dextor's men were buried in the ruins where the land fanned out near the landslide.

In a hastily called council meeting, it was decided that Dextor's followers were free to leave if they chose, provided they surrendered all of their weapons except for a knife. They also had to swear to leave the area and not return to their former home in Dextor's Second Archiva.

More than thirty of them, however, petitioned to stay in

Archiva and become a part of it. The council interviewed each person separately, deciding for or against each one. All but three were permitted to stay. They were encamped in the lower section of Archiva, near the assembly platform.

"We will have to keep close vigilance upon them," Morgan stated to the council. "However, each of these people seems genuine in his desire to follow the path of peace. It may well be that this terrible battle has served to open Archiva to a new aspect of its mission in the world. Only time will judge our decision. May it be a wise one."

By the second week after the battle, Mikkel had healed enough to walk with the help of a single crutch, keeping his leg splinted and stiff but allowing some weight upon it. He proposed to Peregrin that they should lead a squad of Rangers to Dextor's Second Archiva in order to see if anyone had returned there and, more importantly, to look for Dextor.

They took fifteen Rangers with them, as well as Bliss and Curtan. Mikkel rode Carbon, who skillfully picked his way through the trees and rocks as surefooted as a mountain goat. They traveled slowly, sending Rangers ahead to scout for possible ambushes, but they found no one. When they rounded the bend along the hillside, they found the great stone slab door lying open. No one was inside the cavern entrance or the barracks there. Mikkel left Carbon at the entrance and rode the lifter down with Bliss. The rest of the troop descended by the stairways.

Inside the canyon they discovered a few of Dextor's followers, who surrendered immediately. They had not been a part of the battle, being cooks and camp personnel, but word of Dextor's defeat had reached them through those who had fled back to the canyon to collect supplies.

Peregrin and Mikkel showed Bliss the cell in which Dextor had kept them, as well as the hidden crevice that the Waterman had used to rescue them. Bliss even followed Peregrin into the crevice to see the climb they had made in the dark.

Dextor's headquarters showed no evidence that he had returned here. All was orderly and neat. Peregrin felt a sudden pang when they looked into the inner room and saw a bed and a closet with clothing for a man and a woman. He remembered Gabrielle's grace and voice and wondered where Dextor had buried his love.

They searched every dwelling in the canyon and found no sign of Dextor. Mikkel admired the forges Dextor had built, as well as the leather-making house.

"We could use these in Archiva," he said.

"Perhaps we ought to make an outpost here," Curtan said. "It would make a wonderful garrison for the Rangers."

Mikkel folded his arms and looked about. "It would at that," he said. "Still, there's no telling what tomorrow will bring."

They collected all the supplies and weapons they could carry and set out for Archiva. When they reached the great boulder, Peregrin again felt a pang. A light rain had begun to fall, and for an instant it was as if he were crouched near that boulder again, waiting for Gabrielle and Carlin. He could hear the cries of the battle, saw Gabrielle and Sanda fight, and saw them fall again.

"Peregrin, are you all right?" Bliss asked.

He shook his head. "Yes, I was just remembering the fight here."

"Let's move on then," said Mikkel.

"Wait," Peregrin said. "I have an idea. Do you remember, Mikkel? Here is where we separated the night we escaped from Dextor. The Rangers can continue down the trail with the supplies, but I would like to walk that path again. I think we should go that way, just the four of us, to see how Waterman gave his life."

"I was there, Peregrin. I saw," Curtan said.

"I know. I think this can help us heal."

Bliss smiled and nodded. Mikkel nodded as well.

Curtan stretched out his hand. "For Archiva. For Waterman."

Peregrin, Bliss, and Mikkel laid their hands atop his. "For Archiva. For Waterman," they said together.

They set out, rising through the hills along the winding trail. As they went, Peregrin remembered Waterman and his carefree banter. He told the others how, even with all the urgency of escaping Dextor, the Waterman's mood had been irrepressibly joyful. He shared Waterman's pride in seeing the great waterwheel and pump house he had built.

"I remember when he proposed that project," Mikkel said. "I was sure he had lost his mind. But he built it, and we have had water ever since."

"I hope we can rebuild it in his honor," Bliss said.

Peregrin had been expecting this to be a somber journey for all of them. But talking about Waterman and sharing their memories of him seemed to hearten them. Their talk became infused with gladness, as if Waterman himself were walking with them, joking and playing tricks.

They were forced to proceed single file as the trail grew narrow alongside a steep hill. Peregrin was in front with Bliss about ten feet behind him. Mikkel had dismounted and hobbled along carefully, while Curtan brought up the rear, leading Carbon. The slope yawned below them, sliding steeply down about seventy-five feet to a ledge. Beyond that was a sheer drop of at least one hundred feet.

Peregrin picked his way across stones piled to bridge a small crevice in the hillside. He turned to give instructions to his companions when he heard an inarticulate scream, like a hawk swooping on its prey, and someone crashed into him. He had the briefest moment to see the face of Dextor, twisted in rage, before they both tumbled off the trail and rolled end over end down the steep slope.

Dextor clung to Peregrin fiercely with one hand as they tumbled. With the other hand he stabbed at him with a long knife. Peregrin twisted and tried to grab Dextor's wrist as the knife came in. The knife caught him in the shoulder, and he cried out.

Dextor tried to raise the knife again, but the motion of their fall knocked it from his hand. They landed heavily on the ledge. Dextor kicked Peregrin in the face, rolled clear, and sprang to his feet like a cat. He charged at him even as Peregrin rose, still bleeding.

Peregrin rolled to the left, tripping Dextor and sending him flying near to the edge. Both men rose and faced each other. "Dextor!" cried Peregrin. "Enough! Enough have died!"

"Not you!" Dextor screamed, and he attacked with blazing speed, pummeling Peregrin with blows and sending him reeling backward.

Something clicked in Peregrin's mind. A fresh infusion of knowledge poured into him. Dextor was an excellent fighter hand to hand, but now he found he matched him blow for blow. They rolled, kicked, struck, twisted, and leaped with such speed that Peregrin was astonished at Dextor's ability and at his own sudden skill.

Dextor landed a blow across Peregrin's jaw that staggered him. Before he could recover, Dextor had launched himself in a full-body tackle around Peregrin's midsection. The rocks were slippery from the rain, and the collision drove Peregrin backward. Too late, he realized that the impact was sending them both over the edge.

They hung in midair for an eternal moment. Dextor's eyes were fiery with triumph. "Die, Traveler!" he hissed. Then they fell, still locked in an embrace of battle.

Peregrin tried to twist away from Dextor but found himself held fast. He had an image of rocks jutting out from the cliff face about halfway down. The rocks grew at impossible speed. Then there was a terrific impact, and the two of them were tossed outward through the treetops. He thought he could hear someone screaming his name. Then all went black.

He was floating in an ocean. *It must be an ocean,* he reasoned. He was surrounded on all sides by a dark bouyancy that extended all around, on every side of his body. *How nice,* he thought. *I could just float here forever.*

But where was here? And who was he? Where was he floating to? He had been traveling somewhere. Oh yes, traveling. I am the Traveler. I am Peregrin.

With awareness of his name came a stabbing sensation that pushed back all the beautiful dark floating feeling. Peregrin was suddenly aware that he was in terrible pain. His head felt as if it had been split. His body felt crumpled and battered all over. His legs appeared to be twisted beneath him. He wasn't sure, because he really could not feel them.

Am I dead? he thought as pinwheels of light exploded in his brain. *I can't be. It wouldn't hurt this much.*

The pain increased until he felt like screaming. It cascaded upon him in torrents, lashing him as if he were being whipped from many directions. He became aware of his body resting upon hard rock. His arm was twisted beneath his back, but he was unable to move it.

Near the small of his back, he felt a warmth begin to grow. It was but a pinhole at first, in a blanket of pain, but it slowly began to increase. It became a fiery spark. He became aware of noises within his body and a shifting of parts.

His arm twitched unexpectedly, and he drew it out from under him, able to move it now. It began to burn with the same warmth. He suddenly realized that his arm was repairing itself. Feeling returned to it, flowing down from the shoulder, through the elbow, and into the fingers. It burned terribly but conveyed a certain satisfaction that things were being set right again.

He experienced the same feeling throughout his body. His legs, which he had been sure were broken, suddenly twisted out from underneath him, causing him to gasp. They lay straight, and he could feel the fire spread through them.

Something was tapping his eyes. Opening them, he realized it was raining. All was a blur above him. Then the warmth passed through his face, and his vision cleared. He was lying amid a grove of pine trees, staring up through their grim branches at a gray sky. Why was he here?

"Dextor!" he said aloud, and the sound of his own voice startled him. "Dextor and I fought. We fell. We fell..." He grasped for understanding.

Peregrin pulled himself up into a sitting position. His body was still awash with pain, but the worst had subsided. He saw that he had been lying upon hard ground embedded with small boulders. He glanced about him and started in shock.

Dextor lay not ten feet from him, his eyes still open, and his face frozen in a snarl of rage. His body was folded backward over a medium-sized boulder. He was clearly dead.

Dextor is dead, Peregrin mused. *But I am not. What is happening?*

He looked down at his arm. It was covered in blood from being torn open by the fall. Yet, even as he watched, the gash in his arm began to heal at an impossible rate, closing itself and knitting the flesh together as if nothing had ever happened.

There was an audible click in his head. At once, information began to race through his mind at a terrific rate, as it had in the archive. Only this time there was no pain and no dizziness. Knowledge poured into him like the water had poured from the Waterman's release gate, and as if a fog had lifted, revealing a sun-washed valley, everything became clear. He knew who he was. He knew where he had come from. Most importantly, he now knew why he was here. He knew everything. He remained still and allowed his mind to receive to the thoughts raging through it.

Even after the torrent of information subsided, he did not move but continued to bask in the glow of his revelation. All of his questions had been answered.

"Peregrin!"

He looked up to see Bliss running toward him through the trees. Behind her, Curtan helped Mikkel make his way across the rocky ground.

Bliss ran up and knelt beside him. "Peregrin! Oh! We saw you go over the edge. I thought … I thought …" She stopped and looked at Dextor's crumpled body and then back to Peregrin. "Dextor," she gasped. "But how … how did you … ?" She stood and drew back from him, seeing the expression in his eyes.

"Bliss," he said gently, "you were right. It was knowledge that you saw rising in me. I know now who I am."

Mikkel and Curtan joined them. Mikkel surveyed the scene.

"Peregrin," he said softly. "I am glad to see you alive. But I do not understand how. That's a hundred-foot drop. Dextor lies here broken, but you sit here as if you are unhurt."

Peregrin gathered his legs beneath him and stood. "You are right, Mikkel. Though I am covered in my own blood, I am now unhurt."

Curtan shook his head. "How? How is this possible?"

"Let me show you." He reached out his hand. "Give me your knife, Curtan. I lost mine in the fall."

Curtan looked at Mikkel, who nodded. He unsheathed his knife and laid it in Peregrin's hand. Peregrin held the knife up, examined the blade, and then laid it upon his arm and slashed it open.

Bliss cried out, and Curtan stepped forward. Only Mikkel remained impassive, fixing his gaze upon Peregrin.

Peregrin held out his bleeding arm and grasped the flesh, pulling it back from the wound. "Look," he said. "Here is your answer. Here are all the answers."

As they gazed at the wound, the blood flow slowed and then stopped. The flesh began to heal itself, closing the wound before their eyes. But not before they had seen the gleam of white metal where a human bone should have been.

Bliss put her hands to her face and stepped back. "No! This cannot be. You cannot be a ... a ..." She could not finish.

Peregrin nodded. "I am. I am what you call a Sheen. I was built five years before the Great Destruction, in a last desperate attempt to avert it. That having failed, I was reprogrammed to sleep until ... until my father's people needed me."

"Your father?" said Mikkel.

"The man I called my father. The man who built me and programmed me for this day. The man who ... loved me. It was he who invented the Sheens, and I was his greatest creation. He created me, hoping he could save the world he felt responsible for destroying."

"Your father ..." Mikkel repeated.

"The man I called my father, Mikkel. His name was O'Keefe ... Daniel O'Keefe."

Bliss made a small, inarticulate sound. Mikkel took a step backward and looked at Peregrin incredulously.

"True son," he whispered, his voice sounding like a breeze through the pine tops. "O'Keefe's true son."

XIV
SHEEN

No one spoke. Raindrops pattered through the leaves around them, filling the air with a snapping, crackling sound that could have been a blaze rather than water. They stood, staring at Peregrin, staring at one another, in the silence of one who wakes from a dream of light to find the room in utter blackness.

It was Mikkel who finally dared to disturb the silence. "We must return to Archiva now. Let us not speak of this to anyone until ... until we have had time."

They wrapped Dextor's body in a blanket and laid him across Carbon's back, behind the saddle, tying him down loosely so that he would not slip off. Curtan helped Mikkel to mount, and they set out slowly, picking their way through the valley toward the south.

As they set out, Peregrin was surprised to find the knife he had lost in the fall still in its leather sheath, dangling from the lower branches of a pine tree. He pulled it down and tied it around his waist once more.

Though the west entrance to Archiva was only a few miles from the spot where Peregrin and Dextor fell, the remainder of their journey could have been a thousand miles. They spoke little, each one submerged in a mire of thought and emotion. The valley in which the Waterman had unleashed the reservoir had returned to its former state, the water having drained off to the river below. Only the scoured hillside, uprooted trees, and debris from the waterwheel remained to testify to the power of his last act. They passed through the area in silence.

As they entered Archiva, they were met with hailed greetings and cheers. Though still dealing with the loss of so many and the violence they had suffered, the people of Archiva had experienced some jubilation now that the crises had been resolved and Archiva would survive.

Word spread quickly, however, that they had returned bearing a body. By the time they reached the water pump, Morgan and Merida had come to meet them.

Morgan took hold of Carbon's reins. "Peace to your heart, Mikkel," he said. Then, seeing the expression of grief in Mikkel's face, he looked at the body behind him. "Who is this that you bear?"

Mikkel looked about him, eyeing the sizable crowd that had gathered. "It is Dextor, Morgan," he said after a long moment. "We have brought the body of Dextor."

There were gasps and murmurs about them. Curtan came forward and untied the ropes securing Dextor. He laid the body on the ground and opened the blanket.

Morgan gazed at the broken form. "How did this happen?"

"He fell," Mikkel said flatly. "He attacked ... attacked us on a high trail, and in the ensuing fight, he fell from a cliff."

"That is all?"

"That is all I can say now," Mikkel answered. "Our hearts are heavy, Morgan. We need to rest."

Morgan looked as if he wanted to hear more but then nodded. "When shall we hear your words?"

"Call the council," Peregrin answered quickly. "Tell them to convene in two hours time. All will be explained."

Morgan looked at Mikkel, who nodded. He called for two men. "Take Dextor's body into the nearest guest quarters until the council has decided where he will be laid to rest."

Curtan helped Mikkel to dismount. Mikkel glanced at Peregrin and then shook his head. "I am tired," he said. "Curtan, help me to my quarters." He turned and hobbled off in the direction of his home with Curtan at his side. Neither of them looked at Peregrin or said anything.

Peregrin watched them go. Bliss still stood beside him, motionless, as the crowd dispersed.

"What will you tell them?" she said at last. He raised an eyebrow, so she continued, "At the council meeting, what will you tell them?"

Peregrin shook his head. "I don't know. I guess I will have to tell them the truth."

"The truth?" Bliss said. "What is the truth you will tell them?"

He looked at her, feeling as if he were standing upon a wind-scoured barren mountain. "I will tell them what I have learned— that I am not human."

Bliss sighed. "The truth," she said again. She bowed her head. "Mikkel is right. Our hearts are too heavy. I need to rest." She started off and then paused and looked back. "Peregrin," she said, "when the time comes to share your truth, remember my words from when you first stood before the council. Peace to your heart, Peregrin." She turned and strode off quickly.

Peregrin watched her go. "They're both right," he said softly. "I'm so damned tired. Funny thing for a machine to feel."

He slowly walked to his quarters, entered, and bolted the door. He lay down, knowing now that he could go days without physical rest if it were required. Yet he needed rest now. Something within him felt as though it were slowly being twisted, wrung out of every drop of energy or willpower. He closed his eyes and slept.

He found himself back in the cave of white metal, sitting on the edge of the table in the center of the room. O'Keefe was there, gazing at him.

"Now you must sleep, Peregrin, my true son," he said. "How I wish I could be with you when you awake."

"Father, I'm afraid."

"Of course you are. You will face so many challenges when you awake. But they will all seem as nothing when you remember who you truly are. It is then that you must not falter. Although you will possess knowledge of all things, the one thing I cannot give you is hope. This you must find on your own."

"Will it really be that difficult?"

"Mara said it would be like dying. A fearsome thing until you pass into it. Then it is a good friend."

"I miss Mara. I've missed her since she died last January."

A tear teetered on the ledge of O'Keefe's eye. "I know. I have missed her every minute. I am but a hollow shell without her. But it won't be long for me. I will see her soon."

"Do you really believe there is something beyond death?"

O'Keefe paused. "I am a man of science, Peregrin. Yet all my science has crumbled around me. Everything I put my trust in has failed me. It is as if I walk aimlessly in a dark forest, not knowing the trail. But Mara always told me to look for the light through the trees and let it be my guide. She said there was a light beyond the knowledge of science that would guide me when all else had failed me. Just before she died, she spoke of that light, as though it were flooding the room. Yes, I believe there is something. It's all I have left to believe in."

"Will I ever see that light?"

"I do not know, my son. I hope that you may, but that is up to a power beyond mine. I only know that Mara said that when your past was revealed to you, your present would become clear, but your future would depend on the light and the water."

"Did she ever say anything that was not a riddle?"

O'Keefe laughed. "No. She did not." He pushed back on Peregrin's chest, laying him down into the padded frame. "Sleep now, Peregrin. Rest well, my son, my true son."

He opened his eyes. Someone was rapping at the door. "Come in," he said. The door was pushed on but met resistance from the bolt. Peregrin groaned. Hold on. He stood, went to the door, and slid the bolt. The door opened to reveal Curtan.

"Peregrin," he said, and his voice was devoid of emotion.

"Curtan."

"Two hours have passed since we returned. The council is convening."

Peregrin blinked. "Two hours? Already? Are you sure?"

"You're the Sheen. You tell me." Curtan's voice was like shattering ice.

"Something you wish to say, Curtan?"

Curtan gazed at him. "I don't know what to say. I cannot reason like a Guardian or sort out emotions like a Seeker. I am a Ranger. I act by instinct and skill. What you have shown us is beyond me. I do not know how to act."

"Are you angry with me?"

"No. I fought at your side, and you were true to Archiva and the Waterman. I bled with you and would have died for you. No, I am not angry."

"What then?"

"I am afraid of you." He turned and walked off.

Peregrin watched him as he strode rapidly away, tense, as if expecting to be attacked from behind at any minute. He felt a great hollowness within him, as though he were a dry well down which children were throwing pebbles to hear the clattering echoes. "Curtan," he murmured softly. "Curtan, my friend. I'm sorry."

Slowly he set out to the council building. Evening was approaching, and the long shadows thrown by the westbound sun made the valley look distorted. He paused and considered his own shadow stretched out to more than twice his size to the east. *Maybe that's the real me,* he thought, *a long, drawn out shadow of a man.* He shook his head and continued.

The council room was filled with voices when he entered, as several discussions were going on at once. Morgan motioned Peregrin to the chair he had sat in when he first addressed the council. Mikkel sat beside Morgan with his hands clasped before him on the table and his head bowed. It suddenly occurred to Peregrin that he looked old and tired.

Peregrin looked to Bliss's chair and found it empty. A quick glance about the room confirmed his fear. Bliss was not present. *She should be here,* he thought. The vacant space amid all of these living, talking, breathing people was like a glaring accusation. He suddenly felt like running out, fleeing into the coming night, and not looking back.

He heard the door open behind him and did not need to look to know it was she. He could smell her, identify her breathing, experience her without looking. She had stopped just within the door and was standing very still. He saw Morgan look up at her and smile. Then his brow furrowed, and the smile vanished.

Bliss moved around to her chair. Morgan tapped the table with his gavel. All of the Guardians stood. He turned to Bliss.

"Bliss, these days have seen many things. We need to remember who we are. Would you honor us with the Song of O'Keefe?"

Bliss nodded and began to raise her arms. She stopped midway, glanced at Peregrin, and then quickly looked away. After a moment's silence, she dropped her arms and said softly, "I'm sorry. I cannot."

Morgan opened his mouth but closed it again and nodded. "Very well. Who knows the depth of our wounds? Let us be seated."

The Guardians sat down. Morgan looked about. "Guardians of Archiva," he said, "our soul lies bleeding. Though the threat of Dextor is ended, we now stand in the knowledge of violence and death. Many have died. Many have killed. Dextor himself lies dead within Archiva. It is a time of sorrow unparalleled since the Great Destruction. Now is the time for those who bear the guardianship of Archiva upon themselves to work for healing. It is time to renew our dedication to the Creed of O'Keefe. Only by reaffirming our belief that human beings can live without violence and killing can we regain the path of peace."

"But is the Creed true?" said Mikkel. "Are human beings able to live without violence?"

Murmurs rippled throughout the room. Morgan turned. "Mikkel, what do you mean?"

Mikkel gripped the table and pulled himself into standing position, keeping both of his hands on the table for support. "What do I mean?" he said. "I am not sure myself. We tried to hold to the Creed even in the face of Dextor's threat. Still, it was necessary to rise to the defense of Archiva—not a place or a creed, but our spouses, our children, our brothers and sisters. They were worth fighting for and even dying for. When I led the people of Archiva into battle, it was for my children's sake, Cornel and Janel. I realized then that I would even kill if it meant protecting them.

"Perhaps this is the fate of our race," he continued, looking about at the shocked faces around the table. "Though we refuse to embrace violence, perhaps there are times when we cannot avoid it. I wonder if it's just the way we have been created."

The table broke out into an uproar. Many of the Guardians rose, shouting. "You're mad, Mikkel! What of the Creed? You've gone too far! Are you possessed by Dextor?" Mikkel gazed at them impassively.

Morgan pounded the table with his gavel. "Guardians!" he shouted. "Guardians of Archiva! Get hold of yourselves!" The shouting continued, unabated.

Bliss rose quietly and spread her arms outward, as if embracing the entire table. Softly she began to sing a melancholy tune:

> *When the daylight hours wither in the wind.*
> *When the darkness leeches into your mind.*
> *Close your eyes to see the light.*
> *Remember me, remember me.*
> *For I sleep in your heart.*
> *Do not surrender to the dark.*

Slowly, the noise in the room subsided. One by one, the Guardians sat down as Bliss sang the verse again and again, her voice weaving around them like a blanket. Finally, she let her voice fade off, leaving the room in utter silence.

Peregrin looked about the table. The Guardians sat with closed eyes, their hands folded in front of them. He realized he could hear all of their heartbeats. As the silence pervaded the room, he noted that the beats were becoming more and more in time with one another until it sounded like one beat, calm and serene. *So this is what it means to commune,* he thought.

Morgan opened his eyes and sighed. "Once again, Bliss, you have blessed us with a rare gift. Guardians of Archiva, let us follow the Song of Mara. We must not give in to quarreling and accusing one another. We must not let the dark emotions of the past weeks destroy our union with one another. Mikkel, please explain your words."

Mikkel looked about the table. "These past moments explain it better than I can. Where did this furious uproar come from? Dextor lies dead in our midst. Yet he, too, sat at this very table and spoke of peace. He was not evil. But he blamed the Creed for allowing the death of his love, and his resentment and anger led him deeper into darkness. Where did that darkness come from unless it was already within him?"

The table was silent, so he continued. "My love, my Joy, was also killed these many years ago. Her last wish was that I should not kill, even to avenge her death. At the time, I felt I had withstood the greatest challenge of the Creed.

"Yet, when we had defeated all but a small band of Dextor's force, I thought of all the pain and destruction he had caused, and I longed to see him suffer and die. I longed to kill him myself. If it was not for the intervention of Bliss and whatever force that worked through her that day, I believe I would have. I would have irrevocably abandoned the Creed and sought another's death out of revenge and hate.

"Then, when Dextor attacked Peregrin upon the slope, I found myself hoping that Peregrin would kill him." He slapped the table suddenly. "I still wanted Dextor to die! Where does this darkness come from? That has been my question since our return to Archiva. I can only conclude that the same darkness that Dextor followed after the death of Franceen also dwells in me. It was ever present in me. I only had to reach out and grasp it. There was, I saw, no difference between Dextor and myself. I was as capable of great evil, as he was capable of great good.

"Even now I look around at all of you. You sit at this table because you have dedicated your lives to the path of peace. You have striven to live by the Creed. Yet the darkness is there. It is close to each of us. Good and evil are as shadows and light in the early morning. They cannot exclude each other, for they give each other meaning. It has become my belief that we are beings of light and dark, of good and evil. We seek what is good, but we will never be able to truly choose the light, unless... unless we dare to look into the darkness and accept that it belongs to us." He paused. The Guardians remained in silence. Many had bowed their heads.

Finally Merida spoke. "What then? Does this mean our Creed is a lie? Have we pursued peace to no avail?"

"No," Bliss said softly. "Our Creed is true. Yet what Mikkel says is also true. To seek the path of peace means to choose. All who would choose good must first grapple with their ability to choose evil. Only then can the Creed find truth in our lives."

"What does this mean for Archiva?" Morgan said.

Mikkel turned to him slowly. "It means we must come out of hiding. We cannot bring peace to the world by surrounding ourselves with hills and forests, pretending we do not exist. We cannot rebuild a world of peace by indoctrinating our children and the few people we deem worthy to join us."

"What should we do then?" asked Janette.

"We should take our stand in the world," Mikkel said. "Corlee and the Terists have shown us that many people long to turn from violence but do not know there is another alternative. It is our mission to give it to them. We must allow the course of our river to change. We have already begun this process by accepting Dextor's men into our midst. Let us continue around the bend."

"But what of all O'Keefe taught us?" Morgan said, spreading his arms around him. "What of the way of life that he himself established?"

"O'Keefe never meant for Archiva to remain hidden forever," Mikkel answered. "These hills have been our cocoon, to protect us until we were strong enough to come out. It is time to emerge. It is time to evolve beyond our sheltered way of life. As the husk of the cocoon must fall away from the butterfly," he looked directly at Peregrin, "so must life in Archiva as we know it fall from us if we are to fulfill O'Keefe's vision."

He sat back down. The silence settled upon them all like a woolen blanket, binding them beneath a heaviness that was both comforting and oppressive but not easily disturbed. After minutes that could have been lifetimes, Peregrin slowly stood.

"Guardians of Archiva," he said quietly. "I marvel at the strength that you give to one another. From the moment I spoke the name of Dextor to this moment, I have seen you support one another through a complete upheaval of your existence. You have seen fear, rage, suspicion, betrayal, war, death, and despair. Yet here you remain, pledging yourselves to a Creed of peace and to your future. You are a strong people, and I know O'Keefe would be proud."

"How do you know this?" asked Derth.

Peregrin smiled at him. "I know this because I knew O'Keefe. The time has come to share an astonishing truth with you—truth that has been revealed only this very day. It is the truth about myself, about Archiva, about O'Keefe, and about you. It will be a hard truth, but you have the strength for it."

He looked about the table at their puzzled expressions. Mikkel gazed at him steadily. Bliss sat with head bowed and hands clasped. Peregrin took a deep breath and continued. "As Mikkel has said, Dextor attacked us as we made our way along a narrow trail on a steep hillside. More specifically, he attacked me. It was his intention to kill me, even if it meant killing himself. He succeeded. In our fight he lunged at me, and we both fell nearly a hundred feet to the rocky ground below."

Morgan glanced at Mikkel. "Mikkel, what is this? What is he saying?"

Mikkel turned his head toward him. "The truth. Listen to him."

"Indeed," Peregrin said, "listen well. Much of what you have believed before this is wrong. But I can set things straight now. Dextor and I fell together. We died. At least, Dextor did. But I awoke to severe pain and the experience of my body repairing itself with great speed. By the time the others had gotten down to me, I was fully healed and unhurt. It was then that a gate somewhere in my mind opened, and I was flooded with the answers to all my questions.

"The fact is that I am what you call a Sheen. I was built by O'Keefe himself. He built me to help him avert the Great Destruction. When this failed, he programmed me to sleep until the time came for me to return."

Morgan started to his feet, as well as many of the Guardians. "Mikkel, what … ?"

Mikkel held up a hand. "Peace, Morgan. Peace, all of you. It is true. Bliss and I have both seen. Peregrin is a Sheen. Sit down now and remain silent." They sat back down.

Peregrin stretched forth with arm and palm upraised. "If you wish, I can show you the proof of this."

"No!" said Bliss, jerking her head up sharply. "Mikkel and I have seen. It is enough. He is a Sheen."

"Very well then," Peregrin said. "This is the truth about me. Now I must tell you the truth about yourselves, that is, about what happened to the world and how Archiva came to be.

"As the Waterman told it to me, you believe that the Sheens longed to be free of their masters and, therefore, struck a bargain with the Terists for their freedom. This resulted in the Sheen War, which led to the eventual destruction of the world.

"This is incorrect. The Sheens were innocent in this affair because, outside of myself, they were never capable of independent thought or longing. They were used, not by the Terists, but by the leaders who wished to eradicate the Terists.

"Archiva itself already existed, though in a different way. The ruins were a thriving town centering around a government building. What few people knew was that under that building lay a huge vault containing machinery, tools, and weapons of every kind. This town, which we call Archiva, was also a secret place, closed to outsiders. Beneath this very building lies another vault, containing the true wealth of the ages—information on every subject one could imagine. The two vaults formed a government museum of sorts, which no one was allowed to see.

"The tunnels that you use were also built by the leaders. The council building in which we speak was built to monitor and maintain the archives of knowledge and machines that the government had amassed. It was a project that lost interest and funding after the Sheens were created. The whole complex was eventually abandoned.

"O'Keefe always felt responsible for this action by the leaders. He was the director of this entire complex—the first Archivist, if you will. He loved knowledge and would spend days in the archive, pouring over bits and pieces of information that others had discovered. His intellect was vast, and he was able to connect knowledge from different sources. He and his colleagues here built a laboratory. It was there that he discovered how to alter the genetic makeup of tissue so that it could regenerate and duplicate itself. It was there that he built the first Sheen."

There were gasps from around the table, and a few of the Guardians almost stood. Peregrin held up his hand. "I can see this shocks you. But it is true. O'Keefe was the scientist most responsible for the creation of the Sheens.

"The Sheens were perfect imitations of human beings without the limitations that had slowed human progress through the centuries. They were real flesh, blood, sweat, and everything that comprises the human body, created and grown from human DNA. Only they could repair themselves immediately upon injury. They converted food to energy, as did humans, but far more efficiently, thereby needing little food or sleep. They were capable of accessing immense information instantly. Only two components of the Sheen were not human. Their skeleton was made of pure titanium and a beta-phase alloy of titanium and vandium with poly fiber for ligaments. Their brains were really microchip processors embedded in human brain tissue."

Peregrin paused and shook his head. "Poor O'Keefe. His only downfall was that he believed in science as an ultimate good. He cared little for politics and ambition. But others did. While he saw the Sheens as a benefit to humanity, others saw a tool for power and control.

"The leaders seized upon O'Keefe's discovery. Of course, he was handsomely rewarded. He was taken from this place and put in charge of all government genetic research. Believing that humanity was on the verge of a new era, he began to build Sheens.

"O'Keefe's vision was to create servants who could help humanity advance. But they had no emotions. In his youth and excitement, O'Keefe felt this was a good attribute. His creations could work unfettered by the mire of human emotion that, as an avid scientist, he believed to be a weakness in human beings. And his dream was realized. Sheens were used to build underwater laboratories, to work in space, to design and build great skyscrapers. For more than two decades, O'Keefe lived under the illusion that his Sheens could only bring good to humanity.

"Then he began to notice signs that all was not right. Sheens, he found, were being used by the military to develop and test new weapons of mass destruction. Sheens were being used to assassinate leaders of other countries. Sheens were being used to design spying equipment and tracking devices so the leaders could better control the people.

"By this time O'Keefe was married to Mara. She was as intuitive as he was practical. They knew if they protested the government's use of the Sheens, they would be killed. So O'Keefe quietly retired, citing health problems, and together they fled to the very laboratory where he had created the first Sheen. It had been abandoned and sealed, but he knew the codes needed to gain access. That laboratory lies precisely forty-seven feet beneath this room, just above the Archive.

"There he labored to build a Sheen that could think for itself and, more importantly, that could experience emotion. He hoped that this Sheen could reprogram the others so that they would refuse to perform any work that was not for the direct benefit of all humanity.

"Mara began to have dreams, however. She foresaw a terrible destruction that was to occur. She convinced O'Keefe that the greatest hope for humanity lay, not in trying to heal its wounds, but in starting again. The world had come too far down the path of greed and violence, she said. The only hope now was to create a community that would cherish peace and disavow the destructive tendencies of humanity. And so, the idea for Archiva came to be.

"Meanwhile, the leaders had been experiencing more and more difficulty with the Terists. The proper word for them was terrorist—a name that aptly describes them. They lived by disrupting order and spreading fear through planned acts of destruction. They cared little who was hurt or killed, as long as their demands were met.

"By the time O'Keefe had created me, Mara said it was too late to avert the destruction. Our primary task became to try to preserve what we could. The vault of the Archive was already well stocked with books concerning all aspects of science, machinery, trades, and skills. We simply supplemented what was there with poetry, fiction, art, and music.

"We set out to preserve the greatest treasure of all—people. Like Seekers, O'Keefe, Mara, and I searched out masters of every trade and assessed their potential for peace. Many gladly joined us, for the world had become a dangerous and frightening place to live. We laid in supplies and tools of every kind.

"The end came when the leaders hit upon a plan to eradicate the terrorists for good. The Sheens were used to create a supervirus that would attack the human nervous system, causing an increase in a person's primary emotions. Terrorists, it was reasoned, were people of rage and violence. Therefore, this virus would spur them to uncontrollable rage, inciting them to destroy one another. Certain 'hotspots' of terrorist activity would be blanketed with the virus, brought there by Sheens, despite the presence of innocent civilians.

"It worked well. Whole cities destroyed themselves. But the virus was much stronger than originally thought. Not only did it overwhelm the entire cerebral cortex, causing madness and death, but it could survive outside of a host. It spread quickly, and by the time the government realized its mistake, it was too late. The virus had taken root in the general populace.

"The end came swiftly. Madness was the rule of the day. People rioted about in the streets of the cities, burning and killing. The fires raged unabated for weeks, until everything was reduced to cinders.

"O'Keefe and the scientists he had gathered here labored to counteract the virus. Since the virus itself did not destroy its victim, they reasoned that controlling the madness would allow the body to overcome it on its own. By the time it spread to the smaller towns, they had developed a serum that would neutralize its effects during the period of infection until one's own immune system was able to handle it.

"By that time, however, they could only tend to the people within Archiva. The rest of the world burned and raged, with millions upon millions dying. The smoke and ash from the fires blotted out the sun and became so thick that the land was plunged into an unnatural winter. Millions more died from sickness and hunger.

"Many of those whom O'Keefe had brought to Archiva also died during this time. Sickness, despair, and grief took a heavy toll. Seeing all that humanity had brought upon itself, O'Keefe realized that human beings could not be trusted to return to the knowledge they had acquired. Together with Mara and the other leaders, they formed the first council and vowed that those within Archiva should live by a code of peace. They created the Creed, and each person who survived the Great Destruction swore to live by it. This has been the guiding light of Archiva for more than a century—to abhor violence and to embrace peace. This is your story. This is how you came to be. I was there. I am witness to it all."

Peregrin looked about the table. There was complete silence among the Guardians. He slowly sat down. Most of the Guardians were looking down at the table. A few were gazing toward Mikkel and Morgan, perhaps seeking some guidance from them.

Bliss was looking straight at him. Their gazes met, and Peregrin found he could not turn away. Her eyes were not accusing, yet he felt guilty of some great betrayal. It was as if she were studying him, weighing him in some unknown scale, assessing his words. After a lifetime, she rose and looked about the table.

"Fellow Guardians," she said softly, "Peregrin brings to us a story that shakes the very core of our life here in Archiva. Indeed, all that he has done has been a challenge to us. He came to us a traveler not knowing his past, and now he reveals our own past to us. He came gladly embracing our commitment to peace, yet he led us to war. He stands before us a Sheen—a machine created by our own founder, yet he lays bare the human roots of our existence."

"What then, Bliss?" rumbled Stevan. "Are we to curse the day Peregrin came among us? Are we to disbelieve what he tells us?"

"No to both, Stevan," Bliss answered. "It was you, Bernhadette, who spoke of Peregrin as a riddle. His answer was that he was a riddle within a riddle, that is, that Archiva itself was a question mark. Perhaps, as Peregrin faces the answers to his search, we are being challenged to face answers to our own as well.

"But this is too much for us now," she continued. "I can sense it in you all. Let us adjourn for a time. Let us rest this night and come together at dawn. We need to absorb what we have heard. We need to find our balance once more."

There were murmurs of assent around the table. Morgan stood up. "So let it be," he said. "Go forth in peace, Guardians of Archiva. May peace be the bed on which you rest."

The Guardians arose and left in silence. Only Peregrin, Bliss, and Mikkel did not move. Morgan hesitated and then left, closing the council doors behind him.

With just the three of them, the room took on the aspect of a great ancient chamber whose inhabitants were but memories echoing in the vaulted ceiling. They were intruders, daring to disturb the dust of history.

Mikkel spoke after a long silence. "Well, the Wanderer has returned, and Archiva will never be the same. Mara's prophecy is fulfilled."

Bliss turned to Mikkel. "You knew of this?"

Mikkel shook his head. "I knew a prophecy that I was sure related to Peregrin. I was right about that. About the rest—about him being a Sheen and all that about O'Keefe—no, I did not know."

"Nor did I, Bliss," Peregrin said quickly. "The information I just shared is almost as new to me as is to the council. Until Dextor and I fell off that cliff, I had given up on finding the answers to my past." He paused and sighed. "It may have been better if I hadn't found them, but I didn't have a choice."

"What about that memory you had about being chosen for an experiment?" Mikkel said.

"It was a ruse. There was an experiment—cryogenics it was called—but it was a failure. O'Keefe hoped it would allow him to come back himself, but we could not even freeze a chicken and bring it back to life. Still, since there really was an experiment, O'Keefe used it to program a false memory into my brain in case I found the Archive before I was ready to remember everything. It was plausible enough to fool even me, which was its real purpose.

"I think it was just as important that we should not know about all of this until we were ready," Mikkel said.

"What makes you think we are ready now?" Bliss said sharply. "What Peregrin has told us completely changes our understanding of ourselves. I don't think I was ready for that. Looking around the table, I don't think anyone was."

"Nonetheless, Dextor's threat has come to an end," Mikkel said. "Yet the challenge his threat brought to us remains. Do we cringe behind our hills, hoarding our peace and our knowledge? Or we become visible to the world? Yes, Bliss, I think Peregrin's revelation comes at the perfect time."

"How so?"

"Peregrin has told us that our past is not what we thought it to be. If we are brave enough to face a new past, perhaps we can dare to face a new future."

"Bold words, Mikkel," Bliss said. "And what of you, Peregrin? Where do you stand?"

Peregrin gazed at her. Something in his chest hurt. He looked at the table and rubbed his forehead. "I don't know, Bliss. I have received so much knowledge, and I feel as though I know so little. I, too, must face a new past in order to face my future."

Bliss's eyes softened. "Is it hard for you? You have discovered that you are a Sheen. What does this do to you?"

Peregrin shook his head. "I cannot say. Up until the moment I fell, I thought I was a human—a very confused, uncertain human being. Now that I know I am a machine, I feel even more confused and uncertain. And if I'm not human, why do I feel this way? Why does all of this hurt me inside as much as it does?"

Bliss actually smiled. "There's more to being human than being conceived, Peregrin. Don't you remember my words at your first council meeting?"

"No."

"I said I was convinced you were a true child of O'Keefe and a true human being. I still believe this to be the truth."

"How can this be, Bliss? I am a Sheen. How can you say I am human?"

"That is the question you must yet answer." Bliss got up and began to walk toward the door. She paused and laid a hand upon his shoulder. "Do not be afraid, Peregrin. The path lies before you. Walk it in peace." She left and quietly shut the door.

Peregrin looked at Mikkel. "Mara's prophecy is fulfilled? What about *Archiva shall fall around him?*"

"It has fallen," Mikkel said. "When you fell off that cliff, Archiva fell with you. Until you came, each day went as the day before. You come, speak the name of Dextor, and we are plunged into terror, war, and death. Terists have come to live among us, and we find that you are a Sheen built by our most revered leader. Nothing remains the same—not our past and not our future. Yes, the Archiva I grew up in has fallen around you, Peregrin. But now I see that this is not to be feared. Mara foresaw it, and O'Keefe prepared for it. Dextor's threat would have destroyed us, either from within or without. O'Keefe sent you to help us grow past our understanding and our fears. You have brought us survival, Peregrin, not destruction."

Peregrin did not know how to respond. He gazed at the man who had exhibited such reserve toward him when he had come to Archiva and who now so surely affirmed all he had done. He was like a fulcrum on which the life of Archiva balanced. No, he was more like a hinge on which it swung open toward the future. He had suffered the fears and doubts of his people, led them into battle, and now stood ready to lead them into a new world.

"You truly are the Archivist," Peregrin said, smiling.

Mikkel smiled back. "Thank you," he said softly. "Thank you."

"Doesn't it bother you that I am a Sheen?"

Mikkel cocked his head slightly to the right. "No ... no, it does not. This surprises me as well. I now know that you are a Sheen. But you are still Peregrin, whom I came to know as a man. Mara called you O'Keefe's true son. That alone is enough for me."

"How? How can that be enough?"

"You said O'Keefe created the Sheens, but they could not think or feel on their own. Then he labored to create you, a Sheen that could. He labored, I think, to create a Sheen who could know compassion, anger, doubt, and all of the emotions that drive us. I think he wanted to create a Sheen that could choose its own path in life, the way every human being must. You were his true son; not just a machine he built. He created you, but he did not control you. You were free to become Peregrin as you chose, wandering, as all human beings do, through all of the confusing experiences of life."

Mikkel stood up. "By now, the words of this meeting will have swept through Archiva. I must go to assure the people. Try to rest, Peregrin. The dawn will bring new challenges and new hopes." He left the room, leaving the door open.

Peregrin remained seated at the great table. It occurred to him that O'Keefe himself had sat here, at this table, with all of the first inhabitants of Archiva, dreaming of a new world from the ashes of the old. It was not simply the physical existence of human beings he struggled to preserve but, as he used to say, to, "Turn your back on the darkness from within." That's what separated a human being from an animal that looked like one. A human being, O'Keefe said, was a human creature that cherished other human creatures enough to choose the light and reject the darkness—to choose to be truly human.

"All Archiva is here with us," he whispered. He sat in the council room a long while, listening to the silence.

XV
LIGHT

Bliss was waiting for him when he emerged from his quarters before dawn. For most of the night, he had lain on his bed, listening and pondering. For some time he slept, or at least rested. Actually, Peregrin had simply ordered himself to become inactive. He now knew that he could do this.

He rose before the first light of dawn. *It's strange, being a machine that can feel,* he thought as he dressed and girded on the knife he had taken from Crown. *Seems like so long ago, but it was not even a year. Might as well have been a hundred years, though. I'm not the man I was then.* He chuckled. *Now there's a true statement!*

There were so many things he was aware of now. All of his senses had been sharpened in a quickening that began as a prisoner in Dextor's canyon and completed with his fall from the cliff. He could access information about any subject immediately if he desired. Yet emotions were still like a misty spring morning— beautiful, fragrant, and very confusing.

He opened the door, ready to tackle what the day would bring, and there was Bliss. She stood a few feet in front of the door, smiling at him. He pulled up short, caught by surprise and then overwhelmed with gratitude that she was there.

She laughed, free and unfettered like a swooping swallow. The sound of it washed over Peregrin like a refreshing shower, and he could not help but laugh with her.

"Aha!" Bliss said. "Once again I have caught the great Traveler unaware!"

"So it would seem," Peregrin said, and without even thinking he reached out and embraced her, picking her completely off the ground. Bliss hugged him back. When he set her back down, she stepped back.

"It has been a difficult night," she said without accusation. "I did not sleep well, thinking of all that has come to be."

"I know," he answered. "I was awake for most of the night."

"I thought that you and I might climb the elbow before the sun rises. There is something I wish for you to see. It is a difficult climb in the dark, but I'm sure you can manage."

"I'm sure we can," he answered. He took her arm, and they walked together to the elbow. With his heightened senses, he had no difficulty locating handholds with which to climb the stone. He allowed Bliss to go first and instructed her where to reach and step, ready to catch her if she should fall. She listened and followed his guidance, though he had a suspicion she knew how to make the climb perfectly well on her own.

They reached the top and sat down, dangling their legs over the edge. "Look down there," Bliss said. "Outside of a few torches, Archiva is shrouded in night. We sit in utter blackness with our backs to a cliff. Perhaps it will remain this way forever."

"Don't be silly, Bliss. The sun will rise soon."

"How can you be so sure? Perhaps it will not rise today."

"I've seen it rise a thousand times."

"But how do you know it will rise today? Maybe today will be the day it does not rise."

"It will rise."

"How can you be sure?"

"I trust it to rise."

Bliss was silent a moment. Then she spoke softly. "So do I, Peregrin. This was the answer I found in the night. This was the assurance I received. The sun will rise."

Peregrin looked at her. "You are a rare and insightful woman. You are an emerald among the stones."

"Wait till you see me when it's not dark," she said with a laugh. "I will show you a marvel today."

"Bliss, where do you stand with all that has happened? I mean, how are you dealing with the fact that I am a Sheen?"

She looked at him. "That fact was a major contributor to my sleepless night. During those long hours of darkness, I came to this conviction: you are Peregrin. This is your fate. I met you as Peregrin, and it is as Peregrin that I…" she paused. Then he could feel her smile in the darkness. "It is as Peregrin that I love you."

Peregrin was stunned by her words. "Bliss, I—," he began.

"Shh," she said quietly. "Be still now, and let it lie. The sun is rising."

Across the valley from them, an outcropping of rock high on the hillside had caught fire and was beginning to glow with a deep orange red hue. Peregrin realized that the first rays of dawn were peering over the hillside behind him and reflecting upon this rock. Seated upon the ledge as they were overshadowed by the cliff, he had not even noticed the growing light.

"I call that rock *the day-breaker*," Bliss said. "It is the first thing to catch the sun's rays and reflect them back. You can only see it from here on the elbow. Very few people know of it. Waterman and I used to meet here often before dawn to witness this moment. Joy, when she was alive, and Merida as well, would come here.'

She paused. "My heart still cries when I think of Joy. She was more than my sister. We shared a special silence—a language that was all our own. But in moments like this, I experience her presence, and I know she is alive and well.

"She would be glad I brought you here this day. Waterman, Joy, Merida and only a few others—we had our own secret circle beyond the Guardians. Now I have brought you into it as well." She laughed. "You've come to the innermost circle of Archiva, Peregrin."

"And what does one call the circle beyond the Guardians?" he said with a laugh.

"The Circle of Peace," Bliss answered. "Only those whose hearts abide in peace may enter this circle. Only those who have walked through the shadows, trusting that the sun will rise."

Peregrin was silent a long moment as he watched the glow from the rock intensify like pulsing embers. "You are truly a child of O'Keefe, Bliss," he said.

"I am a child of the light," she said in return. "And a child of peace."

They said no more, settling into a deep silence that seemed to lay on them like a blanket woven by a parent's loving hands, watching while the sun gently brushed back the darkness and embraced Archiva. As he sat, hardly daring to breathe lest he destroy the moment, Peregrin discovered that the less he thought, the more he felt a unity with Bliss, Archiva, and all its people.

Most of the council members looked as if they, too, had remained awake for most of the night. *It's not easy to learn that your founder may have been responsible for the fall of civilization,* Peregrin thought.

Waterman would have faced the news with a laugh and gone to bed, but few are so lighthearted.

Morgan tapped his gavel for silence. "Fellow Guardians," he said, "yesterday's council is one we will not soon forget. Our friend Peregrin, whom this very council welcomed and who led us to victory against Dextor, has revealed himself to be a Sheen, created by our very own founder, O'Keefe.

"He has gone on to tell us that it was O'Keefe who designed and built the Sheens, which were then misused by those in power for purposes of control and violence. This caused the Great Destruction and the chaos that governs the world outside of Archiva."

Morgan paused. "I must admit, I always wondered why our Creed included the mention of the Sheens as an imperative. If your words are true, Peregrin, O'Keefe experienced firsthand how something created for good can be twisted to evil."

Peregrin nodded. "My words are true, Morgan. O'Keefe included the word *Sheen* in the Creed to warn you about that very tendency in human beings. As you have correctly interpreted through the years, the command forbids use of any created thing for the purpose of violence. But his reasons were also deeply personal. It was a kind of public confession and warning."

Morgan smiled slightly. "Indeed, I think it helps us to better understand our founder. But this is not all. Mikkel has challenged us to change the course of Archiva's future by becoming visible to the world. Your words about the darkness within us, Mikkel, are most disturbing."

"This is good," Mikkel said. "I would be concerned if you were not disturbed by them."

"Be that as it may, it appears an hour of decision is upon us. First, Peregrin, we must look to you. You came among us a stranger, a wanderer. You quickly became our friend. Next, you became the leader of those who wished to resist the threat of Dextor with force.

You went forth believing that you would give your life in battle with Dextor. You have proven yourself true to Archiva time and again.

"Yet now you reveal to us that you are a Sheen of old, a word that, in Archiva, represents all that went wrong with the world. What are we to do with this knowledge? What does this knowledge do to you?"

Peregrin slowly rose and looked about the table. All of the Guardians of Archiva had their gazes fixed on him. Some seemed eager to hear his words, some seemed half fearful, and some seemed desperate for guidance. Yet none of them expressed any revulsion, condemnation, or abhorrence. He smiled, and many smiled back.

"Guardians of Archiva, I do not know what to say. In the wake of this revelation, I ask myself the same question as you do. How am I to act? Though I was built and programmed as a machine, can I claim to be human? I do not know. I pondered these things for most of the night. One side of me analyzed all of the data and information, carefully weighed it in the balance, and found no answer. One side of me swam in a sea of emotions—confusion, care, desire, fear, doubt, anger—and also found no answer. How aptly Bernhadette named me a riddle. Yet I was a riddle with no answer.

"Then, this morning, quite without any effort or skill on my part, I trusted that the sun would rise—and it rose. It seemed to me then that life is not a riddle to be answered but a gift to be trusted. It was then I came to know..." he paused and gazed at Bliss, who smiled slightly and winked, "I knew that I am Peregrin. That is all. You may treat me as you would a machine, or you may treat me as you would a human being. That is up to you. I am and I remain ... Peregrin."

He sat down slowly. There was silence at the table. Slowly the Guardians began to take their gaze from him and look at one another. The silence deepened like a summer evening. Peregrin could hear their hearts beating.

"I am for him," said a voice. It was Mikkel.

"I am for him," said Bliss.

Morgan smiled. "I am for him."

Like the ripple of the wind on a banner, the same assent was murmured around the table, almost in quick succession, by the rest of the Guardians. Peregrin bowed his head, humbled by their generosity of spirit.

Morgan stood. "Peregrin, the Wanderer, the Traveler, the Council of Guardians is for you. Let no one scorn you for your origins. I declare in the name of this council and all who would follow the path of peace that you are a true son of O'Keefe. You are most welcome among us, my brother."

The table suddenly erupted in a joyful shout. Peregrin lifted his head to see all of the Guardians standing, grinning, cheering, and applauding. He found himself unable to speak as the deluge of their approval washed over him.

Something warm slid down the right side of his face, then again, and then on the left side. His vision blurred. Raising a hand, he touched his face and then looked at his fingers. They were wet. He looked at Bliss, who simply stood gazing at him with great warmth. Even through the hubbub, he could hear her whisper, "Every human being can cry, Peregrin."

Later he reflected that what happened next was much like what he had witnessed when Waterman opened the release gate. Something within him seemed to snap open, and suddenly tears were flowing freely down his face, as if they were cleansing him from all the joy and pain of the past weeks. Great sobs choked him as he was overcome by the experience of being affirmed. He spread his arms wide and cried out inarticulately. The Guardians surrounded him, and he embraced all who came near to him. Most of them wept as well, and all were swept away in the tide of emotion. The grief of so much loss, the fear of change, the exhilaration of victory—all that had been experienced became present and was cleansed in a bath of tears.

No one could say how long this experience lasted. Slowly the Guardians returned to their places around the great table. They sat down, but no one spoke, for they were all still in the embrace of the moment, held in silence until the surging emotion subsided. All remained silent, surrounded in utter peace, gazing at one another.

It was Merida who finally spoke. She rose quietly and spread her arms outward. "My brothers and sisters, I am a healer. Yet I have never seen healing just as we have experienced. May we receive this healing with gratitude, for it is a gift. We may not know the giver, but we may accept the gift with joy. My brothers and sisters, peace be to your hearts."

"And to yours," the Guardians answered in unison.

Morgan rose. "My friends, Archiva is at a crossroad. Whatever gift we have received surely prepares us for the question before us now. Where does Archiva's path lead? What lies over the next hill? Can we return to our lives as before, preserving an ideal of peace and quietly seeking others to join us within the protection of these hills? Or is it Archiva's time to be seen?"

"We cannot go back," Stevan rumbled. "We are not the same. We have seen death, despair, joy, and victory. We have seen the darkness that Mikkel spoke of before. We cannot go back."

"I agree," said Merida. "We believed that Dextor was a child of darkness, and maybe he became such. But we have found that same darkness in ourselves. If we deny it, try to ignore what recent events have shown us, it will fester and grow. Other Dextors will rise from among us. No, we must admit to our darkness; we must name it and declare it to be our own. Only then can we rise above it to become true people of peace."

"I fear this darkness," Bernhadette said. "Dextor was seduced by the idea that Archiva could become a ruling force in the world. We have defeated him, but our victory itself shows that he was right. Those exploding sticks that Mikkel threw turned the tide of the battle. Every man, woman, and child knows about them now. The temptation to use them and even more tech knowledge will torment our children and our children's children. I fear what Archiva may become, especially if it goes forth into the world."

"Bernhadette is right," Derth said. "I felt a thrill within me as those things exploded and Dextor's warriors were knocked down. I felt the power of them. I felt exhilaration as we charged down the hill. If we are threatened again, it will be all too easy to use this knowledge once more. And we will be threatened again."

"So then," said Merida, "the doorway has been opened. Before us lies the means to lead the world back from chaos. Before us also lies the means to embrace the darkness that can corrupt every good intent and turn it into a quest for power. Our eyes are opened now, to the good and evil of what we possess. Perhaps we will walk the path of peace for the rest of our days. But what of our children, and their children? How can we prevent them misusing the legacy we will give them?"

Many voices began to speak at once, creating a din of debate. Morgan tapped his gavel. "Brothers, sisters, be still now. The questions before us are many, yet it does no good to swat at a swarm of bees." He turned to Mikkel. "What does the Archivist say? Mikkel, you raised this matter. Still, it is obvious that many of us have the same thoughts. What is your counsel?"

Mikkel looked about at his fellow Guardians. The corners of his mouth turned upward, and even from the other side of the table, Peregrin could see a twinkle in his eyes.

"Guardians of Archiva, my sisters and brothers," he began, "we have suffered many trials in such a short time. But we have endured, and this gives me great hope. Archiva was well founded a century ago, and it is well led this day. Through danger, death, and war, we remain a people of peace.

"It is my belief that recognizing the darkness of our nature can only do us good. If only we had been wise enough to do so when Dextor first tried to bring it to our attention, none of this might have happened. I suppose we just were not ready. Be that as it may, I believe we are ready now. We will grow stronger by appreciating our weaknesses.

"Still, we need time to absorb recent events. We need time to grieve for our dead, to assimilate our new residents, to be healed as individuals and as a community. We face serious questions about Archiva's future, but we need time to recover from all that has happened. These questions will not go away, nor do they demand an immediate answer.

"Now is the time to turn our attention to more mundane matters. The fields are in need of planting. The Waterman's gate must be rebuilt, as well as the waterwheel and pump house. Many of our families will need special attention, having lost a loved one. Let us rest and bring healing to one another. We shall know when the time comes to resolve these matters. I do not believe it is today. Let us rest now."

There were murmurs of assent from around the table. Morgan looked about. "Your counsel seems well received, Mikkel," he said. "If no one objects, we shall look to the restoration of daily life in Archiva.

"Here is one matter we can deal with now," he continued. "At our table are two empty seats, once occupied by Carlin and the Waterman. Who shall we choose to take their places? Who shall we invite to enter the Circle of Guardians?"

"I would like to suggest someone," Peregrin said. Morgan nodded for him to continue. "The Ranger Curtan has proven himself a true child of O'Keefe. He rose to Archiva's defense and was ready to give his life for Archiva, even when all hope seemed lost. I believe he has earned the right to become a Guardian of Archiva.

"It is my belief that Curtan is a descendent of one of the original Guardians of Archiva: Sakura, the Master of Defense. O'Keefe and I brought this man to Archiva. He was a man of gentleness and peace yet fierce in hand-to-hand combat. It is to the skill of Sakura that most of you owe your defense skills. Curtan bears certain features that lead me to believe he is of Sakura's stock."

"I would add my voice to this," Stevan said. "I fought beside Curtan in the ruins and saw him stand over one of his fallen comrades, protecting him from further harm."

"Two for Curtan," Morgan said. "That is a fair nomination. Does anyone dispute this name?" No one spoke, so he continued. "Very well then, but what of the other empty chair? Who will take the place of our Waterman?"

There was a long silence. Then Mikkel spoke. "Lisel. Lisel the horsetender. She cares nothing for power or prestige. We have had many a talk while feeding the horses she serves. I believe she has the ability to keep the council rooted, as did the Waterman."

Janette added her voice to Mikkel's nomination. After a brief communion, both Curtan and Lisel were affirmed to be invited to join the Circle of Guardians.

Morgan tapped his gavel. "Guardians. It is time to adjourn. Let us look to the restoration and recovery of our people, as well as the inclusion of the Terists who have joined us. Before we depart, however, I must ask Peregrin one more question in the name of our council."

He paused and gazed down the length of the table. "Peregrin, you are called the Traveler, and so you are. This council has welcomed you, and in that welcoming we, too, have found healing for our grief. Yet what are your plans now? Will you continue to travel? You stand among us as our brother. Where will you stand tomorrow?"

Peregrin stood and looked about at the watching Guardians. "Tomorrow I stand as I do today. My friends, my brothers and sisters, I have breathed the light of the dawn. I have tasted the water of tears. I shall wander no more. I am home."

XVI
JOURNEYS

Spring blossomed into a vibrant summer as the days flowed past, bringing joy to Peregrin as he labored in the fields, helped rebuild the Waterman's wheel and gate, and pulled weeds with Bliss in the morning. He felt as if each day were part of a lazy river in which he gently bobbed along. If the night was clear, he would climb the elbow and lie on his back, contemplating the stars. At least once a week, he and Bliss would meet before dawn to watch the sun's first rays strike the day-breaker rock. Sometimes Merida would join them, and once she brought Janette with her. They always sat in silence, absorbing the peace of the moment the rock absorbed the sun's first light.

Yes, peace is a good word, Peregrin thought. The daylight continued to lengthen, the air grew warmer, and the land around them swelled with life. Everything was in constant, peaceful motion. Even the days and nights seemed to be simply an alternating perspective on the same reality, so that there was no time, but only a never-ending, ever-present moment presented in different shadings.

All matters had been resolved. By decision of the Council of Guardians, Dextor's body was taken back to his canyon and laid in the quarters he had carved into the hillside. The door was then sealed with rock, and a monument was erected upon the ledge, bearing his name.

"It is only right," Mikkel had said when he proposed the idea. "Dextor was once a Guardian of Archiva, and even though he turned his hand against it, we must recognize the achievement he accomplished in founding that place."

It was further decided that Second Archiva would become an extension of the original. It would serve as a garrison for the Rangers, as Curtan had suggested, as well as become home to the metal, carpentry, and tool-making trades.

Some of the Guardians had objected to this arrangement. Led by Bernhadette and Derth, they argued that this would result in dividing Archiva by separating the functional, manufacturing trades from the gentler occupations of farming, livestock, and artistry. Most of the council, however, believed this separation would not result in any detriment to Archiva's unity.

A few days after the council, Peregrin was in his quarters when someone knocked on the door. He opened it to find Curtan standing there.

"Is it all right if I come in?" he asked.

"Of course," Peregrin answered, stepping aside to make room.

Curtan walked stiffly past him. He stopped, facing the inner wall. "They tell me you nominated me to join the Circle of Guardians."

"That is true."

"Why?"

"Because you are worthy of it. During the entire resistance to Dextor, I trusted no one more to fight beside than you. I would have been proud to die at your side."

Curtan snorted. "Of course, that would not have happened."

"I did not know that at the time," Peregrin said softly.

Curtan spun around. "How can I know that for sure? I would have died for you as well. I believed in you. I believed in you! That final moment during the battle just before Mikkel showed up, I was certain that death was coming for us both. And I wanted nothing more than to die beside you, as your brother."

He drew a breath before continuing. "Then you did die; only I was not with you. You went over the cliff with Dextor. And you died. When we got to the bottom and found you, the Peregrin I knew was gone. In his place was a Sheen who could not die. And now I don't know what to believe in or who to follow, because I put my faith in a man named Peregrin; but he was not what I believed him to be."

Peregrin remained silent for a moment but did not lower his gaze. Finally, he spoke. "Curtan, I cannot imagine how difficult this is for you. It's difficult for me, I can say that. But I have not betrayed you. I, too, was unaware of my origins until I fell off that cliff with Dextor. And you are right. The Peregrin we both knew died in that fall.

"Still, this changes nothing about how I feel about you. Then, as well as now, I think of you as my brother. And if, by being smashed to pieces, I could save your life, I would do it. There are still battles to be fought; only the battlefield is now the future—an uncertain future in which Archiva will take many risks. Archiva needs leaders like you who are not afraid of action. And I for one would be proud to stand shoulder to shoulder with you in facing them."

Curtan looked at him a long moment, and Peregrin was half afraid he would simply walk past him and leave. Then he grinned. "No frogs in Archiva!" he said.

Peregrin grinned back. "No frogs in Archiva! We'll keep them hopping."

Curtan extended his hand. When Peregrin took it, he pulled him in, threw his arms around him, and embraced him.

⁓

One morning as they pulled weeds from the tomato patch, Bliss stopped and looked at Peregrin. "Are you happy?" she said.

Peregrin smiled back. "Yes, I am happy. Or at least I am greatly satisfied with my existence right now. I could want nothing more than to spend my days in Archiva."

"How long do you think that will be?"

Peregrin furrowed his brow. "What do you mean? Why this sudden questioning?"

Bliss smiled. "I'm not trying to upset you, Peregrin. But you are a Sheen, capable of regenerating. You're already more than one hundred years old, even if you slept most of it. It seems to me that you were built to survive for a long time."

"So?"

"So, do you have any idea how long you can expect to live? How long before you cannot renew your cells?"

Peregrin thought a moment. "I don't know. I suppose, with proper times of hibernation, I could live more than a thousand years."

"A thousand years," Bliss mused. "And here you sit pulling weeds."

"What on earth are you driving at?"

"You say that with proper times of sleep, you might live a thousand years. But I will not. I will live my time here and die. Nor could I imagine living for a thousand years. What will you do with all that time? How will you bear the heartbreak of watching everyone you love die?"

Peregrin stood up. "I do not like this conversation. I am happy now. That's all I can say. Now if you will excuse me, I have to find Mikkel." He turned and walked away.

He wandered for sometime, first to the council building, then the stables, and even to the pottery house, but he failed to find Mikkel. Bliss's questions pursued him like a mosquito, distracting him from his purpose until he would consciously push them away, only to have them reappear less than a minute later as his concentration slipped. At one point he found himself standing near the Waterman's pump and realized he could not remember walking there.

Why does she ask things like this? he wondered. *Why can't she just leave it alone and enjoy the time we have together? Be a lot easier. Why think of things you can't change?*

Still, her words demanded his attention, the way a splinter demands treatment no matter how much one ignores it. He could not deny that he was designed to live for centuries, yet he had never considered that Bliss, Mikkel, Curtan, and the rest wouldn't be there with him. The very thought made something leap in his chest, as if he were suddenly threatened by an unseen assailant.

He looked about, realizing he had been walking again. He was close to the south end of Archiva. A small group of men were conversing near the assembly platform, and he saw that Mikkel was among them. Coming closer, Peregrin could see it was Corlee and about five of Dextor's men who had joined themselves to Archiva.

"I'm sorry, Corlee," Mikkel was saying. "It's too early for any of you to go back. I cannot allow it yet."

"But this was our home, Mikkel," Corlee answered. "We already have homes there that you have no right to take."

Peregrin joined them. "What's the problem?" he asked.

Corlee looked at Peregrin suspiciously. "I would not expect you to understand."

"Try me."

"All right then, we have heard that the council has decided to inhabit Second Archiva. Many of us wish to go back there, since it is our home. We see no reason to wait until homes are dug for us here when we already have a place to live."

Peregrin glanced at Mikkel. "It has been less than two months since you fought for Dextor, Corlee. How could we trust any of you to return to the place where you prepared for battle against Archiva?"

"I knew that you would not understand," Corlee answered. "It is our home; that's all. We still want to live in peace, but we want to go home. The Rangers will be there, and we will come to work in Archiva each day. But we want to go home."

"And I say it is impossible at this time," Mikkel said. "Send you back to remember Dextor and all that he planned? It is madness."

"Nonetheless, it is our right. The men have asked me to bring it to the Council of Guardians. I believe that anyone in the Circle of Belonging can request this."

Mikkel paused. "Very well. You may bring it to the council. I shall inform Morgan."

"Don't trouble yourself," Corlee answered. "I'll tell him." He and the men walked away.

Mikkel watched after them. "I'm beginning to believe that Bliss's little inspirational speech is wearing off. I was afraid this group would become unruly."

"Or maybe they just want to go home," Peregrin said.

Mikkel's eyes narrowed. "These are Terists, Peregrin. Do you want to fight off another army a year from now?"

First Bliss, now Mikkel, Peregrin thought. *What's gotten into everyone?*

"I'm not suggesting we let them go. I'm only saying that it would be natural for them to want to return there, especially now that we have decided to use the place."

Mikkel looked as if he was going to retort, but he caught himself. "Well, it's a matter for the council now. What do you want?"

"Maybe now is not a good time."

Mikkel put out a hand. "No, Peregrin, no. I'm sorry. I'm a little on the edge lately. I'm still afraid of these new 'Archivans,' and we have come to no conclusions about Archiva itself. Please, forgive my rudeness."

Peregrin smiled. "Of course, Mikkel. Listen, I have an idea about that." He took Mikkel's arm, and they walked to the assembly platform. "Archiva is changing, as well it should. But as you said, it needs direction, right?"

"Right."

"Archiva's ultimate mission is to bring order and knowledge back to the world while setting it on the path of peace, am I right?"

"Yes."

"Already we are taking a step by incorporating Dextor's canyon into the life of Archiva. So now Archiva is found in two locations. And whether or not Dextor's men return to Second Archiva, this expansion alone represents an expansion of Archiva's mission and methods, right?"

"Uh huh."

"I suggest, then, that we look toward expanding in other ways, namely by sending Archivans to another community and helping them grow through our guidance. If this place accepts the path of peace through the years, it becomes a springboard for new expeditions. In this way, Archiva becomes visible, as you said it must, without exposing itself to the world."

"You have somewhere in mind?"

Peregrin nodded. "I spent last winter in a small village about ten days' journey from here. The people are not violent, but they are primitive. We could send a band of volunteers there to help them, to teach them about the Creed. I'm sure they are ready. Then we will not be teaching this person or that person and bringing them back to Archiva. We will be bringing Archiva to whole villages at a time. The process of restoration will accelerate, and Archiva will truly take the lead in bringing the world back from the edge as O'Keefe intended."

Mikkel reflected on this. "It's a big change in the way we do things. Will you present it to the council?" Peregrin nodded. "All right then. We will trust in our communing."

Bliss caught up with Peregrin as he returned to his quarters. She stepped in front of him.

"I'm sorry if I upset you, Peregrin," she said.

Peregrin looked at the ground. "You didn't upset me. You just caught me off guard with all those questions."

"Still, they are matters on which you must think."

"Bliss, something tells me there is more to your questions than you are saying."

Bliss raised one eyebrow and smiled slightly. "Why Peregrin, whatever would give you that idea?"

"Hmm. I don't know. Maybe it has something to do with the fact that we seem to commune in silence more than we talk. So when you suddenly start raising questions about emotions and the years to come, I get suspicious. And I say to myself, 'I wonder what's behind these questions.'"

Bliss studied him for a moment before she answered. "I'm not sure if I should tell you. I had a dream last night. It made me think."

"A dream? What was it about?"

"O'Keefe."

"You'll have to be a bit more specific if this conversation will go anywhere."

"I dreamed I was in a small room. The walls were all white, and the light was very bright from the ceiling. In the center was a table with a long box of sorts on it. I heard a noise behind me and turned to find a man entering through a door. He looked startled to see me there; then he relaxed and smiled. He said, 'Oh, it's you, Bliss. I was wondering when you would show up.'"

"I said, 'Who are you?' And he said, 'Come on, Bliss, you know me.'

"It was then I realized that I did know him. It was O'Keefe. He looked a lot like Mikkel, only smaller and with little glass windows in front of his eyes. He studied me through them with eyes that were warm and calculating at the same time. He said, 'It's a time of hard choices, Bliss. I had to let Peregrin go. Now he is in your hands.'

"I asked him what he meant, but he just smiled, turned, and walked out the way he had come in. The door shut, and I heard it being locked. I thought, *I'm trapped in here,* but I wasn't afraid. In fact, I knew I was supposed to be there, but I didn't know why. Then the whole thing faded."

Peregrin looked at Bliss. She had told the story with great zeal, almost joyfully, as if the very thought of it brought her peace. But it did not bring him peace.

"I can see this dream upsets you," Bliss said.

"It's a bit too real for me," Peregrin answered. "That place with the white walls does exist. It's the underground bunker where I slept for the last one hundred years. And O'Keefe did wear glasses."

"So what do you think it means?"

He shook his head. "I will have to think about it. I'm sure its meaning will be made known to me. Have I told you lately you're an incredible person?"

She laughed and shook her head. "Well, let me say it now, before I forget," he said.

＊ ～ ＊

The Council of Guardians met a few days later. Corlee presented his petition, stating that nineteen out of the twenty-eight Terists wished to return to their former dwelling place in Second Archiva.

The other nine had already found their niche and decided to stay in Archiva.

To Peregrin and Mikkel's surprise, the council supported the wishes of these men. "Everyone needs a home," Stevan said. "These men have lived in Second Archiva and should be allowed to return there, provided they continue seeking the path of peace under the guidance of their companions." The other Guardians agreed.

Sanda was put in charge of the Ranger garrison for Second Archiva. Twenty Rangers would be stationed there, with a squad of five rotating back to Archiva each month, so that eventually all of the Rangers spent time there. More than a hundred people involved in various trades would also relocate there.

Peregrin's proposal caused considerable debate. After all had been said, the Guardians communed with one another. Twenty-one voted in favor of sending a group comprised of ten Rangers and two persons from each trade to see if some connection could be made with the village where he had spent the winter.

"It is a fearful thing for us; that is to be understood," Morgan said. "We will make ourselves clearly known to the world at large. Still, I think we cannot remain enclosed within these hills any longer. The time has come for us to allow our mission to grow."

Peregrin gladly agreed to lead the first expedition to the village. After the council had adjourned, he asked Bliss to go with him when they left in two weeks, but she smiled and simply shook her head.

"It is right that you go, Peregrin. You know the way, and you have befriended these people. Also, I can see that you wish to go and see them again. This is your choice. As for me, I have done my share of wandering the world in my seeking days. Besides, who will be left to pull the weeds?"

Peregrin looked at the ground. "I was hoping you would say yes. I would like you to meet them and tell me what you think of them."

Bliss laid a hand upon his cheek and lifted his face so that his eyes met hers. "Karinda and Drum will be with you. They are fine Seekers."

"They are not you, Bliss."

"I know," she said softly. "You have to walk your path now. The falcon must fly with the current of the wind. My path is here." She kissed his cheek and walked off toward the gardens.

He watched her go. *She's so much like Mara,* he mused. *There's a great truth in her words, but you can't quite get it.*

Bliss's answer deflated his excitement about the expedition. In fact, as the day wore on, he found himself wondering if he should go at all. It worried him that she seemed to think their paths were separating. He did not care how much or little time they had together. He just wanted to be with her. Why couldn't she see that?

The real problem, though, isn't Bliss, he thought. *I'm feeling restless again. I thought I had Archiva's future at heart when I suggested going to Jaspar's village. But I wonder now. Did I think it was such a good idea because I wanted to go—to face a new challenge?*

He returned to his quarters, entered and shot the bolt. *Why do I feel so tired?* he wondered, rubbing his forehead. Looking about, he found he was having trouble focusing. *I'll just lie down for a few minutes and re-energize,* he thought as he moved to the bed. He lay down and closed his eyes. A heaviness descended on him like a curtain.

There was a strange noise. It was a rhythmic, insistent sound, growing gradually louder, as if giant footfalls were moving closer and closer. His mind resisted the intrusion, but there was no escaping it. Sluggishly, as if heavy drapes were being pulled open, he came to realize that someone was knocking at his door.

"I only need a little rest once in a while," he muttered as he sat up, trying to shake off the muddiness of this thoughts. "Is that really too much to ask?"

When at last he opened the door, he found Bliss standing there. He blinked a few times.

"Bliss, hello, I, uh, thought you were going to the gardens."

Bliss cocked an eyebrow. "Are you all right?"

"Of course I'm all right. I just saw you a little bit ago. You went off to pull weeds, and I came back to get a little rest."

"Peregrin, that was yesterday."

"What?"

"We talked yesterday. No one has seen you since. I was worried I had upset you, so I didn't come looking for you. But then when the morning and most of the afternoon passed—"

"Bliss, wait! What time is it?"

"It's late afternoon, Peregrin. Almost a full day since we parted."

He gaped at her. "No, that's impossible. I just laid down a moment ago."

"It was yesterday. The council met yesterday; you proposed an expedition to a village; we talked and parted. Since then you've been in your room. Mikkel rapped on your door earlier but decided you must not have wanted to be disturbed. We only knew you were in there because the door was bolted. What's going on, Peregrin? Are you okay?"

He shook his head. "I don't know. I just felt really tired. Maybe all the stress of these past days finally overcame me. I feel fine now."

In the next few days, life continued its lazy pace. The expedition party prepared for its journey. Outside of a few troubling moments of reflection, Peregrin did feel fine. He decided that his day of sleep had simply been a long overdue rest after all of the turmoil of the spring.

The expedition set out on a fine summer morning. Lindah, who had been assigned to guard the ruins, told him that the path beside the river continued on past where he had come over the mountain, connecting with a deer trail that would make the going easier. They opted to follow this route.

Once they ran into Terists, surprising a small band of men in a camp who quickly fled from their superior numbers. Although the encounter was not violent, it reminded them to remain alert and on guard.

On the seventh day, they came to the big river and turned to follow it upward. Four days later, rounding a bend, they came in sight of of the village. They remained in plain sight and approached slowly without threat. Even so, Peregrin could see people in the village quickly grabbing weapons. The headman rode out to meet them with five other men, halting some fifteen feet away.

"What do you want?" he called out. "Why have you come?"

Peregrin stepped forward. He untied Crown's knife from his waist and held it out. "I seek Jaspar the deer tamer. I wish to return his knife to him."

Jaspar reined his horse around and peered at him. Then he threw his head back and laughed. "Peregrin!" he cried and quickly dismounted and strode to embrace him.

"Jaspar, I always hoped I could return. I am glad you are well."

"And our village is well, thanks much to the Peregrin! We have three new babies, five cattle, and two new horses. But what's his? You have not come back alone!"

"Nor emptyhanded. What little help I gave you this past winter these people will share a hundredfold more. Jaspar, I have found my people. And, like myself, they seek to share knowledge to help you thrive." Briefly Peregrin explained the mission of Archiva and how they had come to help them. Jaspar was silent, pinching his chin.

"I am not sure what to say," he said. "Strangers are not usually a good omen."

"Say nothing, Jaspar. Let us come into the village and stay awhile so that you will come to know us. Then your elders can decide if we shall remain."

This was agreeable. The Archivans pitched camp just outside the village. Peregrin and Jaspar called together the people and introduced them. After Peregrin testified as to their intent, the people agreed to allow them to stay for a while.

By the time two weeks had gone by, the people of the village had become fast friends with the Archivans. The elders met and unanimously decided that it would be wise to allow a permanent relationship with Archiva to be established. They immediately set about building homes.

Though the mission was successful and he was glad to see the people of the village once more, Peregrin found he was restless and troubled again. Each night he thought about Archiva and its people. As he lay down to rest at the end of each day, he could see Bliss's face before him. He realized that he longed for the day when he could return.

"Is this what it means to be homesick?" he said aloud to himself one night. "I've always been the Traveler, the falcon without a nest. Now I do not want to be anywhere except Archiva."

Whenever he thought of Bliss and Mikkel and the rest of Archiva, however, he was struck by a quiet melancholy. Though he thought of Archiva as home and did not want to wander anymore, he could not shake the feeling that his place among its people was temporary.

After two more weeks, the Archivans had become such an integral part of the village life that it seemed as if they had always belonged there. Peregrin came to Jaspar one morning and told him that he was leaving for Archiva with four of the Rangers.

"Others will come in time, to replace those who desire to return to Archiva. Learn from them and listen to them about peace," he said.

Peregrin held out Crown's knife again. "Here," he said. "This time I really mean it. This knife has served me well, but I will no longer need it. Keep it, and remember me."

Jaspar took the knife. "As I said before, we will not forget the name of Peregrin."

Peregrin and the Rangers set off, eager to return. Along the way they established certain markers for those who would travel the route. As they approached Archiva, Peregrin's anxiousness to see Bliss grew within him. He had been gone for forty-two days. Summer was near to its end.

As they approached the rockslide at the far end of the ruins, Drek, the Ranger in the lead, stopped suddenly and held up a hand. After a moment, a short birdcall warbled twice. Logan, the Ranger nearest to Peregrin, grabbed his arm and pulled him down into a crouch as the other Rangers did the same.

"What is it?" Peregrin whispered.

"Signal for trouble," Logan said quietly. "Wait."

Peregrin remembered his first encounter with the ruins at this very spot. As he had done then, he listened to the sounds—birds, chipmunks, water, twigs, frogs, cicadas—ah, there it was! Sounds that didn't belong. The crunch of a foot; a distant muttering voice; wood and stone being moved.

After a long minute, the call sounded three times from slightly up the slope. A Ranger stepped into view from behind a tree and beckoned and then dropped into a crouch. Peregrin and the Rangers crept carefully toward her. It was Lindah.

When they reached her, Lindah signaled them to follow her. They continued up the slope, angling carefully along the ridge from which the rockslide had fallen. Once they had traversed about one hundred yards along the ridgeline, Lindah flattened herself onto the ground and crawled toward the ledge that overlooked the ruins. The others followed and peered over the ledge.

A few hundred yards beyond them they could see several people moving about the ruins near the old government building. They appeared to be looking for something. They were also armed, holding knives or swords ready in their hands as they searched.

"There are eleven of them. I've recognized a few of them as Dextor's men. They arrived about an hour ago," Lindah whispered. "I sent Marin back to Archiva for help."

"What are they looking for?" asked Logan.

"I don't know," Lindah answered. "They have been lifting rocks and fallen trees. They even tried to get into the old building there, but it was too well blocked."

"They're looking for an entrance," Peregrin said quickly. "It is imperative that we stop them before they find it."

"Shouldn't we wait for help from Archiva?" Drek said.

"No," Peregrin said. "If they find the entrance they're looking for and get away, it could mean big trouble."

"What's behind the entrance?" Lindah said.

"A big room with a lot of dangerous stuff," Peregrin answered. "Remember those exploding sticks Mikkel used to put Dextor's men on the run? There's that and a lot more. We've got to stop them now. But how are six of us going to stop eleven of them?"

Lindah smiled. "That's where the ruins come to our aid. Drek, you did a turn in the ruins awhile back. Do you remember how to operate the landslide?"

"I sure do. I'll handle that end. You lead everyone else down the shaft."

They followed Drek and Lindah farther up the ridgeline. Once at the top, they followed the arc of the hillside around until it swept back in toward the ruins. Near to the place where Bliss had stood on the day of the battle and the cliff was most sheer, Lindah stopped beside a boulder, resting at the edge of what appeared to be an impenetrable thicket. She leaned against the boulder and pushed. It slid easily aside, revealing that it had been set upon rollers. Behind it was a passage cut into the thicket about three feet in diameter.

"I'll sing three verses of the song of O'Keefe before I use the pipes," Drek said, and he vanished into the trees ahead of them.

Lindah crouched down and crawled into the tunnel. Peregrin

and the others followed until they came out into a small clearing. Before them was a crevice about four feet wide and no more than ten feet long.

Lindah grasped one of several ropes that were attached to various tree trunks around the crevice and went over the edge. After a short interval, Logan followed. Peregrin and the others did the same. They descended quickly for nearly sixty feet until they came to the bottom. A short crawl through a tunnel brought them out into a shallow basin behind a rockslide.

Peering over the edge of the rocks, Peregrin realized they were near to the old building. He remembered his first inspection of this building and how he had thought this way impassable. He smiled. *The secrets of Archiva run deep.*

The intruders were not far away from them. They were scouring the area near to the building, speaking in low tones to one another. Peregrin recognized Crop among them.

Lindah indicated a copse of trees about halfway to the river. "There are pipes from the top of the hillside to those trees. Drek will blow into a device that feeds into those pipes, creating an unearthly wail from that area." She then pointed to the hillside just beyond the building, near to the ledge that Peregrin had slept upon his first day in the ruins. "As they look to find the source of the sound, he will work a lever above that will dislodge a pile of shale on that side to make them think the whole hillside is coming down. That should send them our way in a panic. The rest of the job is up to us."

They waited, remaining still. Suddenly a long screech rose from the trees Lindah had pointed out. The sound was so discordant and shrill, but almost human sounding, that it caused Peregrin to jump up himself. The intruders looked about alarmed, searching for what creature must surely be rising up to attack them.

Just then there was a rasping sound, and a section of the cliff face suddenly gave way and came rumbling down toward them. The intruders were so unnerved that they simply turned and ran, some dropping their weapons in a panic.

Peregrin and the Rangers rose up as the men reached them, catching them off guard. This sudden appearance of forms from yet another direction threw the men into a panic. Many of them simply cowered and covered their heads with their arms. The few who fought were overwhelmed. The fight was over in moments.

They tied the intruders' hands behind their backs and made them sit with their backs against the cliff face. After an hour or so, Marin arrived with reinforcements. Curtan was among them.

"Peregrin!" he cried. He threw his arms around Peregrin in a bear hug. "It has been too long since I have seen your face! Peace to your heart!"

Peregrin laughed. "And to yours, Curtan! Indeed, I am glad you see you! What news from Archiva?"

"Archiva grows stronger each day," he answered. "But what is this gift you bring with you? Eleven Terists? Couldn't you just return in peace without starting a battle?"

Peregrin shook his head, grinning broadly. "You know me. Wherever I travel, trouble is not far behind. But these men were here ahead of me."

Curtan crouched down in front of one of the intruders. "I remember you," he said. "You were one of Dextor's captains." The man glowered at him but said nothing. "Dextor is dead, in case you did not know it," Curtan went on. "You know these ruins belong to Archiva. Why have you returned?"

"I'll go where I want to go," the man spat back. "I don't need permission from anyone."

"You do as long as you're within ten miles of here," Curtan said. "What were you looking for?"

The man looked as if he were going to refuse to speak but then seemed to think better of it. "We were looking to find where you keep the stuff," he said sullenly.

"What stuff?"

"You know what stuff. We all saw those things that exploded. Dextor said there was a whole room full of weapons and stuff somewhere beneath these ruins."

"Why do you want it?"

"Word is out there, you know," the man said. "You've got weapons from the old world. Powerful weapons that could make a man important. Others will come looking too. You could give them to me, and I would make sure that no one else comes."

Curtan snorted and stood up. "Take these fools back to the holding cell outside of Archiva," he said to those he brought with him. "We'll see what the Guardians will have to say about them." He turned to Peregrin. "Come on. I want to see the look on Mikkel's and Bliss's faces when I bring you home."

"How have they been while I've been away?"

"I think the best word that describes it is *miserable*," Curtan said, laughing. "You will bring gladness to their hearts this day."

"And they to mine. I am eager to see them."

Even so Peregrin agreed with Curtan that they should not use the closer, long tunnel into Archiva since it seemed possible that other Terists could be in the area. Also, he was glad for the extra time it took to walk around to the entrance through which he had first beheld Archiva. Curtan caught him up on events, while Peregrin related the success of the mission. Mostly they just enjoyed being in each other's company again.

Peregrin paused as they emerged from the tunnel and surveyed Archiva, remembering that time he stood here beside Bliss for his "first" look. It seemed like lifetimes ago. Then he had felt uncertainty and amazement. Now, looking down at the activity on the floor of the basin below him, he felt immense gratitude and a sense of belonging, as if he had been born here. *I guess in a way I was,* he thought and smiled.

They descended the steps and had not gone more than one

hundred yards when he could hear his name being whispered by the people who saw him pass. *No chance of surprising anybody,* he thought. *Word moves faster than a sparrow in flight.*

They made it almost to the water pump when he heard his name called out by that familiar, welcome voice, and he turned to see Bliss running toward him. She did not check her speed as she came up to him and flung her arms around him, nearly knocking him over. He laughed, picked her off the ground, and swung her around. Without even thinking, he kissed her.

She smiled brightly as he set her back down. "Peregrin!" she said. "I can't believe you have come home! It felt like you would never return."

"I felt the same way, Bliss," he said. "But I saw your face every night as I lay down, so I knew I would come back."

"Peregrin!"

Mikkel came striding quickly toward him. His leg was fully healed, Peregrin noted. He grasped Peregrin's hand in a firm clasp, looked at him a moment, and embraced him. "Peregrin," he said again, "it is good to see you once more."

"Peace to your heart, Mikkel," Peregrin said, grinning. "It is good to be home."

Mikkel turned to Curtan. "Some Ranger you are, Curtan. You say you're going out to ward off Terists in the ruins, and you come back with this one."

Curtan shook is head in mock sorrow. "What can I say, Mikkel? I'm always getting my duties confused. But hey, I took one look at this guy and said, 'There's trouble for sure.' So I thought I had better bring him back for you to handle. You're better with strangers."

Peregrin laughed. "And surely there's no one stranger than me! Come on; let's find a quiet place for a while."

They set off with linked arms. While Peregrin had intended to go to the elbow, Mikkel suggested they go to the stables instead. Once inside, they were greeted by Lisel and a young man she was apprenticing. They walked to the end of the row of stables to greet Carbon, who whickered in response.

Finding a seat on the hay bales, they shared their experiences of the past month. Archiva was recovering well, Mikkel said, and an air of expectation and challenge was in the air. Bliss affirmed that the mood in Archiva was exceedingly positive. Peregrin told all about the mission to the village and his return home. Mikkel's jaw grew taut as he spoke of the Terists searching for the entrance to the vault of machines.

"He said the word was out there, did he? That can't be good."

"I agree," Bliss said. "I have had a troubling feeling about the ruins ever since the battle. We have to do something."

"True," said Curtan. "We have to bring this to the council. Meanwhile, I plan to increase the Ranger presence in the area of the ruins. Two just can't cover it under these circumstances."

"It will take a few days for the council to assemble," said Mikkel. "Morgan, Stevan, and several others are inspecting Second Archiva."

"Oh, I almost forgot about that," Peregrin said. "How are things in Dextor's canyon?"

Mikkel smiled wryly. "Better than I would have thought. Sanda keeps the Rangers well drilled, and they keep an eye on our former Terists. For their part, however, they give every indication that they have truly changed. The craftsmen are pleased with the forges and tools Dextor had stocked there. I guess it all might work out."

"It will, Mikkel," said Bliss. "I spent a week there myself, Peregrin. Despite its origins, a peaceful spirit pervades the air there. I think those Terists might become more Archivan than the Archivans."

"I hope you're right," said Peregrin. "Well, there's little we can do right now. I for one would like to go visit Waterman. How about it?"

"I would like to go," Mikkel said, "but I have to go see to matters concerning the new water pump house."

"And I have to see if our new guests are settled in well," Curtan said.

"I don't have a thing to do," said Bliss. "I'll be happy to come along."

Mikkel and Curtan grinned and exchanged glances. Peregrin raised one eyebrow at them and then said, "Hmmph! It's just as well. I only really wanted Bliss to go along anyway. Come, Bliss, let us depart from these so-called friends." He reached out in exaggerated haughtiness and took her by the arm.

"By all means," Bliss said. "Lead on." Arm in arm they strode from the stables.

When they arrived at Waterman's grave, they stood in silence, and Peregrin was amazed to see a brilliant array of flowers covering the spot.

"The flowers look beautiful," Peregrin said. "Whoever used them to mark the grave was as much a genius as the Waterman."

Bliss blushed. "I claim that distinction. I was certain that Waterman would be better remembered by a living monument than a stone one."

Peregrin nodded. "You thought right. It's perfect for him. He's still giving life to Archiva."

"I see him sometimes."

"In dreams, you mean?"

"Sometimes," Bliss answered.

"What does he say?"

Bliss did not answer right away, and for a moment Peregrin thought she had not heard him. Finally, she said in a very small voice, "He tells me I have to let you get on with your business."

Peregrin wrinkled his brow. "My business? What does that mean? Archiva is my business now."

"Exactly what Waterman says," Bliss answered and fell silent.

They remained at Waterman's grave for a while longer in silence. Afterward they climbed the elbow and sat as the sun tended toward the horizon, laughing and talking about gardens, wind and rain, sunsets, and nothing in particular until the night colored in the spaces between the long shadows and a dampness began to set in. Then they climbed down and ambled to the door to Peregrin's quarters.

Peregrin stopped at his door and turned to Bliss. "Good night, Bliss," he said quietly.

Bliss put her hands on his shoulders. "Your story is not finished, Peregrin," she said. "Of this I am sure, you have many more chapters to live. My days will come to an end much sooner, I am afraid."

"I'm not worried about that," Peregrin said.

"You do not have to be," Bliss answered. "I do not think you will see that day. But remember me, dear one. Remember me." She leaned upward and kissed him on the mouth. "Just remember me," she whispered. She turned and walked quickly into the night, leaving Peregrin quite perplexed.

XVII
ARCHIVA
SHALL FALL AROUND HIM

Though Peregrin was glad to be home in Archiva, the days that followed brought him more turmoil than peace. He replayed his conversation with Bliss over and over in his mind but could not determine why it troubled him so much. He tried to press Bliss for clarification of what she meant, but she only smiled and said, "We both must learn."

It wasn't Bliss's fault, he realized, but her words had sparked a conflict within him. All he had desired was to come home to Archiva. Now he was reunited with Bliss and Mikkel and Curtan, which gave him great joy. Yet he also experienced a growing uneasiness, as if he were being called onward, and the home he had found would now be denied to him.

All this was compounded by a distinct loss of energy. He felt a greater need for sleep yet often only tossed and turned restlessly all night, receiving no refreshment. Other times he slept for hours without any awareness of passing time. The people of Archiva were in constant joyful motion, harvesting and preserving their food for the coming winter, but Peregrin felt as if he were slowing down.

Somewhere in the depth of a restless night nearly three weeks after his return, he was surprised to see the bolt on his door being drawn back. He remained still, watching the bolt slide to the side without anyone touching it. The door opened slowly, and as he watched in amazement, a light grew stronger in the doorway until the room was flooded by a brilliance so strong that he had to shield his eyes.

Peering out from under his hand, he saw a figure step out of the light and into his room. As the door began to close again, he could make out the silhouette of a short, slightly-built person with tousled hair.

"Waterman?" he said. "Is it you? Am I dreaming?"

"Perhaps to both questions," came the answer. The door clicked shut, and the light vanished leaving but a soft glow around the figure.

Peregrin sat up. "It sure looks like you."

The figure laughed. "That will be for you to decide when the sun rises."

"What do you want?"

"I just came to say hello."

"I've missed you terribly."

"I know. But I've never been too far away. I was at the battle. You saw me upon the hill beside Bliss."

"She is pretty amazing."

"I know," the figure said. "I've always loved Bliss with a special affection. She knows the path of the true human better than anyone in Archiva."

Peregrin nodded. "You are right. She does know the way."

"That is why you must remember her: not just because you

loved her, but because she knows the way. You have to remember her path."

"You talk as if I'm going somewhere." The figure remained silent. "Am I going somewhere, Waterman?"

"Not somewhere, Peregrin," he said. "Some time. Look here."

He gestured toward the door, which swung open again. Beyond it Peregrin could see not light or the dark of night, but another room—a room with white walls and a light that came from the ceiling. A room with a table in the center of it and on that table was a long, padded box.

"No!"

Peregrin sat bolt upright and nearly fell off his bed. It was still dark in his room. Although he could see well in the dark, he lit a candle and looked about. There was no one there with him. The door was closed and firmly bolted. Fearfully he slid the bolt back and opened the door. Damp air and the sounds of deep night were all that he found. He closed the door, shut the bolt, and leaned back on it, breathing heavily. *A dream,* he thought. *It must have been a dream. Do Sheens dream? I don't know, but I would think so. My brain is so addled by everything that has happened that it must have created a dream. A dream of Waterman coming through the light*… He paused. "The light and the water," he murmured. "The light and the water." He paced the room for the rest of the hours until dawn.

Bliss found him crouched in the gardens about midmorning, absently plucking weeds, studying them, and dropping them into his bucket. He was almost obscured among the bushy tomato and bean plants.

She approached softly and crouched beside him. "I thought you would come to see the day-breaker this morning."

It was a long moment before he answered. "I thought the dawn would be cloudy."

"The sun still rises behind the clouds," she said gently and reached out to touch his hand. "Peregrin, what is moving within you?"

He looked into her eyes, thinking he had never seen such a comforting gaze. "I do not know, Bliss. It makes me afraid. I thought I had found my identity, my humanity, and my home. I thought it was finished. Then that old feeling of restlessness returns to taunt me."

"Is it the urge to wander?"

"Not exactly. It's more a feeling of incompleteness, like there is some task that remains undone, some choice that has yet to be accepted. I talked to Waterman last night. Or rather, he came and talked to me. I did not get to say much at all."

"What did he say?"

He related his experience with her. "I think it was just a dream, you know, my brain trying to sort out the many things that have happened to me." Bliss was silent at this, so after a pause he continued. "What do you think of it? Wasn't it just a dream? Didn't my mind just create the experience?"

"Perhaps to both questions," she said, rising. "At any rate, you're awake now. I have to find Merida. Janel is sick. Peace to your heart, Peregrin." She turned and walked off.

"And to yours, Bliss," he said softly, watching her go.

When night fell, Peregrin could not rest again, so he left his quarters in the very early hours of the morning and climbed the elbow. Sitting with his back against the hillside, he drew his knees up to his chest and gazed out across the space that was Archiva.

He had sat there completely still for the better part of an hour when he experienced the impression that someone was sitting beside him. It was more of a sense of someone being there than any sensible perception. He did not look to confirm his sense, for he was sure he would find nothing.

"Is that you?" he said quietly after a while.

There was no answer, but he did not need one. "I do not know what to do," he said. "Archiva has turned the corner, I think. I would like to stay with it through the years."

He paused and then said, "And I would like to stay with Bliss. Is that asking too much?"

He let a minute go by before continuing. "Still, the vault of machines needs to be closed off. And Archiva is to the point where it will continue to develop and learn on its own. All that remains is centuries in which to grow. My work here is done for now."

The silence continued to deepen around him. He remained in it for another long pause.

"It's never easy, is it? I mean, the choices we face, we never get any guarantees. But we still have to make them."

He remained still then, through the rest of the night. Shortly before dawn he heard a scrabbling sound of someone climbing the rock. He knew it was Bliss even before her head appeared above the ledge.

"Peregrin?" she said quietly.

"I'm here, Bliss."

She clambered over the top and came to him. She stopped, looked at him, and then seated herself beside him without saying anything.

"Bliss?" Peregrin finally said.

"Yes?"

"Why didn't you ever get married?"

Bliss was quiet for a moment. "I chose the gift," she answered.

He looked at her. "What do you mean?"

Bliss returned his gaze. "It's pitch dark now, Peregrin. It's like that before the dawn. But I can see you. Remember how I told you I could not experience your emotions? And then you told us that you were a Sheen, and I understood. But ever since the council reaffirmed your place among us, I have been able to see you. That is my gift." She paused. "And my burden. I can see and experience another person's emotions. I can commune with others at will."

"Why did that prevent you from marrying?"

"To marry another is to pledge to become that person, to commune only with him, so to speak. If I chose that path, my gift would have been reserved for my husband. I could have gone that route, I think, and maybe I would have been happy. I chose instead, for the good of Archiva, to let the gift grow by placing it at the service of anyone who needs it."

"Has it been difficult?"

"Yes. Sometimes the pain of others is too much to bear."

"That's not what I meant. I mean has it been difficult being alone?"

"Yes."

"Did you ever regret your choice?"

"No."

They sat in silence then until the first light of dawn edged over the horizon. Slowly the day-breaker rock began to glow, promising a fresh day of sunshine.

Bliss stood and dusted herself off. She smiled at Peregrin. "It has been good sharing these moments with you. Whatever your future holds, I will cherish this time as a gift I received." She went to the edge and climbed down.

"Whatever my future holds," Peregrin murmured aloud. "I know what I would like it to hold, but somehow I don't think that's the way it will be. He watched Bliss make her way across the valley floor. "Thank you, Bliss," he said softly. "I wish it could be otherwise."

A few days later, the council of Guardians convened. Peregrin related to them the full story of the expedition. The council listened with approval as he told of how well the people of his winter village had received the Archivans and how the people there had embraced the ideals of peace.

"Peregrin, once again Archiva is indebted to you," Morgan said when he had finished. "You led us in the defense of our home, and now you have led us out into the world. The dream of O'Keefe has become that much more real thanks to you."

There were nods and affirmations from around the table. Peregrin bowed his head. "No thanks is due to me," he said. "It is the wisdom of this Council of Guardians, who dared to risk everything in order to bring peace to the world. May your names be remembered for all ages."

Morgan then asked Curtan to tell of the Terists in the ruins. When he had finished, Morgan looked grim.

"Again, we thank Peregrin for acting swiftly. But these men speak of others who will come looking for the vault of machines. It would appear the question we laid aside after the battle has come back to us."

"Indeed it has," Derth said. "Now we do not dare lay it aside. 'The word is out there,' this man said. How far has the tale of Mikkel's exploding sticks gone? How many will come looking for a way into the vault? We must deal with this now."

"Can we move the contents of the vault?" Merida asked.

"Impossible," said Peregrin. "Some of the things in there are huge, bigger than this table."

"What of more Rangers in the area?" Curtan said.

Mikkel shook his head. "It won't work in the long run. Eventually someone would get hurt. Or maybe a Ranger would decide to take a look in the vault. There is just as much curiosity about the vault here in Archiva as out in the world."

"What do you suggest then?" asked Stevan.

"The vault of machines is simply a repository for things that have been built," Mikkel said. "It is not a true archive of knowledge, but a museum of the former world. You have seen the destructive power that exists there. Below this council building lies the true archive of knowledge. Our future lies there, not in the vault under the ruins."

"Are you saying—," began Bernhadette.

"Close it off for good," Mikkel said. "If word is out there that there are powerful weapons beneath the ruins, word will also get out there that it is impossible to get to them."

"How will you do this?" Morgan said.

"The same way he shook up Dextor's army," Peregrin said. "Dynamite the cliff face and bury the entrance in tons of rock and rubble."

"Those sticks are powerful enough to bring down the cliff?" Stevan asked. He looked stunned by the thought.

"Yes. They are that powerful and more, if someone knows how to use them."

"And you can?"

Peregrin nodded. "Oh yeah."

"What of the vault itself?" asked Bliss. "Will it be crushed?"

"No. The vault is made of the same material as my bones and is heavily reinforced. It was made to withstand the pressure of time."

The council continued to debate Mikkel's proposal. After a period of communing, however, it was decided that the vault of machines should be buried to prevent anyone, Archivan or otherwise, from obtaining and using what it contained.

After the decision was cast, Peregrin stood. "Brothers and sisters," he said, "I believe this is a wise decision. As Archiva continues to go forth into the world, this will become a haven of peace. The machines and weapons within the vault have no place here. Let them be buried and forgotten."

He paused and looked around at them. "Guardians, you are the true wealth of Archiva. As long as you remain true to your course to serve the life of Archiva, O'Keefe's dream for a new world will continue to come to fruition. I am so grateful to have become a part of this dream and to see Archiva's mission evolve and begin to spread into the world. I am grateful to have sat among you and shared your dreams, your fears, your anguish, your joy. I am grateful to call Archiva my home and to call you my true family."

He paused again and drew a deep breath. "Which is why it is exceedingly difficult to say this. Though it is my desire to remain among you, I believe the time has come for me to sleep. When the vault of machines is buried beneath the cliff face, I will be within it."

There was a moment of total silence. Then the table erupted. Several people gasped in shock. Many rose to their feet. "What madness is this, Peregrin?" Curtan shouted. "Have you lost your mind?" Even Mikkel rose up, looking shocked and stricken, and demanded an explanation. Only Bliss did not move, but sat with head down, saying nothing.

Peregrin motioned for quiet. Even so, it took a few minutes for the tumult to subside. "Brothers, sisters, hear me out. You have affirmed my humanity and called me brother. Because of your love and acceptance of me, I know who I am. But I am a Sheen. O'Keefe created me to survive the centuries. I now know that it is my personal mission to return to Archiva again and again, not from a different place, but from a different time.

"Not only do I believe this is my purpose, but I may have no choice in the matter. When I fell off of the cliff with Dextor, my body required an incredible amount of energy to repair itself. Since then I have noticed a sluggishness of body and mind. I thought this might be temporary, but it has persisted and increased. I believe only a prolonged period of inactivity will allow my body to regenerate properly."

"Why in the vault of machines?" Mikkel said. "Why not return to the place where you slept before?"

"I considered returning to that underground bunker," Peregrin said. "However, I have become aware of how intricately connected I am with the life of Archiva. Here I will know the vault is protected. Here I will sleep near the people I have come to love. When it is time for me to return, the vault will be opened, and Archiva itself will call me out."

"You think this is what O'Keefe planned for you?" Curtan asked. "To leave us?"

"Yes. Since I discovered my identity, I have also come to realize that O'Keefe built two archives to preserve the knowledge of the world. One lies below our feet. One lies here. He tapped his head.

"O'Keefe programmed knowledge of all things within my brain so that, should something happen to the archive below, the wealth of humanity would not be lost. My task for as long as I exist is to ensure that this knowledge is dispersed at the proper time. I am meant to monitor human progress throughout the ages to come."

A clamor of voices broke out around the table. Bliss quietly rose from her seat and stood without speaking. One by one the voices quieted.

"There is no one who wishes for Peregrin to remain with us more than I," she said softly. "If I could have stopped this day from coming, I would have. But even before Peregrin left for the village, I knew his time with us was limited. I just did not know why. As he speaks, I can see his path clearly.

"Still, I would wish for him to deny his path and stay." Her voice caught, and she choked back a sob. Drawing a breath, she continued. "But this is not for me to say. There is a greater need than mine here. There is a greater need than Archiva here. Everyone must follow the path given us." She choked again, turned, and walked out of the council room.

Silence blanketed the room. Then Merida rose, walked to Peregrin, embraced him, and left the room. One by one the Guardians followed suit until only Curtan, Mikkel, and Morgan remained.

Curtan rose and came before Peregrin. There were tears in his eyes. "I do not understand this decision. It wounds my heart. What shall I do?"

Peregrin laid a hand on his shoulder. "Trust in Curtan. Make sure there are no frogs in Archiva."

Curtan smiled slightly. "No frogs in Archiva." He embraced Peregrin and left quickly.

Morgan came before him. He looked at him and shook his head. "I am the Speaker of the council," he said slowly. "Yet I can find no words to say." He embraced Peregrin and went out.

Mikkel remained seated, staring at the table.

"Mikkel?" Peregrin said.

"Archiva shall fall around him," Mikkel said quietly. He looked up, his blue eyes glistening. "It wasn't supposed to be literal, Peregrin. I tried to remain distanced from you. From the moment I met you, I felt the attraction as to a brother. But I tried to keep my distance. I failed. You are the brother I longed for, true son of O'Keefe. And now you will go from me."

Peregrin found he could not answer him. "Oh, you must follow your path," Mikkel continued. "Have no fear that you are not doing the right thing. I, too, can see clearly that this decision is right. It's just that it hurts."

Peregrin reached down and touched his face. "Remember me, Mikkel."

Mikkel gripped his hand. "Remember me, Peregrin. Peace to your heart. Now please, leave me. I think I need to be alone."

The following two weeks were difficult ones. Peregrin largely spent the time with Curtan, Mikkel, and Bliss. They traveled to Second Archiva together to see Sanda and were impressed to see how well that community was thriving. He took long walks with each of them, mostly talking about little matters of the harvest.

Bliss and he met every morning upon the elbow to watch the sun rise. They said little, wrapped in silence. On the day before he was to go into the vault, Bliss raised her head as they sat in the darkness.

"I will not be there tomorrow, Peregrin," she said. "I know you have made the right decision. I can see the growing exhaustion in you. But I cannot watch."

"What will you do?"

"Today I will set out to see your village. Merida, Janette, and Jorge would like to have a look at it."

"Jorge?"

"Yes, he is drawn to the idea of Archiva going forth into the world. I think he will do well there."

"You will leave today?"

Bliss looked at him. "It's the only way I can bear it, Peregrin. Please, if you love me, do not make me stay. I can see how tired you are, and I know that you must follow your path, but don't ask me to witness it. Let me say goodbye first. After we leave the elbow, do not seek me again. I don't know if I can bear losing you, and I don't want you to remember me that way." She drew her knees up to her chest, wrapped her arms around them, and began to cry quietly.

He looked at this woman who had done so much for him and for Archiva and found no words to say. He pulled her close, and they held each other in silence, waiting for the sun to rise.

The next day came quickly. Peregrin rose before dawn and collected the things he had brought to Archiva. He put on his floppy hat, opened the door, and stepped outside. Mikkel was there, seated on a chair beside his door.

"Thus goes the Traveler," he said.

"Does the Archivist never sleep?" Peregrin asked with a slight grin.

Mikkel shook his head. "Not this night. Come; let me walk you to the ruins."

"I have another idea," Peregrin said. "Let me show you another way."

He took Mikkel to the council building. Together they entered the secret passage and descended to the Archive. Peregrin entered the code for the door to open. "It's programmed into my memory," he said in response to Mikkel's quizzical look.

They entered the giant vault with its spiraling bookshelves. Peregrin led Mikkel along the wall until they reached the other side. There they found a large portrait of two people meeting along a desolate roadway. Their hands were stretched toward each other, fingertips nearly touching.

Peregrin stood squarely in front of the portrait. "Peace to all hearts!" he said aloud.

The section of the wall on which the portrait was affixed moved inward and to the side, revealing a corridor. Peregrin looked at Mikkel.

"It leads to the vault of machines and opens on the other side the same way," he said. "O'Keefe always had a backup plan. As Archivist, you alone will possess this knowledge. Record it safely so that future Archivists will remember."

"In the Book of O'Keefe?"

Peregrin smiled. "I think it should be recorded in the Book of Mikkel. Archiva has begun a new chapter, Mikkel. It's up to you to preserve its history. Go and get Curtan now. By the time you reach the ruins, I will be in my place. The charges are set. Curtan knows where to light the fuse. And Mikkel...?"

"Yes?"

"Please take care of Bliss."

Mikkel nodded. "I will. I'll bring her down here to see you from time to time."

They stood and gazed at each other for a long time. Mikkel reached out and embraced him and then turned and walked away. Peregrin looked after him a long moment. "Farewell to you, Mikkel, son of O'Keefe," he whispered. "I will remember you." He turned and entered the corridor.

The vault of machines was identical in dimensions to the Archive. As Peregrin entered, light rose from sconces in the wall. Tools, machines, and weapons of all sorts and sizes were arrayed on huge metal shelves. Some of the largest machines occupied a center area. In the midst of these, in the very center of the room, was a padded chair that leaned backward so that one could recline full length in it. Peregrin looked at it and sighed.

"I see that my room is reserved," he said aloud. "Nice bed, but not much of a view." He climbed into the seat and lay back.

Already he could feel his body commanding itself to shut down. He wondered how long he would sleep this time.

Above him, life in Archiva would go on. Generations would come and go and progress in knowledge. He wished he could be a part of it. He felt as if an unseen hand were scratching the inside of his chest. He felt lonely. He felt … human.

As he closed his eyes, their faces appeared before him. Mikkel, so alive and commanding, yet carrying the weight of Archiva in his heart. Carlin, who betrayed the Creed for love of his brother yet found his way back. Curtan, his brother in arms, whose courage would never fail. And laughing, joking, mischievous Waterman, who brought such hope for a weary world.

And, of course, Bliss. Bliss, who gave so much to so many. Bliss, who disavowed personal happiness so that she could share the burdens of others. Bliss, who embodied the path of peace in its fullness. Bliss, gentle and kind. His Bliss, the one he loved above all.

They were all there, inside of him. He would remember them. They were the core of his knowledge. They bore greater wisdom than all the books. They had shown him that the true path of life can only be followed on the path of peace. It was the path of the human being. He would remember them always.

And he would tell others about them. He would return to the surface many times. He would awaken when human beings were ready for more knowledge. He would seek out those on the path of peace, and he would share such knowledge as was proper for that time. Because this was his task. He was Peregrin—the Traveler. Only he would travel across time instead of space. He would return throughout the ages to help humanity become human.

But he would also tell the story of Archiva. And each generation he encountered would know their names and would weave them into their legends and lore. The names and deeds of Mikkel, Bliss, the Waterman, and even Dextor, would be told in every age, to every human being. So that thousands of years from now, their names would still be spoken. They had lived their lives so that human knowledge might be preserved for a time when humans could use it without greed or violence. They had lived to preserve the truth that humans must not kill, nor use machines to kill.

Yes, they would live on, and the Creed they lived by would survive. He would see to that when it came time to awake. He was the Archive, and he was the Archivist. He would see it done.